# The RISE
## of
# RANSOM
# CITY

TOR BOOKS BY FELIX GILMAN

*The Half-Made World*
*The Rise of Ransom City*

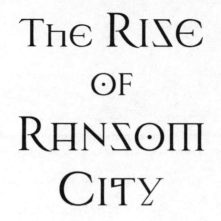

# The Rise

## of

# Ransom City

## Felix Gilman

A TOM DOHERTY ASSOCIATES BOOK

NEW YORK

THE RISE OF RANSOM CITY

Copyright © 2012 by Felix Gilman

A Tor Book
Published by Tom Doherty Associates, LLC
175 Fifth Avenue
New York, NY 10010

www.tor-forge.com

Tor® is a registered trademark of Tom Doherty Associates, LLC.

Library of Congress Cataloging-in-Publication Data

Gilman, Felix.
    The rise of Ransom City / Felix Gilman. — 1st ed.
        p. cm.
    "A Tom Doherty Associates Book."
    ISBN 978-0-7653-2940-0 (hardcover)
    ISBN 978-1-4299-8729-5 (e-book)
    1. Steampunk fiction.   I. Title.
PS3607.I452R57 2012
813'.6—dc23

                                                    2012024837

First Edition: November 2012

Printed in the United States of America

0   9   8   7   6   5   4   3   2   1

*For Will*

## ACKNOWLEDGMENTS

As always, my agent, Howard Morhaim, provided invaluable advice. Thanks to Eric Raab, whose edits made this a much stronger book, and to everyone at Tor for their hard work and creativity and the gorgeous cover, etc. Thanks to Sarah for all the usual, and thanks to everyone who supported or just read the first book.

# Editor's Foreword

## by Elmer Merrial Carson

It seems I have worked half my life on this account of Mr. Harry Ransom and his adventures. I have published more books in my life than I can now recall, I have founded two newspapers and run three into the ground, I have rewritten my own autobiography four times—one of the hazards of longevity—and it seems to me now that this book has cost me more labor than all the rest put together. Ever since I first met him, Mr. Harry Ransom has made my life difficult.

This is Mr. Ransom's story, and for the most part it is told in his own words. I have corrected the man's unorthodox spelling, and in a few places where his pages were torn or fouled or never recovered, I have had to guess at his meaning. Some of his punctuation appears to be of his own invention, and I have forced it into a more standard mold. I have preserved all his digressions from the point and I have corrected only a small percentage of his errors. What I believe Mr. Ransom intended as his title was one hundred and sixty-six words long, which is an abomination that no publisher can abide. I have shortened it.

I do not intend to say anything much about Mr. Ransom here. I do not intend to express an opinion on whether he was a good man or a bad one, a genius or a charlatan, an honest man or a traitor. He was the kind of odd fellow one used to meet back in the century gone by, in the days when the Great War was at its height.

All that is to say that my editorial duties have been light. The labor I speak of has mostly been a matter of tracking down the pages of Ransom's manuscript. But that has taken me half a lifetime.

✳  ✳  ✳

I received the first two hundred pages of Ransom's manuscript thirty-six years ago last month, in one intimidatingly large parcel, left for me at the post office in the town of Colriffey, where I was at the time rooming with friends and working on a novel. Ransom's manuscript promised—as you will soon see—an EXPLANATION and an APOLOGY OF A KIND FOR RECENT EVENTS IN THE GREAT WAR. There was no indication of who had left it for me, and no letter of explanation as to what Ransom meant me to do with it. There was no "Hello Elmer I hope you are well"; there was nothing but two hundred pages of Ransom's outlandish life story.

At the time, nobody had heard from the gentleman in question for quite a few years. His fame was waning, or his notoriety, or whatever you'd call it. I guessed he meant to rekindle it, and wanted my help. He talked about building a city in the wilderness. I wanted nothing to do with the matter. I was tired of war and talk of war and justifications for or against it. The novel I was working on was a light and fantastical comedy, later published as *A Toad's Tale*. I was not at all happy to hear from Ransom, whom I had last met back in Jasper City, shortly before it fell to the Line, and I held him at least partly to blame for that fall. What's more, I had only to read a few pages into the thing to see that it was dangerous stuff, and that if half of what Mr. Ransom had to say was true, then the spies of Gun and Line would be very interested indeed in his story.

Those two hundred pages covered Mr. Ransom's life from his birth in East Conlan, which is a dull little mining town in the eastern part of the Flinders, through his travels out on the Western Rim, with a great many digressions on his fabulous Ransom Process, and up to the famous Incident in White Rock. Along the way, Mr. Ransom managed to claim credit for the exploits of Liv Alverhuysen and the late John Creedmoor and for the beginning of the end of the Great War and for many other things besides. Two hundred pages; he promised more. One part of the story delivered, three to come. He wanted me to publish his story. He was on his way out West to make his new world. He had a typewriter with him, and by the Powers, he meant to use it.

I read his two hundred pages in one night and burned them in the fireplace and left town the next day. Those were dark times and I am not ashamed to say that I was afraid.

✳  ✳  ✳

And that was that for a few years. No more parcels of pages came in the post. Maybe I was traveling too much; maybe spies or censors intercepted them. Maybe Mr. Ransom had lost interest, or found someone else to publish his story, or fallen down a ravine out there in the western wilderness. Wherever he was and whatever he was doing, he was long gone from the known world. I heard from time to time about Ransom City, the utopia that he and his colleagues were said to be building out there beyond the borders of the settled world, though nobody knew exactly where. I wrote another two or three comic novels and made a little fortune and I tried to retire.

In the fall of 1906, a part of the third of the four parts of Ransom's story was sent to me care of my publishers. It came to me from a young lady who had inherited it in the papers of her recently deceased father, who had formerly been a Professor of Physical Science at Vansittart University. The pages were not signed, but she knew they concerned me, because they were the pages of the story in which Mr. Ransom recounted his meeting with me, back in Jasper City, back in '91. I was surprised firstly to see that he had continued his story, and secondly that his account of our meeting was passably accurate.

Well, I cannot abide loose ends, and I cannot abide gaps in the story; and besides, retirement did not suit me. I set out to track down the rest of Ransom's narrative, a few pages here and a few pages there. And that is a story in itself, for Mr. Ransom's pages got scattered all over the world, which was the way of things back in those bitter waning days of the Great War. I have been all over the West in search of the things, and I have spent a lot of money, and I have met with retired Officers of the Line and aged Agents of the Gun and I have been in danger; I attribute my longevity to the exercise Mr. Ransom has given me. The events of Mr. Ransom's story faded into history, and my dangerous hunt turned into an old man's harmless hobby. A few more pages here; a few pages there; the recollections of certain people who knew him, which have clarified some illegible passages. The thing is as complete now as it will ever be. Maybe Mr. Ransom never achieved half his ambitions, and maybe he never made good on any of his promises, but at least he has kept an old man busy in his retirement. And who knows; maybe he did.

# The Rise of Ransom City

AN AUTOBIOGRAPHY, *in Parts,*
WRITTEN ON THE ROAD BETWEEN HERE AND THE WESTERN RIM,
AND MOSTLY ON THE RUN, *I expect*

CONTAINING AN EXPLANATION OF SORTS
AND *An Apology* OF A *Kind*
FOR SOME RECENT EVENTS IN THE GREAT WAR

AND SOME ADVERTISEMENTS *for*
RANSOM CITY, *soon to rise* IN THE WEST,
"THE CITY OF THE FUTURE"

AND SOME INTERESTING FACTS *regarding*
THE RANSOM LIGHT-BRINGING APPARATUS AND
THE "MIRACLE AT WHITE ROCK"

AND A SKETCH OF A DINNER *with*
MR. ELMER MERRIAL CARSON,
FORMERLY OF THE *Jasper City Evening Post*

AND A MAMMOTH

AND A FULL AND FAIR ACCOUNTING
OF THE *Crimes* OF THE NORTHERN LIGHTING CORPORATION
AND OF *The Inner Secrets* OF MONEY AND POWER
IN THIS WORLD

AND A LAMENTATION *for* THE *DAMARIS*
AND *for* MR. CARVER AND *for all of* JASPER AND *for*
ADELA AND *for Everybody Else I have Forgotten*

WITH SOME MAXIMS *for* SUCCESS IN BUSINESS
AND *Some Useful* PRINCIPLES *of* EXERCISE AND DIET AND
*Some Invaluable* ADVICE *for* WHAT TO DO
SHOULD YOU RUN FOUL OF WOLVES.

# THE FIRST PART

## The Rim

## CHAPTER 1

# Introductions

My name is Harry Ransom. Friends call me Hal or Harry, or by one of a half-dozen aliases, of which I have had more than any honest man should. Don't let that shake your confidence in me. I was a victim of circumstance. Often I went by *Professor* Harry Ransom, and though I never had anything you might call a formal Education I believe I earned that title. For the last few years it's been *Excuse me, Mr. Ransom, sir,* from those beneath me and just plain *Ransom* from those above. I never cared for any of that and now I am free and on the road again with nothing but my name and my wits and my words.

If you know my name maybe it's as the inventor of the Ransom Light-Bringing Process, or maybe you believe in all that secret-weapon stuff they wrote in the newspapers, in which case I intend to set you straight. Or you may know me as the man who lost the Battle of Jasper City, or won it, depending on where you stand in matters of politics. If you're an Officer of the Line who has intercepted this in the mails, then you know me as a Wanted Person but maybe you know to think twice before coming after me.

If you're reading this in the future maybe you know me as the man who founded Ransom City. It lies out in the unmade lands, or it will, one day. Maybe as you read this it's a bright new century and Ransom City is a great and glittering metropolis and there's a big bronze statue of me in a park somewhere—if I have any say in the matter there will be parks—well, who knows? I am an optimist. Maybe one day these pages will be read by every boy and girl in the West. Your grandfather will look over your shoulder and say, *I remember old Harry Ransom, I saw him back in Nowheresville one time, that was a hell of a show but the bastard still owes me money.*

I am writing from no place in particular. All I'll say is that it is a big red barn not so different in architectural grandeur from one of those old-world cathedrals you see in picture-books sometimes, although I guess more full of straw and dung. I have never been in a cathedral but I have been in a whole lot of barns. There are thousands like it in the Territory. The fields all around and the mountains in the distance are brown like an old coat. The man who owns the barn and the cows and the horses and all the straw and the dung is a good fellow, not educated but one of nature's Free-Thinkers, and when we strike out West again he will come with us.

I am writing on a typewriter that I salvaged from the old man's office after Jasper City fell. Naturally it's the very latest state-of-the-art machine. Nothing but the best was good enough for the old man. There's a bullet-hole in its casing and some water-damage to its innards. Nobody thought I could get it working again but I did not get where I am today by being a fool, at least not in matters mechanical. In spite of my efforts the letter *R* still sticks one time out of four, and that is no small inconvenience for a man who likes to talk about himself as much as I do. On the other hand the machine types in triplicate, through an arrangement of carbon papers and clever little levers, so that when I type RANSOM it echoes across one-two-three sheets of white paper. The old man used this device to convey orders with the greatest possible efficiency. I want to talk to a lot of people as I go so this is a great time-saver.

Well, we moved on from the big red barn. One of the Line's Heavier-Than-Air Vessels was spotted overhead. It circled, writing a kind of black-smoke question mark in the sky. Most likely it had nothing to do with us—there's fighting not far south of us, or so I hear—but we're taking no chances. We left by night and took the road west. I am sitting and typing under the shadow of a big old cottonwood tree in a valley of rank grass and blackberry bushes and old tin-plated junk and fat dragon-flies. Our numbers have been swelled by the barn-owner's younger son and two of his friends, and I have just eaten one of his first-rate apricots, but the man himself stayed behind to sell off his furniture and settle his affairs. If all goes well we shall all meet up at a certain location on the Western Rim.

I left a triplicate of letters in his care all about who we are and where we are going and what we are going to do when we get there, by which I mean the founding of Ransom City. We are going West. I waxed eloquent about the glories of the free city of the future and true democracy and the Ransom Process and the parks and the tall buildings I have planned in my mind's eye and all the rest of it, and how every person who wants should follow us. One of the letters is to go to my onetime friend the famous Mr. Elmer Merrial Carson, formerly of the *Jasper City Evening Post*,* one is to go to the editor of the *Melville City Gazette*, and because I do not know any other journalists, the third is to go to an editor of Mr. Barn-Owner's choosing.

I thought everything would be easy to explain but it is not. I mean to set the story straight, because a lot of things have been said about me or by me that are not exactly true. It is not easy to tell a true story. Most of my practice with words has been selling things, which is not the same at all, it turns out.

I am not yet thirty but I have had an odd kind of life and I have a lot to say before I go. Anyhow this is my AUTOBIOGRAPHY I guess, and so I will call this CHAPTER ONE, and below that INTRODUCTIONS, just like a real honest-to-goodness book.

---

*Of course, there never was a *Jasper City Evening Post*. I was an *Evening News* man. Mr. Ransom's memory fails him here, not for the first or last time. —EMC

## CHAPTER 2

# My Humble Beginnings

When I was a boy I read the *Autobiography* of Mr. Alfred Baxter, the late great business magnate of Jasper City. We knew him even in the backwater town of my boyhood, and I read his *Autobiography* half a dozen times if I read it once. The book told of how he came up from nothing to triumph over adversity and become the richest and grandest and free-est man in the world. I read it by candlelight and I learned it like it was sacred Scripture. I can still quote some of it today.

> There is a moment in the life of every man of greatness when he sees History clearly; when the Spirit of the Age stands like a woman before him; when he can seize the reins of Fortune!

I would not presume to call myself a man of greatness, but as it happens there were a few moments back there when it was my hand that seized the reins of History and Fortune, if only by accident or because nobody else wanted to or while I thought I was doing something else.

Mr. Baxter also liked to say that things come in threes, in business and history and Fortune. I will go the old man one better. By my count I have held history in my hands on four occasions, and if Fortune favors me like they say she favors the bold then the founding of Ransom City will be the fifth.

First I will tell how I saved the lives of the lovely Dr. Liv Alverhuysen and the horrible John Creedmoor and thereby changed the course of the Great War too, not that I meant to at the time.

But of course when Mr. Alfred Baxter sat down to write the story of his life and how he rose from Rags to Riches, as they say, he very sensibly began in the natural place, which is to say with Rags. You do not start right in with History and Greatness and the Future, that is no way to make the sale. And so in Mr. Baxter's first chapter he told us how he was born in a pauper's room in the bad part of Jasper City and he was the seventh and hungriest of seven hungry children, and so on and so on. So that's how I'll begin too.

I was born in the town of East Conlan, thirty years and a little more shy of the new century. I was the fourth of four children. I do not know the exact day of my birth. My father was scrupulous in his business affairs but did not make note of the date, and my sisters all remember it differently. I like to think my mother would have recalled it had she lived. I believe that I recall my birth as a kind of red light and terrible pressure but when I tell people this they get skeptical, and I do not want to strain your faith in me too soon.

East Conlan is a coal-mining town some four or five days' ride north of Jasper City, on the northern edge of the Tri-City Territory and not far south of the Line's lands. There is no West Conlan and so far as I know there never was. There are two mines up on the hills at opposite ends of a long straight road and the town of East Conlan is laid out in the depression between them. When I was a boy one was operated by the Conlan Coal Company and the other belonged to a Mr. Grady, and sometimes when Grady's men and the CCC's men met in the middle of town there was fighting, and the myths and epics on which I was schooled as a boy were stories of how Big Joe from the Grady mine had met the Bierce Brothers outside Shad's Bar and beaten both of them black and blue with a pick-handle for saying . . .

Well the business of coal never interested me. Once when I was a boy no more than knee-high I met Mr. Grady. He was a very old man even then and there was something dry and dusty as coal about him. He had come to my father to make arrangements for someone's burial—as I remember it the burial in question was his own, though that may be a child's imagination at work. He patted me on the shoulder and asked if I would come work for him one day. I told him that I would sooner flee town and live wild among the Folk, even at the risk that they might eat me. He asked why and I said that coal-mining was always the same: the going down into the dark and the coming up again, day in day out, since men first set foot in the West, and that a new century was coming and I had my eyes on the future, when men would not toil like beasts. Mr. Grady gave me a quarter-dollar, and told my father that I had a clever tongue but no sense of when to use it, and that that quarter-dollar would likely be the last honest money I would earn.

My father was not a miner, and did not work for anyone. He made a living arranging funerals and burials, of which conditions in the mines ensured a steady supply. He was not a native of East Conlan. In fact he was as far from a native as it is possible to be. As a young man he came over the mountains into this western land of ours from the hot and distant country of Juddua, which to me has always seemed unthinkably magical and strange, and whenever I meet a fellow from that part of the world I pepper him with questions until he is about ready to strike me down and flee. I believe my father had been a man of great learning, maybe a priest or a doctor or something of the kind—he never talked about his past. He came West and I do not know what he was looking for but he found my mother in East Conlan.

He was a tall man in a town of short men. You could not imagine him entering Grady's Mines—he did not stoop. He kept his beard precisely scissored in a way that was somewhat too grand for East Conlan, where men mostly either went clean-shaven or shaggy as a moose. For exercise, he took long walks, alone. He was tremendously strong, or so it seemed to me. He hauled stones taller than me and he carved names and dates into them as casually as a man might jot down numbers in a ledger.

Ransom was not his real name. His real name was something a little like Ransom in sound but too hard to say for the simple people of Conlan, so he became Ransom. He spoke little, and as I remember him he was quite bald on the top of his great black head, and though he was not a religious man in any way he tended to the widows and the dead with the dignity of a priest. He often quoted a variety of Scriptures in a variety of languages but he believed in none of them. The miners of East Conlan were not religious either in those days and the plain things he did for them sufficed.

My mother died a little after I was born. She was pale and freckled and pretty and I am sorry that that is all I can say about her. Jess used to say that she had green eyes but in the photograph my father kept everything about her was soft and sepia-brown as if she was looking up from the earth where she lies. I have three sisters: Jess, Sue, and May. Two older brothers did not live past infancy. A reasonable percentage. We the survivors all worked for Father from as soon as we could walk. I was no damn good at it.

One day my father summoned us all into his workroom. There were heavy tools and dust and fragments of stone. There was a human skull on a shelf above my reach and very dusty books in languages from the old country which I could not read but wished I could. There was also the photograph of my mother and some mementos of her in ivory and jade. My father sat behind a desk and looked at each of us in turn, and announced in his deep rumbling voice that he had been thinking about the future, and what would happen when he was gone. He reminded us that nothing on earth lasted forever, but everything sooner or later went down into the dark, and one day he would too. What would happen when he was gone, he said, was that May would go to the church, and Jess should find work in Jasper or Gibson City, and Sue would marry and take over the business and do well with it. I scratched my scabs and I asked what I would do and he was silent for a very long time then said that he had thought long and hard and consulted the wisdom of the ages and of the dark places of the world and of the most learned heirarchs of ancient Juddua and the wisest wizards of the Folk and still he could not imagine what sort of things I might do with myself.

✳ ✳ ✳

Not long after that I fell sick.

The sickness in question was something that originated in Mr. Grady's Mine, something belched up out of a dark recess of the deep earth. It laid low a dozen men with fever, and they were strong men who were used to physical hardship. Most recovered. Some did not. It was probably one of those who died who brought it into our home— no fault of his own, of course. May fell perilously ill for a week and it is possible that that is why she was never able to have children, and maybe that in turn is why she got so damnably Religious. I don't know and I guess now that I have committed this thoughtless and idle speculation to the page I will have to hope she never reads this.

One popular theory—regarding the sickness, I mean, not May—one theory was that the sickness was a curse left by the First Folk. Something they had left behind, a gift for the usurpers—maybe in some deep hidden place Mr. Grady's diggers should not have penetrated. A word carved on the wall. A curse, a poison. Some of Grady's men tried to organize a mob to go scour the hollows south of town, where some families of the Folk lived free, it was said. I know this because they came to my father to see if he would go with them and he told them to go home and stop being such fools, and there were raised voices but they did as he said.

I heard all this from my own sickbed.

Most likely there *would* have been a mob sooner or later, and ugly things would have happened, but within a few weeks the sickness had run its course—for everyone but me, that is. But then I was always an odd child, who had to be different.

Previously I had resided in the same room as my sisters, with a curtain for modesty's sake, but now I was quarantined. What had previously been storage was made into a sickroom. It smelled at first of dust and stone and it was cold. There were two cabinets of battered pine. My father shuttered the room's window, at the advice of Dr. Forrest, who worked for Grady's Mine and believed that sunlight would excite and overtax the nervous system or some such nonsense. Nor were candles permitted. The sickroom was at the end of a long hallway, the shape of which created a sort of big camera obscura mechanism, so that there was real Light only at certain unpredictable times when all the right doors were open at once. Otherwise everything was gray. I sweated and shook and did not eat. The sickness was a great mystery and when Dr. Forrest visited, cloth to mouth and hovering in the doorway, there was something like awe in his eyes. My father could not look at me. My sisters came and went and I don't mean to sound ungrateful but I have to confess that in my state of delirium I could not often tell them apart. Dr. Forrest stood in the hallway and whispered to my father that it was inexplicable that I had not died already. For a time I was scared pretty bad, I will not lie, but after a while it came to me with certainty, as if I had reasoned it out and the mathematics was sound, that I would not die, and I could not die, because I was meant for something greater. After that it was mostly a matter of patience. There was not a lot in that sickroom to do for fun and a lot of discomfort to endure. I do not mean to ask for your pity, because it seems to me that for a great many people life is always like that, and I have otherwise been lucky for the most part.

It was while I was sick that the Line came to town.

East Conlan is on the southern edge of Line territories, like I said. Before I was born it owed its allegiance to no one, and the law was mostly what Mr. Grady said it was. The Red Republic rose and then fell and East Conlan politely declined all offers of federation and would not sign the Charter, but we sold the Republic coal at neutral terms. When I was a boy some people said we belonged to Jasper City, though I never understood exactly what that meant. I have never cared for politics. But we were near to Line territories and even a child could see that we could never be free of their influence. On a clear day if you went up onto the hill north of town, among the storehouses and outhouses and cranes and heaps and unmarked shafts of Grady's Mine—and if you found a clear high place to stand—you could see all the way to a black mark on the horizon that might debatably have been Harrow Cross, oldest and biggest of the Stations of the Line, with its enormous smoking factories and its indescribable fortifications. And sometimes when the wind was just right the sound of an Engine crossing the continent in the distance might be carried into town and there would be one of those moments of nervous silence, as if anyone who spoke too loudly might be swept away in its wake.

Mr. Grady's business belonged to no one but Mr. Grady, but it was an open secret that the Conlan Coal Company was owned by the Line. This was the cause of some of the fights I spoke of, though most were over women or money or for no reason at all. Even Grady sold much of his coal to the Line, like it or not, because their factories were always hungry and they could always outbid anyone else in the world. Otherwise they did not interfere with us much.

One afternoon while I was busy sweating and puking, and my sisters were at their chores, and Dr. Forrest dozed in a chair in the hallway with a bottle at his feet, and my father was in town doing business, three big black cars came up a road that had previously mostly been used for mules or horse-drawn conveyances and led right into the heart of town. The cars' motors kept running as their passengers emerged, and kept running all afternoon, with a noise like a swarm of locusts. Or so Jess said, who said she heard it from my father. However, when Jess went sneaking out after dark to spy on these new arrivals the Linesmen had gone to bed—she was disappointed that Linesmen went to bed like regular people—and their cars sat silent in the road. They were warm to the touch, she said. I do not believe she really dared to touch them.

The Linesmen had taken up rooms in some of the bigger houses on the main road. Rented or requisitioned or a little of both. There were about a dozen of them, which is a unit that Linesmen often come in, I have noticed. Some were soldiers, black-clad and dead-eyed and fearsomely armed. Some were what for want of a better word one could call *businessmen*. It was said that they had with them a great deal of complex machinery of mysterious appearance and function, and perhaps their real motives were ulterior and unearthly, known only to the Engines whose minds are not like ours, but their ostensible purpose in town was straightforward enough. They wanted Grady's Mine.

There was a war on. There was always war somewhere or other, like weather, and at that time it was blowing quite close to East Conlan. Line was at war with Gun, whose sinister and fabulous Agents had infiltrated some nearby towns and were working their corruption in secret. So the Linesmen said, or so Jess told me they said. She snuck into the town meeting where the Linesmen's demands were debated, and heard everything, though she may not have understood it all.

Have I said what Jess looks like? It's been years since last I saw her but she was quite tall, and very beautiful. She was brown and green-eyed and thick-haired. There, now she is immortalized in a way. Let's call that a portrait of my sister. It is very strange this business of turning flesh-and-blood people into words.

Anyhow a neighboring county had thrown in with the Line's enemies and there had been some acts of terror and sabotage, affecting the Line's chains of supply, which were vast and far-flung beyond East Conlan's imagining. To avoid further incidents it was necessary for the Line to assert control over the means of production in the region. The price they were offering Grady was not unreasonable—so Jess said they said—and the alternative unthinkable.

Well, after considering the offer but not for long Mr. Grady stood up in front of the meeting and the old man leaned on his stick and shook with rage like a proper old-fashioned prophet of doom and he said:

"Go to hell. Go to hell and f—— you. The things you serve should never have come up out of hell. They may steal everything else in the world in their greed but they shall not steal a single thing I have built. I will burn and bury it all first. Good day to you and go to hell. Go to hell! And as for the rest of you. Half you provincial dunderheads have never known a damn thing in all the years I have worked for this town, and yet I can see you are trying to *think*. Here are two things you should think about. First, their demands will not end with me and what's mine but they will eat you up too. Second, any man who is not with me who sets foot near my properties will be shot. Good day to you all."

And Mr. Grady stumped on out the back door of the meeting-hall and up the road up the hill, and he settled into his territory with those of his miners who were loyal to him, and they broke out rifles hoarded against maybe exactly this particular emergency, who knows, and Grady's Mine turned into something like a fortress, lit at night by torches. Attempts were made by the town's accountants to calculate the tonnage of explosives Grady might possess up there but they could not come to agreement. Honest traders started to pass Conlan by but we were visited by a plague of life-insurance salesmen. Dr. Forrest fled town without giving notice and I hear he later set up a practice in Sweet Water where he operated drunk and killed a child and was shot by her father, in a duel and in accordance with both law and custom. The Linesmen stayed in town in their rooms on Main Street and seemed to do nothing, which only made everyone even more afraid of what they *might* do. And nobody in East Conlan much remembered or cared that that odd little Ransom boy was still sick, except for my father.

※　※　※

He went into town and he called on the Linesmen. As I imagine it, it was one of those good old Conlan mornings when the sky was gray-black like coal dust, and my father stooped and stared at his feet and held his hat in his hand and tried to make himself look small and forced himself to be humble. For the Line had machines that no one else in the West could begin to understand, and back north in Harrow Cross there were sciences that only the Engines themselves fully comprehended, and while their ingenuity and their productive capacities were mostly turned to War they had medicines too. Certainly they had medicines that old Dr. Forrest could not dream of.

My father was a very proud man, and I do not doubt they made him grovel. The Line gives nothing for free.

Of course I knew nothing of these negotiations, until one afternoon there was the sound of many feet in the hallway outside, and the sound of ugly and unfamiliar voices, and then the door to my sickroom opened and five men entered. One of them was my father, and he stood in the doorway. The others, who quickly and without asking permission encircled my bed, were all short men in long black coats. Apart from various combinations of caps and spectacles and gloves or their absence there was no way I could see of distinguishing between them. One of the gloved ones seized my jaw and turned my head this way and that, and I could think of nothing clever to say. He let go of me and wiped his glove clean on the other glove and said, "He'll die."

"I do not believe that." My father spoke as if from a very great distance, and his tone was very flat.

"It don't make no difference what you believe, Mr. Ransom."

"What is it? What does he have?"

"Don't know. We don't know. Some sickness, some poison. Some defect in the world. Something badly made. Not our business to catalog these things. What does it matter?"

"There is something you can do."

"If there was, you couldn't afford it, Mr. Ransom."

"You could send back to Harrow Cross for help."

"Think they got nothing better to do in Harrow Cross? There's a war on, Mr. R—"

"I know, I know. What do you want? Damn it what do you want?"

"You want to talk in front of your son, Ransom? Makes no difference to us if he hears but the stink in here—"

"No. No. Thank you. You're right. Come away. Please, come away."

They left. They were gone for a long time and I slept, and Jess came and chattered about nothing in particular, and I slept again, and when I next woke the Linesmen were back in the room. My father was not with them. But this time they had one of their machines with them, and I could not make out what it was exactly in the dark of my sickroom but it was the height of a low table, or maybe it was just something that sat on a table. In any case the wheels of it were turning and turning, and there was a terrible stench of burning metal and oil. Two pairs of strong hands—one gloved and one ungloved and cold—seized me by my arms and my head. I opened my mouth to protest and a leather strap was thrust into it. Like an animal my instinct was to bite on it and go silent. They lifted my head and lowered a crown of wood and wire upon it. There was a snap and a sizzle and a stink and then there was LIGHT—

—and to this day I do not know if the Light was all in my head or if it really and truly filled the room but to me it made black ghosts of the Linesmen and splashed everything else white. After the Light there was pain, the way thunder follows lightning. The pain was in every part of my body, every muscle spasming and then bursting with new life, not least my heart, which rushed like an Engine until I thought I would certainly die.

These days sometimes you see people offering the *electric-cure* for madness or a variety of other ailments. In my expert opinion they are mostly quacks or madmen themselves. This was the real thing. I have never seen or heard of its like since.

They packed up their apparatus. As soon as they took the bit from my mouth I said, "What was that? What did you do? What *was* that?" Or I think I said it. In any case they did not answer, but marched silently out, single-file. I could still see the Light as they left, and it was some time before it faded.

The Linesmen demanded two things of my father. The first debt came due at once. I have said that my father had a certain authority in that town. He was not a priest but the next closest thing. He was their link to the next world. When he spoke they listened.

The town was divided. Some people wanted to side with Grady against the outsiders, because he was a bastard but he was our bastard. Some people wanted to get rid of Grady before the misfortune that had fallen on Grady fell on us all. Some thought that if they got in good with the Line it would make their fortune. All along my father had been neutral. Like a priest, he did not involve himself in politics. But now he spoke out against Grady, and for the Line. People listened to him.

And not long afterward some fifty or a hundred men from town set

off up the hill to Grady's Mine. They were armed with picks and a few
rifles. They banged on locked doors and shuttered windows with pick-
handles and called for Grady's surrender. From up on top of a tower
one of Grady's men let fire and in the ensuing daylong skirmish two
men died and many more were injured. Some of the explosives went off
and Shaft Number Three enjoyed a brief but noteworthy career as a
volcano. And so of course the Linesmen had no choice but—for our
own protection and for the maintenance of public order—to intervene
and to resolve the situation by force, with noisemakers and poison gas.
Then in order to maintain the operations of Grady's Mine, which they
said was vital for the War, they were forced to seize it. Mr. Grady was
taken to Harrow Cross for trial and he was an old man and he did not
make it all the way. Since then East Conlan has been a Line town, in
some ways openly and in some ways that are not obvious or easily spoken of. And nobody ever listened to my father in the same way again.
His foreignness, which had formerly been considered a sign of his great
and exotic wisdom, now marked him as untrustworthy—hot-blooded,
a rabble-rouser, of unsound judgment.

The other debt was only money, but it lasted the rest of his life and
he never repaid it. He never came close, though he lowered his dignity
and took on odd jobs and worked himself to death. He sold our better
furniture and what remained did not fit his giant's frame and it is on this
that I blame the stoop that afflicted him more and more, as year by year
he seemed to shrink until nothing was left and he died with nothing. He
and I never talked much and I do not know how badly he regretted his
bargain.

My sister May recalls all of this quite differently and says that bad
business deals were to blame, but I know what I know.

I have worked all day and not said a whole lot of what I meant to say.
I have not talked about how I first got interested in mathematics. That
was while I was still laid up in bed—because though the Linesmen's
treatment set me back on the path to health I did not at once get up and
walk around like in a miracle. My father had some old books and later
I sent off for a set of books published in Jasper City by a company
owned by Mr. Alfred Baxter, some Encyclopedias and some books on
business and a whole lot of almanacs of various kinds. I sold them at a
small profit to the few literates in town and to business travelers and to
some gentlemen who could not read, but who thought the volumes

gave their homes a touch of big-city sophistication. Before I sold them I read them myself. I do not mean to boast but I am what is called an *Autodidact*. That means I taught myself just about everything I know and that is why some of my notions are unorthodox, and it is why when I write letters to the Professors in Jasper City they do not write back. The *Autobiography of Mr. Alfred Baxter* came free with the set and that is how I came to read that book over and over dreaming of greatness and fame and the freedom that comes with them.

I have not talked about how one of Jess's gentleman friends taught me to shoot, though not very well, or about what it was like when Line troops started moving into town, or about the boy in town who fell down an old shaft and stayed down there for weeks and we got reporters up from Gibson City and how I tried to impress them so they would take me back with them, or about first loves or anything of that kind—well, there is a lot I could say about Love but I am writing now about History and the two have little to do with each other. I have not talked at all about the time I ran away and met with the Folk and there is a lot more I guess I should say on that subject if I mean to tell the truth and the whole truth, and I do, but not tonight.

I never did set foot in a mine but I always found work of one kind or another. Most of the money I earned went on my father's debts. He didn't thank me and I guess he didn't owe me any thanks. The rest went on books and later on parts: copper wire and glass and magnets and acids &c. I kept on returning in my daydreams to that Light.

Jess moved away to the Three Cities to find work in the theaters. Sue got married. They both sent back money. May got religion and went off with a traveling revival, from which she sent back occasional optimistic messages about the World to Come. I sold Encyclopedias and swept and mended and dug and scraped and ran and climbed and carried and cooked and did whatever else I could. I worked at night on the Ransom Process. At first, naturally, I tried to create an electrical process just like the one the Linesmen had used on me. I climbed to the top of the disused tower on what some of us had started calling Grady's Hill, in a thunderstorm, with a kite and some nails, though all I accomplished that way was three months of penal servitude as punishment for Trespass. The Encyclopedias were not well informed on the subject of electricity, it being so new and in those days mostly a closely guarded secret of the Line. I made a virtue out of ignorance. I did not know what could not be done. I did not know the names or the words for anything so I made my own. In my fourteenth year I had a piece of good fortune that

I may write of later if there is time. Behind every moment of inspiration there is hard work and good luck. Anyhow what I ended up discovering instead of electricity was something more fundamental than electricity. I did not call it the Ransom Process then. I did not call it anything because it was not the sort of thing one could speak of in East Conlan. It was too big and wild a notion. I did not have the money to do it justice. And besides East Conlan was a Line town now and I did not mean to let the men of the Line steal my idea and make it ugly. I dreamed of heading out West, where I would be free to work and think freely and look for investors who might not know or think they knew that the whole thing was impossible.

I got taller. I exercised daily. I expect I will tell you about the Ransom System of Exercises in due course. I learned from a book how to paint signs and for a time I supported myself and paid down my father's debts that way, making the town colorful until the Line ordered me to cease and desist. I was sometimes happy and sometimes not, just like everyone else. In my eighteenth year the Line installed electric-lighting in East Conlan, like they have in Harrow Cross or Archway or other Stations of the Line. Men from something called the Northern Lighting Corporation placed big arc lights on the rooftops or at the top of wooden poles, at the foot of which they placed barbed wire to discourage sabotage. The sky over Main Street became a cage of wires. The birds departed and were mostly replaced with rats. The lighting increased efficiency and working hours, but the costs of operation were extraordinary and the fee that was assessed on each household in town was so absurd that at first it was widely thought to be a mathematical error, and that is not even to mention the interest on it. Nothing the Line does is for free. Nothing in this world is free. I have never accepted that should be the case. The light was cold and hideous and I took it as a personal insult. I knew I could not stand it for long.

I was nineteen years old when my father got sick and died. In the same year I built the first prototype of the Apparatus, and I will certainly tell you about the Apparatus in due course, because if I am still famous it is what I am famous for. By the time I was nineteen years old East Conlan was a much bigger town than it had been when I was a boy, and when I put an advertisement in the newspaper for a mechanic and an assistant and a traveling companion it was not long until one Mr. Carver applied for the job. Not long after that Mr. Carver and me and two horses and the Apparatus's rickety prototype headed out West.

---

CHAPTER 3

# CLEMENTINE

I see that when I left off telling this story Mr. Carver and I were just setting off on our travels. Not a bad place to leave off. Maybe not a bad
place to stop. Anyhow it has been a week since I wrote those words. I
have not been idle. I am going West again, just like me and Mr. Carver
did five years ago, but this time we are going a whole lot farther. I have
a lot more people with me, all the pioneers of what is to be Ransom City,
and I am busy all the time, which suits me just fine.

In the week since I last wrote we the pioneers of Ransom City have
had all the usual kind of adventures and escapades you have on the
road, with refugees and bandits and unexploded devices of the Line and
the fording of high rivers. Our numbers have swelled to the tune of one
poet one lady botanist a driller of wells two traveling salesmen one deserter from the forces of the Line and the four Beck Brothers, John,
Erskine, Joshua, and Dick, who are handsome and smiling and fair-
haired and good-natured and I guess you could say they have hired on
as muscle. We passed by a town with a very fine Meeting-House of the
Smiler faith, and I nailed to their door a letter regarding Ransom City,
under the title AN OPEN INVITATION TO THE MEN AND WOMEN WHO
WOULD LIVE IN THE WORLD OF THE FUTURE.* We have left the Tri-City

---

*I do not know if this letter ever won Mr. Ransom any recruits, but I have it in my collection,
and it is a fine piece of work! It makes promises about Ransom City that a priest would
blush to make on behalf of the heavenly Silver City itself. I acquired it from the aged master
of the Meeting-House, who had preserved it for twenty years, as an investment, believing

Territory behind us and are traveling across what used to be called the
territory of Thurlow before all the recent unpleasantness, toward the
Opals and the Western Rim and beyond that: who knows.

It is raining. I am sitting on a rock in a tent listening to the rain type
on the canvas as if it too has things it needs to get off its chest. When
the Beck boys ask me what I'm doing I say I am thinking.

There is a whole lot I could say about the time Mr. Carver and me
and the horses spent out on the Rim doing business. I do not know
where to start.

The year was 1890. I was twenty years old.

There've been worse years. Swing Street boomed and theater-people
traveled from all over to Jasper City and some of them made their fame
and fortune there and even the ones who starved did so with a touch of
romance. The Free State of Nod extended the franchise to women,
and opinions were divided on that but I count it an unqualified good.
Down in the hot wet marshy lands of the Delta Karthik the Younger's
Territories seceded from Karthik the Elder's without bloodshed, or
so I read. The Line's laboratories at Harrow Cross began the mass-
production of a vaccine for polio. In the northern mountains the Baron
of New Pisan held an Exposition for the West's Fourth Centennial,
with sharpshooters and lion-tamers and Dhravian rope-dancers and
jousters from the ancient principalities of the far East, and I know it
was a hell of a show because there were photographs, which were of
a new and highly experimental sharpness and beauty. Everyone everywhere that year saw the photographs and after a while nearly everyone remembered it like they were there, or said they did. I won't lie: I
was not there.

That was the good, or some of it. The bad? Well, the Juniper Municipal Bank collapsed, scattering bad debts and lawsuits all across the
world like ashes on the wind. There was an epidemic in Cray, I forget
of what but it was ugly.* There were collections for the victims but I
was young that year and I had no money to spare. Explorers brought
back a monster from the far uncreated West to the Gibson City Zoo—
iron bars could not hold its vague and slippery form and to make a long

---

instinctively that anything so odd would sooner or later be salable to someone. I proved him
right. —EMC
*Rasmussen's disease. —EMC

story short several unfortunate zoo patrons were killed before it was brought down.

On the edges of the world the Great War between Gun and Line raged on. It was always worse on the Rim than it was back home in the Territory and environs. The fighting was worst in the north-west, up around the town of Greenbank—or what was left of it. Greenbank itself was well and truly annihilated right in the early weeks of that year. Some blamed Agents of the Gun, some blamed the forces of the Line. I don't know. I got caught in the crossfire at a place called Kloan between Linesmen and an Agent or maybe half a dozen Agents, I don't know—I kept my head down and saw as little as it was possible to see. That was early in the fighting. After that the Line settled into the ruins and built up an iron-walled Forward Camp there, and laid track, and Engines came back and forth all spring and summer carrying Line troops, until soon there was no place you could go for a drink in that whole hot country without seeing a black-clad squad of them, watching you disapprovingly, taking notes on your movements. Meanwhile the Gun brought its Agents and mercenaries into the hills, and recruited refugees, making its usual promises of revenge. The fighting dragged on toward summer. The Dryden Engine was derailed. A pack of Agents burned the orange groves at Toro-Town so that the Line could not have them, butchering the slaves there for good measure, and afterward posed smiling for reporters and photographs: Gentleman Jim Dark, Rattlesnake Renner, and I forget the names of the others. Bridges were cut, stranding refugees and interfering with business. A brutal Line-made poison-gas rocket penetrated the ornate stuccoed ceiling of the dining room of Melville City's Main Street Hotel, killing seventeen of that town's wealthiest citizens, a number of waiters, and damn near yours truly too. Later it was said to have been an accident, off-target by a number of miles. The Line blamed sabotage but it was most likely the work of some minor military clerk in a Harrow Cross Signals Station who hadn't slept in thirty-six hours and added 2 and 2 and got 7. Or something of that kind. I heard that some small compensation was later paid to the Hotel. None to me.

I was in Melville on business. Everywhere I went that year I was on business. You may find it hard to credit but there was a time when people doubted the efficacy of the Ransom Process, or its wisdom, or even its existence, and I was always on the lookout for investors. At the moment

the rocket hit I was sitting at a large round table, heaped high with silverware and warship-like gravy boats and fanned-out napkins fastened
with gold. I hoped that if I kept talking fast enough I might forget how
hungry I was, and also that the assembled worthies of Melville City
might forget to have me ejected. As I talked and gestured with my left
hand I used my right to sketch on a napkin.

". . . so ask yourselves," I said. "What's going to put this town on the
map? This is a young town, gentlemen, on the very edge of the world—a
pioneer—it stands on the edge of greatness, in my opinion."

Melville was one of the oldest cities in that part of the Western Rim,
which was to say that it was only a little younger than me.

"Now, think about Jasper City back east—what do you think of?—
well, Jasper's got Swing Street and Vansittart U and the yards and the
Brass Bull and all the rest. Gibson's got the Horse Guards and football
and that big statue of the woman with the lantern, you know the one.
Juniper? Juniper's got its Banks—"

"Not anymore," said a scowling banker.

I said, "Crisis is opportunity, sir, I don't have to tell a businessman
like you that."

His wife cleared her throat. She was a very fine-looking woman.
She was, I had learned from listening at the next table, the President
of Melville's Six Thousand Club, whose aim was the increase of Melville's population to that number by the turn of the millennium. I
reckoned that she and I should be natural allies, because we were
both about making something out of nothing, but so far she remained
skeptical.

"What did you say your name was, Mr.—?"

"Ransom, ma'am." I smiled at her. "Professor, if you don't mind.
And I take your point about opportunity, sir, you put your finger on the
very heart of the matter, but what opportunity? What's going to make
Melville City's fortune, that's the—"

"Copper," piped up a little tufty-eared businessman to the left of the
fine-looking President. "We control the largest deposits of copper on
the northwestern rim and my smelting operations are second to none,
and now listen anyhow, Professor, of what exactly—?"

"Copper! Nothing wrong with copper. But it runs out. It costs
money and toil to dig it up and it comes up soiled. I'm talking about
*Light,* gentlemen. I'm talking about *energy.* I'm talking about the Ransom Process." I showed them the napkin. They did not understand or
appreciate it.

"Professor Ransom, there was a salesman from the Northern Lighting Corporation in town a week ago and—"

"The Northern Lighting Corporation are rogues and villains and I
hear tell the Line owns them and they will bleed you dry. I hope you ran
him off like you would a vampire. I hope you slapped him like a gnat.
You may quote me on that, if there's any reporters present, and please
quote me on this too: What I'm proposing to you is the Melville City
Harry Ransom Illuminations, I'm talking about Free Light. . . ."

The smelting-operations gentleman recoiled at the word *Free*. You
have to be careful when talking to rich men. Too much talk of *Beauty*
or *Liberation* or *An End to Drudgery* raises their hackles, makes them
suspicious. You have to speak in their language.

"I'm talking about a once-in-a-lifetime opportunity, it will not come
again, to make your name in the history books, I'm talking about *The
Future*—"

Three things happened at once. I stood, for effect, and began to
pace—a banker harrumphed—and Melville City's future came crashing
down through the ceiling, nose-cone first. There was a shower of brick
and plaster and a noise like the end of the world. Parts of a chandelier
fell where I had been sitting. My dining companions variously threw
themselves to the floor or jumped up and started yelling in outrage.
I believe I cursed but otherwise kept my cool.

I got a good long look at the rocket as it fell—it seemed to take forever. Dear reader, wherever and whenever you are, I hope that you live
in a time when you are not familiar with the weapons of the Line. I'll tell
you that the thing was drill-like, made of black iron, plates, and rivets,
and looked about the size of a mule. It breached the ceiling and fell sideways onto the buffet table like an unwanted wedding guest, drunk and
mean and clumsy, spilling silver soup-tureens and bottles of champagne,
smashing the neck off a big glass swan. Waiters dropped their trays and
screamed.

The rocket groaned, shuddered as if waking from a nightmare, and
unscrewed itself. It vented a greasy white gas, which quickly filled the
room, put out the candles, made women clutch their pearl-necklaced
throats and choke. My dining companions started to go dark in the face
and fall over. The diners and waiters surged for the exit, and fell over
each other, and with awful inevitability they all blocked the doors.

I seized a bottle, poured wine into a napkin, and held it to my face.
I don't know that this was much of a substitute for a gas-mask, and I
would not care to repeat the experiment, but I guess it was better than

nothing, because I stayed standing while others fell. No matter how I tried I could not help them to their feet again.

I do not recall that I decided to run, but I just found my feet carrying me to the door, and best not to think about what I was stepping on, the swan's glass wing shattering underfoot, a woman's necklace, a man's outstretched hand, I don't know what else. I held some woman by the arm as I fled through the kitchens and out into the street where a crowd was waiting, and a cheer went up as she and I tumbled together on the cobblestones. She later turned out to be the President of the Six Thousand Club. I am glad that she survived but I am sorry to report that statistics compiled by the Line's surveyors tell us that Melville has not yet got above Five.*

I breathed deeply, stood, and started back in again, but then someone grabbed me and wrestled me to the ground. I lay on my back and blinked. My sight is very bad in my left eye at the best of times, though you would not know it to look at me. The other eye was so aggravated by the gas that at first I could hardly make out the face of my trusty assistant, Mr. Carver. He looked concerned for my health and safety, as well he might, because I had not paid him in weeks.

A crowd of Melville's citizens stood all around us. A man in a heather green suit and a kind of raffish collar with a gold pin on it crouched beside Carver. He put a hand on my knee and said, "It's hopeless, son. No sense throwing your life away, you can't save them, nobody can now." It later turned out he was a reporter for the *Melville Booster*. Light-headed as I was from the wine and the gas I didn't at first understand what he meant and nearly said, "Save who?" The honest truth is that I had been thinking of running back in for the napkin, which held diagrams of the Ransom Process, and Fortune forbid if it were to fall into the wrong hands. I said nothing. Instead I passed out.

My pluck and daring were much admired. A sketch-artist captured my likeness for the *Booster*. He was kind enough to strengthen my chin and flatten my ears. By the end of the day I could have had investors lining up around the corner. But it didn't feel right. Carver packed up the wagon and we left town that afternoon.

---

*Nor would it until well past the turn of the century, and long after Mr. Ransom had departed for parts unknown. —EMC

This was not my story of heroism. It was just one of the things that happened that year. I don't know why I thought to tell it now.

Adversity breeds ingenuity, that's what they say. It was a great year for ideas and notions and inventions and grand world-changing schemes. In our various travels and escapes, me and Mr. Carver met gentlemen and sometimes ladies who were trying to sell sewing machines, and electrical door buzzers, and a method of hypnotism using magnets, and procedures for rain-making and cloud-seeding and the increase of crops. And of course not least of these grand ideas was the Ransom Process, also known as the Ransom Infinite-Escalation or the Ransom Unmoved-Mover Process, or the Ransom Free-Energy Process, or the Ransom Light-Bringing Engine, or a number of other things from time to time and on various patent applications and sideshow advertisements. Mr. Carver and me, we went from town to town all along the edge of the world, displaying the prototypes, seeking investors. We had what you might call a run of bad luck but remained always hopeful. Or at least I was hopeful, I can't speak for Mr. Carver.

We traveled alongside inventors of procedures for extracting gold from lead, silver, and scat—dog, beetle, and human—and the inventors of cures for cancer using flowers, crystals, exercise regimes, uranium, and magnets. Magnetism was in style that year. We drank and argued with the inventors of several plausible-sounding alternatives to the Gold Standard, and of two or three new religions, and what seemed to be a kind of rural utopia called *Land-Tax Distributism.* They came out West, like us, looking for territories where the future was still open, where the laws were still unsettled—I mean not least what they call *the laws of nature,* which as everyone knows are different on the Rim.

They drank. I did not. I abstain from drink for the most part—it clouds the mind. Coffee is my only vice, not counting curiosity and pride.

We lunched on bread and cheese at a rugged brown-canvas camp overlooking a sweep of golden valley, talking with a man by the name of Thomas, who'd come out West to hawk the prototype of a hand-cranked contraption that was so complex in appearance you might have guessed it could read the future or puzzle out the stock market or at the very least calculate the primes, but in fact it only peeled apples, and not very well, as you could tell from the bandages on his fingers. The thing was beautiful to him regardless, and I wished him good luck. We met a man in Hillsdale who said he was secret business-partners with a great wizard of the First Folk, and that together they could bottle the magic of those people, including the seven-mile step and the drumming up of storms and the trick of immortality. Mr. Carver spat on the sawdust floor and said "Bull——. F—— bull——." I had to agree.

✳ ✳ ✳

So we came to Melville City and we left Melville City in a hurry. We went south to Carlton, where we were nearly press-ganged into the militia. Another story. We fled Carlton for Toro, and Toro for the mining camps at Secchi, and from there south and south-west. Mania had descended all over the western edge of the world. Armies massed on every horizon. The Engines flashed each other paranoid signals from horizon to horizon, and the Guns brooded and schemed in their Lodge. It seemed like every second person sitting at any bar you might care to walk into was a spy for someone or other. Agents of the Gun camped in the woods and sometimes strolled boldly into town, armed openly, larger than life, recognizable from the picture-books and not caring who saw them. It took some fancy footwork just to stay neutral. In the banks and futures-markets in the cities back East there was intense giddy speculation over what would survive when it was done. If you were a bright young fellow but not so bright as to have got to blazes out of that whole unlucky part of the world after the Kloan massacre, if not sooner, then you could make good money sharing your observations by occasional post with the financial speculators in Jasper City or Cray or even Harrow Cross. I was able to pay off certain debts and settle certain lawsuits surrounding the Process, and to purchase a very fine white suit, and also to purchase a new and gleaming white and more spacious wagon for myself and the Light-Bringing Apparatus and Mr. Carver, in which we joined the stream of refugees heading south out of the ever-expanding war zone.

There were rumors. There were always rumors. It was said that both Gun and Line had come out to that country chasing the same quarry. A deserter. A stolen weapon. Secret intelligence. An old man. A beautiful woman. A general. Some secret of the Folk. The war was nearing its end, people said. This battle was for the prize. Somewhere out there was a weapon that might end the war. Well, I was twenty years old in that year and for as long as I'd been alive people had been saying the Great War was coming to an end, that deliverance was knocking on the door. In my view the armies were there for no particular reason at all. The fighting was a purpose in itself. There were scores to settle, and every week brought a fresh humiliation for one side or the other to revenge. They could not extricate themselves, they could not go on or go back, and whatever brought them there was forgotten. I have cousins on my mother's side who are like that.

Anyhow it was the late days of summer when we came down into Clementine.

Clementine was a little town on a flat and vast plain of fields through which a dirt road cut straight west toward the horizon and east toward whatever the next town over was. I forget what it was called and it doesn't matter. The fields looked haphazard, and put me in mind of a man who has been on the road for days and not shaved. We put on a show of the Process in a high-raftered barn belonging to a farmer by the name of Mr. Corbey, the proceeds of which paid for our dinner and a night in the barn for our horses and ourselves.

"One day," I said, as I inspected our accommodations. "One day, Mr. Carver."

Mr. Carver said nothing, as I recall, just thoughtfully scratched his beard. Then he lay down in the straw and slept like the dead. I on the other hand could not sleep—I have never slept easily. By the soft light of the Process itself I tinkered with the underside of the Apparatus until something I did created sparks, so that I was forced to halt the Process and turn my attention to a small but growing fire in the straw. I stamped and cursed and beat with my fine white jacket until it was gone.

"Mr. Carver," I said. "I hope that amused you." He said nothing, and I admit I was exasperated.

It was dark in the barn and I have never liked the dark, and outside there was a bright yellow moon, and so I went walking, out across Mr. Corbey's flat fields and into town.

Clementine had maybe three dozen buildings, counting barns and outhouses. They were arranged like wooden crates laid out carelessly along the side of the road, or like junk scattered from the back of a passing Engine. Every window but one was unlit.

Over someone's store some black birds perched along the top of a black sign. The night was warm and windless. There was a drowsy wilderness silence, except for the sound of my own footsteps, and the occasional insect going about its business, and the clack-clack-clacking

of a typewriter, which somebody behind that one lit window was oper-
ating despite the unsociable hour.

As was my habit I thought how Clementine might look if it got
Illuminated. How the softly glowing lamps of the Ransom Process
might be strung along the rooftops where the birds roosted and how
travelers coming along the road from the huge darkness to the west or
the east might see the constellation of Clementine shining before them
and what they might think it might mean.

The typewriter and the electric-lit room over the general store in
which it sat belonged to three Officers of the Line. There was some of
that old menace in its sound—I hope that if you are reading this in days
to come you will not remember what the machines of the Line sounded
like and you will not know what I mean. Those three uniformed men of
the Line had been at the show that evening, scowling and taking notes,
and now they were no doubt making a report. If I know how Linesmen
operate, they had not paid for the room but requisitioned it according
to the universal Authority their masters claimed. The officers of the Line
were always everywhere that year, out on the Rim that is, watching and
making reports and looking for whatever they were looking for. I myself
had nothing to hide so far as I knew, but nor did I care for the sound of
their report-making, so I took myself off to the edge of town.

Out in front of Clementine's westernmost shack there was a sign
promising FOOD AND WATER AND MUSIC, and beside it a bench. A dog
slept on it. The dog did not object when I sat down beside it.

The bench was as good a place as any to sit and watch the road and
think. The Ransom Process was far from perfected in those days and
there was always a lot of thinking to be done.

I don't know how long I sat there before I first caught sight of someone coming along the road.

The road was a wide flat band of dirt. It was a clear night with a
bright moon and you could see a long way into the west. When I first saw
them coming they were very small and distant. The two of them were
just one speck. More accurately they were at first like a tremor of motion in the darkness, nothing that had a discernible shape or form. A
tremor like a tiny wave or ripple in the Ether—except that the Professors in the big cities will tell you that the dark is a stillness in the Ether,
whereas Light is the Ether in motion. Well, I thought about that for a
while, and about what it would be like if the natural laws of the world
were inverted so that the Dark was motion and the Light its absence.

I thought that maybe if you got far enough out West things might get turned on their head like that. But then would we still call the dark the dark, or the light the light, or would the words change with the things themselves? I thought that *Ether* is just a word for what we cannot name, and maybe *motion* is just a word too.

By the time I had put these speculations to rest and returned my attention to the world and the road the figures were a good deal closer. Now I could see that there were two of them, and they were on foot.

The dog rolled its head lazily to regard them.

Not for the first time that year I regretted somewhat that I was not carrying a gun, because who knew what kind of person might be on foot on the roads out there at night. I might have quietly crept away but as they got closer I saw that one of them was a woman, and I took that as a sign they were not likely dangerous. A few minutes later I saw that the man with her was old, and walked with a stick. The woman was fair-haired and even in the dark you could see she was tired and thin as they stopped before me and I smiled and told them, "Welcome to Clementine."

The old man said, "We're just passing through."

"Harry Ransom," I said. I extended my hand, and the old man took it, somewhat reluctantly but I took no offense. People were wary those days.

"This your store?"

"No. Nor the dog."

"Who are you, then?"

"Professor Harry Ransom," I said, "when doing business. Inventor, businessman, Light-bringer. And I am just about always doing business these days. So tell me, how are things out West the way you came—I heard Clementine was pretty much the edge of things."

"Not quite," said the woman. "But close enough."

"What's business like out there?"

"We're not in business."

She had an accent I couldn't place, and I was widely traveled for my years. She was weathered by long and hard travel but underneath her features were refined.

"Refugees?"

"Yes." She thought before saying, "I suppose in a manner of speaking we are."

From the way the old man was leaning on his stick it seemed to me he should not be walking all night.

I stood. The dog looked up, took a brief interest in me, and then dropped its head back down between its paws.

I pointed back toward the town.

"A Mr. Corbey gave me and my assistant the use of his barn for the night. Ordinarily we sleep in the wagon so a barn is as good as a hotel for us. You're welcome to join us and I doubt Mr. Corbey will mind."

They looked at each other then spoke at once.

He said, "Mind your business, Professor."

She said, "We couldn't pay you—"

"Don't think of it," I said. "I need the company. Mr. Carver doesn't talk much. That's my assistant. A fine mechanic and a trusty hand in our various misadventures but not a conversationalist."

From the look on the old man's face it seemed he did not like me much.

I said, "You are—?"

"Harper," the woman said. "Miss Harper."

"And is this your father?"

He thought for a moment too long before nodding.

"There are Linesmen in town," I said. I pointed toward the lit window, which was a faint star in the distance.

They both had a kind of hunted look to them. That's why I said that.

"Don't mean to imply anything," I added. "Just thought as fellow travelers on these roads you might want to hear the news."

Old Man Harper nodded again. "We'll be moving on, Mr. Ransom."

"Thank you," said Miss Harper.

I figured that they were most likely just con-artists fleeing the law or escaped indentureds or something of the kind—maybe just possibly they were spies, which was interesting to a degree but in those days of War there was no shortage of spies on the roads. Nevertheless my curiosity was roused. Curiosity has always been my weakness. One of my weaknesses. And besides like Mr. Baxter wrote it is true that opportunity can be found in the most unexpected of places.

"There are Linesmen all along the road east too," I said. "And they are checking papers and asking questions about I don't even know what they want to know—who knows how their masters think? Not that I think you have anything to hide from anyone but nobody likes an interrogation."

I nodded to them and made as if to walk away, then turned again and said, "Listen. If you don't mind cramped conditions Mr. Carver and I are setting out before dawn. You may not credit it looking at me but our papers are all in order so far as I know, and we could use a couple of extra hands, the roads being what they are these days."

He said, "No thank you, Mr. Ransom." And at the same time she said, "Where are you headed?"

I waved a hand toward the big black night and I said, "No place in particular. Wherever business takes me."

"Well, Mr. Ransom, we're heading east."

"Any place in particular?"

Old Man Harper said, "It's a family affair."

"Well," I said, "it so happens that right now business takes me back east toward Jasper City."

"You're a long way from Jasper City," said Old Man Harper. "About as far as you can get. You've got a sideways kind of way of going about things if you're heading for Jasper City."

I waved away his objections. "I have business there," I said, and smiled at Miss Harper. "With Mr. Alfred Baxter himself."

That was half-true. As I saw it back then I had business with Mr. Baxter whether he knew it or not. Besides I had thought the name might impress her. It did not.

Something about her said, as clear as if she were branded with it, that she had some secret she wished to tell, that she needed to tell, and that sooner or later she would have to tell someone.

She shrugged, exhausted, and succumbed to temptation.

"Maybe for a little way," she said.

I smiled.

The dog had one eye open and was regarding the two of them calmly and without great interest. It is not true what they say about dogs and their sixth sense.

Meanwhile the man who claimed to be Miss Harper's father looked at me for a moment like he was reckoning the most efficient way of killing me, then having quickly reached a conclusion looked east past me and seemed to be scheming something unguessable.

"But nobody travels for free," I said. "Nothing in this world is free. Can you cook? Can you shoot?"

❋　❋　❋

Well as it turned out later, they could not cook, but he most certainly could shoot.

Mr. Carver wasn't so happy to be woken in the dark hours of morning so that we could pack up and leave town like thieves, especially since for once we owed nobody money. Nor did he seem to care for our new traveling companions, but he kept his own counsel.

The sun rose as we got a couple of miles out of Clementine. There was a roaring noise and a bad smell and a black Line motor-car came up from behind us. As it passed us by it slowed a little, and though the car's window was black too I thought I could make out the gray face of an Officer of the Line examining us. The Harpers were safely in the back of the wagon with the Apparatus and all he saw was me and Mr. Carver and the horses. I nodded but did not wave and the face receded into the black glassy depths as the car accelerated past us into the distance. It frightened the horses, and then it scared up a big family of black birds out of the fields. The flock rose up across the huge pink sky like a lady raising the lace hem of her skirt. Mr. Carver cursed and shook his head. Otherwise he said nothing.

## CHAPTER 4

# ON THE ROAD

It has been a few days since I last returned to these pages. Red ants have made a home in the remarkable triplicate typewriter. I do not have the heart to oust them. Fortunately they do not seem to mind the clatter of the typewriter. I guess these are frontier ants and they know how to make do in tough conditions.

We have been camped for a few days while the Beck Brothers haggle for provisions with farmers. Farmers here and everywhere in these parts mistake us for a lost regiment or unemployed mercenaries and they have a tendency to bring us tribute in hopes that we will move on. It is a constant temptation but I insist that we pay our way. In Ransom City every man and woman will get a fair deal.*

Red ants have also made a home in the Apparatus, where they are less welcome. The Apparatus is delicate and dangerous. I have driven them from their hiding places like an angel of wrath.

It is not easy traveling with the Apparatus. Rivers are a particular problem, so is rain, so are ants. But what good will Ransom City be if it doesn't have the Process lighting its streets?

The Beck Brothers keep asking to see the Apparatus in action. Not

---

*The records of the court of Glendale town, Nevison County, make frequent reference to the four Beck brothers—enough brawls, affrays, breaches of the peace, and insults to decorum to fill another book, ending in Erskine Beck's conviction for horse-theft and the brothers' disappearance from the town's records and one assumes the town itself. One imagines the Beck brothers were not so scrupulous about temptation as Mr. Ransom hoped. —EMC

yet, I say. Not until we get there. No matter how cold or dark it gets at night. It is not to be trifled with.

I guess I should try to say what the Ransom Process is. I hope that in the future when you read this everyone will learn in school about the Process but maybe your education has been deficient.

❄ ❄ ❄

"So what, precisely, *is* the Ransom Process?"

So said Miss Elizabeth Harper, pausing from her work, pushing some strands of golden hair back from her flushed and sweating forehead, smiling.

"You'll see it work tonight," I said.

"You're coy, Mr. Ransom."

"I am wise," I said. "And call me Harry."

We were in the town of New Sydney, or maybe Homeward, or who knows what it was called. A couple of days east down the road from Clementine. I recall that there were vineyards and a bank and the town was nestled beneath a yellow slope of valley. I had negotiated with the Reverend of wherever it was and we were to put on a show that night in his meeting-hall.

He was a Reverend of the Smiler faith, or as they are properly known the Brothers of the New Thought. I don't recall his name because frankly the Smilers are all much the same to me. He was young, pleasant to look at, fair-haired and blue-eyed. It was his job to keep his circle smiling their way through times of struggle—to keep them day-by-day improving their souls, and not falling into despair—and it was putting the first lines of worry on his face.

"Adversity," he said, "is good for the soul." He gave me a strained smile. "But there are limits. The war, Professor, the war and the rumors of war, it's hard for them all—for *us* all—it's bad for business and bad for the nerves, is what it is—"

I noticed how he said *them* and asked if he was new in town.

"Does it show? Well. Well it's all right if it shows, isn't it? Yes. Yes. I was trained at the Inner Circle in Jasper City. This is my first posting. Adversity strengthens us, that's right, isn't it?"

"You're from the big city! I bet you particularly requested this difficult posting, I bet you lit out for the Western Rim to challenge yourself. I did just about the same thing, in fact the way I see it you and me have a lot in common. But maybe I've been here a while longer than you and I know how people are out here. They're simple, not like in the big cities.

They don't get a whole lot in the way of entertainment. They brood, they hole up for the winter, they get the fear. What your circle needs is a diversion. Something that's not war nor rumor of war nor anything they've seen before—something new. I can help you there."

He smiled nervously.

"It must be consistent with the dignity of the faith."

"Dignity is my watchword."

"A month ago," the Reverend said, "a man came through town with an automaton that played checkers. He won bets. But it turned out there was a dwarf beneath the table."

"Is that a fact? I've never met a dwarf. Well—I'll bet it was diverting."

Miss Harper and Mr. Carver and I moved the Apparatus piece by delicate piece into the meeting-hall and Mr. Carver assembled it on the Podium. The Reverend watched nervously. I do not know whether he was more worried about the possibility of blasphemy or fraud or fire. Old Man Harper did not believe in manual labor, it seemed, but he pulled his weight in other ways. For instance, in towns like that I was used to having small boys swarm around the Apparatus and sometimes try to steal small or shiny parts. Old Man Harper's scowling presence was a wonderful scare-crow against such distractions.

Miss Harper asked me, "Are you a scientist or a prophet, Harry?"

"I observe no such distinctions," I said.

"Or a circus-act?"

"Distinctions are for little minds."

"Are they really?"

"No offense intended. How about you just wait till it's dark. That's when you can really see the Light."

The meeting-hall was round, and well-worn, and would have been comfortable if it were not so damn hot. It was conspicuously clean and smelled strongly of floor wax. Sunlight streamed through wide windows. The benches and the walls were carved with Scripture of the Smilers, like SMILE THROUGH ADVERSITY and CLEANLINESS IS THE BEST MEDICINE and THERE IS NOTHING TO FEAR BUT FEAR ITSELF and EARLY TO RISE EARLY TO BED &c. You know the kind of thing. Between these slogans there was a poster urging that suspicious travelers be reported to the nearest available Officer of the Line, which I didn't much like. There was also now the sign I had myself painted in blue and gold and red and white, COME AND BEHOLD THE FUTURE OF THE WEST, THE RAN-SOM PROCESS, &c, &c, which I liked very much if I do say so myself.

Miss Harper was tall and a deft hand with a hammer and a great help when it came time to hang the glass lamps all around the rafters. For much of that time I was otherwise occupied, soothing the Reverend's mounting anxieties regarding the Apparatus and what it might do, explode or catch fire or call down the wrath of who-knows-what. (I guess I could see how it *did* have a certain blasphemous quality, sitting there on the podium.) Still, Miss Harper and I found time for a good long talk. I told her about good old East Conlan, maybe prettifying things a little, and about my sisters and where they'd scattered to with their marriages and work in Jasper City and occasional letters to remind me that I owed them money, and I told her about my big dreams and my big plans. I told her about the incident in Melville City—and maybe I made myself out to be more of a hero than I was—and I told her about some of my other escapades and misadventures in such colorful places as Kloan and Disorder and the like. I had been out on the edge of the settled world for more than a year and I had a lot of stories.

"Fortune and fame," she said, "always on the horizon. And always some pitfall between you and it."

"An excellent summation," I said, "of my life in particular and of the world in general."

She stood by the window where there was a little breeze and she took a long drink of water.

We talked for a time about the War. It seemed she had a great interest in it but she had not been able to read a newspaper or talk to anyone much for a long time, because there was a lot she wanted to know but did not. I told her what I could, which was little enough, and after a while she stopped asking. She asked me instead why I'd come out to the edge of the world, where things were so dangerous, and I explained that I was looking for investors and partners in my great work, and also that if you had it in mind to make something new and strange this was the place to do it.

It is widely known that as one presses West it is not only the people and the land but nature itself that gets wilder and rougher and looser. Many things that are settled certainties in the heart of the world are negotiable on the edge of it. It has been shown that clocks run faster out here, except when they run slower or not at all. The boiling point of water varies from place to place. If you drop a stone from a roof in one town it may fall faster or slower than in the next, or so I have heard: I have never successfully observed this myself.

If you were looking to found a new political order or the city of the future you would go West—that's the standard practice. Or if you were fleeing from the law of law-abiding places, west is the direction in which you would flee. Similarly, if your quarrel was with what in solider and more staid places they might call *laws of nature* . . .

I asked her how far she had gone out West and what she had seen of the edge of the world, thinking of how when I met her she had been coming from that horizon. She gave me no straight answer.

I shrugged and pulled on the jacket of my fine white suit.

She said, "Where are you going, Harry?"

I said that I was going nowhere in particular at that moment except to the doorway, where I wished to be seen in my fine white suit so as to attract the curiosity of passers-by. If she meant where did I plan to go tomorrow, it depended where the road led. I said I was just wandering, going no place in particular, the same as she was.

"I thought you said you were going to see Mr. Baker in Jasper City," she said.

"Baxter," I corrected her.

"Baxter, then."

"I did say that, didn't I? I didn't think you were listening."

"Of course I was listening, Harry. He's a businessman?"

"You really haven't heard of him? I didn't think anyone in the West didn't know that name. Well," I said, warming to my subject, "he's the greatest and most famous businessman in Jasper City and in all of the West and besides he's the author of a book that meant a lot to me when I was young. And more importantly he is famous for investing in promising young men, and he is known to have made the fortunes of the inventors of the slipjoint lockknife and the hand-crank dishwasher. One day—one day, when the Process is perfected—I plan to visit him—we'll go together, eh Mr. Carver?"

Mr. Carver sat at the pedals of the Apparatus, head hung down, half-asleep, as if preparing himself for the labors to come.

"If I have to I'll sit on his doorstep all day," I said, "until his butler has no choice but to let me in. Or I'll jump in his carriage while it rolls down Swing Street among the theaters and before his driver can eject me I'll strike up a conversation. I reckon if I can just start talking they can't stop me."

She laughed.

"Maybe I'll wait for him in his library all night, sipping his brandy. He won't mind, he can take it out of our profits. Oh, don't think I haven't thought of a hundred other angles of attack. . . ."

I told Miss Elizabeth Harper nearly everything I had to tell about my hopes and dreams, and in return she told me nothing about herself except a pack of lies. She told me that she was a schoolteacher from a little town near Gibson City, and that she and the old man had come out West to visit a dying aunt, and some other falsehoods which I will not waste ink repeating. I don't mean to say she was a bad liar because she was not, but I did not believe any of it.

The sun started to set and a pink light came through the windows, and it bathed Mr. Carver as he sat at the pedals of the Apparatus, giving him a sinister aspect. The Apparatus itself was a thing of beauty as always. Brass flamed in the evening light and the domes and flutes of glass were so clear that the meeting-hall's slogans were legible in their mirror-images. The magnetic cylinders had a certain heavy elegance, like prayer-wheels from one of those old-country faiths. The Apparatus began to hum. Old Man Harper had fallen asleep on one of the benches at the back of the meeting-hall with his stick in his lap and he was snoring just out of time with the rise and fall of the Apparatus's unpredictable energies.

Then I stood by the door as the townsfolk filed in for evening Meeting, and the Reverend shook some hands and I shook others, like we were competing for souls. The men in that town mostly wore tall hats, as I recall, and the women dressed plainly in grays and blacks.

※　※　※

The name of the town was Kenauk. I recall it now. A Folk word. Its meaning unknown, at least to me.*

※　※　※

If you've ever been in a Smiler meeting-hall you know what they're like. They are the same everywhere, because it is an article of the New Thought that people are all the same. The townsfolk sat in circles around the podium, and the Reverend welcomed them and everyone forced a big smile and shook the hands of those next to them and pretended good cheer.

_____

*Or to me. —EMC

The Reverend led them in the chanting of their daily Affirmations. When they got to the parts about Wealth and Success and Good Fortune I mouthed along with them, though I have never had the patience for religion of any organized variety. Carver shook his head in disgust and muttered something. I gestured at him to keep his silence.

Then the Reverend spoke. The congregation sat back and held their hats in their laps and slapped periodically at the mosquitoes that had come uninvited into the hall. They stared at the Reverend with an intensity that seemed to make him anxious. The Apparatus took up much of the podium and he had to kind of lean sideways to stand and be heard and whenever he turned too quickly he was always in danger of impaling an eye on the big handle. The theme of his sermon was the War. I don't know that I recall that sermon precisely but I heard many others like it in those days.

He acknowledged first of all that those were dark times and that the Adversity that makes us stronger and is a spur to success may sometimes seem too vast to struggle with, and sometimes it is hard to keep smiling. Sometimes the goodness of the world is not readily apparent. He assumed that everyone had read the newspapers lately and knew what had happened in the north at Melville and Greenbank where the Gun and the Line were fighting hot, and what had happened closer to home in somewhere-or-other that had been seized and fortified by the Line and in some-other-place where it was said the mercenaries of the Gun had moved in and taken over the whole town and turned it into a sink of wickedness and vice and dope and casual drunken violence. Then the Reverend fell very quiet then said very loudly and clearly like he was reading from Instructions from on high that he and the Smilers were neutral in that great perpetual conflict. He said that politics is not the business of the Smilers, they care only that you are strong and happy and zealous in whatever you turn your hand to. He looked at all the windows as if he was being spied on, which I doubt that he was but who knows.

A big man at the back stood and shouted, "What do they want? Damn 'em, what do they want out here?" And then he said that they were poor simple folk out on the Western Rim and had nothing the Great Powers would want and also simultaneously complained that the fighting was interfering with his business and lowering his profits. Some others took up the shout. A fat woman stood and announced that she had to keep her idiot son—her words—locked up lest he run off and join up with the Gun and get himself killed, and who in the meantime would do his chores in the store, and when would it end? These were not questions the Reverend was equipped to answer to anyone's satisfaction, and a number of other people started to stand and shout rumors at each other, back and forth in the darkening room. Secret weapons! Buried treasure of the Folk! Oil! Turncoat and runaway servants of the Line or Agents of the Gun, with secrets of their masters' most terrible vulnerabilities, hiding amongst us!

I strained to make out Elizabeth Harper's expression but could not. The woman who'd been sitting in front of Miss Harper got to her feet and blocked my view, saying in a voice that was disturbing how flat and matter-of-fact it was that the Great War was nearing its final end and when it did the world would end too. Another woman stood and said that the War was ending all right, that her husband said that soon the Great Powers would grind each other down to nothing and what would be left would be called peace.

At last the Reverend began to stamp his foot for attention. This is no easy thing to do while maintaining a smile, even the somewhat waxy one he had, and I admired the man's spiritual discipline.

"Rumor," he said, "is the child of despair. It is the ugly bastard offspring of panic and weakness. Adversity is always with us. Do not look outside yourself for salvation. You will not be saved. You yourselves are strong and you are the workers of your own prosperity and increase, if you only . . ."

The usual Smiler stuff. A man who held a kind of battered and mud-crusted hat in his hand like he was thinking of hurling it at the Reverend stood and stuttered *I I I* until the Reverend fell silent. Then the man said that *he'd* been in the town of I-don't-recall-what recently and they were saying they'd heard a rumor that there was a man on the western roads going town-to-town fleeing the armies of the Powers who had a weapon, a great and strange and unthinkable weapon, a weapon of the oldest Folk magic, a weapon that could destroy the Powers themselves if only he would unleash it, which maybe he would and maybe he wouldn't. Maybe he was withholding that grace from us until we proved ourselves worthy—or maybe he was holding out for money. As that man spoke he turned his hat over and over in his hands until it was upturned, so that now it was no longer like a weapon, but like he was begging with it. And a number of people started looking at me and my Apparatus in a way that made me anxious that there might be a misunderstanding.

"Well," I said, "ladies and gentlemen of Kenauk," and I put a hand on the Reverend's arm and gently steered him aside and into the shadows, where he was happy enough to sit and stare at his shoes. "I am just the entertainment here, but your Reverend has been good enough to make me his guest and maybe I can answer some of your questions."

I felt Carver appear at my back—his timing was always impeccable—and mount the pedals of the Apparatus.

"Sir, nobody knows when the War will end. The Powers do not confide in us. Ma'am, if your son is acting up and talking crazy about becoming an Agent of the Gun why not introduce him to some girls? And you, ma'am, the world has never ended yet and nobody can be sure but it is not the way to bet. You, sir, nothing can destroy the Powers, you know that, one might as well try to shoot a bad idea or kick a foul mood, it is a confusion of concepts. A man who tries to tell you otherwise is trying to sell you something, and I want you to save your money until I've had my shot at you, understand?"

A few people laughed. Meanwhile at my signal Miss Harper was going from one side of the hall to the other snuffing the oil lamps until it was quite dark and it seemed to me that everyone was holding their breath. Mr. Carver was working the pedals with occasional grunting of effort and a noise like a man sawing wood. It made the whole rickety podium sway until I felt as if I was on a boat on a big lake at night.

"Here is an answer to a question nobody asked," I said. "Here is a question none of you even knew was a question. The question is Darkness and the answer is Light. My assistant Mr. Carver here is working up a sweat as you can hear and maybe catch a whiff of, I beg your pardon for that but it's necessary. Nothing will come of nothing. Ever hear that? It was in a poem or something. I'm a man of science not a poet but I know beauty when I see it and ladies and gentlemen, just wait a moment, just wait! Mr. Carver works the pedals because we need an initial spark, just something to excite the energies, set things in motion, grease the wheels, but now—now stop."

Carver stopped.

There was silence, except for the scrape as the magnetic cylinders turned against each other. In the deep places of the machine coils of wire like sigils of the deepest wildest magic twitched and shuddered within the counterposed fields of force. There was a harp-like noise and then a twang as a wire snapped loose. I smiled. There was a hum that ascended in pitch and urgency as the energies of the Apparatus mounted, magnetic and otherwise. I felt a tug on my pocketwatch and belt-buckle, that I always thought of as affectionate, somehow.

"Some of you," I said, "may have been in the Stations of the Line, and seen their electric-lighting. You may have seen the headlamps of their Engines in the distance. An ugly light, cold and nightmarish, and ruinously expensive to produce. I know of towns that have tried to purchase it from them and debt and penury follows. I could warn you about the Northern Lighting Corporation. . . . No. Not here! What you are about to see is my own invention. It is the marriage of my own long investigations into the deep principles of Nature, and my studies into the arts of the First Folk."

I reached in the dark for the switch and threw it and the Apparatus released its power into the Ether, setting each Atom in the air to spinning, all jostling their neighbors to share the good news.

An *Atom* is a word the Jasper City professors use to mean the very small things that the world is made of, that ordinary people do not notice because they are so numerous, like the letters that make up a book or the grains of sand that make up a desert. They are always in motion—like people in a city, or words that are being spoken. They move faster in the West than in the East, but are less dense.

Anyhow within moments there was a soft dawnlike light pulsing from the glass lamps. In each of the lamps there was a coil of metal, which vibrated in resonance with the Apparatus. Like called to like. The lamps served to focus a Process that would otherwise operate everywhere and therefore nowhere. Light expanded within each lamp, shifting and pressing thick and eager against the containing glass.

I could see every face in the hall and they were all now beautiful. I fancied there was something childlike about them.

"No wires," I observed.

Miss Harper opened the shutters on the meeting-hall's south-facing windows. We had hung a single lamp from the roof of the town blacksmith. It was lit now, a single point of brightness in the night.

"The Process is everywhere at once," I said. "Like gravity, or time. It occurs simultaneously, without wires, without loss of power, yes, even unto Kenauk's furthest outlying fields or outhouses. Even beyond, if you can imagine that—I could throw a lever here and set a light ablaze in Jasper City. You'll have to trust me on that."

Mr. Carver sat back and lit a cigarette, which was frowned upon in Smiler circles but nobody said a word.

I heard somebody whisper the word *electricity* and I rounded on them as if they had blasphemed.

"No," I said. "Not electricity—names are important, sir. I'll forgive your error, though, because it's a common one. This is something new.

Something new in the world. It works on the principle of the synthesis of equal and opposite forces, the energy of tension and contradiction, you are watching light struggle with dark and the possible struggle with the impossible, and it doesn't have any name yet except the Ransom Process, thank you very much. And if there's a man or woman in the room who doesn't think it's pretty as a sunrise you can leave now and I'd give you your money back if I'd asked you for any."

The light grew in intensity and shifted through the spectrum, going fire-colored, sea-colored, candy-colored. At the time I could not stop it from doing that. It was a side-effect of instabilities and uncertainties in the Process, of imbalances among the energies it contained. Fortunately it was pretty and so I used to pretend it was a bit of deliberate stage-craft. I glanced at Miss Harper, by the window, and was happy to see that she looked delighted. Old Man Harper mostly looked wary.

"You'll see," I said, "that Mr. Carver is no longer pedaling. And I want any man here, a volunteer, how about you or maybe you, Reverend, to come and see that there is no oil-powered engine here and nothing burning coal and nor is it mule-powered—trust me, Mr. Carver is not hiding a mule under his trousers." Carver grinned toothily and bowed to the audience. "And in fact the Apparatus is now powering itself."

Most times at that stage in the show I would go on for longer about how the Ransom Process worked and what was remarkable about it, which was that once the first spark was roused it worked in perpetuity, feeding only on itself, like a rumor or a religion or a beautiful notion released into the world. I would observe truthfully that it created heat as well as light, and that once you had heat there was nothing you could not do with it. I would not explain precisely how it worked because, first, I wanted nobody to steal the idea. One day I planned to give it away to everyone but not until I had exacted the one price I demanded for it, which was that my name be known. Second, I did not entirely understand how it worked, and third, it did not entirely work. It depended on time and place but as a general matter it rarely lasted more than an hour without Mr. Carver returning to the pedals. I have improved it greatly since and I will improve it more when we get to Ransom City.

And usually I would talk about the money that a canny investor might make on it. But instead that evening I had one of my occasional unsound ideas.

I said, "You were all talking about the War and I said I had no answers. Well, maybe I do. Maybe I do. Maybe we all have a lot more answers in us than we think, once we dig 'em out from under all the questions. You've started me thinking along new lines and I thank you for that."

Mr. Carver must have inhaled wrong on his cigarette because he started coughing.

"Maybe the cause of the War is that people think that nothing is free and everything good is at the expense of some other sucker's suffering, and that if one place gets rich another must be poor. These things are what the professors in Jasper City would call a *fallacy*, or so I believe. That is what I believe. I can prove that to you. In a world with greater abundance the Line would have no power and there would be nothing for the men of the Gun to steal. And maybe—"

I had the crowd's attention and they were evenly balanced between apprehension and excitement. What happened next was poorly timed. The Process became imbalanced and immediately the Apparatus kicked and a surge of power went out of it into the Ether and startled the Atoms and the lamps all burst, costing me a substantial sum of money. For an instant the meeting-hall was filled with blazing light like the Silver City of Heaven itself. Through the window you could see a distant flash of blue-white flame as the lamp on the blacksmith's roof burst, wirelessly and simultaneously and without loss of power. Without finishing my sentence I slammed shut my mouth and leapt for the emergency lever that sent the Process into reverse. It seemed to push back, like the Process had its own ambitions toward increase. My face smarted like I had spent too long in the hot sun. I threw my whole weight on the lever, even to the point of lifting my feet from the floor. It would not move. It may be that the problem was not so much that the lever was too stiff, as that I was not heavy enough. I mean that it is possible that I was getting less heavy with each passing instant—when the Process starts to run wild it plays tricks with Gravity. Sometimes you feel like you are no more than a shadow of yourself, or a paper-thin poster. I regret that I have never been able to study this phenomenon as it deserves, due to the fact that it manifests perceptibly only in conditions of extreme and mounting danger. What I believe it proves is that every kind of force is inter-linked, as I had been trying to explain to the people of Kenauk, and nothing is truly separate or divided from anything else, which was a beautiful notion though this was not how I would have chosen to demonstrate it. One also notices at these moments that time seems to stretch out infinitely. I do not know whether this is a side-effect of the Process or whether it is just because of good old ordinary terror. What I do know is that suddenly Mr. Carver added his weight on top of mine and the lever creaked and dropped a notch and then another notch. There was something solid about Mr. Carver. He was a rock, fortune smile on him—in fact for a moment I could have sworn there were two of him—anyhow the lever fell a third and a fourth notch and then there was a beautiful clunk-clunk and whir as the magnets altered their spin, first slowing and then reversing, and then the lever rapidly dropped the remaining notches to its nadir and the light ceased and Carver and I fell on top of each other. The meeting-hall plunged into an utter darkness which instantly became like Hell itself, or like I imagine the Lodge of the Guns is, by which I mean full of screaming and wailing and pur-poseless violence.

Unless you have been living in a hut in the woods these past few years, dear reader, I guess you have heard how dangerous the Process can be. But the people of Kenauk did not know, not back then. I don't think they apprehended the danger they had nearly been in. I myself only dimly intuited the dangers of the Process in those days. I think the people of Kenauk panicked because after what I had just dared to say the sudden darkness seemed like a blow struck by the Powers themselves—as if the wrath of the Engines had come roaring down from Harrow Cross like a rocket, or like the Guns had spat some vile hex from out of their Lodge. Or maybe it was just that I had raised everyone's hopes and then dashed them. The meeting-hall had been crowded before but now it seemed packed to the rafters with faceless figures, shouting and jostling. Anyhow I got a few good bruises and so did Mr. Carver. At one point I thought I would be dragged down into the mob and torn limb from limb. There were a number of hands on me and they were tearing at my suit. They were all asking me questions at once and I did not know what to say.

A hand gripped mine and pulled me back and when I turned I was surprised and delighted to see that it belonged to Miss Harper. I said to her that I thought she'd fled and left me to my fate and who could blame her and she said, "I did. Who knows why but I changed my mind."

Another thing I saw as we stumbled toward the door was that a man reached out to seize Miss Harper, and Old Man Harper came up out of nowhere and struck that man with his iron-shod stick in the

back of the knee and in the soft parts of his back in a way that was
practiced and efficient and devastating. It made me a little sick to watch
but I am sure it was worse for the man he struck. Then we got outside
and I stumbled and Miss Harper let go of me, and when I got up again
she was gone. Both of them were gone.

❋  ❋  ❋

To my surprise the crowd did not destroy the Apparatus. They left it
mostly untouched, as if they were afraid of it. Me and Mr. Carver waited
until they had dispersed and we crept back in to salvage what we could.
The Apparatus was a little dented and the meeting-hall itself was a mess.
Benches were overturned and the lectern was broken like a lightning-
blasted stump and somebody in a sudden whirlwind of nihilistic despair
had taken their knife and carved F—— YOU in answer to each one of the
slogans on the walls.

The Reverend was sitting on the edge of the podium with a tragic
look on his face. He was no doubt thinking about the cost of repairs,
and when he glanced up at me I could see he was wondering whether I
could be held responsible.

I was sorry for him but I knew that I had to be firm. I sat beside him,
and after some thought as to how to proceed, I patted him on the back.

I said, "I can see how you might feel aggrieved."

"Professor Ransom—"

"I won't tell you that adversity is good for the soul, or that every
disaster is an opportunity, or any of that kind of thing, Reverend. All I'll
say is—"

"Diversion, you said, entertainment—"

"Is this. My Apparatus was damaged too, and you may not believe
this but the Apparatus costs more than your meeting-hall and maybe
more than all of Kenauk"—this was not exactly a lie, as I consider the
Apparatus priceless. "Now I am no lawyer, but I have had run-ins with
the law—I admit it. I have been held accountable for the actions of my
horses, and I was held to be at fault the time my assistant Mr. Carver
insulted a man's wife. It seems to me that you are the master of your
meeting-circle, and the responsibility is yours."

He quoted Scripture. "No man is master of another man."

"The law may say otherwise. Who knows? Courts are unpredictable
devices."

"They didn't teach us the law, Mr. Ransom. Only what's right and
decent."

"Right and the law are not always in parallel, I think."

"There can be no question of that."

"So. What say we agree that neither of us will sue the other, and neither of us will mention the other ever again, and I go on my way?"

We shook on it. He forced a smile. It was not bad but I have to say that I have seen better.

## CHAPTER 5

# BLACK CUT

Today I had to maintain the Apparatus. There was water in it from the river-crossing and one of the new recruits, a young man named Tomasi, had proved to have an ulterior motive and had taken a hammer to it before the Beck boys could wrestle him down. A wrecker. I guess he is still mad about something that I did or that somebody said I did back in the War. And besides these incidents, as we go West the Apparatus needs fine and constant recalibration.

I work alone these days and nobody is allowed to come close. A good time to write.

Today I think I am going to write about Mr. Carver.

Mr. Carver and I spent the night after the incident in Kenauk in the wagon, out on the edge of town. In the morning we went into town and there was a woman there who laundered and mended my white suit. I think I recognized her face from the night before, when she had been yelling. She did not meet my eye. She sold us some tomatoes, which she fried and Carver and I ate sitting on a bench looking out over the vineyard. I remarked to Carver on the astonishing and unlikely feats of irrigation involved, and what that said about the human spirit, but he was sulking over his bruises and my heart wasn't in it either.

I wasn't happy about the damage the Apparatus had sustained or the loss of my time or the discovery of yet another mysterious flaw and instability in the Ransom Process. But worse than all that was the fact that Miss Harper and Old Man Harper had gone on their own way and I might never learn their secrets. I had come to feel that this was more than my usual curiosity, that it was somehow urgent. But I could see that if they were trying to keep a low profile then my antics of the night before would have scared them away. I have never had a gift for keeping a low profile. It is not in me.

"You know," I said to Carver as I mopped up the last juices of the tomatoes with bread, "what *really* makes me unhappy this morning is that—"

"Time," Carver said, and he licked his fingers and thumb clean and stood. "Move on." We went back to the wagon together in silence and moved on.

## A Portrait of Mr. Carver

I hired Mr. Carver back in East Conlan, like I said. I put an advertisement in the newspaper for a mechanic and assistant. Experience with electricity and horses would be considered valuable, I said, and a willingness to travel and face danger was a necessity. No Linesmen, thank you very much, and no felons. Within a week I received visitations from several persons of no fixed abode, some small curious boys, a very elderly man who could hardly walk, a man who looked near-certain to slit my throat and rob me as soon as we left sight of town, a Linesman who informed me that my father's debts remained unpaid and I was on no account permitted to leave town, and lastly Mr. Carver, who showed up as the sun was setting and stood in the doorway casting a shadow that reached all the way across the white-tiled floor to the stove.

At first he did not impress me. He was tall, and thin, and stooped, and wild-looking. He wore something brown that could hardly be called a suit anymore, with no belt. He wore a single suspender, lop-sided, as if he were indifferent to customary notions regarding symmetry, or he was dressing for comic effect like a clown. He had no hat. His hair was very long and very black. He was pale and looked sleepless and the bones in his face were as big and as gaunt and as heavy as the arches of a story-book castle where an old king sulks on a shadowy throne or where a princess gets locked up in an attic.

I said, "Please, Mr. Carver, sit," but he didn't.

He said, "You're traveling. Said so in your newspaper. Where?"

I said, "West, out to the Rim, maybe up toward Melville City. You see, you can't get anything made here, there's no money, there's no opportunity, there's no room, there—"

"I know that country well. Show me the machine."

He had no small-talk.

I went to the window and pointed at where the Apparatus was tethered under a tarp in the backyard. I said what it was and what it did, or what I hoped one day it would do, because at that point it did not work at all.

He whistled. Then he said, "Yes."

I said, "Yes what?"

He stepped out of the doorway and vaulted the fence and approached the Apparatus. Over my protests he laid hands on it. He yanked open the casing. He reached in and began to perform certain small adjustments. In particular he reached in and stretched out a tangle of copper wire and inspected it like a soothsayer reading entrails.

"Hah," he said, as if a suspicion had been confirmed.

I said, "I made it. It owes nothing to the Line or the Northern Lighting Corporation or anyone else, whatever they may try to say."

"Is that right?"

"It is."

He ran his finger across oiled machinery. "Wasn't the Line I was thinking of. You know what? I'll come with you, Mr. Ransom."

"Will you now, Mr. Carver? Seems like that's up to me."

He shrugged, and turned back to the Apparatus.

He did not negotiate, and he did not explain himself.

"Well now," I said. "Well."

We inked a contract in the margins of a newspaper. He signed with a *K* and beneath it I wrote *Carver.*

We left town early in the morning, while everyone was asleep.

We traveled together for a year, and worked together long into the night in barns and hotels and forest clearings and hilltops and gullies all across a thousand-mile stretch of the Western Rim. I talked science and big dreams and he never talked much. There were many things he did not do, such as cook or bathe or take collections, but everything he did he did well. He had an excellent sense of direction and a sense of humor that I never quite understood but believed to be profound. He had a deep and rough-edged voice and a trace of an accent which I could not place. He cursed frequently and with conviction, and without regard to occasion or polite company. He smoked foul cigarettes, which his long fingers could roll one-handed while his other hand was working. He was good with snares and could skin a rabbit so quickly even the rabbit would be impressed. He saved my life a few times—I lost count of how many. He rarely changed his clothes but apart from the cigarettes his odor was not offensive. He was shot at once or twice, we both were, but he was never hit until White Rock. He had no views on politics and as far as I could tell no family. I was not even sure how old he was.

One night in a barn outside a town called Garland I drew up another contract, promising half the profits of the Ransom Process to him, in the event that we made it to Jasper City and got rich, although the name would remain the *Ransom Process*. This gallant gesture seemed to appeal more to his sense of humor than to his ambition. He signed again with a *K* and I wrote *Carver*. I guess since that was most likely not his real name it most likely wasn't binding, not that it matters anymore.

✳ ✳ ✳

Anyhow we took the road east out of Kenauk. It was a thousand miles down that road to Jasper City and Mr. Alfred Baxter of the Baxter Trust but on the immediate horizon there was nothing much except a scattering of farms. After a while the road took a sudden crooked leftward turn for no reason that Mr. Carver nor I could speculate on and entered into a scraggly wood of scrub oak and cottonwood.

The road was bad and we walked alongside the horses and conversed with each other while the horses plodded between us. The names of the horses were Mariette and Golda. I remarked on how the wood was like a metaphor for the nature of the world, by which I meant that the leafy upper parts of it were golden and airy and inaccessible, while down on the ground where we had to toil it was nothing but damn mud and mosquitoes. Carver nodded and said, "F—— that."

As the day wore on and his aches and bruises healed he got into an unusually talkative mood, as if the Harpers' departure had lightened some anxiety he had been carrying in silence. In the afternoon he began to name the trees as we passed them by, and that is how I know they were scrub oak and cottonwood, which otherwise I would not have noticed or cared about. I asked him where he got this surprising learning on trees and he shrugged and said, "I travel."

"I travel too, Mr. Carver. Nobody could say I haven't traveled. I've seen things beyond the wildest dreams of East Conlan. But I could not name a tree if you held a gun to my head."

"I reckon there's a lot everyone can't name, Professor."

"True enough."

Those handsome trees gave way to a third kind, something gnarled and ugly that Carver did not name for me, our conversation having wandered onto other topics. Between the limbs of those trees there were spiderwebs, thick as cotton or the hair in an old man's ears. Then that scene too gave way. The road led us out from the trees and along the edge of a valley that opened out to the sunlit horizon. It was one of those sudden and always unexpected vistas of the Western Rim, that are like seeing the whole world all at once.

"You know," I said, "the man who figures out a way to bottle and sell such a scene to the people back East will be twice as rich as Mr. Alfred Baxter on his best day."

"Could be," Carver said.

We were in the midst of this sort of repartee when he suddenly stiffened and cursed. He halted Golda with a tug on her reins and Mariette with a word. He walked to the edge of the road and he pulled his long hair back from his face and he looked out over the valley.

I asked Carver what he saw and he did not answer me.

He walked to the back of the wagon and took the hatchet down from its hook. Ordinarily we used it for cutting firewood or clearing deadfalls from the road, or we used the blunt back-side for striking the Apparatus when the cylinders jammed. Still it was quite fearsome the way he held it now.

I said, "What?"

He shrugged off his jacket and his already loose neck-tie and hung them from the big lever on the back of the Apparatus and said, "Stay."

It was hard to say whether he was speaking to me or the horses. I was somewhat insulted at being spoken to in that way by my assistant, though I guessed it had been so long since he'd been paid that that word no longer fairly described our relationship.

He turned his back and set off down the slope, with that bow-legged walk people have when they are balancing on a steep incline. It is something like the way bad actors walk to show that they are drunk.

His shoulders sank below the level of the road and then his head.

This was somewhat out of the ordinary for Mr. Carver, who was ordinarily level-headed and solid and silent and stable. He kept his own counsel and I was not allowed to look in his suitcases, but he was not prone to this sort of vanishing act.

I walked to the edge of the road and looked out over the valley. Mr. Carver was a small bow-legged shape moving quickly down and into the distance. Beyond him the ground rolled up and down in the usual way—there were trees and rocks and black bushes. I did not see what had caught his attention.

"*You* stay," I said, patting Mariette's flank. "Keep the Apparatus safe and there's a raise in it for you when I get back."

I set off after Carver.

He was moving fast and I quickly regretted the brief time I had wasted bantering with the horses, because I nearly lost sight of him.

❋   ❋   ❋

The earth fell and rose. I caught sight of Mr. Carver black against the sky as he climbed high ground ahead. He crouched, steadying himself with his left hand on the ground and the ax out in his right.

I followed him. It seemed like we had been walking a long time and I began to worry about the Apparatus and considered turning back, but was unsure of the way. I could not imagine what he had heard or smelled or intuited so far from the road. I strained my ears and I sniffed the air and for a long time all I heard or scented was sun and dust and wind. Then at last there was a faint scent of burning.

When I caught up with Mr. Carver he was standing at the edge of a wide expanse of smooth gray rock. At the far edge of the expanse the rock rose in forms a little like breaking waves and among them there were the dark and narrow mouths of caves. In front of them was a great heap of charred wood.

Mr. Carver stood with the ax loose in his right hand. He did not turn to look at me but I knew him very well and I knew that he was aware of my presence.

I looked down and beneath my feet the rock was carved in the looping intricate designs of the Folk, and I realized that I had stepped on some sign or sigil of theirs, and maybe I only fancied that a sudden pain shot through my leg as if I had stepped on a snake. "Mr. *Carver*," I said.

He ignored me. He strode across the plain of rock as if he were the master of it.

I think I said that there were Folk living south of East Conlan when I was a boy. From time to time one of the Folk and one of East Conlan's men might even meet, uneasily, in the woods. There was little or no regular commerce between us but there was rarely violence, so long as both parties maintained the proper attitude of wary respect for the other's prerogatives. Our world and theirs were superimposed, and there was tension. What I mean is that one did not lightly trespass. There were all the usual stories about the Folk seizing and torturing travelers, out of sheer wickedness or for revenge or for breaking their rules, although I do not think it ever happened to anyone in particular. There were all the usual Folk-tales about curses and the evil eye and my sister Jess used to tell me that before I was born a girl from East Conlan who went trespassing in the woods was transformed into a hare.

"Mr. *Carver*," I repeated.

He knelt down by the mouth of a cave, where the heap of charred wood was scattered—except that it was not all wood. When my curiosity finally mastered my dread and I followed Carver I saw that as a matter of fact some of what I had taken for timber was bodies, burned.

They were the bodies of Folk, and there were seven of them. One could tell that they were Folk because of the long limbs and the useful-looking extra knuckle—though someone had severed the hands and feet from a couple of the bodies, maybe as trophies. The stones of their homes had been scattered and the wood used for the fire. Some other cruelties had been performed on the bodies, either before or after the burning. I will not recount those cruelties except to say that the man who did it was a monster.

I was aware of no appropriate prayers and so I just stayed silent for as long as I could stand.

"They say," I said, "that the Folk do not die the way you and I will one day die. That's the first thing every child learns about them. That they were made from a different plan when the world was different and that death for them is not final, but they return to the world, again and again, clothed in new-made flesh, as I once heard a Reverend put it."

"In the end, maybe," Carver said. His voice was flat. He had put the hatchet beside him on the ground.

"Do you think it's true? Would we know? I don't know, you hear people say it but you hear people say a lot of things that aren't true. Like if you yawn without covering your mouth evil spirits get in and ride you. Or that burning a white calf keeps the rest of the herd safe from sickness. Or, well, you know."

Carver said nothing. No flies gathered on the bodies, but nor did they get up and walk. There were what might be tracks on the ground but they meant nothing to me. There were sigils carved in the rocks and I studied them curiously but I could learn nothing from them.

"It may yet be true," I said. "The world is very large and we do not know the tiniest part of it."

Sure that is trite, but it is true.

Carver stood. He scratched his beard.

I said, "I used to think long and hard about what it would be like. When I was a boy, I mean. It kept me awake at night. The coming back, I mean. Into the dark and back into the light again and again. Like it's said the Great Powers do. Like stars. Around and around. In fact it seemed to me that maybe it was only men like us for whom death is final, and that was a kind of mistake in our making. As if death is only a word and has no meaning of its own. I don't know. I've often said that it was one of the great inspirations for the Ransom Process. You've heard me say that. I said it back in Kenauk."

"Yeah."

I was ashamed that I had started talking about myself again, but it was only to fill the silence of the rocks and the big blue sky above and Carver and the blackened bodies.

"You got questions," Carver said. "Go on then."

"How did you know—?"

"Saw the smoke."

"Is that a fact. I didn't see a damn thing, Mr. Carver. I guess I don't pay you enough."

"Huh," he said. He looked around. He traced one of the signs carved into the rock with a finger. He peered into one of the dark openings in the rock but did not go in. Neither of us did. You don't go crawling into the Folk's secret places if you know what's good for you.

"Was like you knew this was here," I said.

"Was it?"

"It was, Mr. Carver. It was."

"Told you I traveled when I was young. Said you wanted somebody who knew this country. Was I wrong?"

"I guess not. You visited with the Folk often, then?"

"In a manner of speaking."

There was a long silence.

"You know," I said, "I visited one of their places once."

"I know."

This surprised me and I did not know what to say. I was referring to an incident back in East Conlan, when I was a boy, that I have not yet written down here and maybe will not. Mr. Carver and I had never discussed the matter and I did not know that I wanted to discuss it all, and so instead of saying more about it I asked, "Who did this?"

"Someone hunting. Someone questioning. Someone prying into secrets." He glanced at me in a meaningful way. Then he looked around and I guess he saw something I didn't because he added, "Wolves."

"Wolves did this?"

"Wolves were here—led by men. One man. A hunter. A madman. Not the Line, then—the others. F——."

"What did they want?"

"Who knows?"

I remembered the rumors I had heard in Kenauk, of Folk weapons and Folk magic at large on the roads of the Rim. I had not thought much of those rumors, but I guess someone took them seriously.

"F——," said Mr. Carver. "Nothing we can do here and we should move on."

Maybe you'll think me callous but soon enough I forgot about this incident. I have that cast of mind that can only think about a problem when it can be solved.

When we got back to the wagon there was a man and a woman in filthy rags peering into the back of it, most likely wondering how in the world to go about stealing the Apparatus and what they would do with it if they did, and we had a short successful scuffle. We had forgotten the hatchet up there on the rocks and I told Mr. Carver that I would ordinarily take it out of his back-pay, but that I was so relieved at our triumph over the would-be Apparatus-Thieves that I would overlook the matter. We bought a new hatchet in the next town over, and some other parts to mend what had been broken back in Kenauk, including an apothecary's full stock of glass jars. I haggled, Carver mended. He cursed and spat a lot and was back to his old self.

We ate at a saloon where I explained to the owners that I was a Vegetarian, and I explained what a Vegetarian was, and after they were done snickering they fed me well enough. I glanced at the other diners eating pork and beef and hardly thought about burned bodies at all. I struck up a conversation with a man who turned out to be a probate attorney, and I thought about mentioning the news about the Folk just west of town but I suspected from some other not especially agreeable political opinions he'd already expressed that he would say *good riddance*. So that was the last I thought about them until now. Instead we talked about the road ahead and I learned that the James River was unseasonably high and passable only at the bridges, the nearest of which had been destroyed in the fighting. Travelers were detouring a day or two north-east to the Black Cut Bridge. So that was what we did.

Three high iron arches held the Black Cut Bridge aloft of the water. You could see them from miles away because the land around the river was muddy and flat. We approached through waterlogged wheel-ruts and the deep ridged tracks of Line motor-cars, that always looked kind of scaled to me, like they were dug by the bellies of great big snakes. Also there was a considerable concentration of horseshit. Beneath the arches there were tents, and several motor-cars and one monstrous Ironclad with the blind eye of its cannon patiently regarding the road, and among the tents there were men in black uniforms going to and fro or shouting at each other or just standing all day foot-deep in mud and blank-eyed. In other words an encampment of the Line held the bridge. There was quite a crowd of travelers ahead of us waiting to pass, some being questioned and others searched, and among them I saw Elizabeth Harper and Old Man Harper.

The two of them were surrounded by a half-dozen soldiers of the Line. They were being questioned from all sides and it did not seem to be going well. The Linesmen had not yet drawn their guns but you could tell that it was only a matter of time. I saw this as a problem I could solve and I got to work.

"Stop them!" I yelled and I shoved my way through the crowd. "Stop them!" I repeated and I came up to where the Harpers were being questioned, and I held up one hand to dissuade the Linesmen from shooting me and with the other I seized Miss Harper by the arm and said, "Thought you'd got away from me, did you?"

I confess it delighted me to look in her eye and see that for once I knew what was going on, and she didn't.

I turned to the nearest Officer of the Line. They all look alike to me and I have never been able to figure out their ranks. I said, "Thank you for stopping these people, sir. I'm Harry Ransom, inventor and businessman, and these are my papers." And I began to show him the various licenses and passports and authorizations I had had to purchase over the last year in order to do business in this part of the world, which was either Line territory or debatable territory and the Line has different forms for each. He was more interested in the Harpers than in me but a Linesman cannot resist the urge to study paperwork and authorizations.

"I am an honest businessman and I pay my dues, and these, sir, are my servants. I picked her up in Melville where she'd been arrested for

fraud and him in Gooseneck where he was a vagrant and they fled from
me in Kenauk where I had a dispute with the locals over money and
they took with them their papers of service and no doubt they've burned
them. What did they say they were, what lies did they tell you? Sir, they
are mine. Had her for a year and the old fellow for two, I wish I could
reward you for stopping them but . . ."

Well I had to talk a lot longer than I have rendered here, but I trust you
get the gist. The Harpers played along smartly. At first they denied
everything—then they started accusing me of withheld meals and other
mistreatment. I noticed but did not let my eyes dwell too long on a photograph in the Linesman's hand of a man who kind of resembled Old
Man Harper, though younger and handsome and smiling or at least less
worn-out, and anyhow the picture was blurry as if the man in it were
caught in the act of turning suddenly to shoot the photographer. The
Linesman's eyes slowly dulled as he lost what little interest he'd ever
had in me and eventually also the quite considerable interest he'd had
in the Harpers. He filed away the photograph with a grunt and a shake
of his head, and at last the Harpers were released into my custody. I was
so pleased at my daring and ingenuity that I didn't mind when the officer discovered a deficiency in my licenses and assessed me a fine. Nor
did I think much about what might be pursuing the Harpers, or that it
might now be pursuing me, too.

We traveled together for some time after that—through the end of fall
and into winter. At first they had no choice but to come with me, in case
the Linesmen were watching, and after a while I think they decided the
cover I offered was as good as any. They did not acknowledge what I
had done for them and I did not mention it again. Sometimes I tried to
puzzle them out, and other times we were too tired or too hungry or
too hot or too cold or too lost to care about puzzles and mysteries. We
were just on the road together.

## CHAPTER 6

# Some More Portraits

### I. The Western Rim

The world is made up of an infinite number of words, but it contains only a finite quantity of paper and ink. I cannot describe every little town we passed through or every person we met. But for the boys and girls who will be born in Ransom City and for all the generations to come I want to make some record of how things were.

There was a town called Mammoth that is worth recording for posterity. In a big red barn there they had a whole skeleton of a long-dead beast that they said was a monstrous precursor to human settlement or even Folk settlement, from back when the world was hardly made at all. Miss Harper suspected it was composited from bison but I was enthralled regardless. I displayed the Apparatus under the arch of its rib cage and its knuckly spine cast weird shadows on the ceiling.

The town of Izar had more dentists on Main Street than I could imagine was necessary or good for business or good for anyone's peace of mind. New Delacorte was built at the edge of a valley flooded with jewel-blue but lifeless water, stinking of salt and sulfur and dead fish, and nobody was willing to give me a satisfactory explanation as to how this came about. Dope fiends littered the streets of Caldwell, basking like lizards in the summer heat. In Kattagan a dispute over grave-rent threatened to turn violent. There was a store in Hamlin that sold nothing but candy! A hairy-knuckled woman on Main Street outside that extraordinary cornucopia thrust two live rattlesnakes up to my face as I stood sucking a mint and watching Carver water Mariette and Golda.

She cut off both serpents' heads with a single snip of her scissors and purported to read my future in their throes. I had not solicited this service and I was vexed about paying for it.

The fattest man I have ever set eyes on was the Mayor of Ford. Flesh rolled down his body like foothills and if he had a nose I cannot say that it was distinguishable from any other mountainous swelling of his features. I would just as soon have bought tickets for the Mayor as for the Mammoth.

There were at least three Glendales in that part of the world, and one New Glendale. None of them stick in my mind much but the four Beck Brothers, who you may recall have joined up with our westward expedition, Dick, Erskine, Joshua and John, they say that they grew up in one of the Glendales, and they want me to say it was an excellent little town. However when I ask them for details they are stumped too.

In the hills above Marchoun the trees were turning green to red to gold, the same way the light of the Process sometimes does as it grows unpredictable. I thought that was beautiful, and said so. But what held the Harpers' attention was that two big Ironclads of the Line had been abandoned on Marchoun's Main Street, their crews mysteriously vanished, their cannon blind. The townsfolk had resigned themselves to the presence of those hulking machines and business went on around them—certainly nobody dared try to move them. I dallied awhile in Marchoun to pay court to a handsome woman who owned a general store.

Skewbald's Main Street was one long slavemarket where convicts and debtors and captured Folk stood chained to every storefront and porch in silent reproach, and we passed the town by, stopping only as long as it took to re-shoe Mariette. The blacksmith in Skewbald mostly worked on chains and goads, and you would have thought some unease would show in his face, some hint of disturbed sleep or bad digestion, but in fact he was a smiling and handsome fellow. As we walked out I remarked that there is no justice in the world and Old Man Harper remarked that I was too old to be just learning that now.

In that part of the Western Rim there were many Folk still living free, but many in chains too. You did not see the great chained legions you hear they have down in the Deltas but it was not uncommon to see a small family of them, if that is the right word, in the fields of a farm as you passed by or doing the worst work of any particular town. It mostly went unremarked-on. Liberationists did not get much of an audience out on the Rim. That was how it was in Ford, and Hamlin, and Izar, and other places. Ford was also haunted by a Spirit that resembled ball-lightning and darted up and down Main Street at dusk, causing strange moods in women. I did not see it myself but I heard about it and have no reason to doubt it, having seen stranger things in my time.

We stayed at one Mr. Bob Bolton's farm on top of Blue Hill. He was too poor for slaves but he had goats and an ear-trumpet and three beautiful daughters. This sounds like the start of a filthy joke but there is no punch-line. He'd had sons too but they had all gone off to be soldiers for one side or another, and most of them were dead. Down below in Sholl there was a post-office, and I spent all afternoon sitting on a fence beside a cold brown field composing letters to May, Jess, and Sue, and also to Mr. Alfred Baxter, though I did not send that last one. Miss Elizabeth Harper taught me a great deal about spelling and commas.

In the next town over I nearly fought a duel with a man who claimed I had stolen the plans for the Apparatus from him. I was too proud to back down, although I am a poor shot, not least because I have next to no sight in my left eye, as I believe I have mentioned. Fortunately when dawn came, bleak and wintry, he was so drunk that at the signal he turned and walked ten paces at a forty-five-degree angle to true and right into a tree, concussing himself.

In the town after that three salesmen of the Northern Lighting Corporation jumped me in the darkness and beat me for a minute or two.

## II. THE NORTHERN LIGHTING CORPORATION

New Dreyfus was a mining town. It was like East Conlan only smaller and wilder and younger and more crowded, and it was built on lead-zinc, not coal, and there were slaves in the mines, which there were not in East Conlan. There were company stores and saloons all along New Dreyfus's Lead Street. It was a town that was suddenly rich in a way it did not know what to do with. I called in at the most prominent saloon—it had three stories, one more than any of its competitors, and the girls who waved from its balcony were the prettiest and best-dressed in town. I gambled for a while, losing money but making friends, which is my usual practice in a new town. Then I started in pitching the Ransom Process to anyone who would listen.

The saloon's owner leaned back in his chair and put his feet up on the table and hooked his thumbs in a self-satisfied way into his lapels and said, "I'm surprised you haven't heard, Professor. Seeing as you said you knew all about New Dreyfus and what a fine little town it is and how you came here especially to visit us. We have all the electric-light we could ever need, and N.D. does not go dark at night."

My heart sank but I kept smiling.

The saloon owner winked, and got up from the table, and beckoned me to follow him upstairs. He told his lieutenants at the table we would be but a moment, and I agreed, and told them we would talk further when I returned. He led me up and out onto the balcony, where he shooed away the pretty girls and said, "See?"

I saw. While I had been idling in the saloon and drifting from table to table and talking about myself, evening had fallen. A switch had been thrown—I don't mean that as a figure of speech. It now became apparent that all along Lead Street arc lights squatted on the rooftops. In the bustle of the afternoon I had not noticed them. They cast a cold white light that to my eye was hideous.

"The Northern Lighting Corporation fixed us up six months ago," he said. "N.D. does not sleep." There was indeed something manic and sleepless-looking and herky-jerky about the people below, caught in that light.

"I know of the Northern Lighting Corporation," I said. "I know of their work. They are as crooked as the world is wide. They will bleed you, they will ruin you. What did they charge? They say they operate out of the Three Cities but you know what, that is a lie, they are a front for the Line, and that means all that comes with the Line. But what I offer you, sir, is entirely different. For one thing—"

He looked out over the white night of Dreyfus and shrugged. "I don't know much about politics, Professor. But I know what works."

He left me alone out there. I spied Mr. Carver down in the street below, leaning on a fencepost, rolling a cigarette. Our eyes met and we both shrugged.

The same thing happened in Thatcher and Ford. In Thatcher my allegations against the Northern Lighting Corporation were overheard, and three men followed me outside. It was not that late in the day but it was late in the year when we got to Thatcher, and so when the arc light over the saloon sparked suddenly and went out we were in darkness. One fellow snatched the hat from my hand and a second shoved me into the third, who grabbed my arm and told me that if I kept spreading rumors I would regret it. I answered less diplomatically than I should have, maybe, and there was a scuffle and my nose was bloodied and I was knocked to my knees and to tell the truth I was already starting to regret it.

My assailants dispersed when the light came back on. A few minutes later Old Man Harper walked by, on his way into the saloon, and saw me wiping mud from my hat.

"I have more enemies than I deserve," I said. "I am fighting a losing battle, me against the world. The next century is at stake. Time is running out and my optimism is sorely strained."

"Yeah?" he said. "I was young once too." He pushed past me and entered the saloon.

## III. Politics and Religion

I tried not to talk politics or religion with anyone. That is the golden rule when traveling in strange country, doing business with strangers, or visiting with relatives. Little Water was a Line town and Mansel was a Gun town and Slate was divided down the middle and the mere act of eating breakfast in one establishment or another had consequences and implications I could not fathom. There were encampments of the Line all along Gold River and in the shadow of the Opals, and their Heavier-Than-Air Vessels were frequently seen overhead, watching like hawks. In Stone Hill and Dalton and Honnoth there were heaving tents hosting religious revivals of the Smiler, Silver City, and World Serpent faiths, respectively. South of Dalton we must have passed too close to a settlement of the Folk, or in some other way broken one of their laws, because somebody pelted us with stones from up on the rocky hillside until we moved on as fast as the horses could trot.

In Mattie's Town we dined at a hotel whose owners were die-hard old men who had once been soldiers of the Red Republic, you could tell from the relics of that splendid and ill-fated Cause that decorated the walls, torn battle-standards and battered medals and the like, and I did not know where to look or what gestures of respect to make to avoid offense. In Kukri there was a bank that had been robbed seven times by the same Agent of the Gun, the notorious and dashing Gentleman Jim Dark. He robbed it every time he came through on other business, the way a traveling salesman might stop in to visit a woman, and after a while he started posing for photographs, and now Kukri did better business in memorabilia than it had ever done in banking. They kept talking about Jim Dark this and Jim Dark that, and Old Man Harper got unaccountably frightened and made us move on.

In Ruhr and in Tull and in Carnap people spoke with mixed feelings of rumors that nearby free settlements of the Folk had been slaughtered. Eye-witness accounts were not dissimilar to what Carver and I had seen outside Kenauk. Nobody could say who was responsible—but in Carnap I heard that a huge man wearing a foul bearskin over a big gray soldier's coat and filthy breeches had wandered into town. He had a shaggy wild-man's beard and he had more than a dozen long Folk finger-bones and hanks of dry black mane braided into his belt. He had a rifle of incongruous quality slung across his back, and a gun like that on a man like that could mean only thing. He was nearer to nine feet tall than eight. The two hunting dogs that stretched out at his feet were indistinguishable from wolves. He sat at a lunch counter and consumed enough sausage and coffee for six men or as many as twenty, depending on who was telling the story, then left without paying or ever speaking a single word except "Knoll," which might or might not have been his name.

This story frightened Old Man Harper terribly. It frightened me too, though I was not sure why. I did not like the Agents of the Gun but I had no quarrel with them so far as I knew.

I have said the names of the Gun and the Line a lot. Maybe in the new century you will have forgotten what they are. Well—I am an optimist. Ransom City will be free of them if I have any say in the matter. We will build out in the unmade lands where things are not yet made in their image.

I could tell you what I know about the Engines of the Line and their cold greed and the legions of men and machines that serve them. I don't know much but I know more than most men. I could tell you a few things about the Gun. They do not have the numbers the Line has but their chosen few, the Agents, are more than human—like Blood-and-Thunder Boch and Jim Dark and Dandy Fanshawe and all those other colorful ladies and gentlemen of the ballads and the legends and the crime reports. I have met more than one of them in my time, in White Rock and in Jasper, and most of what you hear about them is true. They are strong as bears and faster than snakes and they are not impossible to kill but it is damn hard.

When I was a boy it was always said that the Engines themselves and the demons of the Gun were immortal. They might in the course of their fighting smash each other's bodies of wood and metal but their spirits would always return, after a suitable vacation from history, after maybe one or two human generations had gone by, like a feud reigniting or a touch of madness in the family tree. Nothing could kill them. If that was true the War would be without end. It was best not to think about that for too long.

Anyhow when we got to Garland the Linesmen were going house to house kicking in doors and shouting questions and when they were done with a house they wrapped it in black tape and barbed wire and afterward nobody would look at that house, like it had just vanished. They questioned us and we did the old servant & master routine again and did not stay the night.

When we got to New Boylan Town it was already gone, the buildings leveled by Line rockets and the population evacuated to nobody-knew-where, because there had been Agents of the Gun hiding there, or so they said. And in Sandalwood, which was close enough to New Boylan that they could see the smoke, a man came up to me as I was preparing the Apparatus and said, "I know who you are."

I said, "I should hope so. I put up posters all over town."

He was nervous and thin and did not smile or take my hand when I offered it, only pushed his spectacles up on his nose then fiddled with his tie.

"My brother-in-law saw you in Kenauk and he wrote to me."

"It could take me a moment to recall Kenauk. Would you hand me that hammer?"

"Me, I'm from Boylan. I used to be from Boylan. I had a store there."

"I'm sorry. I am sorry, I really am. So. Ah. Well then. What did your brother think of the show?"

"Brother-in-law."

"Sorry."

"He said you said you had a machine that could end the War. We wouldn't have to. . . . He said you could. That it was a secret, that it was some secret weapon you learned from the Folk. That if you . . . I mean . . . the Powers, the you-know-what and the you-know-who, that you'd found a way to, you know."

"No," I said.

He took off his spectacles and stared at his feet. I was nervous that he would attack me or start crying, and I did not know which would be worse. Fortunately Miss Harper had been watching this exchange as she polished the Apparatus, and now she came around the side of it and put her hand on the man's arm and asked what his store had sold, and after a while he started talking about that instead, much to my relief.

When people asked me about my politics I usually said I was a Free-Marketer, or that I thought the little guy ought to get a fair shot, or if I thought those might cause offense I would just say that I was a believer in Light.

## IV. ELIZABETH HARPER

She was tall, and fair, and blue-eyed. She wore her hair long, tied in a tail. She might once have been pretty but after all the hard and weathering travel she'd done you would have to call her handsome. She did not mind the cold but was short of breath when it was hot. There were times when we ate well and times when we ate badly but she was always thin, in a way that concealed a quite respectable strength and hardness. Her one luxury was expensive tooth-powder. If she ever complained about anything she was too proud to do it in my presence.

The stories she told me about herself were never true, and after a while stopped being even consistent. It was like a game between us. When we had company she was my servant, and very quiet. At other times she was variously a refugee, a botanist, an heiress fleeing an unwelcome marriage, a reporter on assignment for the *Gibson City Gazette,* a missionary come to minister to the wild Folk, an undercover surveyor for the Jasper City Bank, the wife of a famous outlaw in hiding, and the granddaughter of the late General Orlan Enver of the late Red Valley Republic, in hiding from enemies of the Cause. I think she enjoyed being other people. It was a kind of liberation for her. You could tell that she labored under some great responsibility.

She could never quite hide her accent. I guessed that she was from the Ancient East, far away and across the mountains, from one of the cold green northern principalities, like Koenigswald or Maessen or Kees or the like. The way I was raised, that made her almost as fantastic and unlikely as an elf or a troll, and if she'd ever just said she was a princess I might have believed her. I guessed also that she was a scientist, not from anything in particular she said but from the way she said things, and from all the foolish sort of things that most people say all the time but she never did.

She hardly ever spoke a word to Carver except for time-of-the-day pleasantries, and it may be that Carver never said a single word to her. She communicated with Old Man Harper in significant glances and nods. She did not ride well. On the other hand she was cool under pressure whenever we were questioned at checkpoints, which was not infrequent.

When I put on shows she took round the hat for donations and sub-
scriptions, and it turned out that she had a talent for it, especially with
women.

She took a considerable interest in the Ransom Process, and asked
me about it often. I said I would not tell her how it worked until she
told me who she was, and that was that. She also at my urging experimented with the Ransom Vegetarian Diet and my system of morning
Exercises, the Ransom System of Exercises.

She would stare at the Apparatus with a half-smile as if it was a joke
she did not get, and sometimes woke early in the morning and slid
down on her back in the dirt to inspect its underbelly. She was appalled
to discover that I had no regular system of note-taking regarding its
functions. There were times when it ran smoothly for hours and there
were times when it did nothing at all and I said that as far as I was concerned it was a matter of art, like understanding the moods of a high-
spirited horse. She stared at me and I had the sense that I was back
at school again, and being examined, and not doing well. After that she
took on the task of recording observations herself. I think like me she
liked problems that she could solve. Carver seemed to resent this intru-
sion but said nothing.

Soon she reported steady progress, despite occasional setbacks.

"I knew it in my heart," I said, "but it does me a world of good to
hear it from another person."

"Well," she said, "just wait until you get to Jasper City."

Whenever we came to a crossroads she urged me eastward, toward
Jasper City. I still had doubts and misgivings but she told me I was ready
to face Mr. Alfred Baxter and roll the dice on my fortune, that it was
only fear that held me back. I said maybe another year, and she pointed
out that in another year the Northern Lighting Corporation would have
beaten me utterly—would have sewn up every town in the West—it was
now or never. I knew that she had her own purposes for going East, but
I liked hearing it anyhow.

I don't want to be ungallant and the fact is that Miss Harper was
most likely not so much older than myself, but in a way she reminded
me of what I imagined my mother might have been like had she not
died when I was small. I do not mean that she cooked or cleaned or
mended for me, because except when it was strictly necessary to maintain our servant & master subterfuge she did not. I think I mean that
when I was a boy and my mother came to me in dreams she always
seemed to be carrying some secret from the next world, I never knew

whether it was wonderful or terrifying, but either way she could not tell me, there were no words. That is what Elizabeth Harper was like. I wanted to impress her. I boasted even more than usual. Her secrets and everything I didn't yet understand about the Process and her urgency and mine began to get all bound up together in my mind. I would lay half-awake at night sometimes imagining how one problem might be the answer to the other, looking up at the stars and listening to Old Man Harper pissing against a tree and muttering, or whittling ugly pointless nothings out of wood as he kept lookout. One time I felt I was on the threshold of understanding when Old Man Harper woke us all up, shooting into the woods at nothing. Only Mr. Carver slept through it. He could sleep through anything.

## V. THE RANSOM SYSTEM OF EXERCISES

If I am to be remembered at all, it will be for the Process, or the founding of Ransom City, and the System of Exercises will be no more than a footnote. But I am justly proud of it.

Like the Ransom Process itself, the Ransom System of Exercises works mostly by the creation and counter-position of forces. Also like the Process, it may be performed anywhere, without wires or other equipment.

First you stand very straight, like a child trying to steal something from a high shelf. Then you bend, like you are suddenly fascinated by the dirt on the floor. You can do this in a rustic barn, by moonlight under a lonely tree on the western plains, in a Line prison cell, in the privacy of your childhood sickroom, in a narrow attic lodging in Jasper City. You can do it in the presence of strangers if you have a thick enough skin. You can try passing it off as a religious observance—that will not eliminate all jeering but may reduce it. Anyhow the motion is to be repeated, the number of repetitions to be increased daily. This loosens the muscles and the tendons, which otherwise become set in their ways. Then you seize one foot in each hand so that you form a full circle—by now you should be on your back—this is damned hard to put into words!—and now first on one side of your body, then the other, you may set the muscles of your own body against each other. Stand, clasp your hands as if about to wrestle an invisible man to the floor—the angle is important—set one arm against the other with all your might, and more. Repeat and repeat again. Thus you can build strength out of nothing. You would not think it to look at me but I can balance on my own head, and I almost never tire, and I can lift my chin to a tavern's doorframe often enough to win wagers.

I have done these Exercises almost daily—with frequent refinements of the System and with occasional exceptions for emergencies or injury—ever since I was fourteen years old. When I was a boy I tried to sell lessons regarding the System to the miners of East Conlan to finance my greater work, but they regarded the practice with ill-founded suspicion and contempt. Mr. Carver refused to participate too. In the town of Heinberg I was accused of witchcraft on account of the Exercises—they thought it was a Folk-dance to scare up curses. Miss Harper experimented, like I said. Old Man Harper sneered whenever he witnessed me performing the Exercises but once I caught him attempting them himself, puffing, red in the face and furious. It was the day after we heard about the giant Knoll, with the wolves and the bearskin and the big rifle &c, and I think he was still in a panic. Anyhow he was doing it all wrong. I said nothing.

## VI. Mariette and Golda

Mariette was a horse. I do not know very much about her parentage and she kept her political opinions to herself. Golda was also a horse, and she had a certain dignified stubbornness that makes me think she would have fallen in with Trade Unionists had I ever shown her the big city. Mariette was brown and I purchased her in Melville City from a man with crooked teeth. Golda was black and white and I purchased her on a farm south of Disorder after a previous horse got shot. They were both pretty good animals. Neither survived White Rock. So far as I know they were just horses and kept no particular secrets. Though who knows what's important to a horse?

## VII. Old Man Harper

I don't like to speak ill of anyone but Old Man Harper was a mean son of a bitch.

He was of medium height, and solidly built, with the kind of shoulders that could still throw a punch if need be. He wore a long dirt-brown duster and beneath that there was a gray shirt, a curl of gray chest hair, and a thick neck with one or two white scars. He had the kind of face that is either pale or blotchy red or sometimes both at once, and a slightly skewed nose. His hair was still thick and he oiled it. Sometimes he walked with a stick, sometimes not. Often one sensed he was exaggerating his infirmity and the ugliness of his limp, either to mislead his enemies or out of pure bitterness. I always felt that I had seen him before, but I wasn't sure where.

You could tell he'd been handsome when he was younger. That was not enough to explain his huge bitterness. He was like a man who has given up too much and thought he was owed the world in return, and got nothing. I wondered at first if he had failed in business, but once I got to know him I could not imagine him ever doing honest work.

Mr. Carver did not like Old Man Harper, and Old Man Harper did not like Mr. Carver. Most days Old Man Harper had no good word to say about anyone. He could make the word *Professor* sound like the vilest insult imaginable. Then again there were rare days when he was the soul of good cheer, he would encourage me to smoke with him and would walk beside me and tell jokes and stories about things that happened in battles before I was born, and he was so charming one could forget all the slights and the threats of the day before. I did not know what caused these changes of mood, and I suspect neither did he.

He purchased every newspaper he ever set eyes on and scanned first the reports of crimes, then the reports of miracles, then the reports of business, and lastly as if he'd been building his strength for it he read the latest dispatches from the War. He had strong opinions on most political issues—generally that everyone involved was a thief or a damn fool—with the exception of questions pertaining to the War between the Gun and the Line, about which he would only shake his head and say that things were very complicated. He was sometimes generous to children, more often menacing. He could stare down men twice his size and half his age and a hundred times drunker than he was. I saw it happen. He spoke to dogs as if he expected obedience, which he sometimes got and sometimes didn't. He stole, thoughtlessly and often. He was never without a gun on his person, often concealed. He was a keen and deadly hunter.

He was always on the lookout. He rarely slept. Like I said he sometimes fired blindly into the woods at night, spooked by an owl or a rodent or a wind in the trees or the moon or who-knows-what. He read menace in the tracks of animals and whenever he was in town he fancied people were watching him and taking notes. Signs of the Folk fascinated him and sometimes when he thought they were nearby he would set off into the woods or up among the rocks and just stand there impatiently, as if waiting for someone to answer his grievances. Nothing ever happened and he would come back furious and scowling. Sometimes he would vanish for a day or two at a time, as if he had decided to go his own way—but he always found us again, or more precisely he found Miss Harper—I was surplus to requirements.

Once I asked him, "So what brings you back?" I meant this as a pleasantry and did not expect an answer, but it seemed he was in a thoughtful mood.

He shook his head and said, "Someone must keep me on the straight and narrow. I'm too weak to do what must be done. I'm not a good man, Ransom. Without that damn woman's nagging . . ."

"What must be done, exactly?"

"Mind your own business, Professor."

You may recall the story I recounted earlier, regarding the nine-foot giant in the bearskin coat who came into Carnap with trophies of the Folk on his belt and two wolf-like dogs at his feet and who did not pay for his breakfast. This story scared Old Man Harper like I have never seen a grown man scared by anything. He developed an interest in soothsaying, he purchased charms and icons in every town where such things were for sale, he trapped rabbits and consulted their entrails as to the movements of his enemies. I asked what enemies and he said that the great hidden secret of the universe was that the whole thing and everyone in it is your enemy. "You can write that maxim down, Professor, and call it yours if you like." He was told by a patently mad palmreader in Mansel Town that he should avoid river-voyages and mirrors and for the rest of our time together he dipped the brim of his hat to cover his eyes whenever he passed a mirror. As the condition worsened he started to do the same for windows, bodies of still water, even men with spectacles.

If he saw the smoke of a Line vehicle ahead he might make us go miles out of our way. Once he heard two little boys speculating excitedly about rumors that a real live Agent of the Gun had been seen in the vicinty, and he made us leave town at once. A woman who said she was a witch sold him a dried dog's penis on a piece of string, that was supposed to ward off the eyes of the Powers. So far as I know it did not.

He had no interest whatsoever in the Apparatus. He was like a wild animal. Whatever he could neither use nor master frightened him. Whenever I mentioned Mr. Alfred Baxter, he scoffed.

"I could have been a businessman," he said. "Had I chosen to. I was full of big ideas when I was a boy."

"Is that a fact. For instance?"

He gave the question a moment's thought then shrugged. "Buy low and sell high, Professor. It's a simple enough con."

I didn't ask him a whole lot of questions. I tried to puzzle him out by tracking and observation and studying his signs.

I was still sure that I had seen him before. Eventually, and quite by chance, I found out where.

We'd stopped in Durham Town. It was the beginning of winter and the wind was wet and cold and we'd paid to sit by the fireplace in a beer hall and un-freeze our joints and wring chunks of ice from our hair. There were old newspapers by the fire and a shelf of even older books, which the proprietors loaned out for a penny. Mostly they were smut. A few concerned notorious crimes. There was a single ancient copy of the Charter of the Red Republic standing stiff-backed on the shelf like a missionary among whores. Miss Harper found the Charter interesting. Old Man Harper read the newspapers. I got talking to a boy who worked in the beer hall about books and I suggested that an ambitious boy might want to read the *Autobiography of Mr. Alfred Baxter,* or a good Encyclopedia of the natural sciences. And he said that was all very well but he had grander ambitions, and he pointed me to his favorite among his employer's books. It was called *The Captains of Crime: Their Glorious Lives and Their Ignominious Ends.*

It was printed on stiff yellow paper and it recounted the escapades of a dozen Agents of the Gun in tones of both righteous condemnation and ghoulish glee. I read about Dagger Dolly, who once burned a whole town to the ground because a man had insulted her. I read about Blood-and-Thunder Boch, whose legend and whose burden it was that he could never say no to a dare, and who consequently stood athwart an onrushing Engine and shot out its headlamp and was killed. I read about elegant Dandy Fanshawe of whom it was said that no dope was dealt in the West without his taking a cut, and Procopio "Dynamite" Morse, Abban the Lion who dueled a hundred men and could talk to snakes, and then I turned the page and read about John Creedmoor, the charming monster who stole away the heir to the Tyrias Transport Trust, who led the Gibson City Mob for five years, who sabotaged the Line's factories at the Devil's Spine, who . . .

I did not read most of the words. I just stared at the photograph that was reproduced beneath them.

The book speculated that the man was dead. He had done nothing wicked or grand for years, and surely that meant he was dead. A man of John Creedmoor's proud restless spirit would not think of retiring, and besides his masters would not allow it. The only way out of the service of the Guns was by means of a noose or a bullet.

I lowered the book to see that Old Man Harper was watching me. Our eyes met but we said nothing.

I was terrified and did not know what to say. I grew up in a town on the edges of Line territory. We were not important or glamorous and we had nothing much to steal and nothing much worth sabotaging. Except for in books and songs I had never met an Agent of the Gun. Not at that time in my life. But I had seen what they left behind at Toro and I had seen one hanged at Secchi. I had been present at a town called Kloan when there was a shoot-out between an Agent and forces of the Line, hiding behind a barrel—I have nightmares about it still.

Anyhow that night he came into my room. I was not sleeping but did not notice him standing by my bed until a cloud moved from the moon and revealed his silhouette. He stretched out his stick and pressed it against my chin as if to close my mouth. It hurt. The back of my skull was pressed against the headboard, so that my head was in a kind of clamp, like I was about to be the subject of dentistry.

"My fame has found me out," he said.

I could not easily open my mouth to answer, so I did not try.

We stayed like that for some time. I was afraid, and then angry, and then afraid and angry at the same time, and then I started to feel ashamed, as if I had wronged him by snooping into his past. It seemed some of the menace faded from his eyes and he just looked tired.

"That was a long time ago," he said. "I gave it up. I am no longer that man. My bones hurt in cold weather and my hands shake and I sleep badly. I am not the giant that I was. But do not think I am not still a danger to the likes of you."

He turned and left, entertaining no questions.

That was at the beginning of winter, like I said, just a few days before we got to White Rock.

## CHAPTER 7

# THE WOLVES

No yarn of world's-edge adventure and daring is complete without wolves. If I ever got this far into a story-book without wolves I would demand my money back.

For example: in *The Autobiography of Mr. Alfred Baxter,* there are wolves no later than the second chapter. As a young man Mr. Baxter set off into the West to make his fortune and when there were rumblings of War he did his duty and signed up—against the Red Valley Republic, which he regarded as unsound and a threat to Property and good order. He was put in charge of a platoon of brave men but they did not make it to the battle at Black-Cap Valley, on account of being led astray by bad weather or maybe the tricks of the Red Republic's Folk allies. Instead of joining the mayhem at Black-Cap they were harried along frozen plains by starving wolves until they formed a circle, back-to-back, and stood their ground against the snarling fangs. I read all this with great excitement as a boy, though even then I understood that it was only a metaphor for how we must overcome adversity in pursuit of greatness.

It was early winter. There were signs and rumors of impending snow. As the road took us back east it climbed steadily and mercilessly up and into what would soon be mountains. The road was clogged with mud from snow runoff and the woods were glistening and bare. Black clouds leaned in close overhead and were menacing, like policemen. I wore a hooded waxed coat of bilious green that I had purchased in Durham and kept my head covered and did not make conversation. Inside I was in a kind of panic, and had been since that moment the night before, at the fireplace at the World Hotel in Durham, when I learned the name John Creedmoor.

I felt deceived and disillusioned. For weeks I'd traveled with the Harpers and tried to puzzle out their secrets. I'd come to imagine that it would be something grand, something splendid. If they were on the run from the law it was because they were cruelly misjudged, or had stolen from the rich to give to the poor. If the Line hunted them, well that was to their credit, and if they were spies it was in a good cause. I'd been a dupe. I had assisted in a wicked purpose. They were Agents of the Gun. Not only him but also her. I was a fool and the world was worse than I could fathom. It was a terrible injustice. I had been meant to do great and good and beautiful things and this was not my proper fate.

There has never been a man in the West, no matter how upright, who did not sometimes when he was a boy daydream of running away from home and joining up with the Agents of the Gun. I assure you I am no exception. When you are small and weak and poor there are times when your soul seems no big sacrifice to be big and wild and famous and free. But it is one thing to daydream and another to find yourself caught up in the schemes of the Gun for real. It is one thing to see a lion at the circus and another to get in its cage.

How many had they murdered, and how many more would they murder? I was sure that I would be their next victim. I was trouble for them now that I knew and I would be dealt with accordingly. That would be how the newspapers would report it, THE NOTORIOUS JOHN CREEDMOOR STRIKES AGAIN—ANOTHER VICTIM—THIS IDIOT DESERVED IT FOR SURE. They were toying with me. She'd been polite all day but that was her way, it was her little game. We would get far enough out of town and she would give a nod or that quiet little laugh she had and John Creedmoor would turn to me with a smile and faster than I could get my last words in order or even cry out he would cut my throat and roll me into a ditch. Then he would kill Carver and the horses.

Mr. Carver walked beside me, on the other side of the horses. I could not think of any way of alerting him to the danger that would not pre- cipitate it. Creedmoor would be stronger than I could imagine, faster than I could imagine, and his masters might have given him any num- ber of other wicked tricks. It was not impossible that he could hear what I was thinking. I'd heard it said some Agents had that knack. I had been a fool and now Carver would suffer on my account. Or maybe he knew already. I thought over every word he had said to me since we met the Harpers—there had not been many, there were never many—and it seemed every one was a warning. Loyal Carver!

It crossed my mind out of nowhere that I could probably turn both Creedmoor and Miss Harper in for reward money and that that could be a good start toward making my fortune. The idea made me stop in my tracks and I glanced up to see John Creedmoor looking at me in a thoughtful kind of way. All thoughts of profit fled from my mind. I knew I would be lucky just to survive.

I thought about Miss Harper. That was not her real name. Her real name would be a closely guarded secret. Among her fellow Agents she would have her own gloating criminal alias, like Black Casca or Dagger Dolly or Scarlet Mary, something proud and defiant and vile. Somewhere on her person she would have a weapon. I didn't know much about the Agents but every schoolboy knows that each of them carries a Gun, and that weapon houses their master's spirit. I'd never seen her go armed. I wondered where, all those weeks, she'd been hiding it.

It occurred to me in the middle of the afternoon that she might be innocent. I had been duped—maybe she'd been duped too. I started thinking of ways to save her. That helped me to be brave.

She asked me as we walked up the frozen road what had got me so silent and thoughtful-looking and I did not know what to say. I said I hadn't slept all night for worrying about the Apparatus and how it was not yet perfect. I said I had laid awake thinking about what Mr. Alfred Baxter would say if I ever got into Jasper City and showed up on his doorstep like an unwanted child. She told me I had nothing to fear except fear itself.

"Fear," I repeated, being able to think of nothing clever to say.

"In another week the mountains will be impassible," she said. "It's now or wait for spring. We all have places to go."

"She's right," Creedmoor said. "It's time."

I said nothing.

I began to think about how snow was a great thing for hiding a corpse, or how they could shove me off a cliff and pretend it was an accident, and I would go pinwheeling into the cold white light like a bird that never learned to fly, their laughter being the last thing I heard before the rushing of wind swallowed everything.

That was what I was thinking when Creedmoor turned to me and narrowed his eyes and drew his gun.

✳ ✳ ✳

I did not face Creedmoor's gun with all the pluck I would have liked, but I did my best. I stood up straight and swallowed and looked him in the eye and tried to think of some last words that would sound good if somehow after my death the Ransom Process were to become famous and biographies were to be written.

He said, "Get down, you fool."

I looked behind me. A gray beast burst out of the woods. Then there was a splash of red and a whimper and it staggered and fell beside the wagon's wheels. It was a wolf. Creedmoor had shot it.

He knelt down beside the body, wincing as he bent his knee, and inspected it. He had shot the beast in the skull and the light was going out of its remaining eye. He poked it in its mangy ribs with his gun.

He said, "What the hell are you looking at, Ransom?"

The horses were going crazy and Carver was trying to calm them. He had the ax in his hand again.

Creedmoor and the woman had a hissed conversation. I did not know what to do with myself. There was movement in the woods. The gunshot was still echoing in my ears but beneath it I could hear the sound of running feet, or at least I thought I could.

✳ ✳ ✳

There were at least a dozen of them. They had encircled us. Two of the bigger ones came lunging out from the trees, one in front of the wagon and one at the back, where I was. John Creedmoor got off three shots and I entirely forgot what he was and cheered for him. One shot felled one of the beasts—the one closest to me. The second shot hit that same beast again, unnecessarily. The last shot knocked sparks off one of the wagon's wheels. Then Creedmoor scrabbled to reload.

I found that odd. Everyone knows that the Guns of the Agents do not miss, and they are never empty.

The beast at the front of the wagon went low to the ground as Golda reared, then with a strangulated snarl it lunged up at her as she came down again, and then Mr. Carver put his ax into the beast's ribs with a dreadful thump.

There was a silence that seemed to last for hours. Then John Creedmoor dropped his bullets in the mud and said, "F——."

At the same moment a third wolf came out from the woods. It was noticeably smaller than the other two but seemed eager to make its mark. It was growling and snarling and bounding side-to-side. It had three long ragged scars on its ragged muzzle. It came running across the cold wet muck of the road and toward Miss Elizabeth Harper and I forgot all about my fears and threw myself at her too—the wolf and I leaping at almost the same moment, like ball-players—and I landed on her and bore her to the ground beneath me. At once the wolf was on top of me and its claws drew blood on my leg and my chest, but fortune was with me because its teeth missed their mark. It ripped at my jacket instead, with zeal but little effect. Then Mr. Carver put the ax into its back. The first chop didn't slow it much but the second hit the spot. He put a foot on its back and pulled the ax out and hit it again for good measure. Miss Harper cried out for the first time as blood warmed us both.

The horses had panicked and run the wagon into a small ditch so that it stood lopsided and some of my scant possessions had spilled, and the horses had stumbled and struggled to rise and for all I knew might have been lamed.

There was a clack-clack-clack and some cursing as Creedmoor reloaded.

The remaining wolves watched us from between the trees. Then they silently turned away.

Miss Harper struggled out from under me and from under the wolf, and sat in the mud, covering her face with her hands and breathing deeply. Mr. Carver wiped blood from his beard with his sleeve, succeeding only in smearing it all over and making himself look quite mad. John Creedmoor's hands were shaking and he dropped another bullet on the ground again and cursed violently, and in the end left the pistol on the ground as if it had disgusted and disappointed him and went to the back of the wagon, where I had allowed him to keep a shotgun concealed in a blanket. I sprang to my feet and ran jumping over the dead wolf and picked up John Creedmoor's abandoned pistol and turned it on him, then Miss Harper, then on John Creedmoor again.

"Don't be a damn fool," Creedmoor said, and continued unwrapping the shotgun from the blanket.

I fired a wild warning shot, putting a bullet into the ground and raising a little spray of mud. Creedmoor cursed and jumped back and raised his hands.

The pistol had kicked more than I expected, and the bullet had gone nowhere near where I had intended, but I tried not to let either fact show.

"Mr. Carver," I said. "Come here."

Mr. Carver ambled over, scratching his beard with one hand and holding the ax loose in the other. He stood beside me.

"This is the end," I said. "I know who you are. John Creedmoor. I read what you did at, at, well I don't recall—"

"You want me to list my crimes for you, Professor?"

"No. No, Mr. Creedmoor, I do not. I want you to go your own way and I will go mine."

"Hah! Gladly and good riddance."

"I want no part of your plans. I'll tell nobody what I know. Just go."

Miss Elizabeth Harper stood. She dabbed at her face with a handkerchief. I turned the gun on her and said, "Both of you. Who are you, Miss Harper? Don't tell me. I don't want to know. Just go."

"Wolves," she said, to John Creedmoor, not to me.

He nodded.

"No accident—there was nothing natural or ordinary about that—they've found us, then."

"Yes," he said. "Of course. You, Professor, shoot me if you're going to or else let me arm myself." He went back to the blanket and took out his shotgun and I did nothing. He glanced at me with contempt then looked out into the woods, shotgun held ready.

"If I were what you think I am you would be dead, Ransom. I told you I am no longer that man."

"What do you mean—you quit? Is that what you're telling me? You just—"

"I'm not telling you anything, Professor. You're smart, figure it out yourself."

"John," Miss Harper said. "Who is it?"

He shrugged. "The Gun. Its Agents. They have our scent."

"Yes," she said. "But who? Do you know?"

"No. How would I? One of the ones who talks to wolves. It's a vulgar trick and not uncommon. I am not a f——ing encyclopedia. Ask Professor Ransom, he reads the story-books. I knew an Agent once who called herself the Witch of New Rochelle and she talked to wolves but she'd be a hundred and ten if she still lives. A hundred and twenty. Dogs love Scarlet Jen the way everything else with a dick does but she never leaves Jasper City—from what I hear she rarely leaves the Floating World. Are you taking notes, Mr. Ransom? Abban the Lion fancied himself a brother to all predators but the Line got him last year at Greenbank. We were more rivals than friends besides, even before I turned traitor, and he would show me no special consideration, so what does it matter? We come and go. We die young. Could be somebody new. A tracker. Maybe one, maybe more, doesn't matter. One is enough. Could be this big son of a bitch who I hear was seen in Carnap making a spectacle of himself and likes to torment the Folk. I don't know. I was one of the greats. Who the f—— is he? Nobody. In the old days I would have sniffed him out before he sniffed me. I would have heard the whispers and known his name. Does it matter? None of it matters. They have our trail now. We are dead."

This was by far the longest speech I had ever heard from him.

"Huh," said Mr. Carver.

"We have to go on," Miss Harper said.

They discussed the weather awhile, and the road ahead, and agreed on how it was cross the mountains before the snow came or maybe not for weeks or even months. Meanwhile the gun grew heavy and my hands began to shake.

I said, "What do you mean—turn traitor? And who has our scent?"

"Thought you said you didn't want to know," Creedmoor observed.

"I changed my mind. I have the gun, you should understand that, Mr. Creedmoor. Tell me."

"Harry," Miss Harper said.

"Don't tell him," Creedmoor said. "Let him mind his business."

"Harry," she said, "we are not what you think we are."

"I don't even know what I think you are anymore."

"We should have gone our own way back in Clementine," she said, "and again at Black Cut, and I'm sorry you're in this too but if you turn back they will find you and question you. We have to keep going."

Creedmoor turned away from the woods and inspected the wagon.

"We need to move," he said. "Stay or go Mr. Ransom but the wagon and what's in it comes with us. You can keep your damn fool Apparatus."

I was outraged. I looked to Mr. Carver for support but he looked away. He would not meet my eye. His expression was uncertain.

"Harry," she said. "I'm sorry. But it's important, it's so very important. It sounds mad but nothing is so important as that we get back East, and away."

Creedmoor emitted a bitter despairing *hah*.

I kept the gun on her though my arm was trembling.

"Let him go," Creedmoor said.

"They'll question him."

"So? He can't tell 'em much. He knows nothing they don't already know better."

"I was thinking of the danger to him, not only the danger to us."

"I know what you were thinking. What do you think I think of Mr. Ransom's well-being?"

I felt I should remind them that I was there, and who exactly was holding the gun. I said, "Who *are* you?"

"You heard the rumors," she said. "The Line is here and the Gun is here because they are hunting someone with a secret. A secret, a weapon, something that can destroy them both and end the War."

"I've heard that said. It's the kind of thing desperate people say."

"It happens to be true. Harry, do you know the history of the Red Valley Republic?"

I said I knew a little.

"They had a weapon," she said. "It was lost before they could use it. It was a thing the Folk made, or a thing they had from an earlier age of the world. There was a deal between them. You've heard that the late General of the Republic had an ally among the Folk, who—"

"Everyone out here with some unlikely story to sell blames the Folk. Bad weather, good weather, charms against influenza. I've done it myself."

"Shut up," Creedmoor said. "Listen or don't." He put the shotgun down and tried to lift the wagon's wheels out of the ditch.

Mr. Carver shrugged and went to join him. "Here," he said.

"Your servant's got the right idea," Creedmoor said.

Mr. Carver told Creedmoor what he could do with himself. But they both put their shoulders to the wheel together. It moved slowly.

"I'm listening," I said.

Creedmoor stepped back from the wheel.

"I was an Agent of the Gun," he said. "I have done terrible things. They sent me out here last year to bring back that weapon. To destroy it, maybe, or use it themselves. They never told me the truth about anything if they could help it so I don't know. The—Miss Harper was an innocent who had the misfortune of crossing my path. One thing led to another and I turned on my masters and set their business aside."

He said that last thing like it was not so difficult to do for a man of his quality, like he wanted me to be impressed by his daring, which despite myself I was.

"My name is Liv," Miss Harper said. "I was a doctor in another life."

She approached the horses, speaking softly to calm them.

"Huh. What kind of doctor?"

"A psychologist. That means I studied madness and delusion."

"I know what that means. I am an educated man."

I shoved the pistol into my belt and went to help with the wheel.

"So what is this weapon?"

"I don't know," Creedmoor said.

"I like to call it a cure," said Miss Harper—Liv. She put a gentle hand on Mariette's flank. "The Guns and the Engines are a kind of madness, in my opinion. I don't know how it works. It's something the Folk left; that's all I know. The General Enver tried to claim it—instead it fell to us. That's how life is, I suppose."

Carver grunted with effort as the wheel slid in the mud.

"A cure for the world. What does it do?"

"Even the Powers fear it," Creedmoor said. "You know—hold there— you know that the Engines cannot be killed. Nor my former masters. Like a bad idea the bastards keep coming back. This thing kills them for good."

"How?"

"That's all I know. That's all anybody told me. I was never privy to the deep secrets, even when I was somebody."

"You don't know?"

"Do I pry into your secrets, Professor?"

"On the count of three," I said, and with a heave we got the back wheel righted.

"We know *where* it is," he said. "And that alone is enough for us to be hunted all over the world. Line wants it and Gun wants it and we don't intend to let either of them have it."

"You're an altruist, then. No—a profiteer, maybe. So where is it?"

"Buried."

"Somewhere back East," I said. "You said you were going to Jasper, but not stopping there, so further east. Past the Tri-City Territory? And Folk country, right, well, maybe—"

"Shut your mouth, Ransom."

"Maybe you don't know. Maybe I think you don't even know—"

"Maybe you should think more and talk less. Now all right. On the count of three. One, two, push."

Liv reported that the horses were unharmed.

I was not sure whether I believed them or not. Their story had the ring of delusion. I did not have to be a Doctor of Psychology from back

East to know that—I was self-taught, having encountered more than enough maniacs on the road to recognize the symptoms. But Creedmoor was who he was, and the incident with the wolves admitted of no ordinary explanation. I did not know what to think.

I tried to catch Carver's eye again to ask what he thought we should do, but when I succeeded he just shrugged and clapped black mud from off his hands.

I asked what they would do with this thing if they found it, and Creedmoor interjected that they would not, because his former masters were on our trail and we would all be dead before another sunrise. He said that it was only his damn fool pride that stopped him from just lying down in the mud and waiting for death. And Miss Harper said some things about Peace and the end of War and sweeping away the cobwebs of history and waking from the nightmares of the century gone by, and about the promise of the future and all the sort of things that I was used only to hearing from the less scrupulous kind of preacher or the more ambitious kind of con-artist. It seemed she was sincere, but then I often seem my most sincere when I am only trying to make a sale.

# WHITE ROCK

It was a handsome town. It was halfway up the mountains that in that part of their range are called the Opals, on the western side. There was a little comma-shaped mountain lake with piercingly blue water, and houses scattered around that, and a winding Main Street, and then more houses rising up rocky slopes and into the pines. Everything was made of pine. There was a pine schoolhouse, a pine courthouse, and a pine church run by a nun with a face as hard as wood and green needle-sharp eyes.

White Rock was joined to the wider world by two forms of commerce—one that sold, one that took. First, it was a logging town. Second, it guarded the pass across the Opals—travelers coming across the Opals from the east stayed a night in White Rock or re-provisioned there or even if they did not stay it was a rare traveler who got out without paying certain unexpected fees or taxes. Sometimes in the summer rich men from Jasper City or Gibson City came up out of the Territory and into the mountains to hunt or take the air, and though it was winter when we got there White Rock was not so rough or remote or uncivilized as you might expect.

We already knew that we were doomed. Snow had started to fall the day before and the road up to White Rock had been a struggle. When we got to White Rock there was snow drifting in the air, and heaped between the trees and bending down their branches, and the sky was bone-white, and you could not see far in any direction. I will not say that we heard wolves howling in the mountains, because we did not, but there was a sharp wind and with every strange sound of it we imagined the worst. The first man we spoke to in White Rock informed us that the road east was impassable. Snows had come unseasonably early and unseasonably heavy and we were too late. He saw our faces fall but mistook the reason. "I know," he said, "I know. It's bad for business all round. I have lost money because of it myself."

✳   ✳   ✳

There were three small hotels on Main Street but only one was open at that late stage of the year. It was called the Grand. There were muddy snowdrifts stacked by the doorway and ripples of ice on the windows and inside there was a fire. On either side of the fireplace was the mounted head of a wolf, which it gave none of us any pleasure to look at. We were not the Grand's only guests—there were a few stranded travelers, including a handful of businessmen, one missionary in retreat, two sad-looking old women who I think were sisters. The rooms were narrow as coffins and had similar angles.

Mr. Carver went walking. Liv arranged for a bath to be drawn. Creedmoor sat by the fire. With one hand he drank, and the other hovered by his gun, and he stared into the fire as if communing with it. This was the gun I had taken from him, and I do not know when he took it back. The money they were spending on drink and bathing and odd-angled rooms was principally mine and it had been hard-earned but there seemed no point in hoarding it now.

I went out into White Rock, and walked down Main Street. There was no sign of Mr. Carver. There was not much of anyone on the street at all. All the saddlers and blacksmiths and general stores that at other times of the year served travelers across the Opals were locked and empty.

A man walked into a butcher's store with a sack of something over his shoulder, and we nodded to each other as we passed. There was mud and snow on the ground and I kept my hands in my pockets. There was a store that sold thick coats and shoes, but it was closed too and for all I knew I would not need a coat anymore come morning. I felt very sorry for myself.

On the corner where Main Street bent there was a spur of rock, whited over with snow, and next to it was a building with a sign that said it was a bank.

The sign said it was the BANK OF THE OPALS, and there was a painting of a blue-capped mountain. Below that was another sign, which promised WILLS WRITTEN, OCCASIONAL MAIL HANDLED, THE HAPPY BONDS OF MATRIMONY FORGED & ANNULLED, GOODS PAWNED. It was not a particularly remarkable bank, but I felt sure I had seen it before.

I stood on the street for some time with my hands in my pockets looking confused before I realized that Mr. Carver and I had passed through White Rock on our way out West, more than a year ago. I had not stopped for long or noticed much about it. I had been in a big hurry to get wherever I was going. Anyhow it had looked very different then, the mountains had been gray-green and alive and the sky had been blue and you could see for miles west across the plains below.

I remembered that I had strolled down Main Street and into the Bank of the Opals, where I had entrusted to the teller a number of letters, mostly for my sisters Jess, May, and Sue, but also for some creditors back in East Conlan and for a couple of Professors of Science in Gibson City and Jasper and all the way back East, whose names I had plucked out of Encyclopedias.

This was something of a dizzying revelation and for some reason it made me smile. I whistled and looked around and saw things with new eyes and when the dizziness faded I was overcome with sentimentality.

I walked into the Bank. A single teller sat halfway asleep behind a pine counter and a metal grille. He wore a thick horsehair coat and a hat with woolen ear-flaps. I did not recall if he was the same man as the year before, but it pleased me to imagine he was, and I started up a conversation with him like I was a regular visitor to White Rock and just catching up on the gossip. We talked about the weather, and business, and the War, and I asked in a joking way if there was mail for me, and he consulted a big dusty ledger and announced to my surprise that there was. In fact there were four letters. It cost me a dollar to recover them.

One was from a creditor back in East Conlan. It had been there for nearly a year, and its threats now seemed mostly quaint.

The other three were from Jess, May, and Sue. Some of their letters had been there for longer than others, though none of my dear sisters had responded quite so promptly as my creditor.

I had mailed a whole lot of letters to a lot of people over that year I was out on the Rim, but this was the first time I had received a response, and it seemed a kind of miracle, as if I had received communications from the world of the dead, or from the Future.

The Professors had not responded at all. I took that snub in stride

and smiled and gladly paid the teller his handling fee and also a generous tip, and he lent me his pen and I sat by the window and wrote:

*Dear Jess.*

 *This is your brother Harry. I am back in White Rock. It has been
a long year and I wrote you some letters but who knows if you got
them, except the one I guess marked "White Rock." I am not rich yet,
nor am I famous, but the Apparatus has been a big hit in a lot of
places and I have had a lot of good luck along with the bad. Right
now things look bad. My curiosity got the best of me, like you always
said it would. But I am not out of the game yet and we shall see how
things go. I was glad to hear that you are in Jasper City now and doing well. I think I always knew you would end up on the stage. I expect we shall see each other again when I get there.*

*Yours,*
*H.*

I wrote the same sort of thing to May and Sue, congratulating Sue
on the news of her latest child and May on her latest spiritual advances,
then I wrote to my creditor that he might have scared me with that kind
of big talk a year ago but no longer. Then I walked out into the street
feeling that I had accomplished something.

I had to stop a few people in the street before I found anyone who had
seen Mr. Carver. That man was a lawyer, closing up his office, and he
advised me to get indoors and by the fire, because the aching of his joints
told him that it would be a fearful night. He also acknowledged that
from the high window of his office he had seen a stranger answering to
Mr. Carver's general description ambling down by the lake.

The lawyer reached into his coat, and took a swig from a silver flask.
He said it was for the cold, and offered me a taste. Instead I purchased
the whole flask from him. Then I went down toward the water.

I found Mr. Carver leaning against a tree. By then it was nearly dark.

I said, "You must be cold."

"No," he said.

"Well. Maybe I am. I've never liked the cold. Give me warm weather
and sunlight."

He looked at me, and then out again over the lake. The water was
frozen and gray and I could not see the other side of it at all.

I took an experimental sip from the flask, and immediately started to cough. I handed the flask to Carver, who just raised a single thick black eyebrow at it.

"I thought we should drink together," I said. "Under the circumstances. There's a kind of ritual to it. We never have. Indulge me."

He shrugged, and indulged me.

I said, "Do you think they're telling the truth? The Harpers, I mean."

"They think so."

"About what's hunting them. The Gun and its Agents."

"That?" He nodded. "Yeah."

"I didn't mean," I said. "Well, I mean that I never planned for us to. That is, you understand. I'm groping my way toward an apology, Mr. Carver. I mean to say that I did not intend."

I coughed again. "I don't ordinarily touch drink. Bad for the brain. It has been the wreck of many an ambitious young man. Mr. Baxter says so."

"True enough," he said. "I've seen it happen."

"Well then."

He passed the flask back to me and I drank again.

"We were in White Rock before," I said. "On the way out West. A year ago. More than a year. It was not so damn cold then."

"One town is about the same as any other."

"I disagree. I have rarely passed through any place I didn't consider noteworthy in some way. This town has a first-rate lake and a very decent bank and post office. I wrote letters to my sisters and entrusted them to the teller with the utmost confidence."

I drank again. I felt a little less cold with each swallow, but did not yet feel anything I recognized as inebriation.

"Mr. Carver, do you have family?"

"Yes and no."

"Well, you never speak of them."

"No."

"Excuse me." I took a cautious step out onto the ice and was pleased to find that it held my weight. "A first-rate lake. Mr. Carver, if you have family to write to you should do so. I will advance you the money if you need it."

"No, thank you."

"I don't even know how old you are."

"No?"

"I have come to consider you a friend, Mr. Carver."

"Yeah?"

I could not resist the temptation to take a further few steps out onto the ice, slipping a little and extending my arms for balance like a Heavier-Than-Air Vessel of the fixed-wing variety. Then I drank again. The ice continued to hold.

"I'm curious, you know. About you, Mr. Carver, I mean. Your manner invites it. If you wanted to arouse less curiosity you should have told more lies. Or if you'd just said you were on the run from the law I would have overlooked it."

"Not everything has some big secret to it."

I could tell from the closeness of his voice that he'd followed me out onto the ice. I found that very encouraging, and I took a few steps more.

"I wondered once if you might be a Linesman. One of the true men of the Line, born and raised, from one of those awful Stations of the North, in the tunnels beneath the factories, like you hear such awful things about. You have an uncanny knack with machines and you have no small talk. A defector, a deserter, an escapee. If that's what it is I wouldn't mind. What matters is what a man does not where he's from."

"Are you asking?"

"I guess I am. "

"I've lived a long time and traveled. I've learned a lot."

I said nothing, just took a few more steps forward. A little gray snow blew around my face.

"Once," I said, "you told me you had lived among the Folk. Do you remember? After Kenauk. It was when we found that, well, I don't know what to call it—"

"A questioning."

"If you like. A questioning. Well, so—"

"Well, what if I was a Linesman, Professor? A long time ago."

"Mind you, you're tall for a Linesman."

"The Folk are driven from Line lands. Did you know that? The Line will not f——ing tolerate them. A foreign and unpredictable element. A relic of the old world. They fight back sometimes but it's better if they hide. First the Line sends poison-gas rockets then Heavier-Than-Airs then soldiers, then it's fighting in the tunnels, knife-to-knife."

Snow stung my face. The ice creaked underfoot and I shuddered. Carver stepped lightly at my side.

"You could see things down there," he said. "A soldier could."

"I bet you could."

"Things that would make you want to walk away. Change your name. Travel. Things that would make you know the world was bigger and older and different than you thought it was."

I said nothing, just drank. Carver took a drink too.

"Or let's say I was a missionary," he said. "The Silver City church sends missionaries among the Folk. The Liberationists visit 'em. Maybe I was one of them. You could see something that would change your way of thinking."

"That's possible," I said. "There's no shortage of missionaries in the world."

He walked behind me, saying nothing.

"You'll laugh, Mr. Carver," I said, "but from time to time I've thought that you, well, that is, that if you were to grow out your beard a little more, you might look kind of—I mean, maybe on your mother's side some way back, if you know what I mean—kind of like one of them yourself—that is—"

I recall that I slipped on the ice, and he reached out to steady my shoulder, and that I turned so that we were looking into each other's faces.

He said, "I know what you saw, Ransom. I saw it too, once—long time ago. Out of the corner of my eye—you know what I mean, right?"

We were quite far out on the ice by then, and all alone.

"I suspected when I first saw your job-advertisement. Something about it. I *knew* when I first saw the Apparatus. I knew how it worked. I knew what you'd stolen."

"Not stolen."

"I couldn't believe it. I couldn't believe anyone would dare."

"Well," I said.

"I thought, someone has to keep an eye, someone has to see—well, what does it matter? It's over now."

He let go of my shoulder and turned back toward land and was soon lost in the haze of snow.

I did know what he meant, though I guess you do not, because I have not yet found a way to write about it.

I would like to say that I kept on alone across the ice until I found that light on the other shore but as a matter of fact, drunk though I undoubtedly was, my nerve failed me. I was not worried that the ice would break but I couldn't bear the darkness or the solitude. After a little while I turned back too.

❋  ❋  ❋

It was near midnight when I returned to the Hotel. Creedmoor still sat by the fire. He was still drinking. He had his pistol out by his side as if he no longer cared about keeping secrets. Maybe that was why he was alone in the room. With the hand that wasn't drinking he held one of his charms, the head of a big black beetle suspended from a piece of string. I think he'd purchased it in Hamlin. He sipped his whiskey and held the string and watched the head dangle. He sensed my presence but he didn't look away from the beetle.

"There's a trick to it," he said. "It's got warning magic. Folk stuff, you know? It knows enemies. It's alert to vibrations in the Ether."

The beetle's head rotated slightly, but not in any way that struck me as magical.

"I can feel your skepticism, Professor. It won't work if you don't believe."

"I beg your pardon," I said. "I'll try."

I wanted to ask him why he had turned away from the service of the Gun. I wanted to ask him how he had accomplished that feat, since according to the stories the Gun did not let its servants go lightly. I wanted to ask him what the weapon he sought was and where it was. I wanted to ask him what his plans were, and I wanted to know what it was like to have been something more than human and then to be human again, and old.

"You've been drinking, Professor."

"I have."

"Professor Ransom," he said. "There are a number of people I might choose to spend my last night on earth drinking with. All of them are my enemies now and most likely it is one of them who is coming to kill me. You are not among their number. Leave me alone."

## CHAPTER 9

# THE SHOWDOWN

I woke at first light, vomited in the pot, and attempted to perform the Ransom Exercises despite my head-ache and the narrowness and odd angles of the room. Then I went out into the hall and banged on Carver's door.

"Nothing has changed," I said through the keyhole. "The show goes on. Meet me by the water."

I checked on the horses and the wagon and tipped the hotel's boy so generously that he showed no trace of reluctance when I asked him to help move the Apparatus down through the snow to the lake, even when he saw the size of it.

"That's nothing," I said. "Just wait till you see it come alive."

A pair of the hotel's other patrons followed us down. They were business-travelers stranded by the early snow and they had nothing better to do. One of them helped and one of them just criticized the way we were doing things.

Soon enough Mr. Carver came down the road. Despite the cold he was not wearing a coat, only his shirtsleeves. I did not remark on this, or on last night, or on anything else, and nor did he. I was right—nothing had changed. There was still work to be done and it did not matter who had said what or who kept what secrets. There would be time enough to talk again in the next town over, or the next, or on the road. That was my opinion. I told him so, and he thought for a moment, then nodded.

Piece by piece we moved the Apparatus out onto a wide flat rock in a clearing by the edge of the lake.

By daylight I could see that the light on the other side of the lake was only somebody's house. I stood and waved for a while but I don't know if they saw. But somebody from the town noticed us, because not long after that a flock of small children came and sat on the rocks and observed us. One of them got up and ran back into town and they came back with more children, and some grown-ups too. Miss Elizabeth Harper came down to the lake and I greeted her by that name, though I knew it was not truly hers, to show that I did not care. She smiled and asked what I was doing and I said I was doing what I always do, and that I had thought long and hard last night and I saw no reason to do anything different. I said I did not plan to just sit and wait for whatever might come. She looked at the Apparatus for a long time and then she said she agreed entirely, and she started to help too. She and some of the children under her direction strung up the lamps through the trees at the edge of the clearing. She painted THE HARRY RANSOM WHITE ROCK ILLUMINATIONS in red on a white sheet and hung it as a banner between two sticks at the edge of the water. Mr. Carver assembled the Apparatus and tested it, reporting with a thumbs-up and some cursing that nothing critical had been damaged in the incident of the wolves.

I strutted on the rocks and then stepped out onto the ice, as if it was a stage. I was in full flow of salesmanship, in such fine form that I can remember almost nothing of what I said all afternoon, except that I promised them all a show to remember. I promised them an end to the cold dark nights of winter. I promised that nobody would forget the time when Harry Ransom came to town.

John Creedmoor did not come down to the lake. I later learned that he spent the morning stealing blasting-powder from the unattended offices of the White Rock Lumber Company, and readying caches of it about town. I did not know he was doing that and I might have tried to stop him if I had. But then if I had been gifted with foresight I would never have come to White Rock at all.

Afterward I imagine Creedmoor spending the afternoon pacing up and down Main Street in his long coat, hands darting to his guns at every sound and at every passerby, constantly consulting charms and magics that even he knew were worthless.

And I imagine the giant Knoll running all night and all day across the mountains, head down and pushing through waist-high snow as if it was nothing at all, following scents, the whispers of the wolves, the voices of his masters that only he could hear. I do not care to speculate on what those voices sound like.

The Mayor of White Rock came down with a group of local worthies, including the lawyer who sold me his flask the night before, a
butcher, the representative of the White Rock Lumber Company, and a
Nun. They asked what I was doing and I waxed poetic. They asked if
it was dangerous and I assured them it was not. They said that it was a
bad year for business with the early snow, and with rumors of War
scaring off travelers anyhow, and I said that I would not take anyone's
money even if they offered it to me—I said they should see this as a
free manifestation of grace, like an apparition of the Silver City. The
Mayor liked this figure of speech very much though the Nun disapproved.

More and more of the town came down to watch. They wore hats
and furs and families stood close together for warmth, and one or two
small fires were started. Food and drink were shared. I paced and talked
and shook hands and smiled and talked, about the Apparatus and about
Light and about East Conlan and what I had seen on my travels and
about the War. I do not know what exactly I might have promised them.
I do know that I said that this was my last show, that they should gather
their friends and bring their children even if they had to carry them and
drag out their old folks and wrap them up warm because there would
never be another chance to see what they would see. They liked hearing
this but though I think only the children really believed me.

Meanwhile Carver sat on the pedals and smoked, and Elizabeth
Harper stood beside him and they talked together, Carver nodding and
shaking his head and sometimes shrugging. They seemed to be planning
something, or maybe that is just hindsight. Anyhow I did not pry.

The sun moved behind the mountains and night swept across the
lake and engulfed us all.

I turned and gave the signal to Mr. Carver. Most nights the signal
was that I raised my arms, like I once saw a Jasper City conductor doing in a picture-book. That night my mood was different and I stretched
out my arm with two fingers extended toward the Apparatus like a
pistol and mimed a shot. Carver grinned wider than I would have
thought possible and threw the switch and hurled himself into the pedaling. Motes of light swarmed the Apparatus as the Process began. They
swarmed Carver himself and made his teeth shine and his long hair
drift. It occurred to me that I had never really watched him at work
before—ordinarily I would not stand with my back to the crowd. There
was some applause though not as much as one might have liked. There
never was. The light swelled and encompassed Miss Harper, and it

made her angelic for a moment, and then she turned and retreated into the shadows among the trees. Carver ceased his efforts but the light kept growing. It vibrated in the Ether and filled the glasses hung among the trees around the lake in too many colors to name, even if there were names for all of them, which there are not. Now there was more applause. Then there was a distant muffled crash from back up in the town and all heads turned toward that, even mine.

✳   ✳   ✳

While I worked down at the lake John Creedmoor paced back and forth across Main Street. The town emptied out around him until he was alone. I do not think anyone would have stopped as they passed by to invite him down to the lake with them. I can imagine the look on his face. You would have crossed the street to avoid him. I imagine him pacing, alone, not knowing where everyone had gone and not caring. It didn't excite his curiosity. He was pleased to be alone because it meant he could listen more closely for the noises of his enemy. Night fell on him. He drew his gun and holstered it a dozen times. He may or may not have noticed the light coming from the lake but if he did it didn't mean anything to him. I do not know how to describe what he heard when he finally heard his enemy. The growling and the feet of the wolves— it's the animal in us that hears them first, I think. Then there were some scattered screams. Then the pack turned the corner onto Main Street and came rushing down it, and Creedmoor turned and dropped his walking stick and ran as best he could through the snow and into the Grand Hotel. The lobby was empty and dark. He ran upstairs. He was panting already. The wolves were slowed by the front door for a moment but came crashing through the window. Creedmoor lit the taper on the cache of blasting powder he'd left by the door of his room. Then he went up one more flight of stairs with the wolves not six feet behind his heels and out onto the roof where he jumped out across a narrow but deep chasm and onto the second-story roof of the Hotel of the Opals. He hurt his ankle and his hip when he landed. There was a tremendous crash and dust and fire burst from the windows of the Grand and rocketed into the air and then the Grand started folding itself inwards. Creedmoor laughed. He laughed as he got to his feet and started shooting at the wolves that prowled the rubble-choked street below. Anyhow that is how I imagine it.

✳   ✳   ✳

Around this time three wolves came out of the woods near the lake, and that was more than enough wolves to send the townsfolk of White Rock screaming and scattering. The fires were kicked over in the snow and the stampede knocked down the banner that read THE HARRY RAN-SOM WHITE ROCK ILLUMINATIONS and trampled it into the slush. Not every adult had the presence of mind to keep hold of their children. I looked in the crowd and the trees and the swinging stained-glass shadows for a glimpse of Miss Elizabeth Harper but I could not see her.

One of the wolves snapped at the back of a fleeing child and I shouted out and it turned and came bounding toward me instead. I stumbled back and slipped and fell and hit my head on the Apparatus. The wolf circled but something about the Apparatus seemed to scare it or confuse it, or maybe it was Mr. Carver that it disliked, but in either case it circled and circled and then suddenly turned and ran into the trees.

I said, "What now, Mr. Carver?"

He shrugged.

"It won't end well," he said. "Nothing ever f——ing does."

I saw that he had the ax with him. It was sitting across his lap.

✳   ✳   ✳

John Creedmoor shot at the wolves. By now some of White Rock's townsfolk had come back up to Main Street to see what had happened, and some of them saw him at work. Their curiosity did them no good. Wolves snatched at stragglers and brought down the lawyer and the Nun and some old folk. Panicked townsfolk fell in the bloody snow and tried to flee on all fours. Wolves got Golda, the horse. Mariette had already perished in the collapse of the Grand Hotel. Wolves broke the butcher's windows and dragged meat out into the street. Discipline broke down among the pack and the town descended into chaos. Discipline was never the natural state of the Gun's servants and it could not be sustained for long.

A giant turned onto Main Street and stopped to examine the scene.

### A Portrait of Mr. Knoll

If I mean to be honest, and I do, I have no choice but to report that Knoll was not so huge as the rumors described him. He was not nine feet tall. He was probably no more than seven. But he was huge in a way that went beyond numbers and words, huge in a way that the rumors did not do justice. He seemed to brush aside trees and buildings. To be in his presence was to know how small and weak and fragile you were.

He wore a bearskin, like the rumors said, or at least it was something massive and furred and filthy. It was heavy with snow, like a tree. Beneath it was a big gray soldier's coat, filthy and threadbare and torn. He wore stiff frozen breeches stuffed into big black boots.

His head was a giant's head, and oddly triangular in shape, as if he had had a difficult birth and nothing had gone quite right with him since. He had a wide jaw framed by a wild beard, and a tall tapering skull with patches of long black hair growing from it, among patches of pale scalp that looked scarred. His eyes were small and mean but sharp. His nose was large. I dare say it was broken but nothing about his giant's face was quite right anyhow so who knows. There were countless bits of bone wound into his belt and his bearskin and I did not know what any of them meant to him.

He wore his gun in a leather sling over his back. It was long, ornate, handsome, and sinister.

Back then there no books about him, no songs. He had no legend yet. If you could bring yourself to look him in the eye you could see that he was still young—maybe no older than I was. He was new to the service of the Guns. I do not know what cave or solitary shack they found him in. I think they chose him to be a tracker, a hunter. He spoke only with difficulty, like it was a newly acquired skill. He was halfway between animal and man. He was a thing of darkness.

Creedmoor leaned over the roof of the Hotel of the Opals and shot him in the left shoulder.

The giant took a step back and bared his black teeth and snorted with contempt. He lumbered slowly through the snow to the Hotel's front door and kicked it open and squeezed his way inside. Another one of Creedmoor's caches of blasting-powder went off on the floor upstairs and the roof fell in on Knoll's head, as Creedmoor limped off down Main Street, shooting any beast that came too close to him, most likely shooting some of the townsfolk too if they tried to stop him or slow him, dropping his precious bullets in the snow and not stopping to pick them up because his hip hurt too bad to bend.

The second explosion started some fires here and there on Main Street. From where I was, down by the lake, the glow of those fires was just barely visible through the trees, and greatly outshone by the Apparatus, whose energies continued to grow and cycle and feed on themselves unabated. The glass hummed with the strain of containing it all and the air crackled. The light had mostly settled into something golden in color. The Apparatus was warm and getting warmer and Carver and I were in the middle of a slowly expanding circle of thawing snow and glistening wet trees and patchy grass.

Miss Elizabeth Harper emerged from the trees. Her shirt was torn and there was blood on it that did not seem to be hers. She held a small silvery pistol in her hand.

"Harry," she said. "I'm sorry. But we have no choice."

*　　*　　*

The collapse of the Hotel of the Opals did not slow the giant for long. He shoved the rubble aside and walked out of it. He was scorched and bruised and bad-tempered but the demon in him rose up in the saddle and whipped him on, screaming in his head until his eyes went bloody.

Creedmoor was at the far end of the street. He turned, saw the giant standing in the ruins, and took a shot which maybe hit and maybe didn't, I do not know and will not guess, it made no particular difference either way. The giant lowered his head and for the first time broke into a run and Creedmoor had time to do no more than turn his back and take a single step before the giant was on him. He felt the back of the giant's hand cuff his ear and he was lifted off his feet and landed sprawling in the snow on his back.

The giant stood over him. He put his foot on Creedmoor's leg, where his knee was twisted, and pressed down.

"The other one. The woman. Where?"

"I won't help you. I don't serve your masters anymore. I won't go back. I'm free and bigger than all of you. You're nobody. I was doing terrible things before you were born. I am John Creedmoor, I killed a hundred men at Devil's Spine, you're nobody. Who do you think you are? I will not serve. They'll remember me forever, the man who defied you."

That is what I imagine him saying.

"Who asked you to serve? The woman. Where?"

"Go to hell. You're nobody."

"Knoll."

"What?"

"I'm Knoll."

Knoll lifted Creedmoor out of the snow. Creedmoor drew his knife and Knoll slapped it aside, breaking the blade and two of Creedmoor's fingers.

❊   ❊   ❊

When Elizabeth Harper walked back into the town it was in flames here and there, and parts of it were in ruins. The townsfolk were reduced to a state of panic in which they were scarcely more human or less dangerous than the wolves. The town doctor and his assistant tried to seize her and she was forced to wave her pistol at them until they retreated.

The giant Knoll had taken up residence at the Bank of the Opals. The remaining wolves lay at his feet or prowled around, and sometimes he kicked them out of spite and impatience. He had torn open the vault and scattered its contents in the snow, along with all the unsent letters. He kept Creedmoor on his knees and would not let him stand. He had tracked down the Mayor of White Rock and the Nun and nailed them both by their hands and feet to the fence out front with nails from the general store. The Nun survived the night but the Mayor did not. Every few minutes he bellowed out his demand that the woman be brought to him.

As soon as she stepped onto Main Street he scented her. She saw his head loom from the Bank's window, and then she started running.

Knoll stopped to nail Creedmoor to the floor by his left hand, for safe-keeping. Then he followed after Miss Harper. He took his time. He had her scent now and was in no hurry.

❊   ❊   ❊

She burst out of the trees and into the clearing by the lake, into the light and warmth of the Apparatus. I think it had never before worked quite so well as it did that night. It was twice as bright and twice as beautiful as it had been when she last saw it. It was warm enough that the ice on the lake was melting. I like to think the beauty of it stopped her short for a moment.

She was panting and sweating and her clothes and skin had been torn by branches. She stumbled across the clearing to the Apparatus, where Carver waited. They made urgent signs at each other. I stood in the trees on the far side of the clearing and watched her approach.

Seconds later the giant appeared. I caught glimpses of him shoving through the trees and I just about disgraced myself with fear. His heavy shoulders, his heavy head turning this way and that, like he was sniffing.

I think until I saw him I had imagined I might talk my way out of this predicament, as I had so many others, as I had talked my way into it. That would not happen. The thing that came through the trees could not be reasoned with, could not be joked with or cajoled. He belonged to another world, one that I had no business in.

Knoll shielded his eyes as he stepped out into the clearing. The light of the Apparatus seemed to offend him and he let out a deep angry growl. He looked around, blinking, and caught sight of Carver.

Carver spat and raised his ax in both hands.

"No," Knoll said. And he drew and fired. The bullet took off the top of my friend's head before he could speak. Red blood slapped across the Apparatus's innards. What was left of Mr. Carver fell to its knees, then over on its side. The ax fell from the dead hand.

Knoll came over and stood over the corpse. He kicked it with his boot as if to see what would happen. Then he raised his head and grinned hugely, showing broken and yellow teeth, and he turned his gun on Miss Harper.

It was at that moment that I perceived that what had to be done, had to be done by me. It was maybe not unlike the sensation Mr. Alfred Baxter describes in his *Autobiography* as *seizing the moment* or *perceiving the Spirit of the Age*, like the time he bet his whole fortune on Steel, or the time when he determined it was necessary to buy out and destroy the First Bank of Jasper City. It was not unlike the moment when as a boy I first glimpsed the mathematics behind the Process, and woke and hunted for pencil and paper. I am not a violent man or a political man and I never wanted any part in the Great War, but I saw that events had left me with no choice. I knew what plan Mr. Carver and Miss Harper had hatched that afternoon, and I saw that there was no alternative. In fact I was so overcome with selflessness that I forgave them then and there for planning behind my back.

None of this took more than a moment. I ran out from the trees and toward the Apparatus. Knoll turned and fired at me but missed, and since the Agents of the Gun never miss I think it must be that the light of the Apparatus pulsed at that moment and distracted him. I picked up the ax from where it lay at poor Mr. Carver's side and I put it into the heart of the Apparatus, smashing through the glass dome and chopping through the magnets' axle and into the coiled wires beneath. Then I threw myself off the rock and into the water and began swimming

away as quickly as I could. Fortunately I am a quick learner. I found
that it was mostly a matter of kicking wildly and hoping for the best. I
heard the bright sound of all the glass bulbs hung in the trees shattering. I did not see but I did *feel* the unleashed energies of the Apparatus
expand into the air, surge and recoil and snap and twist around themselves, as the Process which was barely predictable at the best of times
went wild and grew and grew and became something utterly new.

The giant Knoll grunted once then went silent. There was a huge
weight and pressure at my back like the sky itself had turned to stone
and fallen right on me. It forced me down suddenly so that I swallowed
water. The lake was cold at first and then suddenly it was warm.

Afterward there was nothing left of Knoll or of Mr. Carver, not even
dust. Parts of the Apparatus could be found embedded in trees for hundreds of yards around, or lying on the streets of White Rock. The trees
themselves in the immediate vicinity were gone. At the perimeter of
the devastation the trees were stripped bare of bark and leaves down
to their green-white bone. The banner that read THE HARRY RANSOM
WHITE ROCK ILLUMINATIONS floated out into the middle of the lake until
I could no longer make it out. I asked Miss Harper if she had seen what
it looked like when the Process went wild and she said that she had
caught a glimpse before she turned away to hide behind a tree, but she
could not describe it.

## CHAPTER 10

# The End of the First Part

I said that I would write about the three times I changed history. You might say that was the first—I mean the time when I saved the lives of John Creedmoor and the woman who I still cannot think of as anything other than Miss Elizabeth Harper. Or you might say it was what happened next.

We walked up to the town together. She was supporting me rather more than I was supporting her. I was crying and also laughing and I kept saying, "Think nothing of it." She said that she was sorry about Mr. Carver and I said, "There's a lot you don't know, Miss Harper."

The wolves by the way fled in confusion and panic as soon as Knoll died.

Snow had started to fall again and the fires had gone out. I do not know exactly what hour of the night it was.

Miss Harper was sun-burned on the left side of her face, and her hair on that side was somewhat charred. I think that her eyes were less blue and more violet than they had been before the Apparatus exploded. I said nothing to her about either of these things.

The street was blocked by the rubble of the Grand Hotel. The big red GRAND sign stuck up from the heap of bricks and timbers and beneath it were the remains of the wagon and of Mariette, the horse. I said my farewells as we circled the rubble.

We found John Creedmoor at the Bank, lying on the floor in his own blood and a mess of scattered notes and deeds and titles and scattered letters. I saw my own undelivered letter to my sister Jess under his boot.

We prized loose his swollen hand from the floor and Miss Harper helped him to his feet. He was bloody and shaking and he could not stand without help.

The two of them had one of their whispered conversations, of which I heard only parts. Creedmoor did not answer any of my questions.

I should confess that most of what I have written here about his conversations with Knoll was guesswork.

The remaining townsfolk gathered around us. They took down the Nun from the fence and were able to save her. The Nun was too weak to do anything but babble and then sleep, and so, with the Mayor dead, the townsfolk had no clear leader. They might have fled like the wolves if they had anywhere to go. It broke my heart to see them, but I was also very much aware that the wagon was gone, and the horses were gone, and the Apparatus was gone, and it was winter and I was ruined.

I looked at the people of White Rock and I felt a surge of hope inside me. It caused me to open my mouth.

"People of White Rock," I said. "You should know the truth."

"Harry," Miss Harper said, and John Creedmoor said, "Shut him up." I smiled at them both and made a gesture with my hand, by which I meant, *Don't worry, I have a plan, you will thank me later.*

"People of White Rock," I said, "listen."

John Creedmoor looked for his gun, but finding himself unarmed was unable to stop me.

✳   ✳   ✳

The truth is I do not remember exactly what I said, but I do remember what the newspapers said that I said, afterward. It was something like this.

*The Juniper City Morning Herald,* —— 1891

### STRANGE NEWS FROM THE OPALS—
### THE "MIRACLE" AT WHITE ROCK

There is strange news from the Opals, where last winter the little town of White Rock, home to the White Rock Lumber Company, suffered the tragic loss of Mayor R. Binion, Mr. and Mrs. William F. Davy, Esq., Mr. Sam Sattel of the Bank of the Opals, and a number of other locally prominent citizens, in the course of a bank-robbery conducted by persons unknown. Witnesses to the tragedy now report that the massacre was the work of one man, most likely an Agent of that power that we shall not name here. The perpetrator's name is unknown, though the fellow is said to have been ten feet tall and, in the words of Mr. James F. Walsh, formerly of No. 19 Main Street, "hairy all over, like he was a —— —— bear." Moreover, the perpetrator is deceased, and not at the hands of any man of White Rock. Rather, the Agent fell victim to what Miss Phelps, formerly of the Bank of the Opals, described as "some kind of —— —— awful weapon like nothin' I ever seen before." The weapon is said to be the property of a Mr. John Creedmoor—perhaps the notorious Creedmoor, whose exploits were well known to this newspaper ten years ago—and of a Miss Elizabeth Allerson, and a Professor Harry Ransom.

Mr. Tom Phelan, formerly the proprietor of the Grand Hotel, describes the incident thus:

"They come to town and I thought as how they was running from somethin', but every body comes to town these days is running from somethin' what with the War an' all. I minded my own business, until that —— —— monster come into town after 'em and starts shootin' and beatin' on the Mayor and carryin' on—all confusion an' consternation—all blood an' thunder an' —— —— wolves—an' used ta keep a gun behind o' the bar but there ain't no man in White Rock can stand agin' an Agent o' the you-know-what. An' then jus' when I thought as how we was all as good as dead anyhow there was this great —— light an' the monster was gone. It was that Ransom fellow. He had a machine with 'im an' it was all glass and wire an' I don't know what-all an' it burned that big son of a —— right up."

Witnesses say that there was a pillar of white light, which the pious Miss Phelps describes as "like a door openin' onto the Silver City its own self." This may be the idle talk of simple rustics, but it is a matter on which many voices agree. Travelers from up and down the Opals and whoever was awake that night as far away as Birnam in the western foothills and Troche in the east say that they saw a pillar of white light flaring over the mountains. This vision has passed already into local folklore as the "Miracle" of White Rock. It is also said that for days after the incident White Rock experienced an unseasonable warmth and an inexplicable absence of shadows and wind, that the survivors of the tragedy glimpsed strange and foreign vistas through windows or half-open doorways, and that small rocks and twigs were seen to levitate and spin of their own accord, and that strangers were seen around town, silent and remote and "ghost-like." What remains of the town is now under the authority of the Line and no further word of these peculiarities emerges.

After the incident Professor Harry Ransom delivered a speech, which Miss Phelps recalled thus:

"He said who he was an' who the rest of 'em was. There was old John Creedmoor, who was a gun-hand lookin' to do good with 'is declinin' years, an' there was Miss Liz Allerson, who was a doctor from the old country. An' he made a speech about the you-know-what an' the Line an' how they was the enemies of all good people. An' he said he was sorry about the Mayor an' all the rest and about all that'd burnt to the ground but that was just how the War was, and how it was goin' to go on forever unless somebody stopped it, because the Powers that make the world the way it is are mad. An' he said that him and the woman an' that bad-lookin' old man had had enough, an' it was time to do somethin', an' that was how come they'd gone out West and brought back this secret weapon that was so damn good it could, never mind jus' killin' an Agent o' the you-know-what, it could do for the demon what rode 'im, and it could knock an Engine o' the Line isself off its tracks. An' they was gonna too."

"He said they was goin' east," recalls Mr. Phelan. "On account of a bigger 'n' better somethin's hidden out East—under the World's Walls, he said—and he spoke all about Folk magic an' magic signs and words that could do who-knows-what an' about that ol' Red Republic from back when I was a boy and about how in the future there'd be peace and plenty and a whole lot of other stuff. He talked about the G—— and about the Engines and all that kind of thing but my ears was ringin' from all the bullets and blood and smoke an' that light so I don't know what-all he said. He was a strange fellow, that's all I know."

"He said they had to make it where they were goin'," Mr. Walsh recalls. "Or it was all for nothin'. An' they'd never make it without we helped 'em, meaning we had to give 'em horses and water and food and a new wagon and guns and new clothes and money for the road and incidental expenses and so on. He said it was a great cause an' a miracle and our shot at greatness an' so on. An' maybe he was tellin' the truth or somethin' like the truth

an' maybe he wasn't but either way we'd had one —— —— of a
night. We took a vote and those as wanted to help 'em was
square outnumbered by those as wanted to stone 'em out of
town and never speak of it agin. So we did. An' me, I packed up
what wasn't burnt and got out mysel' three day later, and that's
how come I weren't there when the Linesmen shown up."

✳ ✳ ✳

We were not fifteen minutes' walk back down the road together and I
was still smarting from my bruises when John Creedmoor turned to me
and shoved me against a tree, dislodging a light fall of snow.

"I should kill you," he said, "Damn it, I should just—"

He had only one good hand and his leg was hurt and he wobbled
but I still did not think I could fight him.

I said, "But—"

"We had little enough chance of success before and now when word
gets out—and word *will* get out—the people of White Rock will not
hold their tongues forever—damn it in the old days I'd have shot 'em
all myself—*when* word gets out then every idiot in every town from
here to the World's Walls will be on the lookout for us to gossip or catch
us for a reward or worse try to f—— help us. This is no game, this is not
a story-book, this is not theater, this is *war*, Ransom. I should kill you.
Damn it, I think I *will* kill you."

He let go of me, and drew his gun.

Miss Harper put a hand on his arm and persuaded him to change
his mind.

"Thank you," I said.

"He's right, Harry."

I said, "But—" again.

"Don't follow us," she said. "Good luck with your Apparatus and Mr.
Baxter and all of that, and I'm sorry about what happened to Carver, I
really am, and I'm sorry we ever dragged you into our affairs. But it's better for all of us if we each go our ways and—well, just, good luck, Harry."

I was for once lost for words.

I watched them walk away.

I would not see either of them again for a very long time.

The rest of that night was very long and cold and that's all I intend
to say on the matter.

# THE RIVER

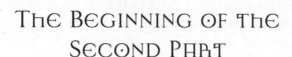

## CHAPTER 11

# THE BEGINNING OF THE SECOND PART

Well. So that was the first part of my story. After I finished it I wrapped two of the three copies in parcel-paper and entrusted them both to young Dick Beck. He has taken them into town, with instructions to mail one copy to my friend the famous journalist Mr. Elmer Merrial Carson, and to leave the other copy in a prominent place, such as a pulpit or doctor's office or saloon bar. The mails these days cannot be trusted and who knows whether Mr. Carson will get it or he won't but if he does I hope it will answer certain questions.* Dick is also taking the usual open invitation to Ransom City. He took a pistol and a knife. The roads are dangerous here. Same as everywhere else these days. Meanwhile I am tinkering with the typewriter and with the Apparatus.

We are camped by a river. I don't know what the locals call it but I have started to think of it as Adela's River, because it is fast and bright and musical like the piano. We have been here for the better part of a week, mostly waiting for Dick Beck's return. The quartermaster of our expedition is a deserter from the Line by the name of Rapp, who is hard at work planning and ordering and who without whom we would

---

* I got it all right, though it took a year to find me. It came in the mail. Subsequent Parts of Mr. Ransom's story had less luck with the mail, and had to be painstakingly assembled over the course of many years, from scattered fragments. I acquired most of the Second Part fifteen years after it was mailed; I purchased it from a retired officer of the Line, a mail censor, and though I do not like censors I honor my promises, and he shall remain nameless. —EMC

surely be doomed right from the start, but I am no good at that kind of work so here I am.

There are more than a hundred of us now, and I no longer know everyone's name. We are dreamers and drifters. The first of us were men and women of science. That's what I say in every invitation to Ransom City that I leave nailed to hitching-posts or meeting-house doors or &c. Nobody will be turned away. It's surprising who finds us. Seventh sons. Refugees. Traveling salesmen. We have more than the usual number of homosexuals. Jailbirds. Soldiers of every side. Men who disgraced themselves back in the War and a few who distinguished themselves. Edge-of-the-world types, for whom a trip into the unmade lands is all in a day's work—solitary fellows who are silently happy to travel in a pack—men who would have been born Folk if they had only had the option. We have a couple of dozen men and women who left their homes back in '91 to follow Liv Alverhuysen and John Creedmoor east, in what the newspapers at the time called the '91 Dash or the Fools' Pilgrimage or the Great Transcendentalist Nonsense, and who have been wandering ever since, looking for the next promise of salvation. We have more adherents of more faiths than I knew there were, not just the Smilers and the snake-handlers and the Silver City types but also—

The truth is that I thought we would have been arrested long since. I am a notorious individual. When I began sending out my letters I would have bet you I'd be arrested within the week. My letters were a poke in the world's eye. I was tired of anonymity.

I cannot believe the Line forgives me for what happened at Jasper. I cannot believe the Gun has forgotten me. And yet here I am, still walking around free and making speeches and telling people how it will be in Ransom City and now I am thinking that maybe it will even happen. Maybe the world is changing faster than I thought. Maybe the Great War really is coming to an end. From time to time wreckage comes floating down the river, like a piece of an Ironclad's tracks or a tangle of barbed wire. Who knows.

Why are they following me? Well, I'm a good talker. I made my living selling the impossible. I have the map—that precious map she gave me, of the way west beyond the settled world's rim. There are not many like it. I am the inventor of the Ransom Process, which is our great strength and our only defense. I am mad in a way that infects others. I want to do one thing perfect and right and magnificent and that does not go wrong and if I have to build a new world for that to happen in then I will do so. I will go out into lands not yet settled by men and I will go out past lands settled by Folk and out past it all if I must.

Ransom City will be arranged in a wheel, I've decided. The circle is a perfect form and rich in significance, and also practical. We will expand in rings as others join us. We will build tall. It will be a city of elevators and buildings that taper into the sky. The spokes of the wheel will be tree-lined avenues, where there will be theaters and on the corner of every street self-playing musical instruments. No one will go hungry and everyone will have their share because there will be abundance for all, and every man will work on tasks that please him and suit his spirit. Women too. Children, especially. Each and every tree will be lit at night by the lamps of the Process. If anyone lives out there already there will be fair dealing—there will be peace between us and plenty enough for all without stealing. I am an honest businessman. It will be a new world.

Dick Beck's back. He got in a scuffle with some fellows who blacked his eye and tore his shirt and bloodied his nose but he could be worse—he does not stop smiling. The letters are in the hands of Fortune now. I told him that in the new city in the unmade lands he'll be Postmaster General, and I do not think he understood I was joking. Well, I guess somebody has to be. Anyhow tomorrow we move on. I should tear this up and start over.

This is the story of my second and third brushes with History. I am going to try to write as much as I can tonight, by the glow of the Apparatus. This is the story of how I got to Jasper City and how I got rich and famous and how it all came to an end.

CHAPTER 12

# The Piano

In the weeks and months after White Rock I wandered, drifting in no particular direction, first out West and then north and then back East. I was hungry for much of the winter. I took hard jobs or sometimes jobs of questionable legality. I presented myself as a man of the Smiler faith fallen on hard times and was given bread and shelter and lectures about perseverance and bootstraps. The Apparatus was gone and my savings were gone and my friend Mr. Carver was gone. Even my name was gone. I did not dare call myself Harry Ransom any more. After White Rock who knew who might be looking for Harry Ransom. I grew a beard and I let my hair go wild and I called myself by different names, like John Norton and Joe Reiser and others I forget.

I wrote a hundred letters. I wrote

*Jess. I cannot tell you where I am so do not even wonder about it. Things have not worked out so well for your kid brother as he hoped and he has got himself into trouble again. The Apparatus came to nothing after all. The future does not belong to me after all. I hope you are doing well in Jasper City and that you are a famous singer or actress or whatever it is that you do on the stage, your letter did not say. Sometimes I wish I could come home. Yours, H.*

Or

*Hello May. It's your brother. I was thinking of your letter and how you said you prayed for me, and I was thinking of the time back in*

*East Conlan when we were children and I ran off into the woods and when I came back I said that I had been living with the Folk there, and I think that is the first time you prayed for me, or anyone prayed for me. At the time I was angry but now I know you meant well. Maybe you are right and I have been unwise. A prayer or two would not go amiss and I would pay you back in kind if I knew how.*

Or

*Mr. Baxter, I have never written to you before but you may have heard my name, I am an inventor or businessman like you. Your book about your struggle from rags to riches was a great inspiration to me and I know it just about by heart. In Chapter Three and again in Chapter Six you said that even in your lowest adversity you never despaired because you knew you were made for greater things. That is a good trick and I wish you would tell me how it works.*

*Maybe you read about what they are calling "The Miracle of White Rock." That was my work. It was not exactly how they wrote about it in the newspapers but it was a hell of a show. One day it will change the world. I would like to talk to you one day. I am kind of in trouble but maybe one day a man of your stature might recognize a kindred soul and help out.*

*Sincerely, Professor Harry Ransom.*

Most of the letters I wrote I did not send. I could not afford to. But I scraped together the money to mail that last letter to Mr. Baxter. Then I left town—I didn't dare wait for an answer.

I stayed for three weeks in a town called Split Hoof, where I went by Joe Reiser and made a small living writing letters for other people, mostly about cows. That was where the rumors first caught up with me. A man came to the market with half-a-dozen goats and the news that a rogue agent of the Gun named John Creedmoor and a wizard called Ransom and a beautiful blond woman had invented an Apparatus that could kill the Engines of the Line or the demons of the Gun, and that they were bringing it slowly along the road east and north to the Station of Harrow Cross itself. He was known as a drunk and nobody believed him. I moved on anyhow. In the next town I read about the incident at White Rock in the newspaper.

✳    ✳    ✳

I had no money to construct a new Apparatus. Even if I had money, I would not have dared. I did not know if I could. I did not remember how it could be done. I had saved a few of my notes and sketches from the disaster at White Rock, but when I looked at them now they were nonsense to me, like childhood poems or riddles. I sketched the mathematics by candlelight but could not make any part of it begin to balance. I could not even recall how the light of the Process had looked. When I passed back through the town of Caldwell I purchased dope from a man in an alley and lay all through a cold bright day in the street trying to recall the Light, and though I saw a great many strange things I did not see what I wanted. I missed Mr. Carver terribly.

Once I wrote a letter to say:

*Mr. Carver. I am sorry that the last thing you said to me was about what I stole. It was not that way. I wish I could explain to you, or you could explain to me maybe. I wish you could come back, so we could talk one more time.*

But of course I had no place to send it. Not even a burial place. No body. The Process had swallowed everything.

✳   ✳   ✳

I went to the town of Domino because I heard they were looking for engineers. The town was built on the banks of the River Ire, just a half-mile upstream from a Line camp. Domino was newly rich and anxious about it. The camp brought in goods and matériel and men from the factories of the north, and some small part of that wealth ended up in Domino's pockets. Main Street sported new and empty second stories and storefronts full of shiny goods nobody knew what to do with.

I stood in a line outside one such building. It was one of those days that is not yet spring, where everything is bright but still bitter cold, and the storefronts glittered. When at last I got to the front of the line and into the building, I was allowed to present myself to a black-hatted man behind a desk, who looked at me like I was a defective part or stray nail that might just maybe be hammered into shape. I gave him a false name and an account of my experience and qualifications that was false in details but just about honest enough in substance. He scratched some quick notations in his ledger and told me he guessed I could be useful and named an insultingly low wage. Domino was to be electrified, he said, in the interests of efficiency and modernization and at the urging of the Linesmen in Camp Ire. He pushed a contract and a pen across the table. There was a space for my name, and beneath it the words *For the Northern Lighting Corporation.* I said that I would sooner starve than work for the Northern Lighting Corporation. He took back the pen and asked me if I was mad. I snatched the pen back from him, I do not know exactly why, and I said that maybe things hadn't worked out so well for me but I had my pride still. He took off his hat and stood up. We exchanged some further words. It was not my finest hour and I do not enjoy recalling it. Two men lifted me by my arms and removed me from the building and threw me down in the street. I jumped up to my feet and brushed down my coat and turned with as much dignity as I could muster, smiling as if nothing in the world mattered to me, and walked down to the riverfront. There I met a man from the crew of the riverboat *Damaris,* who offered me a job, mainly I think because of my smile.

"Why not," I said.

I was sick and tired of the land. It was time to give the water a fair try. If the science existed I would have taken to the air instead.

⁂ ⁂ ⁂

The *Damaris* was a tall red affair, with a great white wheel, and a profusion of lanterns. She looked like an opera house or a whorehouse escaped from the big city streets and gone looking for adventure. She was dusty and creaky and rotting in places—no longer young, but still outrageous. She had no business in a business-like place like Domino, and none of her crew liked being anywhere near the Line's Camp. She resupplied and let off passengers and hired me and moved on at once, which suited me just fine.

The *Damaris* was owned by a man called John Southern. He was missing two fingers on his left hand and an old scar made his left eye droop in a way that was like a wink. He was quite bald on the top of his head but wore his gray hair extravagantly long behind, and his gray mustache hung right down to his collar, which was high and starched but dirty. Altogether these peculiarities lent him a roguish air. I knew at once that I would not be able to help liking him, but also that he was not a good man, and that he would never pay me regularly or fairly.

"Name?"

"Hal Rawlins."

His handshake was crushing. He glared for a moment then grinned.

"Well, I've heard worse, Mr. Rawlins. Charley says you're looking for work. You look like you got a story. Everybody's got a story these days. Don't tell me. You sing?"

"I never tried but I guess I could learn. Charley said you needed a—"

"A man with a knack for machines, yeah. That you? Charley says you can talk like you got learnin'. Say somethin' learned."

"Light," I said, "must be considered a form of energy, not dissimilar in nature to electricity or heat. It is a creative energy, a refinement of the raw Ether; darkness is merely its absence. It—"

I was quoting from the Encyclopedia published by the Baxter Publishing Corporation of Jasper City, parts of which I happened to have by heart.

"All right, all right. You a Linesman, Mr. Rawlins?"

"I am not."

"I'll have no Linesmen on board. Twenty years I've worked this river, since back when *Damaris* herself was alive and dancin'. You a dancer, Mr. Rawlins? No? Never mind. Got a girl for that. Twenty years and every year business gets harder as the Line gets closer. What keeps me afloat right now is defiance and spite."

I had in fact noticed that the *Damaris* was light on passengers.

"I have my own grievances against the Line," I said. "I understand."

"You'll keep 'em to yourself, then. You been to school?"

"Some school. Not much. I'm self-taught."

"We go all the way east to the Three Cities and into Jasper City, where the University is. Sometimes we get rich folks' kids on board. What's that look for, Rawlins, you don't want to see the big city?"

"Let's talk about this machine. What do you need me for? As far as I can tell the wheel turns the, let's say the old-fashioned way."

This was what the learned Professors of Jasper City would call a *euphemism*, which is to say a magic word to make the world seem better than it is. What I meant was that the wheel of the *Damaris* was turned by a team of Folk, below. Mr. Southern gave me a searching look and I thought he might be about to say something on that subject, but instead he nodded and then slapped the top of the piano.

I should say that the *Damaris* had a bar on the upper deck, full of shadows and faded finery and suggestive paintings and a faint sweetish smell of rotten wood. There was also a piano, and we were standing next to it.

"Well," I said. "The piano? That's not what I imagined but I reckon I could learn to play."

"It's not what it looks like, Mr. Rawlins."

What it was, was something I had never heard of. It was a new thing in the world and there were no real names for it yet. John Southern called it a *motor piano* or a *self-player piano* or *that damn thing*. Its inventor had called it a *music box*.

It looked like a large upright piano. It was made of wood, and in keeping with the rest of the *Damaris* it was painted red and black and gold, and somewhat over-ornamented, and covered in dust and grime. There were two wide rows of black and white keys, that were like a kind of terrifying message in a code I could not read. Above the keys there was a window in the piano's frame, exposing bright metallic workings that bore no resemblance to any musical instrument I had ever seen before, or for that matter any machine. A wild profusion of wires hooked into each other at every possible angle and I could see that the apparatus almost hummed with counter-posed tensions. If it resembled anything at all, it resembled an illustration of the Brain and Nervous System that was one of the main attractions of the Encyclopedias I used to sell back in East Conlan—except that that was the lurid pink and vein-blue of human flesh, while the piano was all golden-glittering and immaculate. Immediately my curiosity got the better of me and I reached in and touched a wire, and there was a shivering sound and deep inside something turned over and the wires began to work against each other and the keys depressed as if a ghost was sitting at the bench and the piano played a few notes of very beautiful music, which turned into a few bars of utter cacophony, then silence.

"Useless damn thing," Southern said.

I fell in love with the machine at once.

There was another window you could open in the frame. There were a lot of secret parts, like in a haunted house in a book—I doubt I ever found them all. Behind that window were levers, switches, and several cylinders of hard molded wax, wrapped in stiff yellow paper punched with holes. I did not get where I am today without being a quick study and it did not take me long to understand that the cylinders could control the piano, the molding being a form of secret language that the mechanism could speak, not unlike telegraph-signals.

Someone had scratched KOTAN into the brass, with a flourish, on the topmost winding-mechanism. Beneath KOTAN were the words GIBSON CITY, 1889.

"I guess that's the fellow who made it," Southern said. "Kotan. We got it for next to nothin' in Gibson City last year. A theater didn't want it anymore, they said it made their actors nervous. I reckon maybe they just couldn't get it to work."

"A great year for inventions," I said. I could not stop running my hands over the frame. "A great year for the future."

"We had a piano player," Southern said, "but he was a drunk. I won't tell you what the one before 'im did or I'll get mad. I've had my damn fill of piano-players. I thought, guess we should get someone to fix this damn thing. Least it can't get drunk. You're not a drunk, are you, Rawlins? Can you fix it?"

"No," I said. "Yes."

Fixing the thing was easy enough. A few wires had snapped, a few more had been loosened by the rolling of the boat, some springs had sprung and some mice had made a nest in an unwise location, from which I had no choice but to round up and relocate them. Just replacing the wires and getting rid of the mice was enough to improve its operations greatly—Mr. Southern could have done it himself if not for what I think was a superstitious fear of the machine. By the time I had done that, we were a day further down the river, and I was hired on as a member of the crew, responsible mostly for the care and maintenance of the piano, and for pretending to play it in the evenings.

The performance was mostly a matter of smiling and patter and leaving the machine to do its own work. I could guide it but not control it. I could stop it and start it and gently coax it, through arrangement of the cylinders and wires, in certain directions, but that was all—it would play what it would play. In fact I do not think I ever understood a quarter of the machine's secrets.

I stayed with the *Damaris* until it was summer, until we had left the Western Rim far behind and the Ire had become the Jass and we neared the border of the Tri-City Territory. Our progress eastward was constant but irregular. We stopped in every town, and we followed what seemed like every last tributary of the Ire or the Jass, and we changed direction frequently, according to Mr. Southern's whims, or the cross-currents of business, or because of rumors and warnings about which towns or stretches of river ahead of us or behind us were dangerous due to the fighting. I didn't complain. Mr. Southern provided me with

a russet suit, and though it was old and faded and too big and not
nearly so fine as my old white suit from my days on the road it was
handsome enough in the half-light of the bar. Every night I sat behind
the piano as it worked itself, and mimed the action of playing, and
smiled at everyone.

The passengers of the *Damaris* were farmers and business-travelers
and the occasional adventurous young man or woman who was traveling for no clear purpose that even they understood. There were a few
rough hunting-trapping types returning from the West with spoils. There
was the regular cast of wild-eyed speculators. There were handsome
young private secretaries delivering important correspondence or financial documents, and doing their best to look inconspicuous. There were
wealthy men and women from Greenbank or Melville who had been
displaced when the Line destroyed their towns, and now had nothing to
do but drift and drink until their money ran out. There were some missionaries and a journalist or two. There were some bad men and some
gun-for-hire types and my guess is some of the striking and menacing
men who came and went and commanded a space of shadow around
themselves were Agents of the Gun. Sometimes when I played I wore a
hat low on my head for fear somebody would recognize me.

We had traveling entertainers, including two consecutive magicians.
We had pickpockets, some of whom operated with John Southern's
sanction and some of whom soon wished they did. From time to time
there was a girl who stood beside me and danced, listlessly or with
naïve enthusiasm. They were paid poorly and they usually left at the
soonest opportunity. One or two of them were pretty, I guess. I only
had eyes for the machine. Most nights I slept beside it, on a red couch
at the back of the bar.

The piano was powered by a hand-crank that wound and tight-
ened coiled springs. An hour's work in the afternoon would provide
those springs with enough stored energy to last for the night. I sweated
over the crank the way Carver had sweated over the pedals of the Apparatus.

The music of the piano was not always beautiful. Truth is it varied
widely in quality. Initially it depended on the arrangement of the wax
cylinders and the rings upon them and certain levers and switches—
which on my first night on the *Damaris* I calculated had one hundred
and eight possible permutations or states of ordering, and then on the
second night I understood that I failed to account for the function of
certain pedals and frets, and that there in fact were somewhat more

than eleven thousand such permutations—and then on the fourth night with the piano I understood with a delight I cannot describe that the true number was much, much higher, as big as music or language or the world. Well anyhow however I arranged matters the piano quickly slipped my control. The patterns became unpredictable. Fugues emerged and subsided. Sometimes the piano produced tones and rhythms that no human person would think to produce or enjoy, as if it was amusing itself. It seemed to have moods. Sometimes the noises it produced were like one imagines the music of the Future will be. When it was bad I laughed a lot and told jokes and nobody seemed to care too much. Once or twice a glass was thrown at my head but without particular malice, and I have quick reflexes. Nobody cared much when it was good, either. Southern continued to refer to the machine as *that damn thing*, though he was happy not to have to pay a pianist. Nobody saw what I saw in it. The mind that had built the machine was a subtle and lovely one and I knew that it was a mind that would understand the Light of the Apparatus. It was a mind that recognized nothing as impossible. *Kotan.* I did not know if it was a man or a woman, old or young, rich or poor—there seemed no likelihood that we would ever meet. I did not know if it was a place or a time or a factory, for that matter.

Anyhow this whole period was a pleasant interlude in my life. I collected tips and I saved a little money and I did not mind so much that nobody knew my name. The passengers brought stories of the fighting creeping further and further east, as if it was following us—stories of Line forces commandeering towns, of Agents of the Gun swaggering openly into saloons and murdering as they pleased—stories of Heavier-Than-Air Vessels and Gas and Ironclads and witchcraft and uprisings of the free Folk and of strange new weapons and the Miracle at White Rock. "Not here," I said. "Not tonight. We left the War behind on land." And I smiled and coaxed the piano into something to put them at ease.

The one part of the job I disliked was when somebody would request a particular piece of music. I did not have that kind of control over what the piano would do. Its internal mathematics carried their own implications and it worked them out, like it or not. You could not easily explain that to a drunk. Instead you had to convince them that they wanted what they were going to get anyhow—and so the principal skill the job required was fast-talking and a convincing smile.

The worst of all songs was "The Ballad of John Creedmoor," which appeared at the beginning of spring. The drunks sung it often. They asked for accompaniment and I said no. They asked me why not, was I a loyalist of the Line or something, and sometimes they got belligerent. They sang it anyhow.

*John Creedmoor was a thief and a wicked, wicked man*
*He fought and he killed in the War*
*Till he looked at the blood that stained his hands*
*And it made him cry out, "No more!"*

*Now Liv was a lady of elegant birth*
*A beauty, a kind heart for sure*
*And she came and she saw all this suffering earth*
*And it made her cry out, "No More!"*

*And together they went way out to the West*
*Where the land and the sky are as one*
*Where the wild Folk dwell and each morning is blessed*
*And they said, "Let the fighting be done."*

And so on. There were a number of different versions of this song, and some of them went on longer than others, but however long it lasted the damn thing never got any less bad than it started out. I shall not inflict on posterity the verses that mentioned myself, Professor Harry Ransom, nor the verses about the Miracle of White Rock and the death of the ten-foot monster Knoll.

*Now who can say where they are on this day*
*If we knew we never would say*
*But one day they will come to the place that they seek*
*And one day this land shall know peace.*

"No," I said, when I was asked to play the melody. "We are on the water, gentlemen. We drift downriver. Like I said: we have *already* escaped the War. Why dwell on it?"

## CHAPTER 13

# MAGIC

In a town called Holland, not far west of the Three Cities and about two weeks west of Jasper, we picked up a magician by the name of the Great Rotollo and his wife. For three nights Rotollo and his wife performed their tricks while I played, or rather while Kotan's piano played itself and I mimed. It would be misleading to say that there was a crowd but there were people sitting here and there who could be coaxed into half-hearted applause.

### *A Portrait of the Great Rotollo and the Amazing Amaryllis*

The Great Rotollo did card tricks and he plucked costume jewelry from the ears of business-travelers. He divined the names and dispositions of dead relatives, and he guessed what the speculators were looking for in a way that seemed to encourage them. He did not levitate, he did not cut himself or anyone else in half, he did not disappear or reappear. What he did was simple but he did it well. That is a respectable way to be.

His wife flirted outrageously and danced, in a way that was suggestive, though a little stiff. She was not young anymore. Her stage name was Amaryllis and she had a long neck and a tall beehive of red hair, gray at the roots. She was loud and always smiling. Rotollo, on the other hand, affected a severe and mystical demeanor. His head was shaved but he had a long and sharply trimmed black beard. He wore a top hat and a moth-eaten blazer of red velvet, and he carried two knives, curving in the Dhravian style. One of them was a collapsible trick knife and one of them was not, and I suspected that one day he would get them confused and that would be the end of his wife, and no court would ever be able to prove whether it was murder or not. Rotollo and Amaryllis hated one another in a way that at first I thought was part of their performance, and only reluctantly accepted was real.

Amaryllis wore frills. Her plunging décolletage was strung about with fake pearls like dull lamps. Rotollo wore various rings and amulets, ornamented with stones that he said bore sigils of the Folk, though I had seen the sigils of the Folk and the scratchings he displayed had none of their stark and unworldly beauty. He introduced every trick by saying that he learned it from his visitations among the wild Folk in the farthest western wilderness. I think this impressed some of the more naïve members of our audience, for whom the wild Folk were a source of great fascination, though they showed no interest in the Folk below driving the wheel.

At the end of each night Rotollo would announce that he wished to perform a feat of wonder in honor of John Creedmoor and the beautiful Miss Liv. He was not, he said, a partisan of any side in the War or an enemy of any person. He was a partisan of magic, and of the world to come. And he would remove his hat and his wife Amaryllis would show it around and collect what he somehow managed to imply were donations for the cause of Peace. Then he would retrieve his hat and make some passes over it and release from it a kind of battered-looking dove. The mechanism of the hat was designed to project the bird into the air, gently but forcefully, in case it was reluctant to perform. The first night it fluttered in a panic from side to side of the bar and was hell to recapture. The second night it circled then settled nervously on top of the piano. The third night the mechanism broke and a snarl of wires strangled the poor creature, while the spring launched bloody feathers into the faces of our audience, a half-a-dozen shady-looking business-travelers, who laughed and applauded. Amaryllis screamed and swooned into the lap of a fat businessman. Some of the dove's feathers got into the mechanism of the piano and interrupted its cogitations and it became cacophonous. Rotollo cursed at his wife, like it was her fault somehow, and threw the hat on the floor in a rage. It seemed like the fat businessman was taking more liberties than necessary as he comforted Amaryllis, which further angered Rotollo. I smiled and tried to pass the whole thing off as a joke. When I saw Rotollo's hand twitch toward his knives I got up and went to put my arm around him, making him take a bow and then leading him to the bar. Meanwhile the piano played itself, rising to a crescendo then stopping.

✳   ✳   ✳

Later the Great Rotollo and I stood together on the deck, and he drank with one hand and smoked with the other, while I watched the dark massive treetops slide by under the stars.

"Do you know how much that damned thing *cost*?" he said.

"I can't say I do." I assumed he was speaking of the hat. "Say, what you said about the Folk, is that true?"

"What *did* I say about the Folk now? I don't listen to myself much these days. No, wait, I know what you mean—did I really learn card tricks from some stone-casting shaman of the damn Folk? Well, what do you think? You think my name's really Rotollo?"

"I guess not. You may not think it to look at me but I've traveled widely, Mr. Rotollo, before I ended up on the river."

"It's Joe. And that's all talk, it's all superstition for hicks. Like that horseshit about John Creedmoor and that woman. You know what, you know what, Amaryllis eats that stuff up, I swear she's soft in the head, it's worse than when she decided she was a Smiler. Peace! No such thing. Would be bad for business anyway. Happy people don't need—"

There was a thump in the distance, then a flash of what looked like distant lightning. Rotollo said "huh," then drank.

"If there is some new weapon in the world, it'll be in the hands of the Line or the Gun. It'll only make things worse."

"I guess so," I said. "I try not to get involved in matters of politics. It does nobody any good and it only makes people crazy."

"True enough. But what can you do? Can't hide on this damn boat forever. Got to go places, got to get things done."

"I guess so. Can I see your hat?"

It sat crumpled at his feet. He picked it up and handed it to me, flicking some of the remaining gore off its mechanism with a look of disgust.

"I deserve better than this," he said. "These lousy damn boats, these lousy people, my lousy wife. Wait till we get to Jasper City. Then you'll see."

I studied the hat's mechanism, while the Great Rotollo proceeded to tell me all his hopes and dreams. He was working his way to Jasper City, he said, where word was that the city was booming. Alfred Bax-

ter's factories were the biggest and richest and smokiest outside of Line
territories. Jasper's senate was hiring soldiers and engineers. Jasper's
already crowded streets were crowded still further by people fleeing the
war-torn west in their thousands, all of them hungry for entertainment
and diversion, and the theaters and music-halls of Swing Street were
like gold mines. He started talking about the Ormolu Theater and the
Floating World and a dozen places I'd never heard of before, but which
for him were guiding lights.

There was the sound in the distance of an Engine. At that point the
Line ran parallel to the river, ferrying troops and freight and passengers
between the western Stations and Harrow Cross. The Engine was miles
behind us and far out of sight but you know how they sound, the distant throb and drone that makes your head ache before you can even
really hear it.

"I always thought one day I'd go to Jasper," I said. "Now I don't
know."

"There's beautiful women there, more than you can imagine."

"I have a sister who lives in Jasper. Jess. She was pretty enough last
time I saw her."

"You're what-would-you-call-it, the bachelor type, right?"

"I've had little time for love, I guess."

"Lucky man, lucky man. Women! Well, when we get to Jasper you
can do whatever pleases you, and I can get a new start with a new job
and a new wife. Damn it, that woman—"

I had no stomach to hear his many and varied grievances against
Amaryllis again, and so I interrupted him to suggest how the mechanism
of his hat could be improved. He looked at me first with skepticism,
then with interest. Then, because he had been talking about magic, I
started talking about light, and some of the ideas I had for how light
might be used in the theater, and then I started talking about the workings of the self-playing piano, and about other ideas, many of which I
do not recall, that started coming to me in a rush of excitement that I
had not felt in some time, not since back in East Conlan when the notion for the Apparatus had first occurred to me. It was like a dam had
burst in me. Maybe it was the talk of Jasper City, or maybe it was the talk
of magic. I recall theorizing mechanisms for stage-flight, and card-playing
automata, and mahogany boxes between which the Great Rotollo's
beautiful assistants might be appear to be transported from side to side
of the stage, or maybe they might in actual fact *be* transported, why
not, perhaps by vacuum-tubes or . . .

There was a screeching sound that made me fall silent. I took it for an owl.

"Well anyhow," I said. "That's just how I think."

"You're an inventor," Rotollo said.

"I am. I was."

He sighed. "Times are changing. Back in Hamlin, I think it was, I saw a man who could make rain, you know? He had some contraption of electrical rods and I-don't-know-what. What's card tricks next to that? Nothing, that's what."

"Depends on the card trick, I guess."

"That piano, that's a clever piece of work. I've seen it—I've seen it playing itself. Don't pretend otherwise, I know a trick when I see one— damndest thing. Never seen anything like it before. Did you make it?"

"Well," I said. I did not want to say that I did, because it was not true, Kotan did, but nor could I bear to disown it.

"Damn clever," Rotollo said. "Damn clever. What will they think of next."

I felt I had betrayed Kotan, whoever or whatever or wherever that was, or that I had betrayed the wonderful device, or both of them. I had an urge to run back in and apologize to the piano. Instead I shook my head and said, "To the new century. May it be better than the last."

"Not much chance of that from where I'm standing. It's every man for himself to grab as much as he can before the world falls apart once and for all—that's the mystic wisdom of the Great Rotollo."

"I don't know, Mr. Rotollo. I'm an optimist."

The Great Rotollo pinched his cigarette and sucked deeply on it.

The screeching sound repeated itself. I realized that it was not an owl—it was the Engine, which was now only three or four miles away, which is no distance for an Engine, coming up parallel to us and behind us at speeds that rendered the *Damaris* obsolescent and absurd. We were both men of the world, Rotollo and I, and so we pretended that it did not unnerve us.

"My wife likes you," Rotollo said.

I said, "What?" like I hadn't heard, and I braced for a fight.

He repeated himself, a little louder, over the noise of the Engine. "She mentions in particular your smile. Says I haven't smiled like that in years. Which I don't doubt is true. Do it onstage enough you forget the real thing. Was hoping the two of you might run off together, or get caught in flagrante, quick divorce, I'm free again in Jasper City . . . Don't suppose you'd reconsider?"

"Not much chance of that, Mr. Rotollo—Joe."

He shrugged, then threw his cigarette over the side.

"How does it work? The piano."

"Mathematics," I said.

"Like it's haunted," he said. "You know I've been out on the Rim for a long while—a *long* while—and I've seen things—I've seen hauntings and spirits. I performed at a Hospital once where—"

There was a flash and a thump from over in the direction of the Engine.

"Does it think? Tell me the truth. Is it a machine or something else?"

That was a question I had thought about a great deal, often while working on the piano late into the night, alone but for the rolling of the boat and the murmurings of drunks lying under corner tables. The piano was utterly self-sufficient, making music by and for itself out of nothing. Maybe that is what life is. The truth was that I did not know exactly what it meant to think or feel or live or have a soul, and I did not have any quick answer for the magician. What I sometimes thought about late at night, when the piano seemed to be rearranging itself of its own accord, was about the birth of the great powers of the world. I mean the Gun and I mean the Engines of the Line.

Now I am no great student of history, but I know that there was a time before either of them was here in the world to trouble us. There was a time when a gun was just a gun, and there was a time when men made Engines to serve them and not the other way around. I don't know whether we were at peace then or not, I guess not, but things were better. I have heard some people say that there are spirits in the land just waiting for the right kind of forms to take and that is how the Gun and the Line came about. I have heard it said that we ourselves made them, that something in those forms spoke to us and to our nightmares and obsessions and that is how the world changed, because of us. You do not see these speculations written down often and it takes a certain courage to write them now but everyone hears speculation of this sort. As I recall Old Man Harper was of the first school of thought and Miss Harper the second and Carver stayed silent as if he knew better than everyone. Anyhow sometimes I thought about the piano that way, and what the world would be like if whatever happened back then happened again, maybe right at that moment in the rolling fragrant dark of the *Damaris*.

"It's only a machine," I said.

While I had been thinking, the Great Rotollo had been rummaging in the pockets of his jacket and now removed a small gray stone. It was the size of an egg and smooth on the underside and whorled on the top, a little like a fossil, which was perhaps what it was, or a carving of a tiny city—I do not know, because it was dark. He moved his hands quickly over and under it as if to show that it was attached to no strings, then stretched his arm out over the water and opened his hand.

The stone did not drop.

What's more it became clear after roughly half a minute that it was not falling behind us, but kept pace with the slow eastward progress of the *Damaris*. Or rather, it seemed that the world moved, but it did not—it was hard to look at.

"No trick," Rotollo said.

The Engine was getting closer and very loud. You could see its lights glowing white between the trees. There was another flash and a thump from over in the direction of the Engine and the stone wobbled a little. Rotollo reached out and plucked it back out of the night and put it in his pocket.

"The only thing I've got that isn't a trick!" he shouted. "I don't show it. Never show it. Found it on the side of the road, out on the Rim— *above* the side of the road, you know? Outside a little nothing town called Kenauk. It does what it does. Don't know why. Like a little bit of another world. Like whatever came before. Everything changes all the time. You know, maybe there's something to this secret-weapon thing after all. Everything, all the time, changing."

He said more than that, in fact I think he tried to communicate to me his whole metaphysics of the world in shouting and gestures over the noise of the Engine, but much of it was lost on me.

"Jasper City!" he shouted.

"What?"

"Jasper! When you get to Jasper—don't look at me like that, kid, you're ambitious! I said *ambitious*! You're riding this thing all the way to Jasper same as me and when you do you'll be looking to get rich and famous—do you make weapons?"

"What?"

"You should read the newspapers!" he shouted.

He lit another cigarette. I noticed that he was smoking from a yellow packet stamped with the crest of Jasper City, and the name of the Baxter Trust.

"Come find me, when we get to Jasper!—if you don't want to work for the weapon-makers!"

The Great Rotollo handed me his card. It had his name on it, with a wonderful rococo flourish on the *R*.

"Ormolu Theater! Swing Street! I got a contract! Two months, percentage, continuation! Can hire if want to!"

"I don't know—"

What I was thinking was that I had always seen myself as a man of action, whose destiny it was one day to change the world, not merely to entertain it. But I took the card anyhow.

"I could use a clever fellow! Who knows? Who knows? The future, right?"

At that moment the Engine was passing directly alongside us. I could see its smoke blotting out the stars. There was another thump and a flash of red behind the trees. I recognized the sound of explosives and I think the Great Rotollo recognized the sound at the same moment, because he dropped his cigarette and cursed. Then there was a lightning-strike of white that I took to be the lamps of the Engine flaring in sudden anger. There was a whistling sound in the sky and a thump and a splash not so far away from us, then a thick sheet of water came up over the edge of the boat and slapped into me, making me gasp and splutter. The *Damaris* lurched backwards. The whole immense thing, the *Damaris* I mean, rose up rearing like a spooked horse so that I fell into Rotollo, and Rotollo fell over the side into the water, and several lanterns fell off their hooks and onto the deck and started to burn.

## CHAPTER 14

# The Wounded Engine

I don't know exactly what happened, and I guess I never will.

What I know is that the meandering path of the wide River Jass and the straight mountain-cutting length of the Line between Archway Station and the West came close to intersecting, in the depths of a swampy wood. As the *Damaris* crawled upriver the Kingstown Engine came hurtling along the Line. Persons unknown waited in the wood and when the Kingstown Engine approached they had attempted to derail it by blowing the tracks. Those were the thumps we had heard. It is not an easy matter to slow an Engine and it kept going for some time, and in furious retaliation against its attackers it launched rockets wildly into the woods and into the night, one of which had whistled over the treetops and hit the river just in front of the *Damaris*. The resulting disturbance of water lifted the *Damaris,* throwing her back and to one side. She was an ancient vessel and not equipped to withstand such a shock. Rotten wood splintered, rusted nails turned to powder, frayed ropes snapped. Her tall wheel broke away from its mechanism, which in turn tore a hole in her hull.

The Kingstown Engine survived, later arriving in Archway mostly unscathed, or so the Line claimed. The outrage was officially blamed on Agents of the Gun, but there were persistent rumors that it was the work of John Creedmoor and Liv Alverhuysen and Professor Harry Ransom, putting their strange weapon to work. I believe that it was the first shot of what we later called the Battle of Jasper, which I guess I will write about when the time comes.

The *Damaris* did not survive. She turned on her side and sank, pulled over by the listing wheel. She sank in a stately fashion, as befitted a lady of her advanced years. Lines of pennants and lamps snapped free of their fastenings and slithered into the water. Deck chairs followed. Then the passengers came out onto the deck and held their hats on their heads or clutched their suitcases close like children as they jumped feet-first into the water. The crew followed close behind. The boat's cook had saved a bottle of whiskey and Mr. John Southern hefted a stuffed satchel of valuables. Nobody made any effort to pump out the bilges, as far as I could see, or whatever it is that one does to save a sinking ship. Certainly I did not.

The river was wide and slow, black and warm. Passengers and crew scattered across it in all directions. I saw the Great Rotollo swimming away north, his wake expanding and glittering in the light of the flaming deck. I think I saw his wife Amaryllis heading in the same general direction, while I think Mr. John Southern went south. There was no consensus as to which bank to swim for, or whether to swim against the current or with it. There was no plan. What had held us together was broken.

I do not mean to suggest that there was panic, because there was not, or very little. We had all known the *Damaris* could not last forever. Nothing does. There was a general air of resigned dignity. Mr. John Southern gave one last affectionate nod toward the prow of his boat before he folded his arms over his suitcase and fell backward into the water. The cook jumped feet-first with a deep sigh, as if this happened to him all the time.

I myself turned and ran back into the bar in order to save the piano, or at least a part of it.

The piano was sliding down the slowly tilting floor toward a heap of broken glass and furniture and paintings and plants and cutlery. I staggered sideways toward it. Tumbling chairs tried to tackle me—I dodged and jumped and disentangled my legs from theirs. I cut my hand on a broken bottle. On reaching the piano I found that my own weight was not nearly enough to halt or even slow its slide. I took a butter-knife from a passing cabinet and used it to lever open the piano's frame. The Great Rotollo's other dove fluttered back and forth overhead, I do not know how it had found its way into the room but it was apparently unable to find its way out—I could not help it and besides it was the bird or the piano and I do not regret my choice. I pried out part of the winding-mechanism, a heavy cylinder of brass and wood, etched with the piano's codes, shaped like a sacred scroll. It was the part with *KOTAN* scratched into it.

By the time I had accomplished this I was the last person left on the boat. The upper deck dipped to starboard into the black water. It rose up to port behind me. I held the mechanism tightly beneath my arm and I threw myself into the water.

I sank.

Like I think I have said, I cannot swim, and besides the piano's mechanism was shockingly heavy and unwieldy. I kicked madly to put distance between myself and the sinking boat, which only drove me further down. The strength of the river took hold of me. All I could see was blackness, either beneath the water or above it. I recall that I panicked. I recall that I was quite certain that so long as I held on to the mechanism I would be safe. This was a self-defeating conviction but an irresistible one. I continued to sink.

Slowly darkness gave way and I began to see a red light at the edges of the world.

I do not recall letting go of the mechanism or how I came to be clutching instead a piece of wood that turned out to be a bench from the *Damaris*'s bar. I do recall that when I finally noticed that the mechanism was lost I was too tired even to regret it—regret would come later.

I recall floating aimlessly downstream, all alone in the warm night.

At last the current took me toward the river's bank, where I came to rest in the tangled roots of a huge green tree.

I struck out for solid ground but I found none in any direction. The woods were swampy, like I said. They smelled green and wet. Black water came halfway up my legs. Tall cattail stands horripilated. Every moonlit ripple in the water looked to my imagination like a snake swimming toward me—every vine or frond that dangled from the trees looked snake-like too. There were fever-dream scatterings of fireflies—there were invisible insects that bit. Again and again I pushed through walls of wet fern and reed to look out over yet another expanse of dark weed-thick water.

Eventually I climbed up into the roots of another tree and decided to wait out the night.

The root was thick as the back of a horse, and not as uncomfortable as one might imagine. I sat with my back against the trunk and considered my situation.

I had no means of making fire, no food, very little money, a half-completed letter to my sister Jess, and the Great Rotollo's business-card. I had no weapons—only a small pocket-knife that I used to use to work on the piano, and it was hardly fiercer than a fingernail. I had only one shoe, and it was both soaked and slimy.

I still wore the jacket of the russet suit Mr. Southern had given me when I signed on with the *Damaris*. There had been a dried rose in the lapel but it was gone now. The jacket had been a loan not a gift and I guessed it belonged to Mr. Southern still, but because I saw no likelihood of returning it to him, and because he had not paid me in weeks, and because in any case it was now so vile that he would not want it back, I decided it was mine now. I hung it to dry from a protuberance on a nearby branch. It was like a sort of company. I half-expected it to speak to me in Mr. Carver's voice.

I did not know where I was. I knew that I was on the edges of the Tri-City Territory, south-west of Gibson and west of Jasper. I knew that I was not far from the River Jass. But I did not know what woods I was in, or where the nearest town might be. The River Jass ran westward, and I assumed therefore I had been carried by the current some distance west, away from Jasper City and back out toward the Western Rim. I did not know how far. Far enough that I was alone—whoever else had survived the sinking of the *Damaris,* they were nowhere in evidence.

There were no sounds in the night that I recognized as human.

The piano was gone. I tried to remember how it worked, in some vague hope that I might one day reconstruct it, I recall that I even took my knife and held it poised to carve a memento into the soft root—but I was already forgetting. I mourned it as bitterly as if it had been a lover. I still do.

I think I mourn it more than I do its maker.

I said that I would tell of four times I held history in my hand. Well, this was the second. Had I only held on to the mechanism perhaps the piano could have been reconstructed, and who knows what might have been done with that technology. Who knows how things might have gone differently with poor Adela, and maybe therefore everything else.

I will write about Adela in due course, when I get there.

I never said that this would be a story of triumph. For the most part it is not.

Anyhow there I was. Alone in a swamp, with no prospects and no name.

I tried to recall if Mr. Alfred Baxter of Jasper City had ever found himself in a similar predicament. I did not think that he had. I was without guidance.

At one time in the night there was a sound that might have been feet splashing through the swamp not far away from me, and I thought it might be other survivors from the *Damaris*. I stood, and was about to call out *Here, help me, it's Rawlins, the piano-man,* when it occurred to me that there had been fighting in those woods. Somebody had attacked an Engine of the Line. It might be a soldier of the Line, looking for the perpetrators or it might be the perpetrators themselves. In either case it might be deadly to draw attention to myself. The cry froze in my throat. The noise receded. It was not until after it was long gone that I thought that maybe it was somebody as lost as me, who might have needed my help, whose heart might have leapt at the sound of my voice, and that I had been selfish again, I had been a coward, thinking only of myself.

"When I get out of here," I said to myself, "I will be a better man. I have suffered more than the usual run of worldly misfortune but there is still greatness left in me. One day I will do good things for the world."

I thought of Liv and John Creedmoor and I thought of poor Mr. Carver. I thought about Mr. Carver's last words to me, that I was a thief, and I thought that he was both right and wrong, and I thought about how I would one day make everything right, how I would make everything perfect. I thought about my sisters and how I missed them and how I would explain everything to them if I ever saw them again, which seemed unlikely. I thought about the Great Rotollo and his long-suffering wife Amaryllis and about the Ormolu Theater, which in my imagination was like a great golden palace. I thought about the Apparatus and how much I missed its light and its warmth. I thought about Jasper City, and recalled all my old dreams of how one day I would ride in high style down its triumphal avenues.

I spent a great deal of time on this kind of profitless rumination. Hours, at least. I waited for dawn and dawn stubbornly did not come. Instead there was a flash of white light in the distance, which by the time it came through the trees to fall on the backs of my hands was soft and spiderwebbed. It stuttered, flashing and then fading, like telegraph-signals. There was a coughing sound then a deep roar.

The noise and light was coming from what I guessed to be the north-west, a few miles or so upriver. Fear made me shrink against the trunk of the tree. Then curiosity got the better of my fear and I jumped to my feet and started climbing the tree.

I was cold and tired and my shoulders ached and creaked and cracked like an old boat as I pulled myself up. It was a good tree for climbing, with knots and a thick sturdy mesh of vine and broad swooping branches. I remember thinking as I lay panting on a branch that I could not recall the last time I had climbed a tree. Not since back in East Con-lan, in fact. The town was bare of trees and most of us did not dare go too far into the woods south of town but I recalled incidents of climb-ing, throwing stones, boys shouting. I felt like a boy again but at the same time I felt very old, and very far from home. I stood, slowly and carefully, and pushed my head through a curtain of slimy green leaves, and I saw that flash of light again.

The light flashed, then ceased, then came again. It illuminated a long dark shape behind the trees. I could not properly judge the distance or its size, except that it was huge, and far enough away that I did not think it could sense me.

It was the wounded Engine. Later I would learn from the newspa-pers that it was the Engine that runs out of Kingstown.

Do you know what Kingstown is? Maybe not. I hope no one born in Ransom City will know of the Stations. I hope in the New Century all the Stations may have fallen. But in those days Kingstown was the west-ernmost of the Stations of the Line. It was a town of many thousands of people, mostly soldiers or factory-workers. It was full of industry and smoke and toil. It was a huge machine for projecting the power of the Engines westward. Mr. Carver and I went nowhere near it on our trav-els. Kingstown was thousands of miles west of the place where I stood, but the Engine that was its heart and soul and brain and god went ceaselessly back and forth across the continent carrying men and weap-ons and prisoners and information and . . .

It moved. There was a flash of its lamps, then darkness, then another flash and it had moved. Its long metal body had stretched a hundred yards closer to my hiding place. Each flash illuminated a huge and grow-ing trail of black smoke.

I had seen Engines before, of course. East Conlan was not far from Line territory and we saw them in the north. Carver and I had crossed tracks, seen Engines roaring across the horizon, even considered on occasion traveling by Engine (we could not afford it). They were strange at the best of times, but that night the Kingstown Engine was quite terrifying.

It was injured. Its tracks took it not so very far north of my tree and when its lamp flashed again I could see that its frame was broken. The huge cowl that was its face was dented and twisted. The lamps above the cowl were lopsided, as if some had been blinded. Several of the cars that were its half-mile body were missing, or caved in like broken teeth, or still smoking from whatever or whoever had attacked it. There were cannon on the hindmost car, one of which looked bent.

I don't know why it was flashing its lamps in that way. I have heard that the Engines of the Line signal to each other—all across the continent—with their noise, their thunderous awful clatter, their smoke. Maybe it was signaling its distress, its outrage, maybe it was calling for aid, for revenge, for tightening of control. Maybe it was broken, or mad.

I have always hated the Line. I have written about what it did to my father and to East Conlan and to me. And this particular Engine had destroyed the *Damaris,* and left me stranded, and destroyed the beautiful piano, and had done all this casually, indifferently, the way they did everything. I did not yet know which Engine it was, but I had a particular and specific hatred for it, whichever it was. And yet to see an Engine injured was troubling, and gave me little joy. It made me aware of my own so much greater fragility.

I thought about Miss Harper and John Creedmoor and their weapon and for the first time I thought what it might be like if it were really true. Maybe their weapon could end the War, maybe it could do away with Engines and Guns and their servants. But they would not go quietly. The War would be worse before it would be better. And what would take its place?

For the first time in my life, the thought of the *Future* frightened me.

I do not mean to claim any great prescience. I did not foresee the Course of History. Any man who claims to have such powers of foresight is lying. Truth is I was lost in a swamp at night, and any man's thoughts will turn grim in such circumstances.

The tree shook as the Engine passed. There was a noise that made my bowels turn to water. Leaves were torn loose and blew around my head in its wake. I lost my footing and fell, catching myself painfully on the branch with knees and elbows and bloodied palms, and when I stood again the Engine was already far in the distance, heading northeast toward the Three Cities, toward Jasper.

❋   ❋   ❋

I climbed back down the tree, and I fell asleep in the cradle of its roots.
When I woke it was still dark. It seemed like an improbably long night
but I knew that I was not far west of the Three Cities and the days at
that longitude were mostly regular in their duration, so I guessed the
fault was in my perceptions not in the world. I thought maybe I had a
fever coming on.

The second time I heard the sound of somebody walking through
the swamp nearby, I did not hide or hesitate. I stopped only to take my
jacket and my one wet shoe and I ran out after that faint sound, waving
the shoe in the air and shouting "Hey, hey, help, hold up, I'm with the
*Damaris*, hey, wait" and so on. I waded through the water and crashed
through thick undergrowth toward the sound and burst through a stand
of head-high ferns that scratched at my face and out into a wide open
stretch of moonlit green water. A half-dozen tall thin figures were wad-
ing single file across it. They were all long-legged fellows and the green
did not quite reach their waists. They were stooped and they were pale
and when they turned their heads to look at me I saw that they had the
big-boned faces and black beards of the Folk.

CHAPTER 15

# The Chain

There were seven of them. They stood side-by-side. Two of them leaned together, as if for support, or comfort against the night. In the middle stood one whose shoulders seemed, at first shocked glance, to be hunched. Then I saw that he was wearing something looped around his shoulders and neck, dangling down his back, like an elegant lady of Jasper City might wear a fox-fur stole. I thought perhaps it was a length of rope. Then I understood that it was a chain—a long, long chain— and in the same moment I understood that these were some of the poor wretches who had powered the wheel of the *Damaris*. I had thought they'd all drowned.

That is not true. I had not given them a moment's thought, not until I found myself looking at them face to face, yet now—as I looked into their leader's wide dark eyes now I could think of nothing else.

When I say *their leader,* I mean the fellow with the chain wrapped around his shoulder. I guessed that he was their leader. There was something grand about the way he wore the chain.

I imagined them sinking, pulled down by the awesome weight of the *Damaris,* by the inexorable grip of their chain. They must have been afraid. I know that many scholars and preachers and politicians and businessmen will tell you that the Folk do not feel pain or fear the way we do, but I think that cannot be true.

I shook. All these thoughts took just moments. I guess they studied me too, and drew their own conclusions.

They had been walking in what I thought was a westerly direction. Moonlit ripples still showed the way they had come.

"Jasper City's back that way," I said, "but I guess maybe you're heading out to the Rim, or beyond it I guess. I don't know where you're from. I, well, that is, it's a long way either way and good luck to you."

They continued to look at me. We were alone in the night and the wilderness now and the tables were turned. They could do whatever they pleased with me and whatever it was I could not say it was not just. The *Damaris* and its rules were long gone. This was now their world and I had no say in it.

"I'm glad you," I said. "I mean, well, you know. I'm glad you got out. Got free."

I was afraid.

I had once joined a municipal chapter of the Liberationist Movement, and for two weeks I paid my weekly dues toward the cause of the end of bondage. I wondered whether I should mention that fact. I decided not to.

"I think there was a rocket," I said. "What happened to the *Damaris*, I mean. The *Damaris* was the name of the boat, if you don't know. I don't know whether you. I mean, it was the War again."

The one I took for their leader whispered a word. I did not understand it.

I do not know if they understood me. I think they did.

It was like when I met the giant Knoll at White Rock. Whatever would happen, I could not talk my way out of it.

I thought of the stories of travelers waylaid by Folk, and tortured and killed, maybe for revenge or maybe because they have broken some rule of the Folk's world that they did not understand or maybe for no reason anyone has words for. I thought of Folk-tales of curses and transformations and the evil eye. I did not know if they meant me harm, and I do not know now. I thought they might harm me whether they meant to or not.

"You know," I said, "once, when I was a boy, back in a place we call East Conlan but I guess maybe you have a different name for it, I visited with some of your people. That is, I—"

I had a sudden apprehension of the strength with which they must have torn loose their chains from the wheel, the strength with which they must have split open the waterlogged coffin that was the hull of the *Damaris*, and risen from the muddy bottom of the river—the same strength with which they had turned its wheel for who knew how many long years. A chill ran through me.

I took a step back. They came closer. The fellow who wore the chain was at the forefront. I could see where it had broken, and I could see where it had scarred him.

I said, "My name's Harry Ransom," but of course that name meant nothing to them.

Then I had one of my moments of inspiration. I pulled out the pocketknife and I turned to the nearest tree and I carved into its soft mossy trunk a certain sign, one that I remembered very well and that I thought they might know.

They studied it in silence for a while, looking from the sign to me and back again, and then at each other, while I tried to explain how I came to know this thing and to talk about the Apparatus and about my dreams and my ambitions and my great and wonderful destiny, and why it would be a damn shame for the world if I were to perish in that swamp. All together they began to roll their shoulders and shake their heads, and after a moment I realized that they were laughing, and not especially kindly, that is, they were laughing at me.

✳    ✳    ✳

Well now. I guess I should explain, or otherwise just skip all this thrashing in the swamp and get straight to Jasper City and fame and fortune and the First and Second Battle and all the rest.

I have wrestled for a long time with how I will tell this or whether I should tell it at all, and maybe all I can do is write it all out and see how it looks.

This is about what I call the Ransom Process. I have to go back a way to tell this, back to when I was a boy, in good old East Conlan. If you like you may turn ahead to when I get to Jasper City.

✳    ✳    ✳

I was fourteen years old. It was the summer of '83 or '84 or thereabouts. Conlan was halfway between what it had been when I was a child and what it was becoming, which is an outpost of the Line. I was living beneath my father's roof, or what was left of it—the old house and my father's business having been claimed by the Line. We were lodging on the south side of town. We kept different hours between all of his jobs and all of mine, and we did not speak.

For most of that summer I supported myself painting signs. I learned the trick of sign-painting from a book. The trick of persuading East Conlan's dour storekeeps that there was nothing more respectable or desirable than a brightly colored motto just like the storefronts of Jasper City—a place none of us had ever seen—well, that came naturally to me. I turned the town bright for a summer. My crowning achievement was a bird of paradise over Connolly's store. He asked why and I said why not. It blew down that winter.

Meanwhile my father vanished at night, or sometimes for days, running errands for Conlan's new management to New Foley, which was the next town over. His work, whatever it was, was secretive, unspoken. He was silent and often angry. And after all what was there to say? All day he served the Linesmen in various capacities that were degrading to a man of his pride—what would he talk about? Whatever he had to say I did not want to hear it. I had my own obsessions. I would be free, wealthy, famous, great, I would bring Light to the world. I think I have written about how I climbed the tower on top of Grady's Hill with a kite and some wire in a thunderstorm—well, that was that summer. That was the state of my Great Work at the time. I had burns on both palms and let me tell you that is not a laughing matter for anyone who has to work for a living. My father called me a word in his buzzing old-country language that I guess meant *fool*. I could not or would not explain to him why I had done it.

We were alone in the house except that there was an old woman above us and a large number of feral cats in the rank weeds back of the house. May was the oldest of my sisters and she had gone off the month before with a revival of the Silver City faith. Sue was the next oldest and she had moved to New Foley with an insurance salesman, where she was living in wedded bliss and learning book-keeping. Jess was I guess sixteen at the time, and whatever aspirations she later had to the stage had not yet manifested themselves, except that she loved to dance. She spoke all the time about Jasper City and fame and fortune. I do not think she knew what she would do to get there. She was living at the time with one of the young men who had used to work for Grady's Mine before the Line seized, and having been found surplus to requirements he now did nothing at all so far as I could tell except drink and brawl. His name was Joe or Jim or something of the kind. I disliked him and admired him, both at the same time, and now I do not remember what he looked like except that he was handsome, and dark, and had a curl of hair on his forehead that I reckon Jess liked. He was also stupid. I recall that he used to boast sometimes of his intention to take up arms in the service of the Gun, but the fact was that neither he nor anybody else in our backwater town knew how to do that. I cut him in on the sign-painting business because he was good at carrying buckets and ladders. Sometimes he and his fellows threw stones at the Line's concrete barracks on the north of town. So did my sister. So did I, on occasion. One of my sister's many talents is that she is as accurate with a stone as any Agent is with his Gun—it is mostly because of Jess that I am so quick at dodging stones and glasses thrown at my head, which has served me in good stead throughout my career. I am a bad shot. We all have our gifts.

Anyhow it was as we three were sitting by the old culvert east of town after one such glorious blow for the cause of freedom that the matter of my father came up in conversation. I guess one or other of us was talking about leaving town to strike out for fame and fortune and Joe said something about my father and how he vanished from town from time to time, and I said that he was running errands to New Foley, and Joe said that no such thing could be true, because Joe sometimes went to New Foley to drink away from the eyes of the New Management, and my father had not been seen there in years.

Joe's speculation was that my father was attempting to contact the Gun—or else that he was raising up some black magic of his own, out in the woods, a curse upon the New Management. Joe was a simple fellow and always certain that because my father had come to the West across the mountains from the old country, and because he spoke an old-country tongue, he must be in possession of old-country magic. To him this was elementary, and he did not like it when Jess and me mocked him.

"He's got a woman," Jess said. "Of course he has—a woman in a hut in the woods!"

I did not believe that any more than I believed the black-magic story, and I said so. Not because of the honor of my late departed mother, nor because in my eyes my father was a hundred years old and incapable of romance, but because if he had a woman he would surely be less angry and tired and hollow-eyed than he was. I said that he was going to New Foley to work, just like he said, because the old man had no leisure and no freedom for women or hijinks in the woods.

Jess said, "Yeah—and whose fault is that, then?"

She could be very cruel.

We argued, and Joe and my sister argued, and after a while there was a wager, I do not recall exactly who proposed it first. We were to follow my father and see who was right.

The next night we skulked in the yard with the weeds and the cats but he went nowhere but to bed. After that we forgot our wager for a while. You may recall that after I climbed Old Grady's tower with the kite and the baling-wire I was charged by the New Management and sentenced to a period of penal servitude. My experiment with the kite and the lightning in the thunderstorm on top of the abandoned tower on Grady's Hill was in the view of the new authorities not the admirable curiosity of a young man of genius, but rather an instance of criminal trespass, aggravated by vandalism. I was therefore plenty busy and forbidden to leave town anyhow. My father went off without warning and came back once and then again and nobody thought to follow him. It was not until maybe a month later that my father announced at breakfast that he was leaving the next day to look for work in New Foley and would be gone for a long time, if all went well, and so it was time for me to be a man.

I am sorry to say that I was still only a boy. My servitude had expired the day before and I was free again and in the mood for adventure. Therefore I rounded up Jess and Joe and reminded them of our wager and the next day we followed the old man when he left.

The road from Conlan to Foley had not yet been widened for motorcars. It wound through the woods. It was therefore possible to follow a man unobserved, if one stuck to the trees and if that man was occupied with his own thoughts.

It was the middle of the afternoon, and hot, and the woods belonged to insects. They liked the taste of me and Joe but not Jess. Women have their ways, she explained.

My father walked west down the road for an hour or two. A wagon passed and he refused a ride and did not make conversation. After that he sat on a fallen tree for another hour or more, at a place where the road turned north toward Foley. He had his pack at his feet and his great bald head in his hands. Then he stood very quick like he had seen us, but he had not. He swung his pack over his shoulder and set off west, into the woods, off the road.

I had lost my wager.

The woods south of Conlan are nothing like the swamp I fetched up in after the *Damaris* sank, except in the way that all lonely places are the same. Conlan's woods were dry. Trees stuck up out of the ground tall and thin and regular like the bed of nails I once saw a circus-act lie down on out on the Rim. There was thorny brush everywhere. The ground was stony and uneven and rose up into a hundred tiny hills and shallow gulches, none of which had any names but all of which served to turn you around, so that it was notorious among the people of Conlan and Foley and Haman that to enter those woods was to get lost, sure as anything. We did not get far into the woods before Jess's nerve failed and she wanted to go back.

No—that is not the right way to say it. Truth is that Jess was always brave. But she had better sense than me. Joe did not understand that, and mocked her for cowardice. Hard words were exchanged in whispers. I was for pressing on too, because I could never stand to be thought a coward. In my time I have done a lot of stupid things for reasons of pride. In the end Jess turned back and Joe and me went on. I have mentioned her deft hand with a stone—well, as soon as our backs were turned she buzzed a stone to clip Joe's ear. He cursed. I thought my father would hear but I guess he did not.

Another difference between the swamps and the woods south of Conlan was silence. The swamps were full of strange and wet and unearthly noises, and the woods were silent. My father made no noise, and nor did Jess. Joe grunted and cursed, but he had the good sense to do so quietly. Even the insects were for the most part quiet. Sometimes one of them would make a whining sound that was as shocking in the silence as a gunshot.

Nobody much lived in the woods outside of town and there was little in them of use to commerce or industry. My father stopped at no little huts, enjoyed the company of no women. Nor did he practice any black magic.

We got hungry. It began to get dark. My father produced a lantern from his pack. That made him a good deal easier to follow from a safe distance. Of course we would never find our way back without him.

Joe offered his speculation again that my father was conspiring with Agents of the Gun, and I said that he should hope that was not true, because the Agents would have no second thoughts about slitting the throats of spies.

We were still pretending not to be afraid. As the older of the two of us Joe was naturally determined to show that he was the braver of the two of us, and because I was who I am I was determined to show that it was me. Truth is we were both afraid. In no particular order we feared the dark, hunger, getting lost, wolves, snakes, silence, and Agents of the Gun who might be skulking and scheming in the wilderness and sharpening their throat-slitting knives. Soon enough we added Officers of the Line to that list of bogeymen. On our walk west we twice passed old camp-sites. You could tell they had been occupied by Linesmen because of the kind of junk they leave behind. We did not know what business the Linesmen could have had in those parts but we did not like it. If they found us wandering in the woods there would be questioning.

We lost sight of my father's lantern. After a little argument we agreed to keep walking west, keeping the setting sun at our backs. That might take us in the direction of New Haman by morning.

Joe remarked that it was like we were out on the edge of the world, traveling in unmade lands, and you could not be sure which way you were going or if the sun would come up tomorrow. I told him I was not scared. I was.

Above all else we were afraid of the Folk.

I did not know how many of the Folk lived in the woods south of Conlan. Nobody did. There was nothing very profitable in that wilderness and it was of no particular strategic importance to anyone and so great expanses of it were still unmapped. There was no question though that a sizable settlement of free Folk resided there, most likely in the triangle of land between Conlan and New Haman and the peak we called Old Man Hump. Sometimes a wagon on the road to Foley or Haman crossed paths with a half-dozen Folk going about their business, whatever that was. Once when I was sick a group of the Folk came to the outskirts of town, or so I heard, and the townspeople watched them watch us watching them for an hour or two before they turned back. It was said that Grady's Mine had been hollowed out of caves that had belonged to them. There had been violence back before I was born. Old-timers spoke darkly of witchcraft and curses and strange storms and devils of dust and stone and signs scratched on trees that could drive a man mad—all the usual sort of stories you hear everywhere. Grady brought in a Mother Superior of the Silver City faith to say blessings for his men, and a Master of the World Serpent faith to spit sickness upon his enemies, and in the end religion with the aid of dynamite proved more than a match for magic. Eventually a kind of *entente* was achieved, which is to say that Grady got his mine and the Folk got the woods and for the most part we each left each other alone. But if Joe and me blundered into one of their places there was no telling what they might do to us.

My father was well out of sight and hearing now and so to show each other that we were not afraid Joe and me were talking as loud as we pleased. He told me some blood-curdling stories he had heard about the Folk of the woods and the cruelties they visited on unfortunate travelers. I doubt that there was a word that he said that was not pure invention. I would like to say that I expressed my doubt of his stories but I did not. Truth is that I made up some of my own. Well, I have always been a good talker. I do not remember whatever I said but I remember that Joe's face went pale and he fell silent.

In the silence I began to speculate on the meaning of the Line camp-sites. Could they be looking for my father? Surely not—the camp-sites were old. If they wanted to question him, they would have arrested him in town. Perhaps they had decided that now that Conlan was under their management it was time to drive the Folk away from town, and further into the West. Maybe the camp-sites belonged to scouts, hunters, slave-takers.

It was full dark. To stop and wait out the night would be to admit that we were lost and so we crept along, feeling our way with our hands on thorny tree-trunks and rough rock. The first sign that we had walked into the territory of the Folk was when beneath my fingers I felt carved rock. It was a kind of twisted spiral, like a fingerprint, as I recall. Anyhow you could say it was frightening but now my curiosity was woken too. I had seen fragments of Folk carving before, sold back in town, but I had never seen their homes and I had never set eyes on the Folk themselves. Joe was for turning back. I was for pressing on. I got my way.

Soon enough we heard voices.

We were high up, I think. We had been climbing the slopes of Old Man Hump for some time. There were few trees but there were many tall rocks all around us. There was what I shall call moonlight for want of a better word, though it was somewhat redder than ordinary.

My father stood beneath one of those tall rocks. His back was to us and he was deep in conversation with one of the Folk, who sat cross-legged on top of the rock.

It was a woman. Long black hair fell into her lap. Otherwise she was naked, save for paintings and ornaments.

My father was speaking in his old-country language, that I had never taken the time to learn. He gestured vigorously with his hands, which he always used to do when speaking that language, and never did when speaking mine. I do not know what he was saying. Sometimes the Folk woman responded in her own language, and I do not know what that meant either.

The scene reminded me of an illustration from one of the Encyclopedias—the old-world knight serenading his love at her balcony.

"It is a woman," Joe said. "Jess had that right, all right—, but it's a woman of—that's filthy, Ransom. That's wicked. How could he. That's—"

I told him to shut up.

My father sounded angry. He sounded like he was begging, and he hated to beg. I heard him say one or two names that I recognized—people from back in East Conlan. Officials of the New Management.

The woman stood, and walked away. My father cursed and climbed up after her. I followed and then Joe followed me.

Pretty much nobody ever goes among Folk settlements except soldiers, slave-takers, and missionaries. Soldiers and slave-takers keep their opinions to themselves and missionaries are untrustworthy witnesses, and so few people are familiar with what it is like to walk in one of the places that remain in the possession of the Folk.

It is very hard to describe. Among the rocks there were huts made of stone and wood. They were very plain and simple in their shape but everything was carved, all over, in patterns of surpassing strangeness, that were beautiful from one angle and hideous from another. I closed one eye to look closer as my sight seemed to swim and discovered that when seen through different eyes the carvings took different forms—they changed like they were being spoken. It was like the whole place was one big carving, or the letters in one big word, and I wondered if that was what the whole western world was like before our forefathers all those years ago set foot across the mountains and began cutting down trees and building towns and making maps and damming rivers and naming things &c. There was no other kind of art that I could see, though who's to say I would have known it if I could see it—a cat might wander into East Conlan and stroll down Main Street never understanding the tenth part of anything he sees.

There were no luxuries, and as a matter of fact there were hardly any tools. I guess they had no time for those things. The carving absorbed their attention. They were desperate—they were right up against the wall. They had a whole lot to remember and write down before it vanished from the world. I know how that feels.

Joe kept whispering his disgust for the whole thing and I wished to all the powers that might exist in anybody's world that he would shut up. I did not dare say anything out loud. I did not even want to think too loud in my own head. I'd long since lost sight of my father and the woman and I was exploring for the sake of exploration. I guess I was trespassing but at the time I did not think about it that way.

I began to discern patterns in the carvings. I got down on my knees and I stretched on tip-toes to follow one particular design that ran like a thread through the whole pattern—an endless ever-renewing spiral—it is difficult to describe in words and I certainly do not intend to draw it and commit it to the mails! When the devotees of the World Serpent depict that wondrous creature eating its own tail, I think perhaps they are trying to reckon with the same great truth this pattern spoke of. I recalled a dream I had once had of one of the staircases in Grady's mansion climbing forever and ever in a circle, always returning to itself, and how in my dream there seemed no reason why the world should not be that way. It had that inner light I spoke of—as a matter of fact I believe it *was* light, or at least the word for it. A circle, like the sun, or like what goes on inside the sun. A map of a never-ending world. I struggled to commit it to memory. I fumbled in my pockets for paper and something to write with—something to prick my finger with so that I could write—anyhow that is why I did not see that we were surrounded until it was too late.

Six of the Folk surrounded us—three in front of us and three behind. On either side of us there were tall rocks—we were in a kind of narrow defile. The Folk were not armed but they were none the less menacing for that.

I stood up straight.

"Let me explain," I said. "I am Harry Ransom, of East Conlan—you know my father. You have business with him—I know that—well, that's no concern of mine—but I am here with a business proposition of my own, and I apologize for not entering into this place with the proper formalities but I don't know what they are, and what I have to say is of the greatest possible value to you and me both, not to mention the whole wide world—you see I'm a scientist—I may look young but don't discount me—and my particular study is light. Do you know what I mean when I say scientist? I guess you do. All this stuff here—all this writing, nobody made all this by accident, did they? Well there's a whole lot I could offer you and a whole lot you can offer me, I mean for instance the meaning of this sign right here. . . ."

They looked to each other and began to make a noise that I did not recognize as laughter. As a matter of fact I did not realize it was laughter at all until I heard it again years later in the swamp, after the *Damaris* went down.

I guess maybe Joe was in some ways quicker on the up-take than me, because he took offense. He drew a knife from his belt and drew himself up to his full height and said that he did not see why any civilized and hard-working man should be insulted by woods-dwelling savages, whose proper place was as slaves, and that they might kill him if they chose but he would not be mocked by them. He started this speech in a man's deep voice but it broke halfway through to reveal the boy below. Then he swung clumsily at the nearest man of the Folk, who stepped aside as smoothly as if he was a ghost. I tried to hold Joe back but the next thing I saw was one of the Folk lifting a stone and buzzing it right at my head with accuracy equal to my sister's and with a smooth motion that would make the best ball-player in the Three Cities weep with envy. I spun and fell facedown. Everything went black. I think it is thanks to that incident that I have bad sight in one eye, as I think I already said.

❉   ❉   ❉

I woke to voices. They spoke in the plain old accent of East Conlan, same as mine. I felt relief and despair both at the same time. My sister was there and my father was there too.

They had found me lying in a ditch not fifty feet south of town. All I can guess is that the Folk returned me there.

Joe never did return.

I said nothing about my encounter to anyone in East Conlan. I told Jess that all we'd learned about my father was that he had gone into the woods to drink in solitude, after which discovery Joe and me had a falling out and he got separated and I guess he got lost. My father asked what I was doing in the woods and I said that I was conducting experiments. I said that I had climbed a tree to see where I was going and had fallen out of it and that was how I had injured my head. *Too much cleverness, not enough sense,* my father said, and who could argue with him? The stitches for the injury to my head and the bandages for my eye cost us both a lot more money and I was not able to return to my true calling, by which I mean the study of Light, for several months. When I did I threw out everything that had gone before. I had a new design to work from. Do not imagine it was easy.

I never did ask my father what he was doing in those woods. I guess he went to beg or haggle for whatever power the Folk might have to offer him. Something to settle scores or turn back the clock or make the world right for him again. He must have been very desperate to think they could or would help him but he would not be the first or the last to end up that way. I guess he never got what he was looking for because about a month after that night the Line sent soldiers into the woods. They said it was for our own protection after what happened to Joe but I do not believe that for a moment. They burned down most of the woods and drove the Folk west. We saw the smoke and the flashes and the bangs one morning and that was the end of that. Not long after that my father died—it was his heart that finally did for him.

✳   ✳   ✳

Well anyhow as I stood there years later up to my knees in swamp-water and trembling with fear I remembered all this. The spiral sign that I carved on the tree to show to those Folk was one of the same signs that I had spied in the woods all those years ago. It was just one of many aspects or phases of the pattern that I had seen in the woods that night and every single one of them is carved into my memory. The Apparatus is constructed around a number of such signs. That is why it can do things that the Professors in Jasper City will tell you cannot be done. Part of it is made of the science of a different world. And part of it is mine. Nobody has ever done that before.

Some of the Professors in Jasper City will tell you that the world is made of Ether, and some will tell you that it is made of Atoms. It is my opinion that it is made of words and signs.

Anyhow I tried to explain to those Folk about the Apparatus, talking mostly in gestures.

I was taking a gamble. For years I'd wondered why those fellows back in the woods west of Conlan had spared me and returned me to town. I doubted it was because of my charm and handsome smile, and I doubted that they were merciful, because they were surely not merciful with poor stupid Joe. Maybe they'd found my father too slow a study for their purposes—too old and set in his ways—maybe they'd looked to me instead. Had they wanted me to set eyes on that sign? Was it all an accident, had I stolen it, or was it a gift?

If I had not been meant to see the sign, maybe they would consider me a thief—but then maybe they were planning to kill me anyhow. If I had been meant to take it—and if these fellows were of the same leanings as those back in East Conlan, and who knows what sort of politics the Folk have, it was worth a roll of the dice in my opinion—*if* they had meant me to take it then maybe they would let me go, or even help me find my way out of the swamp. If there was a plan I was happy to go along with it. Anything to get out of that swamp.

I tried to explain all about the Apparatus. About how one day when I had got it working and when I had money to mass-produce it—I tried to explain about *money*—I did not know if they had anything like it, maybe they did—anyhow I said that one day there would be free Light and energy in every town everywhere in the world, and peace and prosperity and an end to meanness and cruelty and jealousy. I mentioned incidentally that it turned out to be one first-class weapon but that was not what I had meant for it. Maybe they had other plans. I did not know. I had sometimes imagined that the Folk of East Conlan had meant me to see that sign so that I could bring peace and prosperity to the world, but their brothers and sisters of the *Damaris* didn't look like they cared too much for the world.

The laughter continued throughout my speech, and for a very long time after I was silent.

I can be a patient man but in the end I got irritated.

"Well," I said. "What is it? What's the answer? This is no joke—I stand before you as a—"

One of them raised a hand. I had visions of stone-throwing and losing my other eye and I ducked. When I stood straight again the Folk had turned and stopped laughing and were walking away.

If there is a moral to that story I guess it is that you do not always need to go to the ends of the world like Liv Alverhuysen and John Creedmoor did to discover wonderful and terrible things—sometimes they are in your own backyard. Or maybe it is that everything in this world is stolen, theft upon theft, and things happen for no good reason at all. Who knows. I can only say what happened.

❋   ❋   ❋

I didn't follow them. I took the knife and cut a few thick lines through the sign I had made, reducing it to nonsense in case anyone should happen upon it, so that it could not fall into the wrong hands, or at least no wronger than it already had.

At first the bark was warm where I had carved the sign, then it went cool. I folded up the knife and walked away.

Eventually I found the tracks of the Line. They were raised on iron buttresses like a bridge, twice the height of a man. The sun had risen by then and I walked in the tracks' shadow, following their straight route north-east until the swamp gave way to marsh, then grassland, then hills. The tracks turned north and I turned east, toward Jasper.*

---

*No part of Mr. Ransom's writings was so full of corrections and backtracking as this fifteenth chapter. Many lines were struck out, many paragraphs written over and over again. In places it is clear that pages were torn up and rewritten, leaving sentences cut in half. I obtained two copies of this chapter, one six years later than the other; I cannot say what happened to the third. Because of Mr. Ransom's copious corrections, they do not entirely match. The impression is one of great anxiety; perhaps a great anxiety to achieve scrupulous accuracy. I have made the best sense of it that I can. —EMC

## CHAPTER 16

## THE END OF THE SECOND PART

One week later I was in Poundstock. It is a little town in the western part of the Tri-City Territory, chiefly notable for the profitable operations of the Baxter Poundstock Clay Mine and a fervent local chapter of the World Serpent cult. Later—after the Battle of Jasper—it became a camp for the Line, and most of its population was relocated.

John Southern had made it there, along with a few other survivors of the *Damaris*. They had no news of the Great Rotollo or his wife Amaryllis, but I was happy to learn that others were unharmed. John Southern was not so upset at the loss of his boat as you might imagine. The Serpent cult had taken up a collection for the boat's survivors, and taken them in, and Southern was well on his way to converting. He had shaved off his magnificent mustache as a sign of piety, and both his hands were swollen from snake-bites. He had given up all his remaining property to the cult, in order to live with the simplicity of the serpent, and also I suspect to avoid lawsuits over the sinking of his boat. I offered the return of his jacket—he said no.

There were soldiers of the Line in town. I submitted to an interrogation as to what I had witnessed of the attack on the Kingstown Engine. Electric-light in the eyes, words recorded by typewriter, the usual procedure. I told them nothing because I knew nothing. I understood from their questioning that they suspected Agents of the Gun, in particular Gentleman Jim Dark, who had been seen in the Territory lately, posing for photographs and signing autographs for young ladies. I suggested as a joke that the attack might have been the work of Liv Alverhuysen and John Creedmoor and Professor Ransom and their terrible mysterious secret weapon, and thereby extended the duration of my interrogation by an hour and added to its unpleasantness by an immeasurable degree.

I took advantage of the snake-handlers' charity, thereby acquiring a second shoe (mismatched) and some pants that were threadbare but less vile than my own.

"Stop your wanderin'," John Southern said. "Settle down. Here is as good as any other place. I see that now. The World Serpent is everywhere. What damn use is all our writhin'?"

Snakes had played a prominent and harrowing part in John Southern's own wanderings in the swamp, and the experience had changed his outlook on the world.

"I'm young," I said, "and not ready to retire."

"The coils of the serpent encircle us all. There's no escapin' your fate. Where d'you think you'll go?"

I did not know.

A coach came into town. It carried an executive of the Baxter Trust from Jasper City, come to oversee the mine, and his wife, and it also carried blasting-powder, salt, rope, pots and pans, and a tall stack of Jasper City newspapers. I had no money but bartered for a newspaper with my own stories of the wreck of the *Damaris*, swamp-wanderings, the Western Rim. I learned from that newspaper that the Jasper City Senate was split evenly on ratification of the Salazar Accord, whatever that was, and that harsh words had been exchanged on the floor of that august body. I learned about ball-games and that Vansittart University had trounced Gibson City College's boys thoroughly, unless it was the other way around. And I read a letter to the editor. I recall every word of it because I read it over and over. It said:

*Dear Sir,*

*Lately there has been a great deal of tavern-talk and gutter-talk regarding what is surely the most preposterous of all the preposterous fancies ever to emerge from the fevered imaginations of the people of the wild Western Rim—I speak of course of the story of the turncoat Agent John Creedmoor, and the foreign doctor, and "Professor" Harry Ransom, and their magical device for the destruction of Engines, or the annihilation of armies, or the creation of free money and whiskey, or what-have-you. Bad enough that this talk should infect the lower orders of our city, but that the newspapers should encourage it defies all reason and propriety!*

*It is disruptive to business and to the balance of power, and it threatens our city's hard-fought-for neutrality in matters of the Great War. Already there are unsound urgings from the mob. Several of my junior clerks have quit their jobs and gone adventuring in search of these unlikely fellows, in solidarity with pure fancy, causing considerable inconvenience. No man of sound mind and more than twenty-one years of age should credit this nonsense for a moment. There should be no demand for a de-bunking. But the City is not short of idle youth, men of unsound mind, and women. Therefore I must reveal that certain information has come to my attention that proves beyond doubt that the man who calls himself "Professor" Harry Ransom is a fraud and a mountebank.*

*For the past year or more, Mr. Ransom—a miner's son of no education or accomplishment—has drifted from town to town along the Western Rim, seeking "investors" in a purported Free-Energy Apparatus of his own devising. In fact the device is nothing more than an ordinary electrical engine, albeit a prototype, stolen from one of my companies that operated in the town of East Conlan, from which he absconded last year. I am speaking of the Northern Lighting Corporation. Investigators retained by the Corporation have followed his trail for the better part of a year. With the stolen electrical device and some pretty words this low criminal has bilked the honest but simple citizens of a dozen towns all along the Rim. Lawsuits for fraud and misappropriation of property and violation of patents await him in Melville, Kenauk, White Rock, Hamlin, Clementine, and Ford, and in Jasper City should he ever be so bold as to show his face here. His so-called Miracle of White Rock is the very sort of mal-function one would expect of a delicate prototype in the hands of a charlatan. Well, let this letter set the matter to rest. This man is no more than a fraud and a thief.*

> *Yours sincerely,*
> *Mr. Alfred P. Baxter, President, Baxter Trust*
> *1 Baxter Street, Isle of Fenimore, Jasper City.*

By the time I finished reading this I was so severely wide-eyed and stricken-looking that several members of the Serpent cult rushed to my aid, afraid I had been bit by one of their sacred snakes.

I could tolerate being called a fraud, but to be called a thief was unendurable. The Process was mine!—well, maybe the Folk of East Conlan had a claim to it, and I do not deny I had creditors, but it was not Baxter's. By the time I got to Jasper City, three or maybe four days later, I had read that letter a hundred times and I was hardly any less angry than I was after the first.

# JASPER CITY

## CHAPTER 17

# NEW IN TOWN

I wasn't sure whether I would rip up all that talk about the swamp and the Apparatus or not. The truth is that I nearly did but at the last moment honesty prevailed. There will be no secrets in Ransom City! I parceled it all up and Dick Beck went bravely forth to mail it again, along with the usual invitations and proclamations &c. And so here I am beginning all over again.

In his *Autobiography,* Mr. Baxter wrote:

> There is no place in this land that so suits the temperament of an adventurous young man as does Jasper City. I have traveled widely and I know this to be no mere expression of parochial loyalty—I am a man of the world. I have seen Gibson and Keaton and the Western Rim and the complacent principalities of the ancient East. I have traveled in the lands of the Line and I have visited the stronghold of the Gun at Log-Town. No place compares to Jasper. My return to that City after my long wanderings— after my soldiering years and my years of self-imposed exile—was not merely a homecoming. Rather, let us call it a Rebirth. As I passed under the shadow of its tall buildings, as I felt beneath my feet the power of that great and wonderful engine that is the City, I understood that it was time to put away childish things, and attend to the business of a Man.

Well, Mr. Baxter and I had our differences. But he was right about Jasper City. I count myself a lucky man to have seen it before the fall.

## A *Portrait of Jasper City*

From a distance, if you came to it from the west, the city looked golden-brown, crown-shaped. (The stockyards sprawled on the east—I did not see them until later.) It was in the heart of the Tri-City Territory, which is to say that it was in the heart of the West. The vast rolling plains of the Territory were a patchwork of farms and grassland, bright green in the early summer sun, green as an accountant's eyeshades, so green they made you blink. The River Jass wound across those plains for miles and miles and days and days, then widened, there were islands, and it forked, going north to Gibson and east into Line lands. Jasper City was built on the island and in the fork of the river, and you could spend all day happily crossing and crossing again the bridges between Fenimore and Rondelet and Hoo Lai and back to Fenimore.

Fenimore was what they called the island in the river, after a long-dead duke from the old country—I don't know which old country. It was shaped kind of like a dagger, or a skinny winged lizard with a long tail, depending on which map one consulted. It boasted tall buildings with countless windows and ornate terra-cotta pediments and sometimes gargoyles. There were the offices of the Baxter Trust and the Northern Lighting Corporation and some meat-packing operations and a few publishers and a whole lot of banks and the smarter sort of mercenary company. In the shadow of the tall buildings the crowds moved in a purposeful way—there was a Jasper City Walk that I never learned to imitate. The Jasper City gentleman wore hats and tails, and he carried a stick, unless he rode in a carriage. It seemed unlikely that I could acquire a carriage but I made it my immediate goal to acquire a stick of my own.

On the north bank of the river were the Bluffs, a wall of tawny sandstone cliffs grown over with deep green pine. The Smilers' Inner Circle was there, perched on an outcrop, gleaming white. The notorious whorehouse they called the Floating World was there too, glowing red at night from behind the pines. There were also mansions among the pines, and I guessed some of them belonged to the gentlemen of Fenimore, and surely one of them was Mr. Baxter's. South of the river in Rondelet there were warehouses and workhouses and streets of tenements, which were arranged in an ever-expanding pattern of concentric half-circles like a sunrise, and there were people in them from every part of the world. There was more filth in the streets than I have words to describe, not just in bad neighborhoods but everywhere, even among the mansions of Fenimore, where there were trees and a policeman on every corner.

There was a ceaseless clamor of advertisement. The storefronts were less brightly painted than I had imagined but they were still something. Every respectable house had a little stone staircase up to its front door, so that it was lifted free of the muck, and sometimes there were wooden bridges across the worst of it. In every district there were parks, sun-dappled by day and dangerous at night, with statuary that was sometimes sacred and sometimes risqué, depending I think on the administration that constructed it.

Speaking of the administration—Jasper was a republic in those days, and a free city, first among equals among the Three Cities. It was determinedly neutral in matters of politics and war and religion and grand ideology—the allegiance of Jasper was to business. The Great War was generally regarded as something rather uncivilized and rustic, a barbaric game of the younger and westerly parts of the world. The men of the Line were not welcome in Jasper except under strict conditions. The servants of the Gun were no more welcome than any other sort of criminal trash.

Jasper was ruled by a Senate of one hundred and three mostly handsome silver-haired businessmen and lawyers and Smilers. They met in a domed building of smoke-stained marble on Fenimore, and I do not know what they did all day, made speeches and formed alliances and schemed against each other I guess. Signed pieces of paper. The building was covered in flags and statues of bulls. A tall pillar rose from the dome on its roof like a spike on an old-fashioned helmet, and there was another bull on it, though all you could see from the street was a glint of gold. The bull was the totem animal of Jasper and you saw it on the flags and on the masthead of newspapers and on the placards outside hotels and bars and there was the famous Brass Bull at the fork of the river, stamping its metal hooves in the red mud, and lowering its huge horns as if to warn visitors that Jasper was not to be messed with, as if anyone would think otherwise. There were legends about how the bull would come to life if Jasper was ever threatened but I think nobody took them seriously, and I can assure you they were not true. There were also legends that Jasper was built on the site of a great city of the Folk, and nobody took that seriously either, because who ever heard of a city of the Folk? Nevertheless there were some tall stones on Fenimore on vacant lots between the office-towers that nobody went near.

Swing Street was in Hoo Lai. You might think it was named for music or dancing but in actual fact there used to be a prison there and a notorious gallows. Anyhow if you have ever whistled a song or laughed at a joke the chances are it was written on Swing Street. It defied the best efforts of city planners and it wound in an irregular fashion back and forth between the regular city streets, stopping and starting, like it was a state of mind as much as a place. Parts of Swing Street were electrified, as were scattered zones here and there throughout Hoo Lai and Rondelet and most of Fenimore. Vansittart University was mostly on its own island, gas-lit in the traditional style, and it was a city unto itself, or like a huge castle, all sharp peaks of red brick and yet more flags, though you could find outlying projections of VU's domain all over town. In the river there were so many tall boats it was like another city, a mobile and fleeting one. The *Damaris* would have been lost among them. East of the river there were the Yards, like I said, the city's ugly shadow, and maybe I will write about them some time but not now.

※   ※   ※

I came into the city from the west, on foot, walking beside the river. In those days everyone who came into Jasper came by river or by road. The nearest Station of the Line at that time was Archway, days to the north and across the border of the Territory. Jasper was not opposed to commerce with the Line but kept it at arm's length. There were coal-barges on the river and wagons on the road, and a lot of drifters and refugees and day-laborers and would-be stars of Swing Street and I guess I did not stand out. I had a little bit of money in a cardboard wallet, and for days I clutched at it tightly for fear of pick-pockets, until I was generously informed that it made me look like a hick and a nobody.

I didn't know what name I should go by. It was a conundrum. Nothing mattered to me more than clearing my name of the slander Mr. Baxter had heaped upon it—yet if I went about openly calling myself Harry Ransom who knew what might happen? Jasper City was neutral but it was not free of the meddling of Gun and Line, and their agents might cause me to disappear. Mr. Baxter himself might have me arrested.

On the *Damaris* I'd gone by the name Hal Rawlins. It had suited me well enough, but some part of me felt that Rawlins had gone down with the ship. One of the great things about the West and about Jasper City in particular is that both are so big you can always start over, or at least you can hope to. So as I drifted through the crowds I eavesdropped on conversations, listening for likely sounding Jasper City names. I muttered them under my breath to try them out.

I walked through the city, not knowing where I was or where I was going, through the narrow streets of Hoo Lai and up toward Fenimore, for no reason other than that it was tall and full of bright flags. I recall that I stood for a while on the south bridge into Fenimore, and watched the water go by. The sun was at its zenith and it was sweltering hot. The river was almost too bright to look at, and it stank. It seemed to me that the water was circling around and around the island, an endlessly replenishing cycle that made me think of the Process, though of course it was only my imagination.

For a while I thought it was all right to have no name at all.

Eventually I noticed that a policeman was looking at me. I knew that he was a policeman because he wore a blue-black blazer and cap, and a brass badge with a bull's horns on it. At first I was afraid he was on the lookout for the notorious fraudster or revolutionary Harry Ransom, but it turned out when we started talking that he was afraid I was going to jump. He did not personally care if I jumped but it was bad for business when people jumped, it upset the office-workers, and so he was tasked with saving lives wherever he could, like it or not. I told him that was not such a bad calling in life and he shrugged. I asked him for directions to Swing Street, and he asked what I was, an actor or a writer or a dancer or something of that nature, and I said I was nothing like that, I was just looking for family.

My big sister Jess left East Conlan two years before I did, in the company of a traveling salesman. Their plan was to get rich in Gibson City in the clothing trade. She got tired of the salesman in a matter of weeks, or he got tired of her, and she ended up heading to Jasper instead, drifting on riverboats the way I did, the way a lot of people end up in Jasper. There she met a man in the theater-business, and soon she started working in the Hamilton Theater on Swing Street, and then in an establishment that was just called No. 88. Her letters never said what she did, only that she was doing well. I remembered the addresses—not because she wrote often, because she did not, but because I wrote so often to her.

Swing Street in the afternoon was near-empty and half-asleep. Would-be actors with no fixed abodes napped in doorways or on the steps outside the theaters. The theaters themselves were jammed tightly together, with dark-windowed bars filling every remaining space. The theaters wore masks—I mean that nearly all of them boasted some brightly colored façade, in the style of a golden Judduan temple or a lacquered eastern palace or one of the ancient ivy-hung castles of Koenigswald. The street looked like it does in the photographs you have seen, except that in the unforgiving light of day you could see how new the façades were, and how thin and flimsy some of them were. Swing Street was meant to be seen after dark.

I didn't know what I meant to say to Jess when I saw her. I had always told her that when I came to Jasper City I would come in style, I would come in triumph, with investors and fame at my back. I guess I hoped we would laugh and cry and embrace and I would not have to say too much about what had happened to me out West. She would know that Mr. Baxter's accusations were slander, and that I was no fraud, and certainly no thief. She would give me a place to stay and a sympathetic ear while I schemed out how I would clear my name, as to which I still had no particular plan. I hoped that she would lend me money without asking what had happened to the money she had already invested in the Apparatus.

I had imagined she would have money to spare. Everyone said that Swing Street was booming and the theaters were machines for coining gold, at least if you were clever or beautiful or musically talented, and Jess was two of those three. Maybe that was true but I was soon to learn that whatever money there was on Swing Street had not found its way into my sister's pockets.

I saw a building covered in pillars and carved masks and peeling gold paint. A sign at the front of it said THE HAMILTON THEATER, and the door was unlocked, so I called in and apologized for interrupting a rehearsal and I asked after my sister. They said she'd worked there checking coats, but had left a year ago and nobody knew where she'd gone. She had not gone by Ransom, but by Gantry, which was the name of her husband.

I called at No. 88. It was closed for the afternoon and the windows were shuttered but there were some young women standing outside it who saw me peering through the shutters, and after we'd established that I was not interested in buying what they were selling we got on pretty well. They told me that they worked at the Eighty-eight, dancing or waitressing or otherwise, and that they remembered Jess—she'd lost the husband and gone back to Ransom—but that she'd left when all those rumors started about her brother.

I said, "Her brother?"

"You know," they said. "Professor Ransom. They say he's an anarchist or a revolutionary or a prophet or something, him and that Creedmoor guy, they've got some kind of secret weapon that everyone's got themselves all excited about."

I said nothing. I was thinking that I had not even thought about how my mistake at White Rock might have affected Jess. Let's ascribe that to the arrogance of youth, and not to any deeper or more permanent flaw in my character.

I was also thinking that I liked the women of the Eighty-eight just fine, but that it was not what I had imagined Jess was doing in Jasper City.

"I heard he's a crook," one of them said. "A fraud."

I said, "Who told you that?"

"Don't play dumb, handsome. You know the story—you're one of them, right?"

"One of them?"

"You're looking for Ransom and Creedmoor and all the rest. You don't look rough enough to be a detective so I guess you're a believer."

"A believer? I guess I am."

"Well we don't know. She just left. That's all we can tell you."

"Did you know her well? Where did she live?"

"What good's that going to do you? You want to cut up her bed-sheets for relics or something? She wasn't anything special. Are you that crazy? Shame. You're pretty."

"Well, maybe I am. Crazy, I mean. But I can pay—for information."

They looked skeptical.

❈ ❈ ❈

Just south of the south-western end of Swing Street was a building that everybody called the Gate. It was a sprawl of old-fashioned peaked towers and blocky outcrops of red brick, stained black. It had narrow windows that made me think of the slits on a zoetrope. In the old days it had been Jasper's largest prison, but in these more civilized times criminals were generally sentenced to work in the Yards, or for Western Rim operations of the Baxter Trust, or pressed into the militia. The Gate had been converted into apartments for refugees or would-be theater-folk or failed theater-folk—it could be hard to tell the difference. They lived two or sometimes three to a cell. The hallways were a maze, painted with strange and sometimes shocking and often beautiful designs. Motifs of the Folk were much in evidence. Music echoed through the whole shadowy low-ceilinged labyrinth. In the apartment where Jess had lived, behind a red curtain, there was a young white woman washing herself with a rag and a bucket. She had dyed green hair like a fairy-tale river-sprite and a lean long-legged body. She cursed at me casually and flicked the wet rag at my face, and I withdrew. A quick glimpse had been enough to confirm there was nothing of Jess's in the room. Apart from the bucket and some charms on the wall that were not Jess's style there was nothing of anyone's in there.

I'd grown accustomed to the wide open spaces of the Western Rim. I had often been poor out there, but even at my worst I slept under the stars or in big open barns. The narrowness and confinement of the Gate was like a nightmare. It reminded me of the worst stories I'd heard about the Stations of the Line, and their lightless factory-warrens. Beneath the incense and the cigarettes there was a damnable stink—actors smelt no better than prisoners. The Gate was not how I'd imagined Jess had been living, and it was certainly not how I'd imagined *I* would live, when the time came for me to come to Jasper City. Yet the terrible truth was that I was not sure I could afford even a cell in the Gate, maybe not even a shared cell. The money I'd offered the women of the Eighty-eight had only made them laugh. Money was worth almost infinitely less in Jasper City than on the Western Rim. I think it is because of the number and density of people there. It takes a greater force to get them to move.

                                    ✳   ✳   ✳

I left the Gate by a different entrance, having gotten myself lost and turned around, and I came back out through an alley onto Swing Street right next to the Ormolu Theater. I knew it was the Ormolu Theater because there was a sign. It was studded with electric-lights, although the sun was still high and they were not in operation at that particular moment.

I took the Great Rotollo's business-card from my pocket, and considered my prospects for a while—not for very long. The math of the situation was not complicated. Working for Rotollo was not as good as visiting with my long-lost sister, but it was a damn sight better than starving in the streets.

The Ormolu's doors were open.

Inside there was a sweeping staircase, and a white stone statue of a naked woman veiling her face, and a lot of brass and purple velvet. There was a young man sitting in a gilded box, but he was asleep with his head on his brocaded arm and did not stop me as I walked through another door and into the corridors behind the stage, until I found a gray-haired woman sitting at a dressing-table smoking a cigarette.

"My name's Randall," I said.

I had tried out a lot of new Jasper City names in my head, and that was what I had settled on.

The woman started but did not turn around. Instead she looked at me in her mirror.

"Ma'am, I'm just going to come out and say it, because people in this city are awful busy and I don't want to waste anyone's time. Time is money, Mr. Baxter always says, and money is time."

I could not break the long habit of quoting Mr. Baxter, even if he was now my enemy.

"I met a man on a boat called the *Damaris* who called himself the Great Rotollo—I guess that wasn't his real name but I don't know what it was—anyhow ma'am if he made it off the *Damaris* and into town he said he was going to work at this Theater, and if he's here I bet he'd vouch for me as a decent fellow and a hard worker, he said I should call on him here. I have his card, it's kind of battered by now but—"

She turned, stood.

"Hal Rawlins!" she said.

"Rand—that is, ma'am, I—"

"Hal Rawlins, don't you remember me?"

I did not, but pretended like maybe I did.

She clapped her hands together and ran toward me and before I could retreat she was embracing me, saying, "Hal Rawlins, as I live and breathe! Fortune is kind, fortune is kind after all, there's a silver lining to every cloud," and other Smiler maxims.

It took me a while to realize that the woman was Amaryllis, the Great Rotollo's wife and assistant. I had not recognized her without her wig and make-up and pearls.

## CHAPTER 18

# The Amazing
# Amaryllis and
# Mr. Alfred P. Baxter and
# Mr. Elmer Merrial Carson,
# and Others

To tell the truth, Amaryllis and I had exchanged no more than half-a-dozen words back on the *Damaris*. But it seemed that she remembered me fondly, as if we traveled together for years and had been great friends. She took it upon herself to introduce me to the manager of the Ormolu Theater, a Mr. Quantrill, and to praise my talents to him in the most effusive terms. She praised my musical gifts, my rapport with the tough crowds of the *Damaris,* my loyalty and hard-working nature, my handsomeness and my pleasing smile, and above all my mechanical genius. She described the wonders of the self-playing piano, and attributed its invention to me. I did not correct her. Mr. Quantrill asked what else I could do, and I said I had some ideas regarding Light. Mr. Quantrill's eyebrows slowly raised as if operated by pulleys in the wings—by which I mean he looked skeptical. Amaryllis then appealed to his sense of charity, painting the sinking of the *Damaris* in the most lurid terms, and characterizing me as a tragic and pitiable orphan of war. In the end Mr. Quantrill shrugged and agreed to hire me for room and board, room being a dressing-room with a bench and a blanket, further wages to be discussed if and when I made myself useful. Then he put on his hat and went home.

"*Well,*" Amaryllis said. She gave me a possessive kind of smile.

Amaryllis had survived the wreck of the *Damaris* by shedding her wig and her fake pearls and her frilly dress, washing up on the riverbank in nothing but a thin white shift—or so she told me. As she lay exhausted on the bank she saw the Great Rotollo struggling toward her, fighting the current. He was too proud and too thrifty to let go of his suitcase full of trick knives and charms and puzzle-rings and weighted dice and watches and cards, and he could hardly keep his head above water. She crawled out onto a tree-root that arched out into the river, and she reached a hand to save him, catching his sleeve—but he struggled, and splashed, and the current was too strong, and all she was able to save was the suitcase.

She dabbed at her eye as she said this, like she was crying, but the corner of her mouth smiled.

"*You* saw how he struggled, didn't you, Mr. Rawlins?"

"Well," I prevaricated. "It was very dark."

I didn't find her story very likely, but didn't want to cast accusations or innuendos. There is always so much we do not know, and it is my rule not to judge unless I must.

Shortly after the Great Rotollo drowned—one way or the other—Amaryllis met some of the other survivors of the wreck. Rotollo's suitcase contained several tricks for making fire, which helped them survive the night. It also contained the Great Rotollo's contract to perform at the Ormolu Theater, and to make a long story short Amaryllis had stepped into Rotollo's shoes and was now performing two nights a week at the Ormolu, where she went by Amaryllis the Amazing.

"This is a new century," she said, "Or near as dammit, and who says women can't do magic? I saw every trick that old bastard ever did and I can do 'em just as good as him. But that's not enough, is it? Not these days. Not for me. Oh no. We have to prove ourselves, Mr. Rawlins, the old tricks won't cut it anymore. Why, just six months ago I met a man with an honest-to-goodness machine for making rain! What's the old bastard's card tricks next to that? That's what we need. The very latest science. The latest ideas. Like your piano, or what-have-you. A man who can do that can do just about anything, I reckon. My very own genius! You and me together, Mr. Rawlins. You and me, Hal, you and me."

She tried to kiss me. I extricated myself as politely as I could, and shut myself away in my room.

Sometimes my words get away from me. I will say no more unkind words about Amaryllis. She did me a good turn when I was in a bad spot, and she had many admirable qualities, including grit and drive and a natural facility with the Gazzo Shuffle and the Log-Town Drop. And besides the lady is no longer able to defend herself, having perished in the Battle of Jasper.

✻   ✻   ✻

The room was windowless, but from long habit of wandering I woke at first light anyhow. I shaved, and I washed, and I found a pair of clean pants in a wardrobe, thinking that clothing was implicit in my deal with Mr. Quantrill. Nothing could be done about the unruly black explosion that was my hair.

Theater-folk are late risers. If anyone else was there in the Ormolu at that hour, they were asleep. I wanted to make myself useful and show that I was a hard worker, and so I poked around in closets and dusty back rooms until I found a broom. I swept the stage and I polished the stage's gas lamps until each one of them gleamed.

Behind the stage I found a number of painted backdrops. One of them was painted like red rock, ornamented with designs that I guess were supposed to resemble the carvings of the Folk, except that they were neither beautiful nor meaningful. Another was painted like a forest, and another showed a starry night, and another was a lurid yellow desert scene, with more ziggurats than seemed plausible. Behind the backdrops there were chests and wardrobes and heaps of props. There were guns that were probably fake and guns that were probably real, there were mirrors that were really cabinets, there were mechanisms I could not identify that looked a little like mantraps. There was a scrapyard's-worth of interlinked metal rings, and there were enough trick hats to start a trick department store. Amaryllis was not the only magician who worked the Ormolu. There was the Wise Master Lobsang, and there was Doctor Agostron, and there was Mr. Barnabas Busby Bosko, Wizard of the Western Rim. The big city had a boundless appetite for magic at that time. I might speculate at length as to why but I will not, except to say that if they wanted the real thing all they had to do was head west. Anyhow in addition to magic the Ormolu boasted dancing girls and two nights a week it showed a hastily written play called *The Story of John Creedmoor*, which was a big hit, I am sorry to say.

I tinkered for a while but I could find no tools and I could only guess what anything was meant to do. I grew bored and restless.

The front doors were locked, and no-one had yet thought to give me a key, so I squeezed out through a window at the building's rear.

I walked north and over the bridge, toward Fenimore. I got kind of lost seeing the sights, which I will not recount here, and by the time I got there it was mid-day. The streets thronged with workers leaving their offices for lunch. The air buzzed with conversation about money, about business, about how the Old Man might be eased out of his position to make room for young blood, or about what was wrong with young people today—or about matters of state—there was speculation about what the fighting out on the Rim might mean for trade, or whether Jasper might get involved, or whether it was true what people were saying about this secret weapon the Line was afraid of, and if so whether there was any way of making money off it.

I pushed against the crowd until I found my way to the offices of the Baxter Trust. They were easy enough to find. Baxter's Tower was the tallest building in Jasper, taller even than the Senate, even including the pillar on the Senate's dome. I recalled that Mr. Baxter's first fortune had come from his invention of a newer and more efficient form of elevator— his Tower was a great advertisement for his invention. It occupied a full city block, though it was set back from the street by a high fence. There were a number of policemen at the gate.

I stood across the street and I watched the workers coming back from their mid-day meals. In many parts of Jasper there was lunchtime drunkenness, but Mr. Baxter's workers were notably sober. Perhaps it was because of the policemen.

I cannot easily describe what I felt standing there, before that place I had so long dreamed of.

I heard the hateful words of Mr. Baxter's letter over and over in my mind, until it seemed that every man in the busy street could hear them too, until it seemed like they boomed from loudspeakers behind the windows of Mr. Baxter's tower. I could not understand why he had slandered me so. I could not understand why he had betrayed me.

The obvious explanation, I told myself, was that Baxter wanted to crush a competitor. That was not just my pride talking. I knew from his letter that he owned the Northern Lighting Corporation. If my Apparatus were perfected and popularized it would render the NLC obsolete. That was reason enough for slander. But I could not accept that Mr. Baxter had acted from so petty a motive. The hero of the *Autobiography* was a sharp businessman, but he was not a cheat.

I considered another possibility. He was an old man, and a rich one, with much to lose. Perhaps he feared the rumors of Liv and Creedmoor's world-upending weapon—the world as it was had been good to him. But I could not accept that either. The hero of the *Autobiography* was not afraid of progress.

I recall that I watched two pigeons squabbling in the street, and I thought that perhaps Mr. Baxter's letter was a kind of joke, a rich man's whim, a game he had decided to play with me for some eccentric reason. If so, much might depend on how I responded. Perhaps I should show that I was a good sport. But no—I did not believe that, either. You heard of other rich men playing that sort of game, but not Mr. Baxter. He did not play games at all.

There was a darker possibility, one that I did not want to consider at all. I knew that Mr. Baxter owned the NLC, and I had heard that the NLC operated on the Western Rim in concert with the forces of the Line. It was possible—I could not deny that it was possible—that even Mr. Baxter had surrendered his pride and independence, and was acting in this matter as a servant of the Line. If so, he had slandered me only in passing, the better to deny the existence of Liv and Creedmoor's weapon, and he had done it only at the orders of the Line. Perhaps he had not even read the letter before he signed it. Perhaps I was nothing to him, not a competitor, not a game—just a name on a letter written for him by some faceless Line attaché.

I paced back and forth. Some part of me thought that if I could only speak to Mr. Baxter face to face, man to man, we could resolve our misunderstanding. If only I could somehow speak to him without the company of policemen and bodyguards. If I could ask him: *Why?*

I paced and paced. Crowds and pigeons came and went. Shadows lengthened and an evening chill crept into the air but I did not see Mr. Baxter himself emerge. It occurred to me that he might not look like he did in his pictures, and perhaps he had left without my noticing. Or perhaps he never left, preferring to work all night—there were electric-lights coming on in some of the upper windows of his fortress.

I say it was a fortress not only because of the high fence and the policemen, but because I recalled Mr. Baxter's *Autobiography,* in which he wrote:

> The future belongs to the tall buildings and the great cities! For the man of destiny there is no substitute for the hard work and the big ideas of Jasper or Gibson or the other pioneer metropolises that are a-grow today in this great land of ours. The man of business—if I may be excused a digression into the romantic—the man of business is the lord of this realm, is the questing knight, and the office-tower is his castle, his fortress on the borderlands.

The way these things are traditionally resolved on the Western Rim is by the duel. Matters of property and ownership, matters of pride of authorship, matters of insult, matters of honor—all come to the same resolution—ten paces and turn, gentlemen! But there were a number of things wrong with that plan. First, this was not the Rim, this was Jasper City, and the duel was illegal—second, I had no gun—third, there were too many policemen about—and fourth, Mr. Baxter could not be less than ninety years old, and even in the wildest and least civilized parts of the Rim it is not manly to shoot a nonagenarian dead, regardless of what he has said about you.

The way these things were traditionally resolved in Jasper was by the lawsuit, which is all right for some people, but I had no money and my adversary was the richest man in the city. Besides I could hardly sign my name to papers in open court—I was a fugitive.

The sun fell toward the eastern horizon. One by one each window all the way down the side of the Tower flashed golden fire then went dark. Shortly after that the sky blushed with violet, and there was black not far behind. Mr. Baxter still did not emerge.

Hidden motors coughed and thrummed, drawing the Tower's gates slowly shut. Two policemen walked beside the gates as they curved inward like men leading cattle home to pasture of an evening. Both of them wore long coats and one of them held a bright cigarette in his hand.

Just as I was about to turn away there was the noise of a motor-car. Moments later a long black automobile emerged from between the closing gates.

I was suddenly sure that it contained Mr. Baxter himself. Who else?

I ran toward it and on the way inspiration struck and when I stood beside the automobile and knocked on its black window I shouted, "Mr. Baxter? Sir? I am a writer for the *Jasper City Evening Post*—sir, would you care to talk about what you wrote about the White Rock Miracle, sir, excuse me—"

I stumbled a little as the automobile turned and accelerated. In the blackness of the window I saw mostly my own face but also someone else looking out at me. It was a thin face with sharp eyes and a long nose that swam menacingly toward me out of the black.

I knocked on the glass again. The nose did not move.

One of the policemen from the gate tackled me to the ground. I hit the cobbles with my head and cried out in shock.

The automobile moved on a little way, then stopped, like it was thinking.

After a few moments the automobile started moving again. I was unaccountably relieved, even though the policeman was none too gentle in the way he pulled me to my feet and sent me staggering off with a blow to the stomach and a kick in the ass. He did not trouble himself even to insult me as I limped away, he just lit his cigarette and slipped in between the gates as they closed.

※　※　※

Halfway down the block from the Baxter Tower there was a small hotel. A man stood on its steps, leaning against a wrought-iron rail and smoking. He wore a rumpled suit of red and green linen, and a sloppy bow-tie. He had an impressive black mustache, that was shaped somewhat like the cow-annihilating cowling of an Engine, or the design on an old-world knight's shield that is called a *cheveron*. He had a nose that was probably eagle-like before it got broken, and he had very blue and very clever eyes, with which he had quite clearly been watching me watch the gate of the Baxter Tower for some time.

He was utterly unembarrassed to be caught spying. As a matter of fact he smiled and waved me over, like we were friends.

"Your head's bleeding," he said.

I touched it. "So it is."

"So," he said, "new in town?"

I saw no reason to deny it. "It shows, huh?"

"It does. No harm in that. Everyone was new in town once. I myself was born down in the Deltas, more years ago than I care to remember."

"Hamlin," I said, naming the first Rim-town that popped into my head.

"Not familiar with it."

"Rim-wards."

"Uh-huh. Fleeing the fighting out there?"

"In a manner of speaking."

"Too bad. Cigarette?"

"No thank you. You know, I was told that people in Jasper were unfriendly to strangers."

"Well," he said, and smiled. "My motives are ulterior."

I could at that point have run away. But it is not in my nature to spurn friendly conversation.

"I heard that about you big-city types."

"So," he said. "You've got a keen and patient interest in Mr. Baxter's Tower. I have been watching you from the window of my room since lunchtime. I have watched mystics meditating on the empty throne of the Silver City or counting the innumerable coils of the World Serpent and few of them have the staying-power you exhibit. What could possibly account for it? Are you just seeing the sights? Or looking for work?"

"I have work, I think. On Swing Street."

He raised one eyebrow. I don't know if I mentioned his eyebrows before but they were as impressive in their own way as the mustache. Throughout our conversation they bristled and flattened as he spoke so that they could express good humor at one moment, curiosity the next, fulminating wrath when necessary. Sometimes I felt I was conversing with the eyebrows and he was merely taking notes.

"It's not what I expected," I said, "but it's better than nothing."

"They let you spend all day staring at Mr. Baxter's Tower?"

"Theater-folk keep irregular hours."

"They do," he said. "That's very true."

He lit another cigarette.

"So," he said. "Maybe your fascination with the Baxter Trust stems from anger. The Smilers will tell you anger is bad for the soul but I disagree—sometimes a good spell of anger is just what this damn awful world calls for and there's no alternative. Maybe the Trust foreclosed on your farm or maybe they dammed your river up-stream—or maybe it's political, maybe you've come all the way here from out West for reasons of politics?"

He leaned back against the rail, stretching out an arm to toy with one of its little wrought-iron spearheads.

"I don't even know what you mean by politics, sir. I make it a rule to stay out of that stuff. It does nobody any good. Maybe I'm just seeing the sights, like you said."

"Uh-huh, uh-huh. What *kind* of revenge, though? You're not carrying a bomb. You don't have a gun—do you? No, I didn't think so and that look on your face confirms it. I mean no offense—a lot of crazy people come to town these days. But you don't look crazy, not in the ordinary way. I've been watching you for a while and I can't figure you out. Something tells me it's worth the effort, and my instincts are rarely wrong."

"Let's get one thing clear, friend—I said I don't want revenge, and I meant it. So if that's all you wanted to know—"

He held up a hand.

"Maybe there's some confusion here—I get used to being recognized. Fame, son, it gets into your head, never pursue it. I'm not a policeman, if that's what you're thinking, and I don't work for Mr. Baxter, fortune forfend that the day should ever come I should be reduced to that. My name's Elmer Merrial Carson."

"Hal Rawlins," I said, cautiously taking his hand.

"I won't take offense that you don't know my name. I guess you *are* new in town."

Of course I have learned since then that Mr. Carson was somewhat famous in Jasper City and throughout the Tri-City Territory, as the writer, reporter and sometime publisher of the *Jasper City Evening Post*. He was known in particular for his broadsides in support of Liberationism and the five-day week and the re-apportionment of the Senate, and against the cruel conditions in the Yards for labor and livestock, and against the meddling of the Line in Jasper City affairs. He was also known for his pen-portraits of Jasper City's ceaseless influx of eccentrics and immigrants, portraits that were sometimes comical, sometimes pitiable, sometimes inspiring, sometimes alarming, sometimes all of these things at once. When I met him he had mounted seventy-seven such heads on his wall, so to speak, and I was to be—he said—his seventy-eighth.

"Are you hungry? You look hungry—don't deny it."

"I travel a lot," I said. "On business. You get used to irregular meals."

"The same is true of the journalism racket, Mr. Rawlins. Well, it's decided then. I'm going to buy the both of us dinner, and you're going to tell me what brings you to Jasper, and what brings you to stand outside Mr. Baxter's Tower all damn day, and how come I heard you tell those policemen that you are a writer for the *Jasper City Evening Post*, which I know you are not, on account of I am Big Chief editor and part-owner of the *Post* and I don't know your face, son."

He pushed himself off from the rail, pointed down the street with his cigarette like an officer directing his men once more unto the breach, then set off walking.

Of course I had no intention of telling him what brought me to Mr. Baxter's Tower. But I was very curious as to why *he* had been watching Baxter's Tower all day, until he had been distracted by watching me.* And besides I had heard about the extraordinary example of

_____

*I had my suspicions, like everyone else. I thought I was on to a story about Mr. Baxter; I was half-right. The details hardly matter now. I have written about the Fall of Jasper else-

Jasper City's financial magic that was the *expense-account,* and I was eager to experience it for myself.

### A Portrait of Mr. Carson

I've remarked already on the great journalist's eyebrows. I will not attempt to describe him any further. How could I compete with the man himself? He publishes an autobiography every other year, and I bet he has published another since I last looked. You may purchase and read *Early Attempts* or *Midstream* or *The Wildcats* if you want to know more. If I'd read his books when I was a boy instead of Old Man Baxter's who knows how things might have turned out.*

We sat on fine leather seats in Mr. Carson's favorite booth in a place called Strick's Tavern. I dabbed with a napkin at my forehead. It bled for longer than you might imagine, then stopped without warning. There was a painting of some hunting-dogs behind Mr. Carson's head, and behind mine there was a painting of one of those big red-sky-red-rock-edge-of-the-unmade-world vistas that people in Jasper City like so much. Outside a madman was yelling about the end of the world, but the window-glass was thick and the noise muffled—I think I heard my name, but I do not know what he was saying about me. Strick's Tavern was squeezed in under the arch of the Fenimore Bridge and Mr. Carson's favorite booth seemed to lean out over the water in a way that was reminiscent of the prow of a boat. Down on the river below, boats came and went through the mist and rain, emerging briefly into the light, their sails seeming to unfold flower-like then shrink again as they passed. I started thinking and talking about the *Damaris.*

Mr. Carson laid open his notebook like a hustler slapping down cards. He wrote in what I guess was short-hand, fierce little strokes of the pen that resembled no language I had ever seen.

I started with the sinking and worked back westward with the current, giving him as lively a description as I could of Mr. John Southern and the Great Rotollo and the ship's cook (on whom I bestowed a parrot) and the rest of them. It seemed like the better the portrait, the fewer

---

where. I will let Mr. Ransom tell it here in his own way. —EMC

*Maybe worse. I make no promises that my books are Improving Literature for little boys; they are true, for the most part, but that is not the same thing. —EMC

pen-strokes he thought it deserved, and I recall being somewhat annoyed.

I described the self-playing piano in great detail, the way a poet might
describe his lover's face—the shimmer and twang and delicate counter-
position of its wires, the ingenuity of its construction, its uniqueness, the
elegance of its mathematics—or what I understood of its mathematics—
and I enlarged upon the promise of automation for other fields of human art or business.

"You're an inventor, then," Carson said.

"I am, though my field is more—well, I guess I am. Yes."

I did not say that I had created the piano, but nor did I say that I
hadn't.

Mr. Carson's eyebrows expressed skepticism.

"There's a lot of people in town calling themselves inventors these
days. I don't mean to sound cynical Mr. Rawlins, but I guess this wondrous thing went down with the *Damaris,* and that was the only example
of it in the whole world?"

"No," I said.

"No?"

"No." My pride was stung—he had meant to sting it. Moreover I
was a little drunk, in contravention of the principles of the Ransom
Diet and the Ransom System of Exercises, the big city being as corrupt-
ing as everyone always said.

"It went down with the *Damaris,* yes," I said. "But. But. Now listen.
I told you I worked in the theater, didn't I? Well, as a matter of fact I
have hired on with the Ormolu Theater. Do you know it? Well, you will,
sir, you will. Write it down, *Or—mo—lu.* It's just about the best place on
Swing Street right now. For two nights a week you can see the Amazing
Amaryllis, who for the last few years has been the greatest magician
touring the Western Rim—now, Jasper City people may think that Western Rim crowds are easily impressed, but let me tell you that is not the
case when it comes to magic, there are so many wonders and oddities out
there already to contend with. That's ay em ay arr uh I guess why double-
el uh eye ess. Yes—she's a woman. It's unconventional but I see no reason why women shouldn't do magic. The coming century and all."

I moved a candle aside and leaned in close.

"Now, Mr. Carson, I have hired on as an assistant to the Amazing
Amaryllis. In the world of theater that's maybe the most sought-after
position in all of Jasper City right at this minute. I said that I'm an inventor—we may not have Vansittart University and all its Professors out

on the Western Rim, but we have Encyclopedias, and better than that we have big open skies and empty days to fill with thinking, and we are too ignorant to know what can't be done—anyhow together Miss Amaryllis and I intend to bring the latest science to bear in the service of entertainment. We *will* re-create the piano. You can come see it. But the piano is only the start of it—write this down—we have plans for automata that can walk, and sing, and dance, ceaselessly and tirelessly and with perfect precision—or an automaton that can calculate so finely that if you give it your name and date of birth it can tell you how you will die—or illusions made of pure light—or levitation of the human body, light and heat and what the Encyclopedias call gravity have more business with each other than you would think, being all of them kinds of energy—and, well, there's a lot more I could say about light but not now—and, uh, well, write this down, I believe I have an experimental method for actually sawing a man in half without injury—and—"

I recalled that I should be talking about Mr. Baxter.

"It'll be the biggest thing in Jasper since the Baxter Trust," I said, leaning back in a nonchalant yet swaggering manner. "I thought the old man might want to invest while he still can. I guess I didn't reckon with the Jasper City police—I've been out on the Rim for a long time now and we didn't have policemen out there."

"And?" Carson said innocently.

"And what?"

He wrote something down, waiting for me to speak.

"Listen," I said. "I'm new in town. Like I said I've lately been out on the Rim, where people speak plainly. If you're hinting at something I don't know what it is. What did you mean, politics? What's your interest in Old Man Baxter? I know him only as the inventor of the elevator and the man who broke the Jasper City Bank. What's going on here?"

Mr. Carson used one of the candles to light another cigarette. He exhaled slowly in the general direction of the window and the river.

"Gentleman Jim Dark himself once sat where you are," he said. "The notorious Agent of the Gun, I mean—you may be innocent of politics but I'll bet you know the name. I wrote down every word he said. He can boast and preen better than any ordinary mortal—not that you didn't do your best."

"I don't know that I'm flattered by the comparison, Mr. Carson."

"I don't care for the Agents of the Gun myself but it sells newspapers. Huh. Who knows? Maybe one day I'll be lucky enough to speak to the famous Mr. John Creedmoor or his associates. I forget their names."

He stopped like he was waiting for me to name them.

Behind me and behind Mr. Carson moved waiters in black and white carrying silverware stacked so high it was like a first-rate magic-trick.

"I heard about him," I said. "Says he knows how to kill the Engines, win the war. I don't put much stock in that kind of talk."

"Well, you've learned wisdom the hard way, I bet, out on the Rim. Here in Jasper City it's the latest thing—I don't mean wisdom, that's never been much in fashion, I mean the secret-weapon mania. There hasn't been such excitement about politics since the Red Valley Republic came and went, back in our fathers' day. It's said that Mr. Creedmoor and associates are heading east, under cover of secrecy, to a place where their weapon can be perfected—popular opinion has it they're going to Founding, where the first crossing took place, but who knows? A gentleman claiming to be John Creedmoor was caught and hanged in Kallut two weeks ago. The woman's name has been heard in Lenderman and in Conant Water. A Professor Harry Ransom, that's the other fellow's name, was photographed beside the road out to Gibson, selling trinkets."

He removed from his breast-pocket a sheaf of newspaper-cuttings—one of which contained a photograph of a grinning sly-looking fellow with two missing teeth. Needless to say he was not me.

"It seems like every second restless young man in Jasper City is heading out in search of them, whether to find them and help 'em or to get there before them or to catch them and thereby make their name. Mr. Blevins at the *Jasper City Herald* called it the '91 Dash, after the gold rush of '81, I wish I'd coined that name—I called it the Fools' Pilgrimage, seeing as how the phenomenon seems to me to have a religious element. It seems to partake of what they call the *eschatological* up at VU—though you can't put a word with that many letters in the newspapers, it would cause fainting and panic. It reverses the ordinary course of things, mind you—in the ordinary course mad young men with visions of a better world go west. These fellows go east, mostly, or north. Why is that, do you suppose?"

"I don't know, Mr. Carson. I don't even know what eschata-what-you-said means."

"And that's not to mention—of or pertaining to the last days, Mr. Rawlins, the end of one world and the beginning of the next—that's not to mention the people who've come *into* Jasper in the last few months—there is a school of thought that says that if Ransom and associates exist, they will surely come to Jasper sooner or later—Jasper being the heart of the West, how could it be otherwise? Personally I doubt it—if you're looking for magic Jasper is not the place for it—what would bring Professor Ransom here of all places?"

Two men came in out of the rain and threw raincoats at a waiter without looking to see if he would catch them—he did. One was very old and looked rich and the other was very young and looked ambitious. I said that I wouldn't know what might bring Professor Ransom anywhere, or even if there was such a person.

"Mercenaries, adventurers, assassins, lunatics, detectives, idealists—inventors, like yourself. There is a mania for weapons—the secret weapon is the fashion of the summer. I hear Mr. Baxter is hiring engineers—buying them up, whether they like it or not."

"Is that a fact?"

"The Senate's afraid. One hundred gout-ridden old men quaking and quavering with fear like barnyard chickens—an unlovely sight. Jasper City's business is business, like they say, not war, and most certainly not war against the Powers. Line troops have been seen in town—you know, or maybe you don't, being new in town, that there are protocols and treaties and agreements of neutrality, that their presence violates a hundred ways at once—and who invited them in?"

The eyebrows interrupted Mr. Carson to express their outrage. He thought for a moment and then agreed.

"How dare they? I have seen what the Line makes of those places it devours, I have seen it and written of it, it will not happen to Jasper while I have any strength in my body. The Senate plays dumb—not unlike chickens, like I said."

It seemed he was expecting me to say something, but I was not sure what. Politics is and always has been over my head. I played it safe.

"Chickens," I said. "I grew up with chickens—back in Hamlin. Curious creatures."

"If I said I have reason to believe these men of the Line are guests of Mr. Baxter, would that be of interest to you, Mr. Rawlins?"

"I guess it's a puzzle, Mr. Carson. What reasons?"

He sighed, and extinguished his cigarette.

While he spoke the rain outside grew so dark and heavy that you could see nothing of the river or the world outside the window. In the window itself I could see the reflection of a man at another booth watching us, and I guess he was an associate of Mr. Carson's watching in case I acted the fool somehow, because something in the gesture with which

Mr. Carson extinguished his cigarette caused him to nod, get up, and walk away. I took this to mean that Mr. Carson had decided I was not dangerous, nor was I especially interesting.

Mr. Carson looked at the window. He had nothing more to say but I do not think he wanted to go home, mostly because of the rain.

"Tell me more about this what's-her-name, then, the Amazing Amaryllis," he said. "And the piano, why not."

✳   ✳   ✳

I guess one day Mr. Carson may read this whole *Autobiography*, in which case I hope he will take my remarks regarding his eyebrows in the friendly spirit with which I meant them. History already judges me too harshly and I do not need any more enemies, especially not ones who can write.*

✳   ✳   ✳

When I returned to the Ormolu Amaryllis was in something of a panic, having convinced herself that I had decamped for a rival theater, like the Hamilton or the Horizon or &c. I assured her of my loyalty. She fussed over my head-wound and I told her I had fallen over. I told her I had met the famous Mr. Elmer Merrial Carson of the *Evening Post* and sung her praises to him and he had promised to write her up in his column, and though she did not believe me she seemed flattered that I had taken the trouble to lie to her.

In the morning I set to work in earnest. For a few days I was busy cleaning and polishing and running errands and learning all the tricks and implements of the magic business. Stage-magic is a science as complex as the study of electricity or light or anything else. Sometimes I thought it would be easier to learn the genuine article. Most of the Great Rotollo's most treasured implements had been lost when the *Damaris* went down, and the truth is Amaryllis was at that date entertaining crowds mostly through sheer grit, and the novelty of her sex.

I set to work reconstructing those lost devices, scavenging parts from scrapyards and the sweepings of blacksmiths all over Hoo Lai. I learned through experimentation about clockwork and the confinement of pigeons and—but I could waste words on this forever, and it would do nobody any good.

I gutted one of the Ormolu's broken-down old pianos, one which I thought Mr. Quantrill would not notice the absence of, and harvested

--------

*Worse things have been said. —EMC

wire. Slowly and cautiously I began to acquire the parts for the reconstruction of the Apparatus—I was developing a great many ideas about
stage-lighting and illusion, and if I did not yet have the parts I could talk
about them so well that Amaryllis almost believed they were real and
even Mr. Quantrill was curious.

I pushed my plans to settle accounts with Baxter to the back of my
mind—I was too busy to think of loitering outside his offices or pester-
ing him with lawsuits or attempting an assassination. The newspapers
reported that two men who'd claimed for the benefit of autograph-
hunters to be Harry Ransom and John Creedmoor had opened fire with
handguns on the Dryden Engine near the borders of the Territory, and
been annihilated—I hardly noticed.

Two weeks after I arrived in Jasper I was the subject of one of Mr.
Elmer Merrial Carson's famous newspaper pen-portraits—you may read
it for yourself, if any copies survived the Battle of Jasper. He portrayed
a series of amiably eccentric inventors, including the usual cast of rain-
makers and virility-enhancers and lead-to-gold types and lastly a Mr.
Rawlins of the Ormolu Theater, self-proclaimed survivor of the *Damaris*,
and his wonderful—though, Mr. Carson implied, most likely imaginary—
automated self-playing piano.

Despite my best efforts, and despite my promises to her, the Amazing Amaryllis was not mentioned by name. That caused her to sink into
a mild depression. She had never believed me when I said that I had met
Mr. Carson but as soon as she saw the column she became convinced
that her hopes and dreams had depended on it ever since arriving in
Jasper City. That night her performance was off—in fact she fouled the
Gibson City Gaffle so badly there was jeering from the audience.

She was still in a state of mild depression some days later, when a
member of the audience forced her way backstage through the curtain
after her performance.

I thought this uninvited intruder meant to complain—it had been
another bad show—and I attempted to intercept her.

I said, "Now, miss, if you have anything to say, it's—"

She said, "Are you Hal Rawlins?"

I acknowledged that I was.

"Ah-hah! So there you are."

She was young, and short. She had black curling hair and brown
eyes. She spoke in the slow and musical accent of the Deltas. She looked
ragged and hungry and sleepless. I cannot say that I noticed immediately
that she was pretty, maybe on account of the way she was glaring at me.

"How dare you—how dare you, sir, how—I am Adela Iermo, Adela *Kotan* Iermo. You know that name, sir, yes I can see that you do!"

I knew part of it. *Kotan* was the word etched into the uppermost winding-mechanism of the self-playing piano. Was this its first owner? Could this be its creator? If so, how many hours had I spent admiring the genius of this young woman!

"Did you think you would never face me?"

"I confess I never did—why, ma'am, I *dreamed* of—"

"The *Damaris*—the self-playing piano—that is *my* work, sir. Did you think I would not find out—did you think you could boast and lie and claim it as your own and I would let the matter be—I am looking you in the face, sir, do you still claim it as your own?"

Amaryllis and a pair of stagehands watched us.

"Listen," I said. "We should be friends, Miss Kotan, you see I—"

I extended a hand toward her, in what I reckoned was a friendly way. She slapped it aside. I soon learned that this was a gesture recognized in the Code of Dueling of the nobility of the Deltas, but at first I took it as mere rudeness, and was nonplussed.

# CHAPTER 19

# THE DUEL

"A *duel*," Amaryllis said. She swayed like she was about to swoon, but since nobody moved to catch her, she decided not to.

"A duel," Mr. Quantrill said. One of the stagehands had summoned him, or perhaps he had been alerted by Adela's shouting. In any case he stood stock-still with his arms folded, attempting to intimidate.

"Not in my theater," Mr. Quantrill said. "This isn't the Rim or the—what are you, Miss Kotan or Iermo whatever it is, you sound like you're from down in the Deltas, I know things are done differently there but this is Jasper City, you know? The duel has been banned for thirty years or more."

"It's a question of honor," Adela said.

"It's a question of aiding and abetting plain murder," Mr. Quantrill said.

She seemed to give this serious consideration. They say in storybooks that *her brow furrowed*. Well, that is what happened.

"My quarrel is with Mr. Rawlins here. I don't—"

"Listen," I said. "You and me should talk, Miss Kotan—Adela—I mean—"

"Enough *lies*," she said.

Mr. Quantrill had been signaling with his eyebrows to the stagehands for some time, and they had been pretending not to understand for as long as they plausibly could, but now they sighed and stood and stepped toward Adela, meaning to subdue her. She drew a gun from beneath her coat and they sat down again at once.

Her coat was so battered and road-worn I could not to this day say what it was made of. It was a dusty rose-red. It had no buttons and loose threads. She wore a white shirt and stiff trousers and no jewelry. Despite the poverty and disarray of her clothing—I shall not mention the condition of her hair—there was something unmistakably aristocratic about her. Above all her accent, which was that of the landowning classes of the Delta territories, as Mr. Quantrill had observed—but also the way she stood, and the way she held her pistol, firmly but carelessly, like it was meant for art or sport and not for killing. I guessed that she was newly arrived in town.

Amaryllis said, "Hal, what's going on—who is this?"

"A good question," Mr. Quantrill said. "Mr. Rawlins?"

Before I could say anything Adela interrupted. "Mr. Rawlins is a thief—the worst kind of thief, the thief of another's hard work and genius and good name. The self-playing piano is mine. You cannot imagine the work that went into it. You cannot imagine what I sacrificed to be capable of it. I made it two years ago in Gibson City. I have no papers, only my word—which should be good enough for you people. I—I pawned it."

She said that like she was confessing something awful.

"I had no choice," she said. "And then after what happened in Gibson I thought I should never see it again—well, I came to this city thinking to begin again, and what do I find as soon as I arrive but that *this* man is boasting that he created the piano himself and—"

Her eyes suddenly widened still further.

"Oh—are you *all* in on it?"

"Well now," Mr. Quantrill said, raising his hands. "Well now. This is between you and Mr. Rawlins, I think."

Adela turned to me. "Where is it?"

"It sank," I explained.

She laughed scornfully. Few people can accomplish this trick. I guess it is one of the things they teach young ladies of the Deltas, along with comportment and poise and table-manners.

"I don't believe you."

"Do you see it here, ma'am? I tried to save it, but it went down with the boat. There was an incident involving an Engine."

"How can I believe a word you say?"

"It isn't what you think it is," I said. "You're seeing wickedness where there's only the usual run of accidents and bad luck and confusion. Listen—"

"I've heard enough."

Well, this all went on for some time. I tried to explain. Adela accused and demanded that honor be satisfied. I want to say that I made a decent effort to talk her out of that course of action. I said that we should resolve our dispute through words. She accused me of cowardice. I said that I did not know how things were done down in the Deltas but out on the Rim young women did not duel—well, of course that was not the right thing to say—my excuse is that her gun was still menacing me and I could not think straight. I was in fact starting to get angry myself. I offered to write a letter to Mr. Elmer Merrial Carson at the *Evening Post* correcting his misunderstandings and giving credit where credit was due. She said that made no difference—the insult was already given— she was not here to haggle or litigate, but to resolve things with honor. Besides, she would not believe that the piano was lost, but maintained that I had hidden it somewhere or dismantled it for parts.

I was not sure whether she was very brave or whether she was a young woman in a kind of panic—it seemed likely to me that she had not eaten right or slept in a safe place in many days, and I knew what it was like to have one's one and only scrap of pride and hope in the whole big hostile world snatched away. I did not want to be shot and I did not want to shoot her, because *first* I am not a violent man, and *second* she was a woman, and *third* I recognized her predicament and understood that my careless boasting was partly to blame, and above all *fourth* because the mind that built the self-playing piano was too precious and beautiful to waste.

On the other hand I am only human and you can call me a thief and a liar and a coward only so many times before I get mad.

I said "All right, damn it—you'll have your duel."

She instantly calmed. It was as if I had promised her something of great importance. She lowered her gun and said, "Thank you, Mr. Rawlins."

"I don't know how they do it down in the Deltas, ma'am. I'm no aristocrat. I was raised without land or any particular kind of honor and while you were probably learning deportment or how to hunt with hounds or something I was selling Encyclopedias. But I've been out on the Rim for long enough to know a thing or two about honor and about guns. You should know that this won't be my first duel."

In my time I had done a lot of stupid things for reasons of pride, but I had only fought one previous duel. That was also over a question of pride of authorship—that time it was over who had first invented the

Ransom Free-Energy process. Right was on my side and fortune favored me. My opponent had stumbled drunk into a tree and passed out. That was the way things were done on the Western Rim. I was kind of hoping that something similar might happen here.

"Not in my theater," Mr. Quantrill said.

"Of course," I said. "We'll need to find some suitable location."

"Of course," she agreed.

"Good—well, what's more, ma'am, out on the Rim when we do this we do it at dawn. Only murderers shoot each other by night—it wouldn't be honorable."

She pushed back her hair and scratched her head. It was obvious that she had not thought very hard or very carefully about her plan. That is often what happens when people get their heads all filled with honor, I have noticed.

"That's true," she said. "I believe you're right."

It was a little after midnight, and mid-summer—dawn was several hours away. I thought this might give her time to change her mind.

"Besides," I said, "I don't have a gun. You're new in town, right, ma'am?—well not everyone here carries a gun all the time, you'll find. I assume you don't mean to shoot an unarmed man. I don't know much about how things are done in the Deltas but—"

One of the stagehands interrupted to observe that Mr. Barnabas Busby Bosko, Wizard of the Western Rim, used two guns in his act, one of which was fake but one of which was real, and that Mr. Bosko surely would not mind if I borrowed it.

"Thank you," Adela said.

"Yes," I sighed. "Thank you very much."

✳    ✳    ✳

A small party emerged from the back of the Ormolu Theater into the warm summer night. Adela and I led the pack. Mr. Quantrill walked behind us. I think he was mostly concerned to ensure that we did not simply shoot each other on his premises and cause him trouble with the police. The Amazing Amaryllis walked beside him, sometimes leaning on his arm, wearing his coat over her frilled and sequined stage-clothes. She said that she was concerned for my safety and I think that she was, but that also she was worried about her investment, and the plans we had made and what I had promised her, the very latest science &c.

The two stagehands brought up the rear. I guess they had nothing better to do. They tried to make a wager, whispering, but I think they could not come to terms on odds. They made ungentlemanly remarks about Adela and unflattering remarks about me. They had a bottle of wine each, which they shared with the Amazing Amaryllis and Mr. Quantrill.

The sky over Swing Street was a cloak of black velvet, sequined with stars. I remarked on its beauty to Adela, thinking I might distract her from her plans.

"You talk too much, Mr. Rawlins."

"One of these days I guess I'll get myself into trouble."

She didn't find that funny.

"We need some place quiet," she said.

"This is Swing Street," Mr. Quantrill said. "It doesn't get quiet."

"The bars never close," I agreed, "and there isn't a single alley that doesn't contain at least one drunk. We'll need to head east."

Mr. Quantrill wanted us away from his theater, and I wanted to postpone the moment as long as possible, in hopes that I might talk some sense into her. She did not strike me as naturally the killing type and I wondered what had happened to her to make her that way.

I suggested that we head toward Reynald Park. That was an expanse of unkempt lawn with some scraggly trees and persistent tent habitations on the eastern edge of Hoo Lai. Well, when we got there, there were policemen. I had guessed that there would be—I often go walking at night when I am thinking and I cannot sleep, and I had noticed that there was a police-station next to the park and a bar where the policemen drank. So we turned back.

We walked down streets of houses, lit or unlit windows, the occasional gas lamp illuminating stone steps and narrow gardens and addresses.

"You can't duel on somebody's doorstep," I said. "Not without an invitation. That would be vulgar."

Next we found ourselves near an expanse of warehouses and workhouses with the banners of the Baxter Trust on their square ugly roofs, and though the streets were empty dogs behind fences set up a racket, and the lights of nightwatchmen drifted toward us, and we drifted away.

"The cemetery," Mr. Quantrill said. "Up on Wyte Hill—it's a long walk but—"

"You can't duel in a cemetery," Adela said. "The Code forbids it."

"Besides," I said, "it would be bad for morale."

You *may* duel in the vacant yard of a Smiler meeting-house, or so Adela said, the Code of the Deltas cares nothing for the Brothers of the New Thought, but there were policemen around in the street outside the meeting-house.

The policemen were going door to door down the street, waking men in nightshirts and women holding babies and asking questions. I do not know what they were looking for but they stopped and questioned us too. We said we were theater-types and that seemed sufficient to explain what we were doing wandering about aimlessly in the small hours of the morning—by that stage the sky was beginning just subtly to lighten in the west.

I was scared—I do not mean to deny that I was scared both of being shot and of shooting someone. But nor did I want to be a coward in anyone's eyes, least of all my own. I asked Amaryllis if she would take word, if I was shot, to my sisters, and she asked what sisters, and I had to say, well, forget it, and that it did not matter.

We headed toward the river. There were more policemen in the streets. It seemed there were more than was usual. I did not know what to expect in the way of policing from a town like Jasper, but Mr. Quantrill did and he also seemed discomforted. He wondered whether maybe another Senator had been assassinated, or an Agent spotted in town.

The omnipresence of policemen began to frustrate me and unnerve me, so that I almost forgot that the policemen were the only thing between me and the duel. Amaryllis speculated jokingly that maybe the notorious John Creedmoor or Harry Ransom themselves had been spotted in Jasper City. Amaryllis had been drinking too. One of the stagehands suggested that maybe they were experimenting with their secret weapon in a basement somewhere and were about to blow up the whole damn city if the cops didn't catch them in time. The other stagehand said that wasn't funny.

When I say *policemen,* I mean that some of them were policemen, and some I think were members of the Jasper City militia, you could tell because they wore different uniforms, and carried rifles not handguns, and had a different kind of dully gleaming copper badge. Some of them wore no uniform at all, or no uniform any of us could recognize.

❋  ❋  ❋

I guess you could call this A PORTRAIT OF ADELA. It's what she told me about herself, anyhow.

## A Portrait of Adela

"It's an extraordinary creation," I said. "The piano, I mean. How did you come to—?"

She shook her head. "It's a toy."

"You'd shoot a man over a toy?"

"It's a question of principle, Mr. Rawlins. It's the last thing I have left."

"I know that feeling, Miss Adela, I know that feeling well. I am a kind of entrepreneur and inventor and traveler myself, and I know what it's like to be down. I'm from a town called Hamlin. You sound like you're up from the Deltas."

"You know that's true, Mr. Rawlins. Why do you care to ask? What business is it of yours to interrogate—?"

"I'd like to know where the piano came from. It was just about the most beautiful thing I've ever seen—maybe the second after some work of my own—and I don't get many chances to talk to anybody who understands about that kind of work. Anyhow I'd like to know who's about to shoot who."

"My name is Adela Kotan Iermo. I am the third daughter and the fifth child of the sixth Baron of Iermo. I was taught to shoot by one of my father's retainers. He did not want to teach a girl to shoot but my money was good. Have no doubt about who will be shooting whom, Mr. Rawlins. Because you apologized I will aim for the leg—the Code permits that mercy."

"Well that's a fine offer—I'll try to do likewise but I make no promises. Put a gun in my hand and just about anything might happen. Nobody ever taught me to shoot unless you count my sister Jess and that was only throwing stones at cats. My father had no retainers nor money. What's Iermo like? I've never been to the Deltas."

"It's the seventh or the eighth wealthiest of the Baronies. It produces sugar and rice; my father or my brothers could tell you the tonnage, the revenues, the number of retainers and field-hands and men-at-arms—I don't know—I have been away for a long time, Mr. Rawlins, and things change fast these days. Do you want to hear about the sunsets or the dances or the rainy season or the sounds and smells of the jungle?"

"Oh," Amaryllis interrupted, "the *jungles*—is it true that—?"

Adela ignored her.

I said, "What does *Kotan* mean? It sounds like a Folk word."

She shrugged. "It's a name. I have others—Adela Kotan Mor Chatillon Iermo and so on—each one a family of some small note and wealth
in the Deltas—Kotan is named for some ruins. Now let me ask you a
question, Mr. Rawlins—why did you lie about the piano? Was it pride?
You had to have something to boast about and you did not care if it
was yours or not—I've known many men like that."

"It was a misunderstanding. My own accomplishments are plenty
noteworthy, ma'am, as a matter of fact. I have lived by my wits since I
was a child. I built my own electrical engine at the age of fourteen—"

"Well so did I, Mr. Rawlins."

We traded boasts like that for a while, as we walked down toward
the river. Some of the stink of the yards was in the air. I learned about
her youthful investigations into electricity, magnetism, musicology, and
logic. I told her about some of my own exploits, suitably disguised. I
learned about the peculiar arrangement that governed her peculiar childhood, which was this. As is the custom among the land-owning classes
of the Deltas, her father settled a trust upon her and each of her siblings.
In the case of Adela Kotan Iermo the family's lawyer—having recently
contracted one of those brain-eating poxes that are fashionable in the
hot & wet climate of the Deltas—committed an unpardonable drafting
error, on account of which the young Adela acquired control of her fortune at the age of twelve, not twenty-one.

She was future-minded. She hired tutors, some from as far afield as
Gibson City or Jasper. She learned mathematics, logic, music—of these
only music was a fitting activity for a princess of the Deltas. When she
began to learn mechanics and electrical engineering her father threatened
to disown her. She caused a new house to be constructed for herself down
beyond the fields at the edge of the floodplain—she was fifteen years
old. She hired servants. Her father ranted and raved. Her eccentricities
embarrassed the family. Her brothers tried to seize her—she hired
guards. She joined the Liberationists and she purchased and freed Folk in
order to spite her father, and she attempted to learn their language because it could not be done. She conducted a precocious correspondence
with the professors in Jasper City and Gibson, and unlike when I wrote
to them she got a reply. She conducted experiments with magnetism and
electricity. All of this sounded like just the life of freedom and greatness
I had dreamed of back in East Conlan but Adela was unhappy about it,
and I thought as I guess everybody sometimes does about how big and
strange the world is. I told her about my vision of Light and she told me

about her vision of the coming century, which was Automation. She said that in the century to come there would be no fields of toiling laborers—there would be leisure for all—there would be steam-power and clockwork. That tiny woman had row upon row of big mechanical men constructed, all stooping and cutting in unison. She made a kind of life. Nature does this sort of thing so easily the world is over-supplied with bugs and beetles that do just about nothing but move mindlessly and she did not see why human ingenuity should not do at least as well. Rust, balance, weeds, all gave her trouble. I imagine the mud-plain outside her house filling up with ranks of half-finished metal men who when the plain flooded looked like the victims of the kind of disaster that gets written about in the newspapers as far away as Jasper. It is possible in this way to burn through most of the fortune of a princess of the Deltas in less than ten years.

By the time she was nineteen years old she'd abandoned these clumsy early experiments, and was deeply engaged in the study of Mind. She fell in and out of love with one or more of the tutors. She developed a kind of analytical engine and a kind of complex abacus that played chess, though not well. She was accused of various kinds of witchcraft and of digging up the lost arts of the Folk. Somebody shot out one of her windows and somebody threw flaming torches at her door. Her father went to court to have her declared mad as a matter of law. I said that her father sounded like a terrible old monster and she took offense, informing me that her father was a brave man who had fought and won a half-dozen duels before he was twenty-two.

By the time she was twenty years old nearly all of the money was gone. The tutors had all gone back north, including the one she had thought she was in love with. She confessed to me that she did not understand love as well as she understood machines and I said that most people understood neither, so she had nothing to be ashamed of. She developed theories of pure mathematics regarding the operation of the Mind and its relationship to language and to music, and regarding the relationship between language and perception and naming and the creation of the world and the unmaking of the world that was here before and why things change as you press further west into what we sometimes in our arrogance call the unmade lands. All of this was intriguing to me but she could not explain it very clearly because we were interrupted firstly by policemen, and secondly by the Amazing Amaryllis, who wanted to know if Adela could build automata for her that would dance and sing and do coin-tricks, and thirdly by the increasingly urgent need to find a quiet and unobserved place in which to shoot each other. It was nearly dawn.

With the last of the money she bought a ticket north out of the Deltas on a riverboat called the *Swan of Guthrie*. The ticket took her to the Three Cities. After that she did not know where to go or what to do with herself. The food in the north was too bland for her taste and the sky too pale and cold and the people too rude. She was too proud to throw herself on the charity of the tutors who for years had consumed her fortune. She considered suicide. She lived for the better part of a year in Gibson City where she learned that being a princess of the Deltas meant nothing outside of the Deltas. She went hungry. She got into business with some people who cheated her. They did not believe she could do what she said she could do, so she made the piano for them to prove herself. They cheated her out of the last of her money but they could not figure out how to make a profit from the piano and so they did not bother to steal it. She pawned it and that is how I guess it came to pass into the hands of John Southern of the *Damaris*. Adela would have retrieved it but before she could scrape together the money Gibson City had fallen to the Line and Adela herself was under arrest.

Mr. Quantrill interrupted. "What do you mean? The Line? Gibson City's neutral—same as Jasper—the Tri-City Territory, all three first among equals, you know . . ."

"The Line, Mr.—I apologize, sir, I forget your name, it's been a long strange night—the Line sir and ma'am has held Gibson City for six months or more. Nobody admits it but it's true. Their Senators still walk and talk like it's still their city but I have seen the soldiers in the street and the Heavier-Than-Air Vessels overhead and the Senators know who their masters are if no one else does. The Line came in six months ago and nobody dared say no. There's a silence about it. Nobody writes it in their letters or in the newspapers but they know. People here in Jasper are pretending not to know—or do you really not know yet?"

One of the stagehands cursed. Amaryllis drew Mr. Quantrill's coat tighter around herself and shivered.

"They were looking for someone. They came up into Gibson because they were hunting and nobody knew who or why. Then we started hearing rumors about that turncoat Agent Creedmoor and the woman whatever her name is and that bloody Ransom charlatan—and the rumors said they were coming east, past Gibson—well, I don't know. The Line's mad with fear. The Engines jump at shadows. I know because

I spent three months under interrogation. The things they asked me were mad."

As she said this Adela was walking ahead down the stone steps at the east end of a street so remote from the city's heart that it had no name but only a number, and that number was preposterously high, two or three hundred or more. The steps were slippery with muck and night mists and Amaryllis in her high-heeled shoes nearly fell. The steps led down to an isolated stretch of riverbank, where nobody lived or did business.

"The old century was theirs," I said, "and three or four before that. Who knows what the next will bring. No wonder they're afraid."

"Word got out that I was a Scientist—like this Professor Ransom, if indeed he exists. A garbled account of the piano got to the ears of the mob—you know the mania that has got into the masses for secret weapons, magic machines to win the war. I didn't think the authorities of the Line would be equally credulous but they were. First a lawyer told me that the Baxter Trust had brought suit against me and when I told them to go to hell they arrested me and handed me over to the Line, to be questioned and questioned over and over. They wanted to know all about the principles of automation and how I came by my learning, I said that's all I will tell you, my family name and my given name and my genius. Well, they did not like to hear that. Are you in league with Professor Ransom, they said. As if there is some world-wide bloody brotherhood of tinkerers. Had I ever been west or east or just about anywhere. Ridiculous things—what did I know about the Folk. What did I know about the Red Valley Republic. Once they start questioning you they can't stop. I was moved and moved again and questioned—they make you, they make you nothing but questions—they make you nothing— they had machines for questioning—until you're released without any kind of reason or warning and the world is . . ."

She looked up and down the length of the river. We were alone, unwatched, unpoliced. There was mud leading down to rushes and then wide black water. There were some empty shacks with caved-in tin roofs and a disused jetty. There was a bad smell—it can best be described as a sad and frightening smell—which I guess was because on the other side of the river were the Yards, the pens and slaughterhouses and wirefence mazes and red pinpricks of fire all dimly visible like the camp of a vast besieging army. This figure of speech did not occur to me until later.

We were quiet for a while, thinking that it was now or never. I was thinking that I was sorry I had caused Adela to be arrested—though it was hardly my intention—and I wondered what the Line had done to her to put that desperate look in her eye. I still believed that the mind that had made the self-playing piano was a beautiful one but I was afraid it had been damaged. I thought about the machines the Line might use for questioning, and I recalled the flash of light with which they had shocked me back into life, so long ago back in East Conlan, and I shivered at the thought of what such a device might do if used as a weapon.

By rights she should be the hero of this story not me, but right has nothing to do with anything.

"Well," I said, and drew my gun and pretended to clean it with my sleeve. It was a stage-gun, like I said. Mr. Barnabas Busby Bosko, Wizard of the Western Rim, had two of them, one real and one fake. He used the real one to put a hole in a plank of wood, to demonstrate its deadliness, then secretly switched it for its double, which flashed and made a noise but did nothing else. Both guns were big and ornate, with fake-gold in-lays and embellishments that were intended to be visible even from the cheap seats. I had checked and re-checked it but was still not entirely convinced that I had the real gun and not its double.

"Well," Adela agreed.

I didn't know what she was thinking. Later she would confess to me that she did not think that she was thinking at all, just listening to the sound of her awful father and her brothers laughing in her head, to the sound of Linesmen interrogating her over and over.

Anyhow I said, "Let's be done with it, shall we?"

Mr. Quantrill took Adela's coat and Amaryllis took mine. Amaryllis dabbed a handkerchief at her own tearful eyes, and also at a mark on my face. The stagehands offered around cigarettes, which both duelists declined. All this seemed to take a very long time. Adela saluted and I mirrored her gesture. We turned back to back. I walked slowly down-river, one pace, two paces, three, four . . .

Adela said, "What's that?"

I turned. I did not mean to shoot but my fingers had a mind of their own and pulled the trigger.

❋   ❋   ❋

Well. The gun was the real article and it fired all right, but the shot went nowhere near Adela. One of the stagehands threw himself facedown in the mud and Mr. Quantrill stepped bravely in front of Amaryllis, but both these gestures were unnecessary—the bullet went no place in particular, out over the river. There was a theatrical flash and a cloud of smoke. The gun made a deafening noise, which was not swallowed by the night as we'd hoped but instead echoed in it, so that we all instantly understood that every policeman for a mile up and down the river would have heard us. Three geese launched themselves skyward out of the rushes. The stagehand who had not thrown himself down in the mud broke into a run without a single word or a glance back. Mr. Quantrill raised a finger like he was about to start yelling at somebody for incompetence and irresponsibility but didn't know who to blame. Adela stood where she was, her back to me still.

What Adela had seen as she looked up-river—as she paced her ten paces—as she studied every rush and reed and ripple of black water with that precise awareness that comes to a person in the face of death, or after committing an enormous irreversible blunder—what she saw was one of the Line's Combustion-Powered Submersible Vessels rising from the river.

The C.S.V. is unique among the vehicles of the Line in that it makes very little noise—they are infrequently deployed, but the Line makes use of them for missions of reconnaissance, sabotage, and clandestine transport—and preoccupied as we were we had not noticed this Vessel approaching or surfacing.

The C.S.V. is long and black and glistening and bullet-shaped, except for two turrets and one steam-vent. It is unnerving to see it rise from the water in the same way that it is unnerving to see the Heavier-Than-Air Vessels rise up into the air—it speaks of the Line's terrible indifference to human limitations and boundaries—it suggests that no place is safe.

This particular C.S.V. operated under the orders of the Archway Engine, and carried between ten and sixteen soldiers of the Line in conditions of hideous discomfort, and was engaged in the covert delivery into Jasper of communications equipment, weaponry, and personnel. I learned all this later, of course, from a memorandum that happened to cross my desk, after the Battle. At the time all that was apparent was that the river was no longer empty, but that it had suddenly spawned this nightmarish metal behemoth.

What's more, a hatch in the side of the thing had opened. The face of an Officer of the Line peered out from its reeking red-lit innards. No doubt he'd expected to see a quiet stretch of undesired riverfront, empty of witnesses. Instead he saw Miss Adela Kotan Iermo &c with her weapon cocked and lifted, and me behind her with a theatrical cloud of black smoke still wafting from my ridiculous ornate gold-inlaid pistol. The way I remember it I saw his eyes widen and then his eyebrows lift, first one then the other.

"Run," I said.

Adela did not run. Amaryllis, hiking up her skirt and kicking off her shoes, did. The stagehand who lay in the mud crawled on his knees and elbows into the rushes to hide. To this day I do not know how Mr. Quantrill escaped.

I stood beside Adela, and together we stood there pistols drawn long enough to permit Amaryllis and the stagehand and Mr. Quantrill to escape, although I will be damned if they ever thanked us.

The Officer of the Line had ducked back inside the C.S.V. so quickly that his hat fell off. There was a minute of silence then his men came tumbling out through the hatch, all of them crouching low to the ground and all of them holding weapons of their own.

Adela and me, we fled too.

I guess this surprised the Linesmen, who had no doubt assumed they were being ambushed by bloodthirsty battle-hardened Agents of their adversary. They did not immediately pursue us. We made it to the stone steps before they gave chase, where Adela slipped and I steadied her, or maybe she steadied me.

Anyhow in the face of a common enemy we had utterly forgotten about our duel. I do not pretend to understand the intricacies of the Code of Dueling but it seemed that honor had been satisfied. We were shot at—maybe that was all that the Code required. Three or four bullets whirred and cracked at the stone wall beside us as we made it to the top of the steps and ran down the street. Adela shot back wildly, not meaning to kill but only to scare—I did likewise. Someone shouted and then they stopped shooting at us—maybe so as not to alert the police or maybe because they hoped to capture us alive. After that they just ran after us, not quickly but tirelessly, heads down, ten or more men in ranks. The sun rose. We did not appreciate the beauty of the morning mist or the lively street-scenes of bakers and butchers and newspapermen opening their businesses and starting their days—we just ran, Adela and me dodging around bakers &c and the Linesmen behind us bowling them over and trampling them. I will not say that I was not terrified. The Linesmen seemed as implacable as Engines. I had visions of the stamping of their boots on my face and Adela's. Adela and I led each other this way and that, with a hand on the arm or a nod of the head. The Linesmen kept coming. The sun was like an electric lamp had been switched on in the sky. It was instantly hot and bright and the buildings and the lampposts and Kotan and me and all the scattering pedestrians and the Linesmen behind us cast very sharp shadows that lengthened and receded and chased us when we turned street-corners. I sweated and so did Miss Adela Kotan &c &c Iermo—I cannot speak for the Linesmen. I recall the sounds of panting, street-muck splashing underfoot, Adela gasping with laughter, and how at that sudden unexpected sound I started laughing as well, until the pain in my sides and my shortness of breath made me stop. I recall a big handsome woman who wobbled between me and Adela like a bowling-pin as we ran past her on either side shrieking as she fell on the street and then the different sound of her shrieking again as the Linesmen trampled her, I guess—I did not look back. I had already looked back at the Linesmen a number of times and every time I looked I saw all of them staring at me, in a way that gave me a chill, a row of gray eyes in red sweating angry faces, and I found their expressions strange until I realized that each of them was trying to fix my own face in his memory so that he could make a full report. After that I kept my head forward, glancing only to the side to see that Adela was still with me.

I would like to say that we eluded the Linesmen through some ingenious stratagem on my part, some piece of story-book cleverness, but as a matter of fact all that happened was that the Linesmen steadily fell further and further behind. I have already written about the Ransom System of Exercises I think and this was an advertisement for its benefits— and Adela had good breeding I guess—and as for the Linesmen, I guess that living bent double in a submersible cannot be good for anyone's health. They looked smaller and smaller as they ran, not only because they fell behind but because they got more and more hunched. Slowly terror ebbed away and relief mounted, the balance tipping in favor of elation some time around our entry into the district of Hoo Lai. The Linesmen were determined but the flesh can do only so much. Each time we turned a corner there was a moment until they turned it behind us, and each time that moment got longer. We could all of us understand the mathematics of this situation but the Linesmen kept coming anyhow, determined to play it out, until eventually we turned a corner and the Linesmen did not appear behind us until we'd already turned the next. The C.S.V. by this time must have long since submerged itself and retreated up-river, its cargo undelivered. It is possible that our interruption of the C.S.V.'s delivery delayed the Battle of Jasper, at least briefly, though of course it did not stop it. I do not know what happened to the

Linesmen—whether they were retrieved, or whether they just hid out in Jasper until they could be reunited with the invading forces. I do not care. Anyhow by the time Adela and me turned onto Swing Street the Linesmen were long gone, and we were no longer afraid at all, in fact we were both pretending that neither of us had ever been afraid. We had forgotten our differences. We were congratulating each other on our courage under fire and our cleverness and our mutual genius. We'd survived the Linesmen together and were now firmly allied, neither of us alone in the world anymore or afraid of anything. The voices in Adela's head were silent. We started talking big plans, though to all outward appearances we were just a young and bohemian Jasper City pair staggering home after a long wild night on the town, laughing and arms around each other's shoulders and quite naturally after all we'd been through together turning and doing what in the romance-novels they might call locking our lips together, with her tugging at my wild & unruly hair and me running my hand down her back. I stumbled on the sidewalk and fell back with her pressed against me, hearts still hammering, the both of us falling together against the ornate façade of Harriman's Theater and causing a sign that advertised A NIGHT OF WONDER to swing back and forth. Some small boys hooted. Delicacy forbids me to say more.

CHAPTER 20

# The Ormolu

When we got back to the Ormolu Mr. Quantrill yelled and threatened to send both of us away.

"You're fugitives. The you-know-what is looking for you."

"The Line," Adela said. "Those were men of the—"

"Stop that—don't talk politics in my office—get out the both of you before you ruin me."

"The way I see it, Mr. Quantrill, you're no less a fugitive than the two of us."

"I'm not—I didn't—they didn't—ah, but at least *I* wasn't carrying a gun."

I said nothing. I guess Mr. Quantrill was thinking about whether that would make any difference to the Linesmen if they tracked him down, and I guess he decided it would not, because the fight went out of him.

"We're in this together, Mr. Quantrill. The best thing we can do is to go on as before."

"What business does the Line have in Jasper?" Adela said. "Why would you let them tell you what you may or may not do? Back home we would never have—"

Mr. Quantrill took that as an insult and started to yell again, and kept yelling until suddenly a wicked smile crossed his face and he sat down.

"Well, Mr. Rawlins. Maybe I'm stuck with you. But I was promised an inventor and since the two of you don't seem to be able to agree on which one of you that is I guess I'll have both of you—at one wage, mind."

Adela looked so surprised and happy that I could not bring myself to protest. Besides, I could not forgo an opportunity to work with the inventor of the self-playing piano, even if she was a little mad, and even if it meant that I would go hungry.

"Don't look so shocked, Mr. Rawlins. Count your blessings. At least you've got work. Now go and do it."

Well, nobody likes to hear that but it is usually good advice.

※  ※  ※

It was a good summer.

Together Adela and I made a device that could be hidden beneath the Amazing Amaryllis's frilly sleeve and could project one of half a dozen cards into her palm, the selection being made by firm gestures of the wrist. Amaryllis said that it was clever but not a whole lot of use, and besides it made her wrist chafe. We made a mechanical orange tree that appeared to bloom on command. Amaryllis liked that more. That was the first difficult thing we made together, and Adela was surprised and delighted to find out that I was not a fool, that in fact I maybe was what I said I was. She kissed me. We made a mechanical dove—I regret to say that it could not fly, but it appeared to fly, which was good enough. It swung on wires out to the cheap seats and back. Its feet could hold and release rings or watches, returning those items to the audience-members from which they were borrowed with passable accuracy. We made these things for the most part out of junk. It is astonishing what kind of junk can be found in Jasper City.

Adela acquired new clothes and cut her hair. At first she stayed in one of the rooms at the Ormolu, same as me. Later when Mr. Quantrill increased our wage she moved into a tiny room in the Gate. I said I guessed it couldn't compare to the mansions of the Deltas. She said it didn't matter.

We made flashes and bangs. We made more contraptions out of mirrors than I can possibly recall, some of which were designed to conceal and others to spy. Some of them were cleverly hinged and folded so that they could make doubles, so that they could reproduce Amaryllis in shining sequined triplicate. Some of them were so tiny they could fit in the Amazing Amaryllis's other sleeve, some of them were cabinet-sized, and some of them were so big that nobody in the theater would ever understand what they were looking at. The theater was always full, sometimes so full that boys and girls sat on the steps or perched precariously on the balcony. If you doubt me you may consult the newspapers. We

got favorable notices. Once a full row at the front was occupied by
serious-looking young men in brown or gray suits, who I was told were
a party from the Baxter Trust. Mr. Quantrill was making money and so
he was happy, though in truth it was not really because of Adela or me
or any of the things we built but because it was summer, and Swing Street
was booming, and like I have said there was a mania for magic. He increased our wages anyhow.

We made secret weapons—we made smoke, fire, and light. That was
what people wanted and that was we gave them. Very modern-looking
devices that spun gears and flashed sparks, or things that looked like
ancient runes of the Folk and emitted stinks and vibrations at frightening and exciting frequencies. It was not required or expected that these
devices *do* anything, merely that they be strange and wonderful and a
little alarming. Adela and I drank in all the coffeehouses on Swing Street
until morning every morning sharing wild ideas, challenging each other
to greater and greater feats of impossibility and absurdity. That was how
Adela came to make the Automated Orange Tree, which I have already
mentioned, and the famous Calculating Serpent. Both were more hers
than mine.

On three occasions we were interrupted while we were dining by rep-
resentatives of rival theaters looking to hire us away. We would not. We
dined together frequently—I had developed plain and simple tastes out
on the Rim, she craved fine food. On this, as on most matters of politics,
we agreed to disagree. On another occasion while dining we were approached by a representative of the Baxter Trust looking to purchase the
patent for some of our flashes and bangs, but the price he named was an
insult—we agreed on that. Once I saw Mr. Merrial Carson in one of the
bars on Swing Street, and he saw me and tipped his hat and waggled his
extraordinary eyebrows at the two of us in a gesture I did not quite understand. Not once did we see any soldiers of the Line on Swing Street,
and we decided that we had escaped them entirely. We were both very
proud of that.

Together we made four different kinds of transforming or traveling
or vanishing cabinet, and though my vanity makes me want to describe
their mechanisms, we both signed papers to the effect that we would
not, and those promises are still binding, or so I believe, despite Amaryllis's death and Mr. Quantrill's and the razing of the Ormolu itself. We
discussed a great many more ideas which we never had time to bring to
life, and never shared with anyone. We were like a corporation or conspiracy of two, the best in the whole city.

The Beck brothers, Dick and Joshua, both read the preceding pages. Both of those excellent fellows are now grinning like bandits and Dick Beck keeps winking. So let me be clear. With the exception of that first instance after the duel, and one other occasion after the first delirious perfumed performance of the Automated Orange Tree, there was nothing of the romantic sort between the two of us. That came later—too late. While we were together at the Ormolu our communion was on a higher plane. She was the first person I had met in all my life who I thought might—if I could only tell her—understand my dreams & notions &c. That was more than enough. As a matter of fact I spent much of that summer pursuing the affections of an actress at the Dally Theater, who later escaped the Battle of Jasper unharmed—I shall not name her. She was pretty and good-natured and she did not ask difficult questions about who I was and so far as I know never once thought of shooting anybody for any reason. Adela received flowers backstage almost nightly from a young insurance agent, who I regret to say did not—escape Jasper that is. I have nothing against him and I was not jealous and when I warned him what he was getting into it was for his own good. Anyhow I shall not wax romantic. There is too much History and Politics I still have to write about.

The truth is I was sometimes somewhat terrified of Miss Adela Kotan &c &c Iermo. She was brilliant and beautiful and ingenious but I could hardly forget that on our first acquaintance she had been quite determined to shoot me—though she seemed to have forgotten that incident entirely.

Her temper was fiery, her ambition and her curiosity were at least the equal of my own, and in intellect she exceeded me. She could not understand why I was content to idle away my summer working for tricksters and theater-people, who she regarded as a very low form of life. As soon as she was fed and housed she began planning greater things.

She attempted to reconstruct the self-playing piano. She marked out a zone of space backstage like a conjurer drawing his magic circle and she filled it with wires, and paper punched with holes, and strange unmusical sounds. Black and white keys were scattered about its perimeter. At first I was delighted to watch her work, but we both pretty quickly understood that she could not rebuild the piano. The plans were lost and the moment of inspiration was lost. In my experience it is often harder to rebuild than to build for the first time. Anyhow it hurt to watch. I do not know if she still blamed me for the loss of the prototype. She said she did not but sometimes she had a look in her eye that frightened me. I have spent a lot of time in war-torn places and I have seen the look in the eye of mothers who have lost their children, and that is what it reminded me of. It was her soul. I wish I had saved it.

She said it didn't matter. She visited the Yards and took notes on the deplorable working conditions and began to talk about Automation of the processes there. She wanted me to go into business with her. She wanted to approach Mr. Baxter with her ideas. I advised her against it.

"He's a thief," I said. "He will steal your ideas and give you nothing."

She frowned. "I haven't forgotten that *you*—"

"If you want another apology it's yours. Just steer clear of Mr. Baxter and his untrustworthy Trust."

"You always talk as if you know more than you're willing to say, Hal. Here you are working for play-actors for pennies—"

"There are worse fates. Let the stage-lights fall on the Amazing Amaryllis, let Wise Master Lobsang and Mr. Barnabas Bosko struggle with fame. I'll work backstage and be happy. That's hard-won wisdom, Adela—"

"There it is again—you drop hints. You talk as if you know Mr. Baxter personally, you talk about politics and about the Great War as if you played some great part in it, but all you are is—oh, I don't mean it that way, but—"

Of course I did not explain the reasons for my low profile. Nor did I like to lie. I waited for her to depart, then I returned to my work.

I had commandeered a corner of the Ormolu's basement, hidden away behind rows and rows of costumes and painted scenes. In one corner of the ceiling there was a little light from a hole up at street-level, and in another corner there was a trap-door that led to the stage above. Behind my workplace there was a door boarded over that led who-knows-where. Probably like most things beneath Jasper there was some picaresque ancient history of crime or politics behind it, but I did not investigate. There were rats, with whom I was willing to establish friendly relations if only they would meet me halfway.

I started to reassemble the Apparatus down there.

I can't say I had any real plan for what I would do if I could re-create it. As I worked I daydreamed that I might confront Mr. Baxter with it. I wrote letters to him in my head, telling him that my spirit was unbowed.

I imagined showing it to the world, refuting his libel in one bright un-
deniable flash of Light. The truth is that more than anything else I
needed to know if it *could* be re-created. I was not certain.

I stripped wire from junkyards. I liberated springs of all kinds from
conjurers' top-hats and mirror-tricks. I sawed wood. I was able to com-
mission the blowing of glass personally, after Mr. Quantrill showered
us with money on account of what Mr. Elmer Merrial Carson wrote in
the *Jasper City Evening Post* about the wonders of the Automated Orange Tree. I had no choice but to steal the magnets I required, I confess
it, from the electrical generators stored in a warehouse belonging to the
Northern Lighting Corporation. This theft too was written about in the
newspapers, though it was beneath the notice of Mr. Carson. It is hard
to do anything in Jasper City that escapes the attention of the newspapers, I have found.

I brewed up the acids and alkalis I needed in an old porcelain bathtub, which had previously been used as a prop in risqué comedies. This
process caused Mr. Quantrill some anxiety, not least because it produced
odors that could be detected by the more sensitive members of the audience upstairs. Adela was curious. I told her to wait and see. That made
her angry, as I recall—at that time her own work on the self-playing
piano was frustrating her.

I built the frame. I used parts of an old typewriter and I used some
old brass breastplates that had formerly been employed in opera, and
which Mr. Quantrill did not miss.

Lastly I reproduced that red-sun-of-creation sigil that had always
been at the heart of it. It was there in the wires and in the tubes and in
the play of the magnetic fields. The snake eating its own tail, the always-
ascending staircase &c &c. It was warm to the touch. When I passed a
charge across it there was a glow so faint that it was visible only by
night, and then only if you closed one eye and stared. Adela asked again
what it did and I said it did nothing so far. I did not want to tell her what
it was. I kept on working.

You may recall that when I first came to Jasper, I tried to find my sister
Jess. I failed. She had left her last known address, maybe because after
Professor Harry Ransom And His Terrible Secret Weapon got famous it
was hard being his sister. Well, I do not want you to think I am a quitter.
I kept on asking around after her. I came up with this ingenious plan: I
persuaded Mr. Quantrill to authorize me to hire dancing girls and con-

cession girls for the Ormolu Theater, and under cover of that purpose I made inquiries all along Swing Street. I felt like a story-book spy, an Agent-in-training. Rumor had it she had left Swing Street. I followed her trail to a low and sinister hotel in the worst part of Fenimore. I shall not describe that place. From there rumor pointed the way to the Floating World.

The Floating World, if you have never heard of it, was a very famous—I shall be blunt—it was a very famous whorehouse. It stood on the top of the bluffs overlooking Jasper City, and sometimes at night you could see the faint red glow of its lanterns, taunting all the respectable and religious people of the city below. I was told by two or maybe three people that Jess or a woman answering to her description was working there now.

I no longer needed to borrow money from her but I believed I owed her my help, or at least an apology. You may think it would have been better if I had left her alone, but that was how I felt.

What stopped me from venturing up that well-worn trail to the Floating World was that rumor *also* had it that the Floating World was a front for the activities in Jasper of the Agents of the Gun. In fact this supposed secret was so open that hardly anyone in Jasper had not heard it. If I set foot in that place, might they recognize me? Professor Harry Ransom—confidant of Liv and Creedmoor, inventor of the terrible weapon that killed the giant Knoll—I could not take that chance.

Some of the Ormolu's crew were regulars at the Floating World. I asked them about it, but declined invitations to join them.

Adela, overhearing my questions, raised an eyebrow.

"If I asked what your interest in that place is, would you tell me?"

"I guess not."

"You're impossible, Hal. You and your secrets."

"I'd tell all if I could."

"You won't even tell me what you're building down in the cellar."

"Well—maybe not yet."

I did not confide in her. I wanted to—I longed to talk about her theories and mine—but I did not dare. I did confide in the other occupant of the Ormolu's basement, who was a ghost.

This is a difficult subject. On the one hand maybe I have strained your credulity enough already. Ghosts are not uncommon on the Rim but nearly unheard of in crowded old Jasper City, and you may think

I am stretching the truth. On the other I once said a long time back I would try to write the truth and the whole truth. So I will, even if it sounds unlikely. I keep my promises, when I can.

He first showed himself on my seventh night in the basement. It had been a long night and I was still crouched over the Apparatus. It was not working. That was no big surprise. I had no money and the thing was made of junk. I had few waking hours to work on it, I was so busy making toys for the stage. Nevertheless I was in an ill humor. It seemed that I would never recover what I had had out on the Rim, when I was free. It seemed like a very long time ago. I stood and sighed and turned, meaning to bring the lantern closer to its workings.

A black man in a tall white wig and old-fashioned red velvet coat stood behind the lantern, its light turning his skin gold. He was wide-eyed, watching me. I jumped back, cried out, lifted a hammer to defend myself. He shook his head, then vanished. I lowered the hammer and persuaded myself that I had imagined it, perhaps mistaking a row of old coats and props for a visitor.

He came back two nights later, again appearing behind me just as I turned off the Apparatus. That time I seized the hammer and swung at his head. What I learned from that experience is that when you swing a hammer at a ghost it does not, contrary to the way it is in that one famous ghost story Mr. Elmer Merrial Carson wrote, pass as if through mist. Instead the ghost is simply not there, and he never was, but instead he is somewhere else, six feet away, then he is behind you, then he is gone, leaving you dizzy.

The third time he came back I asked him his name. He opened his mouth but no sound came out. Then he sat down on my bench, arranging his coat-tails beneath him, and looked so very sad that I felt sorry for him, and put down my hammer. Shortly afterward he was gone.

He only appeared by night. He often opened his mouth but was never able to speak. It will no doubt have occurred to you to wonder whether he was a real ghost or simply an unexpected effect of the Process, and I do not know exactly what to tell you.

I did not think I had encountered any such presence before. Sometimes when I worked on the Process back in East Conlan I had felt like I was being watched—well, I was being watched, I guess, I had three sisters. But sometimes out on the Western Rim when I'd worked late through the night there had been motion at the corner of my eyes—I'd guessed rabbits, or cats on the prowl. I had never seen a ghost.

I asked the employees of the Ormolu if there were ghosts in their establishment and all of them said that there were, but that's just how theater-people always are and it did not necessarily mean anything. The ghost himself could not answer my questions or explain himself.

He had no visible wounds or cause of death. He was dressed in old-time finery and I imagined he might have been one of the founding generation of Jasper City, a nobleman or nobleman's private secretary back in the ancient days when Jasper had noblemen. If so he had lived in the days before Gun and Line, before the Great War, when our world was still being made and everything was possible. Like I said, he could not answer my questions.

I called him Jasper.

"Jasper," I said, "this device you're looking at is the notorious Ransom Light-Bringing Apparatus. Tell no one."

Jasper nodded.

"You should have seen it in its heyday. That was out on the Western Rim, under the big skies, the big red plains and the jagged wild hills and all that, like in the paintings. It lit up like the sun. You should have seen everyone's faces."

Jasper was sitting on the bench, studying the innards of the Apparatus. I was pacing.

"Do you see anything, Jasper? Anything at all?"

He shook his head.

"It's harder here—here in Jasper. Out on the Rim it all seemed to work so easily. I shall not say there weren't setbacks and frustrations because there were, oh there were, but somehow everything and anything seemed possible out there."

He nodded again, and looked thoughtful.

"I guess maybe you're thinking about days gone by, when the world was new-made, and Jasper City was new too, and you were all building a future where anything could be possible. Assuming you are in fact one of the founding generation of Jasper City and not just a shadow of a shadow of who-knows-what. Assuming you can hear me."

He seemed to look at me.

"If you are from those days maybe you should know that everybody hates the Senate you made. Just yesterday there was a riot on Thirty-second Street."

Sometimes I read to him from the newspapers. The topic was generally struggle and strife. Two more Senators were assassinated over the course of that summer. The Senate itself appeared to be in the painful process of splitting in two. So was the whole Tri-City Territory, for that matter.

It was now generally reported, as Adela had told us, that Gibson City had gone over to the Line. The Tri-City Territory had always understood itself to be neutral in the Great War. Gun and Line meddled in the heart-land, but they did not operate there with the wild open abandon they allowed themselves on the Rim. The fall of Gibson shocked the Territory to its core.

In response to the news Juniper City had cut ties with Gibson and with Jasper both, and announced that henceforth nothing would ever compromise its splendid independence. Juniper had expelled foreign businesses, including those of Mr. Baxter. The Juniper City Greater Council declared that it had acquired a terrible and unprecedented new weapon, capable of destroying the Engines themselves or laying siege to the Lodge of the Guns, and that if their affairs were meddled with they would make use of it. This was generally thought to be a bluff but no-body could be sure. One faction in Jasper City's Senate was for throw-ing in with Juniper City. Another was for preemptive surrender to the Line while it was possible to do so on favorable terms. Some of the news-papers railed against the Senate for failing to provide Jasper with its own secret weapons, some of them speculated that such weapons al-ready existed. Meanwhile Liv and Creedmoor and myself were sighted all over the world. We were said to be raising an army, or rebuilding the Red Valley Republic. We were said to be whispering in the ear of the Juniper City Council or hiding in mountain caves. Pilgrims and drift-ers chased us all over the world. I was by now getting used to thinking about that other Ransom as somebody quite separate from myself, and I could read about him in the newspapers with only the tiniest chill.

I reported the news to Jasper whenever I saw him. It generally made him look sad, then disappear. I wondered if he understood me at all.

"Try signs," I said one late summer night. "Nod for yes, shake for no. Did you die here in this basement? No? In the Ormolu? You don't look like an actor—was the Ormolu once something else, I don't know, like . . . Well, in Jasper? _Are_ you dead? Do you have some purpose here, something to communicate to me about the Process, maybe? Listen—if you shake your head for _everything_ I don't know if you understand me, do you understand?"

He nodded.

"Are you here with word from the world of the dead, maybe? Mr. Carver—do you know him? Does he forgive me? Yes? No? My father, maybe? What about Miss Harper and John Creedmoor—are they in the world of the dead yet? Do the dead have news of them—that's where the action is I guess—did they make it? If what they said is true, if they have a weapon that can kill the Powers, maybe there's a whole lot of Engines and Guns down there now—what's an Engine like out of its shell? Say, *is* there a world of the dead? I've never speculated much on religion."

He shook his head. I do not know what that meant exactly, or if it meant anything at all. Take it for what it's worth.

"The truth is I don't much care about politics and I don't care hardly at all about religion so if you are here to tell me something about the Great War or anything of that kind I don't want to hear it."

I mopped sweat from my brow—he did not. It was hot in the basement. I guess it was not hot wherever he was.

"I don't know," I said. "It's hard to get it to work here. This place is older, harder. Conditions are different from the Rim. Have I told you how I found the sign—the word—I did, didn't I?—well, don't imagine it's easy. Don't imagine that's all there is to it. Bringing that world into this. Opening the door. What was possible then is impossible now. No words for it, even, damn it. What'll I even do with it if I can rebuild it, except get myself hunted down and shot?"

Jasper stood.

"You've seen me build this thing. I guess you can see me, anyhow. If I go to law with Old Man Baxter over it will you be my witness? No? I guess not."

He folded his arms behind his back.

"Well, you must be here to teach me some kind of a lesson. In his *Autobiography* Mr. Baxter—damn him—says that to a man of greatness everything's a lesson. Maybe I should find my way toward a theory of ghosts and spirits like yourself. Maybe—"

Suddenly there was an expression of panic on his face. He was not looking at me, but past me, maybe at the Apparatus, maybe at nothing visible in this world or time. Anyhow he turned right around and as soon as his back was to me he vanished.

I will tell you right now that though I tried and tried I have never understood this phenomenon, or what it is about the Process that causes it, or whether it is good or bad or if there is any way of doing anything with it. It is just one of those things that happens. Maybe in the future there will be time to investigate it.

Adela appeared onstage, two nights running, alongside Mr. Barnabas Busby Bosko and his show of Western Rim wonders. It was not a success. She was too proud and too unbending to perform for a crowd. She had no craving to please. The experiment was not repeated.

She stopped working on the piano. She did not say why and I did not ask. She abandoned her little cell in the Gate and moved into an apartment a half-mile from Swing Street and overnight she became a Jasper City patriot—a true daughter of the Bull, as they used to say. She cursed the foreign influences that meddled in Jasper politics and she spoke urgently of the need to defend the city's honor and independence. I said that politics was a fool's game and that we had work of our own to do. She bit back the word *coward*, but her eyes said it. She went all over town to listen to speeches or shout herself hoarse at Senators or businessmen or the offices of the *Evening Post*. She developed a very thorough accounting of which Senators were brave sons of Jasper and which Senators were weaklings and traitors and pawns of the Line. I do not remember any of the names she spoke of. To this day all Senators or suchlike people are the same to me, like cats or dogs. Anyhow I did not accompany her on these ventures. While she was marching or waving flags I was working, or when I wasn't working I was paying court to that actress I mentioned, who I said I would not name and I will not but she was both statuesque & fair, and blissfully uninterested in politics. I who had once in the by-gone days of my youth ranged all across the Western Rim and slept under different stars each night now lived just about my whole life within the confines of Swing Street. When I left the Street it was an occasion and I dressed up in my go-to-meeting best.

Some days I would go and loiter outside the gates of Mr. Baxter's Tower on Fenimore with my hands in my pockets like an orphan child. I never caught a glimpse of him. Yet he haunted me anyhow. Twice that summer he returned to the pages of the newspapers, repeating his libel against me. He assured the readers of the *Evening Post* and the *Clarion* that detectives hired by the Trust were closing in on the fraud and thief Harry Ransom, who had so disturbed the peace of the simple folk of the Rim. . . . I wrote letters of my own. I wrote what I thought of his lies, you can be sure of that. I did not mail them.

Some days I would go visit the campus of Vansittart University. Vansittart U is gone now like so much else that was good in Jasper City but in its day it was a treasure-house of knowledge. It was a paradise of idleness and luxury and good fortune. I snuck into lectures on electricity, the light-bearing Ether, the history and society and science of the First Folk as revealed by their artifacts, and other topics of great interest. If only I had forever I would recount it all here. Instead I have only two pieces of advice. First, if you ever have cause to visit a University you should watch out for ball-players. Those beautiful green lawns are a menace if you do not understand the nature of the territory. Cross the wrong line and at any moment a football may tumble from the heavens and knock you off your feet and if you survive that then a half-ton of well-educated and well-fed Senators' sons will follow it, and they differ from stamped-ing buffalo only in the way that they apologize afterward. Second, if you have trespassed into a lecture concerning the Etheric Flow by a very proud gowned and mutton-chopped Professor, do not raise your hand to contradict his errors or you will be ejected from paradise, never to return.

The lecture halls of VU were full of empty seats. The teams of the ball-players were always a few men down. Even some of the Professors were absent. Idealistic and vigorous youth, intellectuals—those were the kind of people most likely to set off for parts east or north or who-knew-where chasing after rumors of Liv and Creedmoor—or following stories that the Red Valley Republic was rising again in the west or the south or in Juniper City—or digging up Folk ruins, chasing after wondrous weap-ons of their own, poking their nose into Folk business and if they were unlucky getting run through with spears for their trouble. Some of Jas-per City's gilded youth had joined the militia, ready to defend the Bull's City against all comers.

The armies of the Line moved south from Gibson across the Territory, toward Jasper, seizing small towns and bridges and roads, suppressing unrest. Flights of Heavier-Than-Air Vessels were seen in the skies over the Territory's rolling golden fields. Combustion-Powered Submersible Ves-sels were spotted along the meandering River Jass by night and mistaken for sea-serpents. The front moved forward. Agents of the Gun confronted Ironclads at Melnope—when the news hit the *Evening Post* there were riots in the streets of Fenimore. Mr. Baxter hired private detectives in large numbers to guard his factories and his offices. The Baxter Trust warehouse that I stole the magnets from that I used for the Apparatus was piled high with crates containing weapons, fuel, gas-masks &c. I did not notice that at the time, but I learned it later from a memorandum that crossed my desk, after the Battle.

I waited for my ghostly friend Jasper to reappear. He did not. There were rats down in the basement with me but they were not so conversational as the ghost, and I missed him. By late summer the reconstructed Apparatus had grown to the size of a grand piano or a small church-organ. The bathtub had been incorporated into it and a number of other bits of stage business, including spears, a cartwheel, a mirror, and dinner-plates. It focused all the unstable energy of the Process into a sealed glass jar which I had placed, because it amused me, in the arms of a plaster statue of a half-naked nymph.

Sometimes I thought Jasper had returned to me, but it was only Mr. Quantrill or Amaryllis coming to check on their investment, to demand explanations. Sometimes Adela interrupted me. Once two stagehands came into the basement to perform intimate acts together—well, it's a free city, or it was back in those days. Once I thought I glimpsed a man in a ragged soldier's uniform watching me from a far corner of the basement but it was possibly only an old coat. On another occasion I recall I stood over the Apparatus for more than an hour, scratching my new-grown beard and just thinking about the Process, and then about how things had been out on the Western Rim, and about all my adventures out there and the Harpers and Mr. Carver and everything, and when I finally turned to sit on my bench there was a man already there. I jumped back in surprise and stumbled into the Apparatus, causing it to ring like a bell. The figure that sat on the bench held his head hung low, like he was tired, and a long mane of black hair fell to his knees.

I said, "Mr. Carver?"

The figure raised his head. For a moment I saw the face of a man of the Folk. Then the Apparatus began to hum and throb behind me, and I turned back to it to see that when I stumbled into it I had knocked it on its side and set the cylindrical magnets spinning. Their spinning did not slow, but instead gathered speed, as the energies of the Process accumulated out of nothing and fed upon themselves. The acids in the jars and tubes started to bubble and the wires started to glow. I glanced back to see that the figure, if it was ever there, had vanished. The alarm I had felt at his sudden appearance had now been transformed into alarm at the sudden springing-to-life of the Apparatus, and now its increasing instability.

Well I have already said what it is like when the Process gets unstable, back in the good old town of Kenauk, and if you are curious maybe you can look back there, if any of these scattered pages are reaching anybody. All I'll say here is that the Process is not magnetism but it is kissing cousins with magnetism, like it is with all other energies. The basement was full of old stage-weapons and doorknobs and magic-tricks and forks and I do not know what else was flying at my head, but you can imagine the chaos. There was a great flash of light. I wrestled with levers. From the Theater above I heard the sound of applause and cheering and then screaming.

What had happened was that at the very same moment that the Apparatus had taken it into its head to start running wild, the actors upstairs were performing *The Story of John Creedmoor*. This terrible play had been written in haste in the months after White Rock. It portrayed John Creedmoor as a noble but misunderstood hero who, with the aid of his lover Liv and his side-kick Harry Ransom had quested into the deadliest western wilderness and stolen a wondrous weapon with which to &c &c. The part of John Creedmoor was played by Mr. Barnabas Busby Bosko. Bosko was in the middle of booming out a speech about how *all the Great Powers of the Earth will tremble when I hold this sign before them* when suddenly a fountain of white light burst up through the trap-door that connected the basement to the wings of the stage. The audience was delighted at first by this trick but they quickly turned fearful. As the power built the gentle tug of the magnetism became violent, yanking watches from pockets and snatching eyeglasses from faces and necklaces from throats, roughly, like what in Jasper City they call a "mugger." Mr. Elmer Merrial Carson described all this for the readers of the *Evening Post* as a wonderful though vulgar coup de théâtre. I know for a fact he was not in the audience, though in his newspaper he implied that he was. A minor sin, in my estimation—I know what it is like to be a showman—and anyhow he was kind enough not to mention the screaming, the fainting, the stampede, or how the actor portraying John Creedmoor dropped his gun and said an unprintable word. Riot or worse disaster was narrowly averted when Adela come running down into the basement to investigate, and with her assistance I was able to tame the Process again.

# A VISIT TO THE FLOATING WORLD

That was the end of my summer on Swing Street. Now it is time to write about the rest of my time in Jasper, and how it all ended. The typewriter is very stiff tonight, as if it has not got much traveling left in it, or as if it does not want to tell the rest of the story.

Adela and I sat on the floor of the basement in the aftermath of the incident. We were both of us breathless from exertion and panic and relief. The basement was hot as an oven. The floor was hot and the wall we rested our backs on was hot. The contents of the basement were strewn all around us, swords and pennants and spears and tables and chairs and wooden trees and picture-frames and broken crockery and machinery like there had been a battle or a tornado or I don't know what. The Apparatus was in pieces again. It had suffered some damage during the instability, and further damage during our struggle to stop it. There was a smell of salt and surf and burning. The shadows cast by Adela's candle moved in a way that did not look exactly right.

We were alone. Mr. Quantrill appeared at the stairhead but Adela told him to go away, and her tone brooked no argument—he went away. My ghostly friend Jasper did not join us, and I cannot say why but I knew that after that incident with the Apparatus he was gone from the Ormolu for good.

Adela said, "Don't you dare lie to me."

I gave her my most honest and open expression.

"I don't—well, I mean—well, I guess I won't. No."

"That thing—that thing you've been working on all this time—what is it?"

"It makes light. Heat too, and magnetism, as you can see, and a whole lot of other things. Free and perpetual, in theory, and without limit. In theory."

"Does it work?"

"In theory."

"What is it? How does it—?"

"There isn't a name for it. I discovered it. Any of the Professors at good old VU will tell you it's impossible by all the laws of the world. Impossible not to mention indecent. Well, I made my own laws."

She stood and paced through the wreckage. I saw that her dress had torn in the struggle with the Apparatus. Her hair was unpinned and damp with sweat. She took the candle, leaving me in shadow against the wall. I knew what she was thinking and I was waiting for her to say it.

There were fragments of stone and metal and wood in the wreckage— doorknobs, nails, stage-medals, branches from a painted tree, the brass leaves of the Automated Orange Tree. Some of them moved as Adela kicked them aside. Others still moved on their own account. A few floated a little way above the floor.

Adela turned over a bit of hot brass with the toe of her boot.

"I heard about White Rock," she said.

"I guess just about everybody did, from the World's Walls to the Rim or beyond."

"When the Line held me they asked me about—they *questioned* me about—White Rock. Harry Ransom. The east-country woman with the strange name and the turncoat Agent and about secret weapons and devices and science. I told them, I don't know—I didn't know."

"They were scared," I said. "The future belongs to them, or that's their opinion anyhow, and they don't care for competition."

"They say he's seven feet tall, this Professor Ransom, and he dresses like a sorcerer out of the far far East."

That was how I was portrayed in *The Story of John Creedmoor*, upstairs on the Ormolu's stage. The actor was a fellow of Judduan descent, with a thick and unfortunate accent of Gibson City's docks. Sorcerer's robes were easy to come by, backstage at the Ormolu. The tallness was accomplished with high shoes.

"A lot of things they say aren't so."

"They say," she said, "that at White Rock this Professor Harry Ransom had a weapon like nothing else in the world—something there is no name for."

"It's not a weapon," I said.

She turned a full circle, surveying the wreckage as she went.

"Are you sure?"

I told her the whole truth as I knew it. That is everything I've written here. I told her everything I knew about Miss Harper—Liv Alverhuysen—and about Creedmoor. I told her everything about how the Apparatus worked, and what I had learned from the Folk. I said that I thought maybe they had meant me to see what I saw, that maybe they meant for me to make use of that knowledge. I said that I believed that my Process would one day change the world for the better, and maybe that was what they wanted.

She said maybe, or maybe they wanted me to bring the world to ruin. After all why should they have any love for the world we'd made? I acknowledged that that might be the case, but I said that we all have to do what we think is right, and none of us know how any of it will end.

Mr. Quantrill showed his face again at the stairhead. He was now accompanied by several stagehands and by Mr. Bosko and by the actor who played the part of Professor Harry Ransom. Quantrill was huffing and puffing and threatening to evict me. My double was glaring at me as if he was in actual fact a wizard of the far East, and could give me the evil eye.

I told them all that the Apparatus was an experimental device for generating brightly colored smoke for the stage, and that there had been an accident with some chemicals but no harm done. Adela confirmed my story.

Mr. Quantrill seemed to believe me, or at least he did not ask any more questions. From the look on his face as he surveyed the room I think maybe he could not imagine what questions to ask. His eye fell for a moment on one of the brass leaves of the Automated Orange Tree, which was levitating some three feet above the rest of the wreckage and turning softly as if in a breeze, and he looked away sharply, the way a man might look away from the sun.

He chewed it over for a while and then fell back to the old familiar things he was sure of.

"This is coming out of your wages, Rawlins."

✳ ✳ ✳

Quantrill left. The stagehands left. Lastly my double left, gathering his robes around him.

Adela investigated the floating brass leaf.

"The shadows," she said. "Look."

I did not get up. "Let me guess—it has no shadow?"

"On the contrary. It has too many shadows by far."

"Ah."

"What causes that?"

"Truth is that I do not know."

"Can I touch it?"

"I guess so."

She plucked the leaf from the air, carefully wrapping it in a piece of torn cloth and putting it in her purse.

"At my present wages," I said, "I believe I could work for Mr. Quantrill for a hundred years and not pay him back for the damage."

"To hell with him," Adela said. "What does it matter what he thinks? Or his money?"

"I used to talk that way. Then I learned that a man needs to eat."

"You should give notice. We both should."

"You have another employer in mind?"

She waved that objection away, as if it was nothing.

"Not all of us were born rich. . . ."

She did not take offense at that, she was so distracted by big ideas, and so I knew that she was serious.

"You've got something in mind," I said. "Dally's Theater, or—"

"No. Hal—Harry—this is more than a toy. Look at it! We have to go to the Senate."

I think I have said that Adela had become, over the course of the summer, a true patriot of Jasper City. I guess that it was because her own country was lost to her. She gave me quite a speech, a real honest blood and thunder stump speech, about how the Apparatus could be just what poor beleaguered Jasper City needed to fend off the encroaching forces of the Line. She spoke of driving the Line back, crushing its ambitions, humbling the Engines. She spoke of independence, power, wealth, freedom for Jasper from the great forces of the world. I said that

that was all very well, but firstly the Apparatus was in ruins, and secondly what if I spoke up, what might Mr. Baxter do? What if Mr. Elmer
Merrial Carson's insinuations were accurate, and Mr. Baxter was in
cahoots with the Line?

She observed that if the Line was on my trail, the recent incident of
flashes & bangs & blazing light would most likely have alerted them to
my presence anyhow. She was right, of course. Anyhow we argued for a
while. I was kind of annoyed to be told what to do, as if it was any business of hers, but I was kind of happy too. I had been alone with my secrets for too long. I missed Mr. Carver and I missed Miss Harper and
I even missed John Creedmoor—I began to see why the two of them
traveled together, though surely they did not like each other. I missed
my sisters.

I longed to talk to her about the Process, about words and language
and names and the world. She only wanted to talk about politics and
war. Not for the first time I wondered at what the Line had done to her
to arouse such anger, and I wished I could have known her when she
was young.

Anyhow in the end we came to an agreement. We would leave Jasper
and go to Juniper City, on the other side of the Territory. Juniper had
declared open defiance of the Line. We would offer that city our services,
and the use of the Process. To hell with Mr. Baxter and his libelous accusations. If the Line feared us let it have reason to fear—those were
Adela's words, not mine. I agreed that it would be good to be on the
road again. She kissed both my cheeks. I understand that to be a sign
among the landowning classes of the Deltas that an agreement of great
significance has been reached.

Back in the days when I traveled with Mr. Carver out on the Rim, we
would have left at once, before dawn, without a word or a look back. If
we had done that who knows how things would have turned out! But
I guess I was slowing down in my maturity. First, I said, I had business
to resolve. She asked if I was talking about that fair & statuesque &
blissfully unpolitical actress I have mentioned, except that she described
her less kindly. I said that no, it was a family matter, although I would
not deny that I would miss the fair & statuesque &c.

❋   ❋   ❋

I passed the day after that mending the damage the Apparatus had done
to the Ormolu's basement, until I was exhausted and hungry and filthy
with the sweat of a hard day's work, and all in all I was in no fit state to

do what I did next, which was to dress up as smart as I could in borrowed clothes and swallow my fear and strike out for the Floating World.

To get to the Floating World from Swing Street you had to walk north toward the river. On the Fenimore Bridge I was importuned by flower-sellers, match-sellers, beggars, recruiters, and prophets of the end times. A devotee of the World Serpent informed me that one day very soon that famous reptile would swallow itself up entirely, and us with it, and he illustrated that proposition with a gesture that reminded me uncomfortably of the Ransom Process. I gave him a half-dollar.

The evening was hot and the sky was the color of the deep sea, with ink-blot clouds of black. If you stood on the edge of the bridge and looked north and waited for dark to fall you could see the Floating World. It stood on the cliff's edge atop the bluffs north of Jasper. It was a tall building of many rooms, sprawling like a millionaire's mansion, and at night it was lit by a thousand red lanterns that hung from its eaves or from the trees or from the arches in the rose-gardens. . . . Anyhow as the city below darkened the Floating World lit up and it shone through the trees.

My coat was made for an actor who was bigger and taller than me. I carried a gun beneath it. I do not know why. If the rumors were true, and the Floating World was a haven for the Agents of the Gun, and if they sniffed me out, it would do me no good.

When the city was fully dark and the stars were out and the Floating World was burning red like a coal I set off again.

North of the river the city climbs the foothills. The city thins out as the road gains altitude until there is just one path that winds up among rocks and the trees into the heights. At first that path is dark. Later there are lanterns. It is wide enough for the narrow sort of coaches, and you had better watch your back in case one comes thundering past. Some men walk up alone, like I did, and others go in drunken packs, laughing and joking and slapping each other on the back.

The Floating World is a thing of the past now—a long-gone monster, like the mammoth. That is why I mean to take the trouble to describe it. In those days it stood in the middle of lawns, rose-gardens, white marble statues and other such luxuries. There were men in the garden and arm in arm with or sitting beside them on the benches there were women, most of them in scarlet and black, in all kinds of states of undress. I followed a twisting path, glancing from side to side. I met the cold and indifferent gaze of a woman who stared right through me like I was a ghost, while a silver-haired gentleman slobbered at her throat. Three women curtsied in the elaborate old-fashioned style for the entertainment of a Reverend of the Smiler brethren, whose grin was not of the spiritual kind. And so on and so on.

Now I have traveled all over the Rim in wild and lonely places and I do not claim to be an innocent, but I did not like the Floating World. It was as if I saw my sister's face in the face of every woman there, and I did not like it at all. I have done things I am not proud of to get by and I do not judge what anyone does to make a living, but nonetheless I did not like it.

The path led me to two big doors with glass windows spilling light. Soon as I stepped through them it felt like I was washed away in a swell of music and perfume and alcohol and cigar-smoke and laughter both false and real, but mostly false, and then I was standing by a counter of some lacquered and intaglio'd red wood and a woman with a smile as wide as the World Serpent's must be was wishing me a wonderful evening, and inquiring as to my desires. She had a tattoo of a serpent all up one arm and around her wrist, and she was toying with the corner of a page of a ledger of some kind. My desires were mostly not the sort she could service, being more along the lines of striking one of those gentlemen of Jasper in the face or running away at once or both. I held my hat to my chest and stammered like a hayseed.

"Well, ma'am, I don't know, I don't rightly know, I am new in town, it's all just about more than a body can . . . I mean I don't know, miss. I feel overcome. Back in Hamlin we never had any such . . . or I mean to say . . . Well maybe I should sit down . . . may I?"

I sat heavily on a bench and began to dab at my forehead with a handkerchief. Another guest took my place in the woman's attention.

I sat with my hat in my lap and I watched the crowd.

It was an immense room, with paintings and green plants and fireplaces on every wall and shadowed corners. I shall not say who I saw in it because I do not always know who survived Jasper's fall and who did not, and maybe those who did not survive had wives or children who did. Suffice it to say that many of the great and the good of Jasper attended the Floating World. It was what the sophisticated people of the big cities call an *open secret,* I guess. I did not see Mr. Baxter but I saw men who I believed from what I overheard of their conversation were notable in just about every other business or faith or union in town. That is not to say that I did not also see hayseeds and rubes and prospectors with filthy hands and their hair slicked back attempting to ape what they imagined were the manners of city gentlemen. Desire is a great leveler. I saw no fewer than half a dozen Senators, or I think I did, because like I have said all Senators look much the same to me. Three of them were laughing together over some joke, which the women they'd bought pretended to find funny. A fourth came and joined them and said something and suddenly none of them were laughing.

A very tall and very beautiful red-haired woman walked across the room and the crowd parted for her. She met with a man in a fine white suit and they spoke together for a while, arm in arm. It looked like a very important conversation, and I was sorry I could not hear what they were saying.

Half an hour had passed while I watched. No Agent of the Gun appeared behind me, weapon pressed to my back, all evil grin and twirling mustache and sulfurous breath whispering in my ear *There you are at last Professor Ransom.* . . . I got emboldened. I bought a drink for a young lady.

"I mean no offense," I said to her. "No one could say you're not pretty. But I'm kind of homesick, you see. Where I'm from everyone has a color kind of like mine—it's a little place out West, you won't know it—and I'm looking for a girl of a similar complexion. The heart wants what it wants, you know? Is there—?"

That kind young lady pointed me to another young lady who pointed me to a third, who I approached through the crowds and heat and smoke of the room. It was only when I got close to her that I realized she was not a flesh-and-blood person, but a remarkably lifelike part of a painting on the wall. I am not sure whether I had been pointed toward her as a joke or whether I had got turned around. I stood by the wall for a while and studied the painting. It was a mural, depicting a scene in the garden of an old-world prince's palace, and as a man of the theater I took a professional interest in the tricks of perspective it played.

There was a scream from the other side of that wall. Neither the music nor the laughter stopped for it. Still emboldened, I investigated. I explored along the wall until I found a door, in the midst of a painted grove of ivy and shadows. I breathed deeply, touched the gun beneath my coat for luck, and opened it.

The door opened onto a very long corridor, with many doors on either side. It was lit by two red lanterns at its mid-point and beyond was a hazy red darkness. Out of that darkness a figure came forward.

Well I shall not play games. It was my sister Jess. She was a little thinner than when I last saw her and her hair had been cut short, and I guess all I could say about her outfit was that she has always been her own woman and it is no business of mine to judge. I was so overjoyed to see her that a tear came to my eye.

Speaking of eyes—hers widened. At the same time her mouth drew tight and thin. She made a gesture that when we were young and always sneaking into things meant *get out*. I guess you could figure out what it meant too, if you saw it. It was forceful.

There was that scream again, from behind one of the many doors.

Another figure came up behind my sister. It was that tall and beautiful red-haired woman, for whom all the crowd had parted. It made me dizzy to see her, because only moments before I'd seen her, or I'd thought I'd seen her, back in the room behind me, talking to Senators and Reverends and businessmen. She put a hand on my sister's shoulder. My sister was still miming *go* but now only with her eyes. I did not. I was frozen. It was not until the moment I saw her that I recalled John Creedmoor speaking of his onetime colleague *Scarlet Jen of the Floating World*. I tried to push the thought from my mind. I felt like that woman could read what I was thinking the way Amaryllis pretended to and for all I know she could.

Behind me there was the sound of a gunshot, then cheering and laughter. Somebody stumbled backward into me. I shoved him aside.

I swear I did not see either of them move but the next thing I knew the red-haired woman was on the far side of the big room, directing her guards to seize and question the unlucky gunman, and my sister was gone.

The gunman, as it turned out, was drunk and had pulled out his weapon and shot at the ceiling not out of malice, but by way of celebrating a piece of very good news that had just been whispered to him. Now that good news was leaping from ear to ear all across the room and back again, and although I was more concerned with what the hell had happened to my sister it found its way to me soon enough. Like they said in the newspaper the next day:

### THE BATTLE OF JUNIPER CITY

Events in our one-time peaceful sister city of Juniper are on the march too quickly for your humble correspondent to keep pace. Last I wrote Governor-Elect Voll had declared independence from the Three Cities. Two days ago Governor-Elect Voll declared Juniper's support for the reborn Red Valley Republic, that ill-fated empire of the western territories, that we had all thought long-gone. Reports from the High House are that Voll is now dead, murdered mid-speech by an uncaught assassin. Yesterday the forces of the Line came to Juniper, with Heavier-Than-Air Vessels and Ironclads and marching men. Today those forces have been beaten back, all the way to the banks of the River Ire, where it is said that the Angelus Engine itself was destroyed. How was this impossible feat accomplished? Lieutenant-Governor Bloom denies that the city's armies were assisted by that Adversary of the Line, but also of all Decent People, which I shall not name here. Instead he says that the notorious Doctor Eliza Alferhussen and the one-time Agent John Creedmoor have entrusted their mysterious "weapon" to Juniper. Rumors fly thick and fast. Your own humble correspondent his own self has been pressed into the Second Juniper Irregulars, and writes from a tent on the banks of the Ire.

I guess by the time the news was out and had filled the whole room all the best business-deals were already made, and all that was left was for the yahoos and bumpkins who were last to hear it to celebrate or panic as they saw fit. There was only one gunshot but a whole lot of hooting and hollering and fists slammed on tables and glasses thrown and women treated roughly. I could not see my sister in all the chaos. The red-haired woman was surrounded by several Senators who all wanted her ear, and she seemed to have forgotten about me. The flames in all the room's many fireplaces leapt higher and higher, cracking and snapping and charring the edges of rugs and couches and scarlet dresses and the feathers some of the women wore in their hair, not to mention their hair. I cannot say if the flames were celebrating or panicking or both. I fled, out through the back doors and through the rose-garden and down into the city below.

I ran all the way to Adela's apartment. I was eager to tell her the news about Juniper. I changed my mind a dozen times on the way down, sometimes thinking I would say that we should flee at once, sometimes thinking I could enlist her in a scheme to save my sister—I entertained a number of wild schemes involving disguises, tunnels, rope-ladders, hot-air balloons, and I don't recall what else. I do not know what I had decided or if I had decided anything as I knocked on her door. Anyhow I regret to say that she did not answer.

I started to worry.

I went back to the Ormolu. It was late and dark and even Swing Street was empty. I was afraid with every step that Scarlet Jen of the Floating World would swoop down on me, red dress billowing like wings—well, it had been a long night and I have a fanciful kind of imagination, as I guess you know by now. I held on to my gun under my coat. I entered the Ormolu and fell into bed. I was too tired to undress but could not sleep in my own attic room because of the light of the moon and the bigness of the sky and the occasional sounds of shouting from the street, so I went down into the basement and lay on my back on the warm earth where the Apparatus had been. That was where I was when Mr. Baxter's detectives caught up with me. They had Adela and Mr. Quantrill with them.

## CHAPTER 22

# THE DETECTIVES

"Harry Ransom?"

"Professor Ransom, if that's what you call yourself."

"Is this it? This junk? Is this it? Is it? Answer, damn you. Wake up. On your feet."

"Don't move. Stay on the floor. Don't you *dare* move."

"What? Who are you? Who are you people? All right—I'm not moving—I said I'm *not* moving."

"You bastards—how dare you."

"Listen, Ransom. We know who you are. You've led us all on a hell of a chase and fair play to you. Don't make trouble now."

"I'm not—leave that alone."

"This is the so-called Ransom Apparatus? Well then this is the property of the Northern Lighting Corporation and the Baxter Trust and Mr. Baxter his own self, Mr. Ransom, and as their deputized agent I'll touch it if I please."

"How dare you, you ——."

"That is the property of the Ormolu Theater, sir, and—listen, Hal, what is this, what do these people mean, Ransom?"

"Listen, Mr. Quantrill, I guess you don't have much reason now to trust me, but my advice to you is not to ask questions and to get out of here while you can."

"You stay where you are, Quantrill—is that your name? Quantrill. All right. Stay where you are. And will somebody gag that f___ woman? Hite, Copper, what's the problem, she's hardly five feet tall."

"She bit me, boss. She's real mad."

"Leave her alone."

"What's her name? Who is she? Quantrill—give a name."

"Adela Iermo something Kotan something else, I don't know. That's what she said. I don't know. I don't know what this is all about. Take 'em both."

"Don't tell me my business, Quantrill."

"Have your men pack up everything in this room, Detective Gates. Carefully."

"Right under our noses. Right in Jasper. All this time."

"Hal, is this about what happened the other night—that light—what is it?"

"Shut your mouth, Quantrill."

"I have my rights. I'll sue—your boss doesn't scare me."

"Shut your mouth, Ransom."

"Get up."

"Stay where you are."

"Mmmpphh. Mmmm-mmm. Mrrrgg."

"Harry Ransom, sometimes *Professor* Harry Ransom, my name is Charles Elias Shelby, attorney at law. My *colleagues* here are detectives in the employ of the Baxter Detective Agency. I represent the Northern Lighting *Corporation* and the Baxter *Trust* and Mr. Baxter *personally*."

"I know what you represent, Shelby. Your boss works for the—"

"I'd *advise* you to avoid further slander, Mr. Ransom. Now this here is an *order* of the *high court* of Jasper City, Mr. Ransom, *enjoining* you from further infringements on the property and licenses and good name of Mr. Baxter and the NLC. You may consider this *service of process*."

"Careful of him, Mr. Shelby."

"This is all a lie—the Process is mine, nobody else's, your boss and his bosses may think they own the whole world but they don't."

"Mmph. Mmph."

"The law is the *law*, Mr. Ransom. The voice of authority has spoken and the game is over."

"Careful, Mr. Shelby."

"All of this is *over*, Mr. Ransom. That is the meaning of the word *injunction,* which you will see *here*, and again *here*, on this order. Only a word, all of it only words, but words of *great* power. I think you understand about words, Mr. Ransom. Why, what else is there? Now in this instance the power of this word is the power to set the world back on its proper course, to put an end to these *shenanigans* and japes and nonsense and to say who's who and what's what and who owns what. This is a word that commands you to be *silent*. To be still. We are going to seize your device, Mr. Ransom, and what's more you shall never be permitted to build it again, or *anything* else, no matter where you go. The law is the law the world over, Mr. Ransom. Furthermore—"

"Now, Mr. Shelby, just hand him the paper and don't—"

"Hey—what's that—under his coat?"

"Bastard's got a gun, damn it!"

"Get him."

"Wait—I wasn't—"

"Get it!"

"Ugh. Ow."

"Mmmphh!"

"Got it—got it."

"What were you planning with this? Eh? Ransom? What are you doing in Jasper City anyway?"

"Conspiracy to murder I'd call this, what do you say Mr. Shelby?"

"Why, that may *very well* be, Detective."

"I didn't know. I swear on my mother's grave I didn't know."

"Listen, Quantrill—you shut your mouth and you keep it shut, understand? This man is a thief and a fraud, who stole from Mr. Baxter, and nobody wants it to get out what kind of people work here, do they?"

"No sir. No sir. My lips are sealed. He was never here, as far as I'm concerned."

"You coward, Quantrill—you still owe me money."

"The Injunction commands your silence, Mr. Ransom. Don't make me ask the detectives to *enforce* it."

"That's lawyer-speak for shut your damn mouth, Ransom. Now stand up."

"Please, Detectives, don't damage him. Now. Now listen. My employer wants to talk to you, Mr. Ransom. *Frankly* I have advised him *against* this course of action but he says he likes to look a man in the eye when he deals with him."

"Mr. Baxter wants to talk to me?"

"Who else? Will you come peacefully, Mr. Ransom?"

# MR. ALFRED P. BAXTER

It was the first time in my life I had ever traveled in a motor-car. The windows of this conveyance were made of dark glass. The interior was shadow and murk and seats of a black substance that was unpleasantly soft and uncomfortably hard, both at the same time. I was watched from across the shadows by the faces of Mr. Shelby, attorney at law, and Mr. Gates, officer of the Baxter Detective Agency. Shelby's face was round and pink and moist, like a new-hatched chick, or a tub of ointment. Gates was brown and stubbled and hard. He wore a blue blazer with a military collar, brass studded. I could not make out the meaning of his insignia. I could not make out the operations of the motor-car, either. You will understand that my curiosity was elsewhere. I can report that there was a bad smell and a nauseous vibration, and that the driver operated his horn so often to clear the streets of donkeys and carts and small boys that it was like one long continuous note of alarm, somehow perpetually rising in pitch and volume.

I was removed from the motor-car and led across an expanse of concrete in the shadow of Mr. Baxter's Tower and through a servant's entrance into a long corridor of smooth stone and electric-light that ended in a row of a dozen or maybe more ornate and fabulous brass doors, each of them numbered.

This was also the first occasion on which I rode in an elevator.

Of course it was no surprise that Mr. Baxter's Tower should be so equipped. As everyone well knows, Mr. Alfred Baxter made his first fortune with the elevator, at the age of no more than twenty-five. The ingenious invention had made possible the tall buildings of Jasper and Gibson and Juniper, an explosion of commerce—what he called in his *Autobiography,* "the conquest of the sky."

We took the last elevator. Inside it was made of red leather and polished wood and gold and brass. A hot electric-light hung from the ceiling. Its motion was as smooth and silent as the car's had been herky-jerky.

I guessed that we were in Mr. Baxter's private elevator, because the thing stopped nowhere between the ground and the highest floor of the building. I could not say how many times over the years I had day-dreamed about riding that elevator! But I had never day-dreamed about Mr. Shelby, or Mr. Gates, or Mr. Gates's two ill-favored associates, who stood with their hands on their nightsticks and did not bother to disguise their eagerness to beat me.

Adela had been left behind at the Theater. I was both pleased and sorry that she was not with me. So had Mr. Quantrill. I did not miss him at all.

There was a sensation in my head and feet as we ascended that I cannot describe to anyone who has not had occasion to ride in an elevator.

Mr. Gates lit a cigarette and Mr. Shelby shook his head in disapproval.

The doors opened and Mr. Gates shoved me forward.

✳   ✳   ✳

How shall I describe Mr. Alfred P. Baxter? First I'll say that he existed, and that by itself was something of a surprise, because I had sometimes suspected that he was nothing but a name, with no body attached. It was not much of a body but it was not nothing.

You saw the room first, not the man. It was a wide and high-ceilinged room with curtains on the windows and bookshelves on the walls and a number of writing-desks, on one of which sat a typewriter of unusual size. On another sat what I later discovered was a telegraph-machine. Electric-light spilled from a corner across a floor of gray tiles and long black shadows. Two young men in white shirts stood in another two corners, both fairly quivering with eagerness to be useful. I knew their type and quickly disregarded them. In the last corner of the room a man in a black suit with close-cropped black hair stood beside a leather chair. At first I thought *he* was Mr. Baxter, but of course he was many years too young. Mr. Alfred P. Baxter could not have been less than eighty years old.

The old man himself occupied the leather chair. When he moved I started in surprise, and I felt Detective Gates stiffen.

Mr. Baxter's thin arm reached from beneath a blanket—and not to beckon me forward or acknowledge my presence in any way, but only to pull closer the mouthpiece of a small metal tank, from which he inhaled or imbibed something or other. Then he coughed.

The man in the black suit beside him said, "Ransom's here."

It was unmistakably the accent of an Officer of the Line.

Mr. Baxter's eyebrows twitched.

Gates shoved me forward.

"Ransom," Mr. Baxter said. He was almost too quiet to hear. "Ransom."

"The man who says he built a free-energy process, Mr. Baxter," Shelby explained. "The man who stole from—"

"Yes, yes. I know, I know who he is. Well, let's look at you, then, let's see you, thief."

"I am not a thief."

"Course you are, son, course you are. This thing of yours is mine, I have a piece of paper says so—isn't that right, Shelby? Eh, Watt?"

Shelby murmured obsequious assent. The Linesman nodded, never taking his eyes off me. I took it that he was Watt.

"I will not tell you anything about John Creedmoor," I said, "Or Liv, or anything—I do not know where they are, except for what I read in the newspapers, same as you. I—"

"Too late for that, son. Eh, Watt? Too late. Cat's out of the bag, barn door's open. That's business. Spilt milk. In business you don't cry over it, you hit back harder. You compete. That's what you're here for, son."

"I am a free man, Mr. Baxter, and the Process is mine. I can do what I like where I like. Once upon a time I dreamed of working with you—no more. You may have money but I have truth. I intend to stand on my rights—I will litigate if I must."

Gates laughed. Nobody else laughed until Mr. Baxter laughed, after which everyone in the room except the Linesman followed suit.

Shelby stopped laughing and pretended obsequiously to wipe tears of laughter from his eyes.

"Let us be *clear*, Mr. Ransom," Shelby said. "Who did or did *not* make the Apparatus is beside the point, should this come to a court of law. At the time that you—ah—acquired possession of the device, you were a resident in the town of East—ah—Conlan, were you not? And you were I believe *indebted*, you and your family, to the management of that town, which is to say a debt that was acquired by the NLC, which of course is the property of the Trust; and accordingly, should the matter of *authorship* be contested, you will find that *ownership* of all such works belongs incontestably to the Trust; indeed by absconding from Conlan with the debt un-paid you have inflicted a very present *injury* upon the Trust, which . . ."

Mr. Baxter reached for the mouthpiece again while Shelby talked and he drew in a deep breath from it. His eyes did not leave me.

"That is a lie," I said. That was a feeble answer, I know. What Shelby said was not a lie. It was unfair and absurd but it was not a lie.

Baxter exhaled. "Not a question of truth, son. All a question of power. We have it, you don't. Future is ours and will stay ours. Better that way for everybody."

"We? Ours? Mr. Baxter, I admired you for so long—ever since I was a boy—the elevator—the ammonia-ice machine—the cash-register—all of it—freedom, fortune, fame—well, I always imagined one day I'd come here and you'd see the greatness of the Ransom Process and together we'd—laugh if you must, sir—laugh away—but how could you work for this man—why, when *did* you sell yourself to the Line, Mr. Baxter—?"

Detective Gates hit me in the small of my back, making me gasp and fall silent. I do not blame him. At least he spared me from further embarrassing myself.

I reflected that I did not understand the world at all. My eyes watered. I recalled the time I had caught a glimpse of the world of the Folk that lay behind or beneath or before or on top of this one, and you could not quite see it because you did not have words for it. That was what it was like in Mr. Baxter's room.

The telegraph rattled and the two young men rushed from their respective corners of the room to be first to take down the message. The victor presented his text to the Linesman, who shook his head, not seeing fit to share it with Mr. Baxter. The old man himself inhaled or imbibed or whatever it was he was doing from his pipe, and then when he was done coughing he looked at me and said, "So are you ready to talk business like a man, Professor Ransom?"

## A Portrait of Mr. Baxter

Talking business with Mr. Alfred Baxter was not the great joyful exercise I'd imagined, but it sure was an education. If all the Professors of

Vansittart University could somehow be crowded into that room they would not have taught me as much about the world as Mr. Baxter did—may he rot in hell.

How long had Mr. Baxter worked for the Line? Since long before I was born. As a young man himself he'd taken up arms and fought for the Line at Log-Town and Comstock and at Black-Cap, in the armies of the Archway and the Gloriana and the Harrow Cross Engine in turn. This, he gave me to understand, was by way of promotion, or climbing the ladder closer and closer to the heart of the Line at Harrow Cross. That Engine was oldest and therefore first in their hierarchy. The multitude of ordinary citizens may not distinguish among Engines any more than you can tell one thunder-cloud from another but among themselves there is a strict hierarchy. The Line is nothing without hierarchy.

Another misconception that the multitude have is that the Line has no use for clever or handsome or ambitious men. As a matter of fact the Line can make use of anything. Everything in the world can be turned to advantage. Out on the Rim where things are still unsettled and crude the Line operates big and fierce and brutal—here in the heartland the Line finds it efficient to put on a somewhat kinder and more human face. That was what Mr. Baxter was for. Harrow Cross gave him his start. They gave him his capital and his patents. They greased his path to success. He had never sold himself to the Line because there was nothing to sell. He and the Baxter Trust and the Northern Lighting Corporation and the Baxter Detective Agency and all the rest were the creatures of the Line through and through, no less than the rocket that had come crashing through the roof of the Grand Hotel in Melville all that time ago. He was not ashamed of this, and nor was he proud of it. He spoke of it as if it was a mathematical or logical truth. *A is A* and two plus two is four and power is power. Fortune had nothing to do with it. Grasping the reins of history had nothing to do with it—it was entirely the other way around. As a matter of fact he had never written nor troubled himself to read a word of his own *Autobiography*.

He had very little hair, and what there was was bristly, and his skin was just about yellow. I think he had been a handsome fellow when he was young but he was not anymore. His eyes were sharp but his body was just about used up. I need hardly say however that Mr. Baxter was not your everyday octogenarian. He was stick-thin and he rasped and he was racked by coughing—I believe he may have been mostly deaf—yet he did not shake—he did not fidget or twitch. He made no unnecessary motions. He was steady as an Engine.

✳ ✳ ✳

They gave me no place to sit. I had to bend almost halfway over to hear Mr. Baxter's dry and worn-out voice. Detective Gates and Attorney-at-Law Shelby and the Linesman Watt all watched me closely.

"Those damn—and their weapon—stamped out the Red Valley Republic when I was hardly a boy and now we got to do it all again. Nothing ends. Nothing ever ends! If I had my way I'd burn all the newspapers. Look at you. Look at you. Where are they? Eh? Mr. Watt wants to question you, look at him. And now Juniper—I said I should have run Juniper too, didn't I always say that? Free and independent, what nonsense, they're working for the Adversary, Professor Ransom, I would stake my fortune on it. There is us and them. Yes or no. Right or wrong. Future or past. Us or that bitch at the whorehouse. They have their weapon and we must have ours. This thing you have. This thing you found."

"This thing I invented, Mr. Baxter."

"No you didn't, Ransom. This thing—this thing is nothing natural. Heard what happened at White Rock. Gates here saw the aftermath with his own two. That right Gates?"

Gates nodded. "Hell of a thing, Mr. Baxter, sir."

"Hell of a thing. Hell of a thing! Gates has a way with words. Know what it did, Mr. Ransom? Didn't just kill the Agent. Killed its master too. Never happened before. Left an empty chair in their Lodge. Hell of a thing! Nothing made by the rules of our world."

"All that was an accident, Mr. Baxter. I meant to give them illuminations. That's what it's for."

"No—nothing from our world. That means you found it—something of *theirs*—you went digging. Digging in places best left forgotten. Where was it? Eh? Out on the Rim somewhere I'll bet. Nonsense! Poppycock and nonsense. You know what it is, son? You know what it is? It's a disease. It's madness. Poke around in old dark places and you'll get sick, sure enough. Things we built over for a reason. But we must have it. Right, Watt? They have it so we must too. Must show the world. Future is ours. Even if it must be annihilation."

"Build it if you can Mr. Baxter, it's none of my business."

"Stupid boy. Stupid clever boy. Want you to come work for us."

"How can you expect me to—?"

"I was like you once," Mr. Baxter said, smiling. "Not like Watt here—a military man. Not like Shelby—a university brat. Nor even Mr. Gates, salt of the earth but a simple man. I see something in you—"

He stopped speaking, inhaled again, and when he was done the twinkle in his eye had been turned off, and that was the last and only time he ever troubled himself to flatter me. He should have kept trying—I was susceptible back then to flattery, and I still admired the old man.

"It *hardly* needs to be said," Shelby said, "that the terms of your employment will be generous. Nor I hope does it need to be *repeated* that under the terms of the Injunction you may not work for anyone else; nor may you work on your 'Process' or 'Apparatus' on your own behalf; *furthermore—*"

Shelby named sums of money that meant nothing to me. Nothing about Shelby was admirable to me.

The telegraph rattled again and the Linesman Mr. Watt went to see what new messages had come from his master.

Detective Gates admitted that he and his colleagues had been unable to secure control over the person of my sister Jess, but informed me that my sister Sue and her family remained in New Foley, while May was bringing the word of the Silver City to the Delta Territories, and that both were under close and constant observation.

Mr. Baxter croaked something so quiet that I had to bend very close indeed to hear him. The stink of him made me sick. It was mostly old age and oil and medicine.

❋   ❋   ❋

We talked terms. I can never resist haggling.

They wanted the Process only as a weapon. As a matter of fact talk of free energy made Mr. Baxter's lip curl. What use did they have for free anything? All the wealth in the world was already theirs. But they were desperate for a new and better weapon. Liv and Creedmoor had found something out there, after all. Or somebody had. The Angelus Engine had been destroyed at Juniper. They could not or would not tell me how.

They needed me. The Line had thousands upon thousands of engineers and scientists—it had Heavier-Than-Air Vessels and Submersibles and all manner of wonders—it had the ice-cold minds of the Engines themselves. But it was what it was, and could not be anything else. It could never speak in the language of the Process. I was therefore valuable, and that is why they were willing to bargain with me almost as if we equals.

I said that the Process must bear my name, not Baxter's. They were willing to agree to that term, and so I said that we must light all of Jasper City, and in addition the Northern Lighting Corporation must be dismantled, and furthermore each and every one of the Folk held in the possession of Mr. Baxter or the Baxter Trust or any subsidiaries thereto must be released and restored to their homes and their freedom—and I kept on piling impossibilities upon impossibilities like that for a while. Impossibilities are my stock-in-trade, after all. Mr. Baxter told me I was an unreasonable and unruly child.

I bargained because if I had simply told them all to go to hell, who knows what they would have done to me and to May and Sue and Adela and Amaryllis and Mr. Quantrill and the fair & statuesque actress and who knows who else.

I bargained because I was badly tempted. Despite everything I now knew about Mr. Baxter and Line I was badly tempted, and full of pride to be dealing with him, even if we were not exactly equals. As our negotiation went on I even began to think I might come out ahead. I began to think I might walk out of that office with Baxter's blessing, and the backing of his factories, and enough promises of independence from his masters that maybe I could sleep at night. I began to think that maybe Mr. Baxter might even agree to my terms. I began to think that I might turn Mr. Baxter's power to good, and so make myself great. Mr. Baxter was still human, I thought, he was not an Engine, he had his own dreams and desires, he could be reasoned with.

What Mr. Baxter had whispered in my ear, when Mr. Watt was for a little while distracted by the telegraph, was this.

"With what you found—bigger than the Engines, son, bigger than the Engines themselves. Where do you think they come from anyhow? We made 'em—before we made 'em there were the others. The ones you stole it from. We can be like 'em, son, and never die, never get old—"

Those were his words, or as close as I can recall. I never got to find out what he was planning. I do not know if he was really planning to rebel against his masters, or only dreaming of it. He never committed any such blasphemy to writing in any of his files, as far as I was able to tell.

While we talked Mr. Baxter inhaled again and again from the mouthpiece of his apparatus. Whatever it was that was in it stained his ragged lips reddish-brown and made his breath sickly-sweet. Each time his eyes were a little duller, his voice a little softer. At last his eyes closed and he fell asleep. His head did not move.

"Well," I said.

Mr. Watt looked me in the eye.

I have not described Mr. Watt's appearance because I cannot. There was nothing about his face that stuck in my memory.

"It doesn't matter what the old man says," Watt said. "You know that, right, Ransom? It doesn't matter what he promises."

"But—"

"We let him talk because he likes to talk. You're dealing with the Engines themselves, Ransom. You'll do what you have to do in the end. No promises, no deals. You'll do what you're told and you'll do it on the Engines' terms."

"Get out of here," Gates said. "Go sleep on it, Professor. We know where to find you now."

## CHAPTER 24

# SCARLET JEN

Well I was younger back then and naïve, but not so naïve that I could not figure out that they had let me go only so that they could follow me and see who I talked to. As a matter of fact I did not know where Liv and Creedmoor were and I did not have any contact with Juniper City or whoever it was who was claiming to be the Red Valley Republic reborn and in fact I did not even know if such a thing existed, but I guess Detective Gates did not know that. A Vessel took off from the roof of Mr. Baxter's Tower far overhead as I exited onto the street, and it circled for a while then departed north. I guess whoever was following me was on foot, where I would not notice them. I walked all over the city all afternoon, mostly to confuse and annoy the detectives, but also because I had no place else to go. I could not return to the Ormolu or the basement there or my attic room. I did not want to lead the detectives to Adela, and nor did I want to face her and apologize to her or explain myself.

It was a warm night and I was well-used to sleeping rough. I went to the park and I sat on a bench by the river. That was where Scarlet Jen found me.

She was as beautiful as all the stories say. Her laugh was a temptation all in itself. I shall not write down everything she promised me because there was something about her that made it hard to think straight and I do not remember half of her words, only how I felt.

If Mr. Baxter's detectives were following me, they did not dare intervene—or maybe she'd quietly killed them before she sat down beside me. I do not know. Either's possible. I have seen with my own eyes what the Agents of the Gun are capable of.

She sat beside me on the bench, gathering her dress beneath her with a silken whisper that it confuses me to recall even now.

I said, "No."

She said, "Listen to me, Harry."

I did.

Now, Mr. Baxter had believed, or had said he believed, that whatever extraordinary weapon had been unearthed out there was in the hands of the Gun, and had been used against the Angelus Engine at Juniper. Scarlet Jen told me with a similar urgency in her voice that Creedmoor was a traitor, that his discovery had been sold to or seized by the Line, and that the spirits of the Gun Marmion and Belphegor and three or four other unearthly names I do not recall had been snuffed out like candles and no longer burned in their Lodge. The Line now had its Vessels and its Ironclads and its legions of men and it had the unstoppable weapon of the new century and the doomed cause of the Gun was more doomed than ever before, unless I helped it. She promised me fame, vengeance, freedom, power. She told me that the Line would weigh me down with law and money and Injunctions and duty until there was nothing left of my genius but dust. I wanted to say that one master was much the same as another but it was hard to argue with her or put my thoughts in order. She told me that Mr. Baxter might make promises but the Line would never keep them, it was not in their nature to deal with men as equals, whereas her masters positively loved to barter. I said I was sure that they did but I was afraid of the price. She said that I might think of myself as a mere tinkerer or businessmen, but that was only cowardice speaking—I was born for greater things. She would kill Mr. Baxter for me, she said, she would kill the lawyer Mr. Shelby. I said no. She said that she would give me the strength to kill them myself if that was what I wanted. I said I would rather not. She said that all I had to do was whistle—from now on she would always be watching.

✳ ✳ ✳

When she got up and walked away I breathed for a moment and wiped the sweat from my brow.

I called after her, "Wait. Ma'am—my sister. My sister Jess—she's with you. At your place."

She turned her head and smiled a little, like I had done something to please her, and that gave me courage to speak a little more.

"Now I don't need to know what she's doing these days and I do appreciate that you didn't make any threats to her person—you've got a nicer way about you than the other fellows and I'll tell that to anyone who asks—and I will not say that I'll give you the Process for her because I don't know whether I would or not but if you would just let me talk to her—all I can do now is beg, ma'am."

She kept walking along beside the river until the dark swallowed her up.

A few minutes later my sister came walking up that path.

"Jess—"

I ran to embrace her. She was trembling.

She wore a long and plain black coat. Beneath it I guess was the uniform of the Floating World.

"Long time," I said. "Why, I haven't seen you since the day you rode off side-saddle with that salesman from Gibson—I don't count the time I saw you in that place, we don't have to speak of it—you know I forget the salesman's name—you don't look a day older than you did that day. You don't. I feel about a hundred years older, Jess. Two hundred. Did you get my letters, ever, any of them?"

She stopped trembling and she shoved me away. She was always a strong woman—I stumbled.

"I won't apologize," she said. "I won't apologize for a damn thing, Harry."

"Oh, Jess, I wouldn't ask you to—it's my fault, I know, don't think I haven't figured it out—after I got famous I guess they took you to get to me, or you went to them to hide from Mr. Baxter's men—I understand."

"Oh, you've got it all figured out, have you?"

"Not yet but I will. I'll get myself out from this trap and you too, I'll spring us both, I just need a little time—"

"Who says I need to be *sprung*?"

She gave me a defiant look.

"You should give her what she wants, Harry."

"You don't know what that would mean."

"I know plenty."

"You don't."

"Oh don't I?"

✳  ✳  ✳

I guess this is none of posterity's business, and it gives me no particular pleasure to recall it, and besides we were interrupted in our conversation before too long. I was just starting to reminisce about the good old days back in East Conlan when we used to sneak about together in places where we weren't allowed and always got away with it, and she was just starting to tell me all about the wealth and fame that the proprietor of the Floating World would give us both if only I were less of a fool, and I was recalling how my sister and I loved each other but did not always particularly like each other—well it was not long before we were interrupted by the sound of somebody whistling. I guess it was Scarlet Jen herself. It cut through the night of the city like a noise some beautiful hawk might make out on the emptiness of the Rim. Anyhow my sister turned and heeled like a dog. I hated to see that. She walked off briskly in the direction of the whistle, stopping only once to look back.

I sat with my head in my hands and watched the river go by.

## CHAPTER 25

# The Injunction

Let me tell you about Mr. Baxter's Injunction. The *Injunction,* as Mr. Shelby indicated, is an ingenious kind of legal device or weapon. It is made out of words but backed by force, in the form of policemen or private detectives or sometimes armies. By means of the Injunction a man or a hundred men or a whole Territory at once may be compelled to do something or not to do something or to do nothing at all, by order of the Law. There are towns out on the Rim whose whole existence is mandated and measured out day-by-day by Injunctions backed by the Law of Jasper, or the Northwest Territory, or Harrow Cross. Injunctions have broken Baronies and strangled the Keaton City Labor movement and built fortunes out of nothing. I am not a scholar of the law but so far as I know there is nothing the Injunction cannot accomplish. Under the terms of the Injunction Mr. Baxter had conjured up against me I was forbidden to work on the Process or claim it as mine, and I was forbidden to do about a thousand other things. Mr. Baxter was not kidding about any of it.

I soon learned to pick an undercover employee of the Baxter Detective Agency out of a crowd passably quick, and I could get it right nine times out of ten. They were always there, always watching. I went back to the Ormolu to bang on doors and demand my possessions and my back-pay and to tell Mr. Quantrill what I thought of his disloyalty. Detectives watched me from across the street, and when I emerged they stopped me and searched my possessions. I moved into a room in Hoo Lai and by way of welcome they kicked in the door and confiscated my suitcase.

They menaced the fair & statuesque &c until she thought that some performance of hers had somehow offended a deranged admirer, so she left town for Keaton City and so ended that affair of the heart. Ordinarily I am the one who leaves town and I took it hard.

They harassed Adela. They interfered with her employment. They searched her premises, confiscating a number of her scarce possessions but as luck would have it overlooking the brass leaf from the basement of the Ormolu Theater, which she kept in a drawer wrapped in undergarments to prevent it from floating away. Anyhow I guess they were not satisfied with what they confiscated, because for good measure they brought an Injunction against her too, claiming that the self-playing piano was also stolen from Mr. Baxter. Like Atoms or like the Angels that the Sisters of the Silver City posit, a million Injunctions can occupy the same space. Adela flew into such a rage at this injustice that I was scared of her.

They wouldn't let me seek employment. Nor would they let me leave the city. I walked out along the west road—the detectives followed and brought me back. Nor for some reason that they never troubled themselves to explain or justify would they permit me to me purchase a newspaper, and so it was only through what Adela told me before the litigation and the rage &c that I learned that there was still fighting at Juniper City, and also that several of the fiefdoms of the Deltas had declared themselves in support of Juniper and in support of what everyone was now calling the Red Republic, and that the Second Army of the Archway Engine had been stationed outside Jasper for a week—for the city's own protection, of course. I was not permitted to approach the Senate Building or Vansittart University. For the first time in my life I yearned for the comforts of religion but the detectives stood between me and meeting-circle and I was forbidden to set foot in a Church like I was a Vampire.

I do not want you to think that I did not stand on my rights. I am a free man of the West and I have my pride and I know my rights under the common law, or at least I thought I did. With the last of my money I attempted to hire a lawyer. I was not permitted to do so. The terms of the Injunction forbade me to discuss the terms of the Injunction with anyone, and what's more the thing itself was sealed so that neither I nor anyone else could know its contents. The whole matter was cloaked in secrecy. Anyhow no respectable lawyer in Jasper City would ever cross the Baxter Trust, as one such respectable gentleman was honest enough to inform me, in a whisper, before having me ejected from his office.

My life became a maze of rules that I did not understand. If they could have reached into my head and forbidden me to think or dream they would have done that too. I confess that I began to drink. Drink was permitted to me under the terms of the Injunction, and despair was encouraged. I began to recognize the faces of particular detectives, and because they would never give me their names, even when I confronted them in public places, I began to invent nick-names for them, like *Plug-ears* and *the Pig* and *the Mosquito*. All I had to do was come work for Mr. Baxter, Plug-ears said, and I would be free of them. But that was not true. If I succumbed they would be on my back forever. I daydreamed about revenging myself on them. I am strong and fit but they were numerous and bull-necked and hard and well-armed. All I had to do was to give the sign and Scarlet Jen and her comrades would come swooping down on them. She had promised to help me, and she was not afraid of any Injunction. But that would be even worse.

There was no one to help me and no one would give me a fair deal. I had no choice but to cheat.

## CHAPTER 26

# How I Got to the Top

The day after I was ejected from the law offices of Hines & Wilks I woke before dawn and performed the Ransom Exercises. At that time I was living in a tiny room above a disreputable tavern not far south of the Yards, and within the penumbra of the Yards' stink and smoke. The Injunction did not forbid the practice of physical exercise, although my landlord disapproved. When I felt sound enough in both body and mind I dressed and set off into the streets. My friends Plug-ears and the Pig were watching from across the street. Plug-ears leaned against a fence and smoked a cigarette, while the Pig paced in circles like a penned animal. I wished them both a very good morning and walked briskly up the street. The detectives made no particular effort to conceal themselves as they followed. I led them toward Swing Street and then in a little circle around some streets I do not recall the names of and then as crowds emerged I led them west along the river. We arrived as the sun was rising at the premises of the Jasper City Mail Company, which was by the way the property of Mr. Baxter, I have since learned though I did not know it at the time. Anyhow the Mail Company had a big building on the outskirts of the city with stalwart postmen carved on its pediment, leaning forward into hail and snow and staring down wolves and wild Folk, armed only with sticks and mail-sacks and good old Jasper City grit. In the shadow beneath those carvings a lot of somewhat less square-jawed postmen were hefting sacks back and forth across the yard and loading them onto mail coaches, which one by one rattled out of the yard and onto the road to parts west. As the fourth and last coach of the day moved out I produced a piece of paper from my pocket and waving it in the air I raced after the coach, calling out over the clattering of wheels and hooves, "Hold up, hold up, I'll double your pay if you just hold up."

It is a good thing that I have always kept up my Exercises because mail coaches are faster than they look. The motto of the Jasper City Mail Company that is carved onto their big building is WE STOP FOR NOTHING and it is no joke. As I ran alongside the coach the coachman did not stop, but he did graciously permit me to throw up the letter and a dollar into his cab.

I stood there with my hands on my knees, panting in a cloud of red road-dust, and I watched the coach go. I also watched with great pleasure Plug-ears and the Pig racing past me after the coach and the letter, both of them red in the face and shouting, "Stop! Stop in the name of the law! Stop! That letter contains the property of Mr. Alfred Baxter!" Plug-ears held his hat to his head and looked panicked and the Pig glared at me like he would have liked to stop and beat me dead, and maybe he would have if only he had time.

The coach did not stop. I do not know whether the coachman could hear them or not. All three of them receded into the red dust and distance like the rising sun was swallowing them up—I lost sight of Plug-ears and the Pig first, then the coach.

If and when they ever caught up with the letter they would have found that it said:

> *"A great man seizes the reins of History—he does not let the world move on past him. No problem in business or in life is without a solution to a man of daring and ingenuity." I learned that from you, Mr. Baxter, or whoever wrote your* Autobiography. *I guess a lot of it was lies but not that. By the time you read this we will both know better where we stand.*

I had no time to gloat or enjoy my freedom. It would not last long. I reckoned I had no more than a few hours of privacy at most. Soon Plug-ears and the Pig would give up the chase, or stop somewhere to wire back news of my trick to their employers, and when that happened their colleagues would find me again quick enough.

I ran just about all the way back to Swing Street. It was morning and the street was silent. I ran past Dally's Theater and the Ormolu and the

Nightshade and the Golden Dawn Dancing Society and the Gate and then down a side-street corner to where Adela's apartment's window opened high over an alley that so far as I know never had any name. She'd become a late riser since falling in with theater-people and I was betting she was still at home—but when she did not respond to my shouting and throwing of stones I got impatient pretty quick. By bracing myself against both walls of the alley I was able to climb to her window. I banged on the glass. I caught her half-dressed.

"I'll apologize later," I said.

"What in the world do you want—what's happening?"

"I gave the detectives the slip."

"They're watching me too, Harry—"

"I bet they are. No time to talk. Do you still have the leaf?"

"What are you talking about? I'll get my clothes and—?"

"No time. From the basement—from when the Apparatus blew up—you took I guess you'd call it a souvenir, or maybe you meant to study it—not that that matters now —anyhow it was a little brass leaf, about—?"

She did not wait for me to finish. She unearthed the brass leaf from her drawer and threw it to me—it twisted in the air and cast a multiplicity of shadows all over the walls—and just as I caught it somebody started banging on her door. I let go of her windowsill and let myself slide down the walls into the alley, where trash saved me from injury.

I ran back into town and across the bridge into Fenimore, where I had a vague notion that the offices of the *Jasper City Evening Post* might be found. Well, that may be, but not by the likes of your humble correspondent, no matter how long I searched or who I stopped to ask. Did I despair? Truth is I did, but not for long. Ingenuity, I said to myself, and resourcefulness, and never-say-die. That was how we did things out on the Rim, before I got softened by city living. That was what Mr. Carver would do, and Liv and John Creedmoor. I muttered a whole lot of such things to myself as I walked through the streets and the truth is those words did me a power of good. I realized that I did not need the offices of the *Evening Post,* but only Mr. Elmer Merrial Carson himself.

I found him in his usual haunt, Strick's Tavern down by the river, where we had spoken back on my first day in Jasper. I was not dressed anywhere close to right for that fashionable establishment and to gain entrance I had to first trick and then plead and then when both of those failed shove my way past the doorman. He threatened to call the police.

I told him that the police were the last thing I feared. He pulled himself up off the floor and pursued me into the dining-room and laid hands on me as I got to Mr. Carson's usual table, where the famous journalist was taking lunch with someone who had the look of a Senator. Up went Mr. Carson's eyebrows. The doorman tried to twist my arm but I was not in any mood to be trifled with and I showed him how things were handled out on the Rim.

"Hello, Mr. Carson," I said. "I don't know what story this fellow's got to tell you but I know it's got nothing on mine. Get rid of him and call off this doorman and I'll make it worth your while."

The silver-haired Senator-looking fellow snatched up his napkin like it was a weapon and stood to protest my insolence. I will not record what he said because I did not listen to it. Instead I sat down across from Mr. Carson and fixed him with my frankest and most persuasive expression.

He did not move.

"I remember you—Rollins, right? Or was it Rawley? You said you went down with the *Damaris*—you said you'd invented a what was it now?"

"Rawlins," I said. "That was the name I gave. It was a lie. I hope you'll forgive the necessity. At the time I was in hiding and in fear for my life but now my enemies have found me out anyhow so the way I figure it I have nothing to lose. Truth is I'm Harry Ransom, as in Professor Harry Ransom, inventor of the Ransom Process, perpetrator of the White Rock Miracle, confidant of John Creedmoor and the good doctor Alverhuysen, et cetera and et cetera."

He raised an eyebrow, and said nothing.

"That's the truth," I said.

"Last I heard you worked for the theater—I think I recall you saying that. You know—you're not the first fellow I've met who claims that name. You'd be surprised how many foolish young men are desperate for that dubious notoriety, and how many of them find their way to me."

"Nothing surprises me anymore."

"These are difficult times, Mr. Whoever-you-are, and people in this city are desperate—if I publish your story and you turn out to be just another madman, I'll be a laughingstock—that's if I'm lucky—there are people in this city in a shooting mood."

"I can prove it."

"You can? Well for the love of all that's holy don't blow up this restaurant, Professor Ransom, it's precious to me."

"Don't worry about that. I lost the Apparatus."

"Did you now! Ain't that a surprise."

"Stick with me for an hour or two, Mr. Carson, while I tell you my story—and I'll bet you the thirty-two dollars that is all I have in the world that before I'm done we'll be interrupted by Mr. Baxter's detectives—I guess I should warn you that I'm violating Baxter's Injunction just talking to you. They sure as hell think I am who I say I am and they are not people who play games."

"Lunch with a madman and assault by detectives! I've rarely had such a tempting offer."

"You want proof? Well . . ."

I took the brass leaf out of my pocket and held it in front of his face. When I let go of it it hung there, turning slowly.

Mr. Carson did not take his eyes off it for more than a minute, but after a little while he reached out with his finger and thumb to snuff the table's candle, thereby reducing the number of shadows the leaf cast hardly at all.

The Senator, who had returned with waiters, I guess to have me removed, stood by the table and watched the leaf levitate.

"You could have found this," Mr. Carson said. "You could have scavenged it from White Rock."

"Well, take it or leave it, Mr. Carson, we're all busy men here."*

❊  ❊  ❊

And that is how I got famous.

Mr. Carson caused the story to be rushed into print while Mr. Baxter's lawyers and detectives argued with the lawyers and muscular ink-stained apprentices of the *Jasper City Evening Post*. The more they blustered and threatened and slandered me the more they convinced Mr. Carson of my good faith. Suits and counter-suits flew until my head was spinning, and the next day the *Post*'s presses were seized but it was too late—the story was out. It was mostly my own words and mostly true. I told Mr. Carson everything I knew to be true about Liv and Creedmoor, and I told him a few things besides. I said that they had found an ancient and buried weapon of the Folk, and that I myself had seen it. I

---

*I seem to recall I had a great deal more to say about all this, and that Mr. Ransom gave me a great many more promises and assurances in return for my aid. But just as Mr. Ransom observed, we were both busy men. I expect he forgot.

The brass leaf was as he describes it, though I cannot vouch for its provenance. —EMC told him that the Ransom Process itself was a marriage of the latest modern science and the Folk's science. I told him that Liv and Creedmoor had gone West to defend Juniper from the Line, while I had come to bring Jasper free energy—light and warmth in winter for every man, woman and child—and above all an unbeatable super-weapon against which no aggressor could stand. If only, I said, I could be free of these legal struggles with Mr. Baxter. . . .

I promised the Apparatus free of charge to Jasper City. I thought if I could make Jasper love me it might buy me some insurance against assassination or kidnapping by Baxter's goons or the Floating World, and I guess it worked at least for a while, because I am still here. As it happened the silver-haired Senator with whom Mr. Carson had been taking lunch was up for re-election, and he was so taken with my whole speech about the defense & prosperity of Jasper City that he thought it a good deal to be photographed with his arm about my shoulder, smiling and thumbs-up as if he had invented me himself. That was the picture everyone in Jasper saw the next day.

That afternoon a mob attacked the Ormolu Theater, under the misapprehension that I still resided there. Most of them I think were looking for my autograph or for me to promise them that I would save Jasper from the War or cut them in for a percentage of the profits. Some of them wanted me to cure their cancer—within hours of the *Evening Post*'s story the rumor had developed that the Process cured cancer. I do not think I am to blame for that. A couple of fellows wanted to make themselves famous by shooting me, and there was some unpleasantness in the course of which Mr. Quantrill got hurt. He sued me and Mr. Carson and the *Evening Post*. As for me—I was not there. The first I heard about any of this was when Adela tracked me down and slapped me in the face.

"How could you," she said. "Why didn't you tell me you were going to—what about our plans? We were going to go to Juniper. We were going to slip away. I was going to slip away. They'll destroy you now, Harry, they'll have to."

"They were going to do that anyway. Anyhow I've survived worse. First time we met you yourself tried to shoot me, as I recall—"

"They'll destroy us all."

"Things will work out. See, things are finely balanced right now—there's a strange mood abroad. Everyone who's traveled this last year knows it. I know it and I know you know it and I know Mr. Baxter knows it and I know the minds behind him have compiled statistical observations on it—and who knows what gets overheard in pillow-talk beneath the roof of the Floating World but I bet *she* knows it and her masters know it too—it's whispered in their Lodge. They're scared to name it but I'm not—it's change, it's uncertainty, it's the new century to come—I'm speechmaking but I can't help it, Adela—what I mean is that the city is on the brink of revolt. So is the whole damn territory. Either side might lose its grip, or both. All eyes are on me. If I disappear now the whole thing could explode. They won't dare. Don't look so skeptical—I can keep this under control."

I do not recall where I was when Adela found me. Those days were a whirlwind. At first Mr. Carson put me up in one of his properties on the bluffs but then he was arrested, and even after he was released without charges it did not seem proper to return. I was summoned before the Senate to justify my claims and I reckon I made a decent showing of it, because at least half of those gentlemen applauded me and came up afterward to shake my hand, and no more than half of them jeered me or denounced me as an unscrupulous opportunist. I was invited to the opera, where I was prevailed upon to get up onstage and take a bow. A senior executive of Mr. Baxter's Trust was there with his wife—they walked out. After the show was over Plug-ears and the Pig tried to lay hands on me and were swept away by a well-dressed but angry mob and I never saw their unlovely faces again. Two Senators competed to offer me lodgings. I was invited to the Jasper City Museum to donate the floating brass leaf to their collection. I was invited three times to Vansittart University to speak. On the first occasion I spoke to a flag-strewn lecture-hall full of natural scientists on the subject of free energy. On the second occasion I spoke to the VU Union regarding the political situation on the Western Rim, and on the third occasion I spoke to the Chatterton Debating Club on how it was up to young people like ourselves to build the New Century, and on the fourth occasion I was ambushed and presented before a roomful of solemnly nodding doctors as a classic example of *xenomanic paranoia*—that is the word Jasper City's doctors use for those unfortunate souls who are driven mad by an unhealthy obsession with the secrets of the Folk, and the syndrome is said to be caused by guilt or by suppression of the sexual urge. I did not know this either until a doctor in a black gown pointed at me with a stick and said it.

I returned to the Ormolu in triumph, this time onstage, under the lights—two nights only, and you may be sure that I drove a hard bargain with Mr. Quantrill, who I had not yet forgiven for his lack of loyalty. The crowd squeezed into the Theater until I thought it might burst. I showed them the automated orange tree and all the rest and I told tales about the Western Rim and the Miracle at White Rock and about Liv and Creedmoor and I guess I made some big promises I could not keep. Amaryllis joined me on stage—Adela would not. Big Charley Browder re-enacted the role of the giant Knoll—a gentler man you could never hope to meet—I do not know how he fared in the Battle of Jasper but he was big and gentle so I guess not so well. My friend Mr. Carson described my performance as "eccentric." Anyhow two nights of tale-telling in Jasper City made me twice as much money as I had made altogether in my life so far.

I was recognized in stores by sales clerks. Cabs stopped for me in the street. I received more letters than I could count—threats, pleas, propositions, challenges, invitations to speak or play cards or go into business—I read through heaps of the damn things looking for word from my sisters that never came. I was questioned in the Senate by a row of silver-haired gentlemen in green leather chairs, all alike, both the chairs and the gentlemen, at least to my eye, about the War and about the Process and about my dispute with Mr. Baxter. I denounced Mr. Baxter as a liar and a fraud, and then since I was there I took the opportunity to lecture the Senate on my philosophy of Life and Business and the Future. I shall not deny that fame had its pleasures. That night I was forced to attend a ball thrown by some Senator's wife and only Adela's assistance saved me from humiliation—I never could dance.

I sat for photographs. If you have seen a photograph of me it most likely dates from that summer. There are two photographs in which I sat between flags, there are several with Senators, there is a photograph in which I am standing beside a pile of junk which was assembled to pass for the Apparatus. There is one in which I am standing on the Ormolu's black stage in a white suit, arms outflung and smiling so care-free you could almost imagine it was the good old days and Mr. Carver was by my side. There is another in which Adela stands stiffly at my side, and the expression that appears on her face seems in hindsight to be a warning of what would happen. I don't know. I have never trusted photographs. Light was meant to move.

✳   ✳   ✳

What happens when you are famous and much-loved in Jasper City in summer is that the city suddenly becomes full of beautiful women, to a degree of disproportion that defies the laws of chance. It was as if some statistical demon like that hypothesized by Professor Fenglin of VU—I told you I was a learned man!—as if such a demon had set itself squatting at the gates of the city to throw out ordinary women and yank in the beautiful. Well anyhow I could not go any place in the city without being approached by one or more beautiful women with insincere smiles. I am only human and I will confess that I was often tempted, even after one such beauty who'd got me on my own laughed and leaned in close and whispered, *"Jen wants you to know, Ransom, we're still watching. We'll have you in the end."* That ruined the romantic mood—truth is I ran away, leaving her laughing on a barstool.

Meanwhile Mr. Baxter had gone silent. The stock of the Northern Lighting Corporation fell to next to nothing. Baxter's detectives no longer followed me—in fact they were nowhere to be seen. The *Tribune* reported that a man in uniform who resembled Plug-Ears was found dead in the river down by the Yards—I can only speculate as to how he came to that end. I was quoted in the newspapers as to how Old Man Baxter could not hold back the future forever. His lawyers would not comment on our dispute. I thought I had humiliated him, scared him into retreat. I got so confident and proud that I sat down and I wrote a letter to the proprietor of the Floating World, demanding the release of my sister—and I mailed it too. I received no response.

News of my doings and speculation as to when I would deliver on my promises drove the War off the front pages of the newspapers, so that Jasper hardly remarked upon the siege of Juniper, or the fighting down in the Deltas against the so-called Republican Baronies, or the birth of the Gibson Engine. The *Tribune* started to describe my Apparatus as a *bomb,* the word *Apparatus* being too many-lettered for their readers, and though this was both inaccurate & offensive to *me* it became popular, so that people sometimes shouted at me "Jasper's got the Bomb! Jasper's got the Bomb! Give 'em hell, Ransom!" The fair & statuesque &c actress returned to the city and went to the *Clarion* to inform the public that she had always loved me, and had always known of my secret. Shortly thereafter she left the city once again and once again I can only speculate as to the reasons why. Truth is fame had gone to my head and I had kind of forgotten about her.

The Agent of the Gun Gentleman Jim Dark sent this letter to be published by the *Evening Post*—

DEAR SIR *I read with great entertainment all about how your friend Mr. Harry Ransom says he did for my comrade in arms Mr. Knoll at a place called White Rock. Now the world knows that I am a sporting man and I want it to be known that in my opinion White Rock was a fair fight and there are no hard feelings on MY account. Mr. Ransom has no need to fear revenge from this quarter! But if we fancy a fair fight of our own against Mr. Ransom and his Apparatus then I do believe he is a sporting man too and as a sporting man he will not begrudge us that. As a matter of fact I do not see how I can well offer anything fairer.*

I was showered with money from benefactors and investors and patriots and small boys who mailed me pennies wrapped in touching notes. I could have rebuilt the Apparatus a hundred times over, I could have gone into mass-production, I could have lit up all of Jasper City, except that I could not think straight or find time to work. I was always on the move. I was always waiting for Baxter's next move, or the Agents'. The chant of *bomb—bomb—bomb* was in my ears and I could not sleep right.

The *Tribune* was the first of the newspapers to question whether I was ever going to deliver the bomb. "The War presses ever closer. The clock stands at midnight and Jasper stands alone." After that the mood of the public turned and for a bad week or two not all of the things that were shouted on me in the street were friendly. A woman who was later discovered to be a refugee from the Rim and a widow chained herself in protest at my dallying to the railings of what I guess she thought was my workshop but were in fact the premises of the Ransome-with-an-*E* Textile Co.—no relation. My investors demanded explanations from me. Mr. Carson wrote a story for the *Evening Post* all about the '91 Dash and how throughout the history of the West well-meaning people have looked to mountebanks and charlatans for salvation while the forces of wickedness get on with their business. His portrait of me fairly dripped venom. I have forgiven him now.

I do not know if Mr. Baxter's people had a hand in this change in the public's mood—I suspect so. Worse, Adela and I had a falling-out.

It was late summer. We were standing on the Rondel Bridge in a light afternoon rain. Adela had an umbrella and I did not. I used to say that after the sinking of the *Damaris* I had got as wet as I was going to in one lifetime and a little rain could not touch me. We looked down the river toward the place where she and I had nearly dueled—where we saw the submarine. The river was slate-gray and lonely—there was no traffic anymore from Juniper or Gibson City. She asked me what I thought I was doing and what I was going to do next. I said that I did not want to be a bomb-maker. She said that I had left myself with little choice. I said that I did not know about that, but I was sure I would think of something, and she said that I was not a boy anymore and it was not a game. I took that badly and I told her that I believed she was just jealous of my sudden fame. She flushed and bit back whatever words came to her and turned and walked away. All I could see was the umbrella, joining a crowd of its fellows. I did not call after her to apologize. That is all I am willing to record of that conversation.

I guess fame had made me prideful and boorish. That does not take very long, as it turns out—it is as quick as a pot boiling over or the Process suddenly imbalancing and running wild. Anyhow I did not see her again for a while.

❄   ❄   ❄

I continued to receive correspondence, and if the proportion of flattery was waning and the proportion of threats and condemnation was on the increase, well, it might always shift again tomorrow. I do not know how the letters all found me, wherever I was. There were letters pleading with me, there were letters accusing me of fraud, there were letters from people who said they remembered me from White Rock or the Rim. I received a letter from my sister May, at long last. It said that she had been removed from her religious community in the northern Territory and was being held in the custody of the Line at Archway Station, but that although the Linesmen were not religious and their machines were a form of blasphemy, she was not treated cruelly, and she prayed that I had not gotten myself and her into trouble that I could not get out of, because she could not help me and she did not think God was inclined to. The next day I received a letter from Mr. Baxter—it was the only letter he ever wrote to me, and it said nothing but

*Ransom. Are you ready to talk?*

I got letters in bulk from my fellow inventors. It turned out that I was by no means the only entrepreneur or independent thinker whose work the Baxter Trust had attempted to steal—there were dozens of us. I got letters from the inventors of pedal-powered flying machines, miracle cures, moving images &c—all of them laboring under Mr. Baxter's lawsuits, forbidden to pursue their true calling, forbidden to call their work their own—most of them deeply mired in litigation in Jasper City's courts, some of them in the ninth or tenth year of their hopeless struggle. Mr. Angel Langhorne was from the Deltas and had invented a process for making rain, and a whole new mathematics for the description of clouds, and he wrote in a jagged hand that suggested that he had just recently been struck by lightning from one of his own Cloud-Seeding Rods. Mr. Bekman was a Jasper City native and had invented a form of risk-free financial insurance. Miss Fleming had invented the perfect pendulum. Mr. Lung had invented a new kind of soap. Mr. Catchet had invented a new kind of machine-gun, as if there weren't enough of those in the world already, but the muse cannot be denied. Miss Hazel Worth had invented a kind of asparagus that could grow in the most barren unmade lands of the Rim, boosting yields by an estimated factor of I-forget-what. Some of these people were in Jasper City—others were writing to me from the sticks. All of them were being crushed by Mr. Baxter's greedy hand—I guess it is not the worst thing the Line does by a long shot but it did not sit right with me. Anyhow they heard of my fame and of how I was for a while the toast of the town and how for a while even Mr. Baxter seemed scared of me, and I guess they looked on me as a kind of leader. They looked to me for inspiration. I did not want to disappoint. I wrote back—I wrote them all great long letters full of advice about sticking to your guns and never giving up and grit and drive and how the future belonged to the free-thinkers and the dreamers. In fact I did little else but write those letters for about a week. I wish I had one of them now because they were good words and I may never wax so eloquent again. It was while I was writing to Mr. Angel Langhorne that I first came up with the notion that all of us free-thinkers and dreamers together could quit the Territory and leave behind Mr. Baxter and his money and his Injunctions and leave behind all the armies of the world and strike out for the West and build Ransom City.

Adela found me again. I did not answer my door when she first knocked, because I was busy writing to Mr. Lung about Ransom City, and because most people who knocked on my door in those days were not people I much wanted to see. The last time I opened my door a woman spat in my face. The day before Adela knocked on my door a smiling gentleman had passed me in the street and tipped his hat to me and I was very much afraid that it had been Gentleman Jim Dark.

She knocked again, so loudly and fiercely that I thought maybe it was the detectives, my old friends the Pig and the Mosquito—poor old Plug-Ears having passed on to the next world, in which I hope he will be a better sort of person. You would not think such a small woman could make such a racket.

I sealed my letter to Lung and put it in my pocket and considered departing through the window.

She called out my name. I ran to unlock the door.

"Adela," I said, "you look—well—I don't know, my manners have deserted me, it's the big city I blame for it—I don't know how to say it right."

Truth is she looked tired.

"Anyhow listen, Adela, listen to this, I want to tell you about Ransom City."

"Harry—"

"A change of plans. Forget Juniper. Forget fighting. No more fighting. A new place—out on the edge. We'll go together, you and me. Like back in the good old days with me and Carver."

"Harry, listen."

"Just let me read this letter to you. It's to Mr. Lung. Let me tell you about Lung, he's got ideas about public sanitation—"

"Who cares about Mr. Lung? Who's Mr. Lung? Harry, you have to help me—"

"I have a plan. I've got it all worked out. It's good you came, so you can hear it—I'm going to see Mr. Baxter again. Maybe tomorrow."

"You're going to make a deal with him?"

"I'm going to make him an offer. I've given them something to think about I reckon—the old man hasn't been spoken about in the newspapers like that in sixty years I bet and his masters cannot be pleased with him. Do you know what my father once said to me—he said, 'Harry, you're more trouble than you're worth.' I believe Mr. Baxter knows that now."

"His men came to visit me last night again, Harry."

"What they want is the Process. They must know they can't have it by now, and the harder they try the more trouble I'll make, until the whole city's one big riot—now see what they really want is to be sure that the other side doesn't get it. So my offer is that Baxter gives me my apology and we square our accounts and I leave town—leave the Territory—head out West to the Rim and beyond the Rim—an undisclosed location—me and a few brave souls who want to build a new place. Lung's in, and Langhorne's in, so we shall not want for rain or soap."

She walked over to the bed and sat down on it. Adela weighed next to nothing but the thing was old and sagged anyhow, with a noise like a badly tuned organ.

"My father's in debt," she said.

"Isn't he a rich man—a baron or something, I can never remember how things work down there—"

"Richer men have bigger debts, Harry. Not all of that debt but a whole lot of it is held by one of Mr. Baxter's companies now, and his men let me know last night that he may just call it in. I don't think they were lying. They showed me the papers."

I sat down beside her, making the bed lurch like a ship at sea.

"I said I'd talk to Baxter—I said I'd come work for him, if that's what they want. I said I'll make whatever they want, and they can call it his. They said he doesn't have time to talk to me. They want you—they want your bomb."

"It's not a bomb."

"They'll talk to you."

"I guess they will."

I thought for a while.

"I don't know that I care much for your father from what you said about him, but I can plead his case too when I go see Mr. Baxter."

"I'm coming with you."

"You don't know what that place is like. It's full of their machines—it feels like the Engines themselves are watching you."

"I'm coming with you and that's that, Harry."

✳ ✳ ✳

The next day we went together to Fenimore Island and Baxter's Tower.

I wore my finest white suit. Adela wore a long black dress with dull sequins and frilled sleeves, that looked like she had taken it from the Ormolu's ridiculous wardrobes. She was silent and grim.

It was hot and it rained. It had been raining for a few days. The sky was the color of a Vessel's smoke-trail, with flashes of silver light behind. That is what Jasper City is like at the end of summer. The upper reaches of Baxter's Tower were clouded and gray. You could make out what I guessed were two or three Heavier-Than-Air Vessels roosting on the distant roof, and there were bars on the window and more guards than ever at the gate—the whole thing had a kind of militarized quality. Whitewater rivers formed between cracks in the streets and trash rode the rapids. There were few people about. When I stood up on the steps across the street from Baxter's Tower I did not get the kind of crowd I would have hoped for, for what might be my last speech. Anyhow I said, "You know who I am—I guess you're wondering why I'm here."

A little group of office-workers watched me. Their umbrellas made them look like glistening black mushrooms.

Adela stood beside me, and urged me in a whisper to keep quiet and say nothing foolish.

"If you don't recognize me from the newspapers, my name is Harry Ransom, inventor of the Ransom Light-Bringing Process, et cetera et cetera. I've told you I will give my Process to Jasper City and that is not a lie."

Somebody shouted, "The bomb!" I did not like that but I kept talking.

"Now you'll have heard that Mr. Baxter and I have our disagreements. That is no lie either. There are questions about ownership and money and patents—you know how they say it's better not to learn how sausage is made—well, it's better not to know how the future is made, either. Suffice it to say that Mr. Baxter and I may be about to come to an agreement."

A few more umbrellas converged through the rain and joined my audience.

The guards at Baxter's gate wore caps and raincoats. They watched me with interest. I shouted so that they could hear me over the rain.

"Mr. Baxter is a reasonable man—I don't care what you've heard about him. He is not a tyrant. You may have heard some people allege that Mr. Baxter is just a front-man for the forces of the Line, a traitor to the city that has made him great all these years, that he wants the Process for his masters—well, maybe—who knows?—not me. I have no evidence to prove that. He is a free and independent business-man—his *Autobiography* says so and why would he lie? All we want is the best interest of the city and the future. That is why we are meeting today. If Mr. Baxter were in league with the enemies of this city, would he let me, the inventor of the Ransom—ah, Bomb—would he let me just come and go? Of course not. Anyhow I expect to return to you in one hour with news—you can wait for me—you can tell the newspapers if you like—one hour!"

I jumped down from the stairs and walked up to the gate, smiling at the guards.

"Well then," I said. "It's me. I know he'll talk to me. And she's coming too. Take us to him."

Scowling, one of the guards reached out for my arm and I stepped back—and in the same instant a shot rang out behind me and a ragged hole appeared in the bronze-like metal of the gate, right where my head had been. I turned to look at the street behind but I could not tell who had fired—every single man and woman in the crowd looked just about equally sinister at that moment. The gate-guards ran to surround me and Adela while I was still reeling and numb and they took us inside in much the same way ants might carry a leaf.

＊　＊　＊

The elevator took a very long time to reach the upper floors. The machinery ticked like a clock, creaked like an old house in a storm. I have taken riverboat-rides that did not seem to last so long. There were two private detectives in there with us, one at Adela's side and one at mine, so we were not free to speak. She looked afraid and unsure. I tried to buck up her spirits, through signals of my eyebrows and fingers and significant glances. The detectives were well trained and discreet and they said nothing. Adela stared ahead. After a while she took my hand and squeezed it, maybe for comfort and maybe just to shut me up. I recall that her hand felt cold.

＊　＊　＊

The detectives searched us twice, at the beginning and the end of the elevator-ride. I blustered and cracked jokes to show I was not intimidated.

＊　＊　＊

Mr. Baxter's room was the same as it was before, except for the addition of a second telegraph device and a few more assistants. The curtains were drawn. Cold electric-light came from white tubes that hung from brackets from the ceiling—that was different too. The lawyer Mr. Shelby was present, looking disheveled, his hair all gray and wild, like a man who has been woken in the middle of the night or a Vampire who has been woken in the middle of the day. The representative of the Line Mr. Watt was not present. The detective Mr. Gates appeared behind us without warning, closing the door. He was a consummate professional.

＊　＊　＊

Baxter did not rise from his chair. He looked even smaller than last time, and I was not sure that under his blanket he had any legs at all. He cleared his throat for a while before he could speak.

"Ransom," he said. "And who's this?"

"Listen Baxter," I said, "I'm here to—"

"You're here to come work for us. I know it even if you don't. Are you tired of being played with yet, Professor Ransom?"

"Damn right I am. The first thing I want is an apology. The second thing I want is—"

"I don't mean by me, Professor—I am not a sporting man and I don't play games. I mean *them*."

I was kind of bewildered by this line of conversation, and looked to Adela to see what she made of it, but she just stood with her hands folded into her sleeves and her head down like a Silver City Nun at evening prayer.

"Not the whore up on the hill—not that buffoon Jim Dark, either—and by the by Professor Ransom I heard you got shot at down below. It was Mr. Dark, of course. I don't have a lot of fellow-feeling with Mr. Dark but I understand the temptation—though in this case I imagine he wanted to stop you talking to me. My detectives can do only so much to police and protect you. That's why you won't be leaving here again, Mr. Ransom. You won't be making any more of your damn speeches—"

"Now wait—now just wait—the whole city will soon know I'm here, Mr. Baxter—"

Adela said something but I did not stop to listen—I said, "You can't—"

"No, I'm not talking about the Adversary at all. I'm talking about the others. The Folk, as the vulgar call 'em. Dragged kicking and screaming, they should be. I'm going to be straight with you now Professor Ransom because there's not much time left. Trouble-makers at Juniper City. Gone too far. Listen. Last chance before the Engines take matters into their own, what's the word—last chance to deal with the human face, Professor Ransom. Don't look at me like that, Gates—I know my own business. Ransom, I know what the Process is. I know even if you don't. I know where you found it. You think it was an accident, Ransom—you think they don't have plans? You think they weren't watching—you want that? You like being used? Them or the Adversary or the Engines. Ransom, this is your last chance and your best offer. You've played a good game and you've made things hard for us here in Jasper—you've shown me I have to make a deal. Well, this is the deal. I'll tell you the truth. This is as good a deal as you'll get. You're at the top now—well done. I'll tell you things even the Adversary doesn't know. I'll tell you how to take your destiny in your own two hands like a man and—"

There was a sound of metal scraping. Mr. Baxter and Mr. Gates both turned to look at the telegraph devices—I guess they thought it was a message coming in. I knew better. The sound was familiar, happily so, and for a fraction of an instant it made me feel like I was back home backstage at the Ormolu, and I smiled.

It was the sound of a certain spring-powered device that Adela and I had developed for the use of the Amazing Amaryllis and Wise Master Lobsang and Mr. Bosko and the other players of the Ormolu Theater. It could be hidden under a long sleeve—like the ones Adela was wearing— and when triggered it could project a variety of items rapidly into the hand, including watches, cards, rings, flowers, and in this case a tiny silvery pistol, hardly bigger than a finger. The pistol must have been her work alone—it was not mine.

Onstage the device had seemed almost silent. In Baxter's big tiled room it echoed like an Engine accelerating, or maybe that was just my imagination.

Anyhow Adela had the gun in her hand in an instant and she fired. She got Baxter in his chest, cutting short his speech—his head fell back and his shirt turned red.

Then one of the telegraph machines *did* begin speaking—I do not know what it was saying but it was very fast and high and ugly.

Adela said that she was sorry, so very sorry, then she lifted the silvery little weapon to her own chin. She pulled the trigger and the silvery little cylinder rotated and there was a crack and a puff of smoke and a red hole opened in her left cheek. Her eyes rolled back and she moaned but did not drop the gun. The cylinder rotated again.

I jumped for her and grabbed her arm. So did Mr. Gates. I guess we had different reasons for trying to keep her alive, and I do not think he had her best interests at heart. We got her arm down and then I did not like the look on Mr. Gates's face, so I took a swing at it. Gates grunted, spat, and hit me back. I fell over.

"He's dead," Mr. Shelby said. "He's dead. I don't believe it. He's— he's dead."

The security men were holding Adela now, and they held her with blank expressions on their faces as she struggled, making noises that were not at all like words, and as Mr. Shelby began to berate them mercilessly for their incompetence. Gates strode over to the telegraph machine and tore off the paper, cursing at Mr. Baxter's assistants, who all stood around looking like puppets. My nose bled.

"Somebody get Watt," Gates said.

"Don't," Shelby said.

"Do it—they got to know. They got to know now."

"How did this happen? What do we do now? What will they do?"

I could not think very clearly or very well down there on the floor. I got up and made a play for Mr. Gates's gun—that was not my worst idea ever but it was a long way from my best and pretty soon I was back on the floor again.

"You stay there, Ransom. You think it's over now? This was your plan, Professor? The old man was telling the truth—he was the last chance at the human face. What'll happen now—shit, I don't even know what'll happen now."

❃   ❃   ❃

I guess the rest is history.

## CHAPTER 27

# The BATTLE OF JASPER CITY

Even while Mr. Gates's security men dragged me out by my arms, the late Mr. Baxter's office was already filling up with anxious assistants—with ambitious young schemers—with elderly executives crestfallen and hunched under the burden of the secret they now had to bear—with Officers of the Line, blank and professional. The telegraphs had both started to speak, like the Engines already knew what happened. I kicked as they dragged me down the hallway, the security men I mean, not the Engines, while meanwhile secretaries' made-up faces peered out of half-open doors, watching me go. They just about hurled me into the elevator, the security men, and then that whole rattling brass contraption dropped like a man being hanged. My breakfast got away from me.

I won't record for posterity the sub-basement cell in which they held me, except to say that in Ransom City there will be no jail-cells, not ever.

I was there four days before Mr. Gates came to visit me.

"Where's Adela?"

"Not a social call, Professor."

"Where is she?"

"You don't know how much trouble you've caused, Ransom. You and that bloody woman. What were you thinking?"

I protested—"I didn't know!" As the words came out of my mouth they struck me as un-gallant and so I said—"But I don't regret what she did."

"No? You will, Professor, you will."

"This is kidnap, Mr. Gates. Let me go. Let her go."

"Don't be childish, Ransom. Now sign this."

What he put in front of me was a letter to the *Jasper City Evening Post,* announcing that I had taken employment with Mr. Baxter. Not a word about the man's death.

"Sign it."

"I will not."

"Sign it and get ready to speak to your admirers—there's a crowd of 'em outside the tower—sign it or we'll have to take other measures to get rid of 'em."

"Let me see Adela."

"Sign it and we'll see."

For five days after the death of Mr. Baxter, a crowd waited at the foot of the Tower. The last of my true believers—an odd bunch of people, by all accounts. They endured the late summer rain and occasional lightning with the calm patience of obsessives. Some of them were die-hard Jasper City patriots who were still sure I would deliver the Bomb that would ensure Jasper's freedom and preeminence once and for all. Some of them were paranoids with various kinds of delusions. Some of them were my friends my fellow inventors. I know that Mr. Lung was there—the soap-inventor, with whom I'd corresponded—and Mr. Bekman, another correspondent, the inventor of financial instruments—and Mr. Angel Langhorne, the rain-maker. Lung is short and round and round-faced while Bekman is tall and thin and stooped. Mr. Langhorne is of average height and build and in every other respect he is of average appearance, except that he shakes and he stutters and his red-black hair stands up on end like he is being electrified. The Amazing Amaryllis was there too, it touches me to say, in full stage finery and eager to talk to reporters. Together they must have made an odd picture!

Mr. Gates summoned his detectives from far and wide to scare them off but the crowd only grew. Mr. Carson wrote about them—he made a lot of comic business out of Mr. Lung's roundness of body and baldness of head and poor Mr. Angel Langhorne, who as Mr. Carson observed "can no more easily look you in the eye than I"—that is, Mr. Carson—"can stare at the sun."

The crowd grew. Some of them were there to demand my release, and some of them were there to demand that I come out of hiding and explain myself, and some of them were just there to see what would happen. The news of the fighting in the rest of the Territory had been bad all week and I think some of them were expecting the Tower to explode like a big rocket and wanted to be there to see it when it did.

The Tower was sealed. Linesmen came and went by motor-car through the big brass gates or by Heavier-Than-Air Vessel from the roof, but the clerks and secretaries were as much prisoners as I was. This was by order of the Linesman Mr. Watt, who meant by doing this to keep the news of Mr. Baxter's death a secret. Of course it only attracted more attention.

I do not know who first floated the rumor that Mr. Baxter was dead, but the way Mr. Carson wrote about it in his newspaper was that the crowd all moaned at once and looked up at the cloud-wreathed Tower like they expected it to fall over on them. Even the people who hated Mr. Baxter did not want to see him go—they could hardly imagine Jasper City without him. Some of them ran away like rats while others charged the gate. The ones who ran away commenced to trigger an immediate run on the Jasper City Bank that did more damage to the city than any Bomb yet known to science or sorcery. The ones who charged the gate accomplished nothing except that they provoked the guards into shooting. The Amazing Amaryllis—who I guess was with the gate-chargers though I cannot easily imagine it in a woman of her age—got shot. Subsequently she was carried to a hospital by Mr. Lung, among others. Crowds do strange things to people.

✳ ✳ ✳

The Jasper City Bank locked its doors and posted guards at the vault and on the ornately pedimented rooftop and it hunkered down to defend itself against the public, many of whom were on the verge of open riot. One by one bits of the machinery of Mr. Baxter's Trust failed. The Northern Lighting Corporation fired its workers. Half of the Yards shut down—the workers went home and the killing engines stopped and the cattle were left to starve in their pens. A significant percentage of the detectives deserted, and Mr. Baxter's closest loyalists on the Senate mostly left town or retreated to their mansions on the bluffs. "At this time of Crisis," the *Evening Post* said, "we are without leadership."

Well, nature abhors a vacuum and so does politics. Scarlet Jen moved to take over. In the first three days after the Jasper City Bank collapsed four Senators—the last of Baxter's loyalists—were murdered. Two died in their beds, one was shot while he gave a speech urging calm, a fourth died when his mansion burned down. On the fourth day Scarlet

Jen appeared before a crowd of frightened and angry citizens in Tanager Square, on the steps out front of the Bank. She was wearing a red dress and some accounts have her wearing a hat with a red feather in it—anyhow Gentleman Jim Dark stood smiling at her side, and the Agent Rattlesnake Renner leaned his long thin body against one of the Bank's marble pillars, and scowled and toyed with a knife. I do not know how many other Agents were there.

"You know me," she said.

I have spoken to men who were there. They say she spoke plainly.

"You've always known me. This city's known me since before most of you were born. You've always known the score even if you pretended you didn't. You know who's who and who runs things. Well now the time for pretense is over. This city must take sides—us or them. The forces of the Line are coming—you know who I am and you know that I know what I'm talking about. They let Juniper slip from their grasp; they won't let Jasper go too. But they move slow—don't be afraid. We'll take care of you."

"They move slow," Dark said. "You have a week to be ready for them. Will you let them take your city from you? Are you cowards, to roll over like Gibson, or are you sporting men with a bit of fight in you?"

"It's all changed now," Jen said. "The old bastard's dead and everything's yours for the taking, if you have the balls for it."

"First we take the Bank," Dark said. "Who's with us?"

Twelve died in the taking of the Jasper City Bank, but the operation succeeded. Coin and bullion were shared among the mob—notes and stock were already worthless. Later that day Dark led the same mob against the gates of Baxter's Tower, without success. Fifteen died. I have no doubt that for Mr. Dark it was all great good fun.

※　※　※

For sixty years there had been a kind of truce in the Territory between Line and Gun. The War was fought on the Rim and in the north but the Territory was spared. That had all begun to change months ago, when word of Liv and Creedmoor's secret weapon got out—and of my Process—oh, why not call it the *Bomb*. They were not the same thing exactly but I guess there was a lot of confusion on that point—anyhow the great powers of the world wanted both of them. In the scramble to be first to claim control of the weapon the Line broke the truce and seized Gibson City. Then there was the uprising at Juniper City, where Liv and

Creedmoor's weapon was deployed for the first time—unless you count the Miracle at White Rock, which I did not, since I do not believe that the Process was the same thing as what Creedmoor and Liv found— anyhow it was at Juniper City that the Angelus Engine was destroyed.

With Baxter's death the Gun moved to consolidate their power in Jasper, and not long after that the Line moved to retake control. It didn't take a week.

The greater part of the Line's armies in the Territory were still camped all the way over by Juniper City, but the Line had been moving elements of its forces into Jasper all summer. On the evening of the second day after Scarlet Jen and Gentleman Jim Dark raided the Bank and handed out spoils to the mob, four Submersible Vessels surfaced out of the River Jass at the point where the Senate looked out over the sunset- reddened water. Each C.S.V. disgorged a dozen Linesmen, who jumped from the backs of their vehicles onto the Senate's private dock. Two policemen were shot. The Linesmen charged up from the dock and across the Senate's rear lawn and they smashed down the rear doors of the Senate building itself—they have a special device for smashing down doors, that I have never seen in operation and know only by a code-name. There was fighting in the corridors and a few more policemen were shot and the marble busts of who knows how many dead and venerable Senators were smashed in the crossfire before the C.S.V.s deployed the noise-making weapons and pacified the whole street. The Linesmen took down the Jasper City flags and they took the big brass bull down from the building's dome and they settled in to occupy the Senate. The next morning as flocks of Heavier-Than-Air Vessels flew back and forth between the Senate and Baxter's Tower an officer of the Line by the name of Mr. Lime stood on the Senate's steps and issued a statement, to the effect that the Line had been forced to act to protect its holdings in Jasper and to protect Jasper itself from any further slide into chaos.

Mr. Watt had by that time been shot, as punishment for letting Baxter die. He was replaced by a Mr. Nolt.

The city split three ways—I mean both ideologically and geographically. Some people sided with the Linesmen, some with Jen and Dark, some stood for Jasper against both sides. The Linesmen held Fenimore and Jen and Dark's mob held Hoo Lai and the bluffs and the neutrals held on wherever they could, I guess.

✳   ✳   ✳

Mr. Nolt came to see me in my cell. He looked just like all the rest of them.

"I won't sign your damn letter," I said.

He waved that away. "We're past that, now."

I confess that I was frightened to hear him say that, and part of me wanted to plead *No, I've changed my mind, I will come and work for you.* I fought back that craven instinct and instead I said, "Where is she?"

He didn't answer. Instead he stood so close to me that I could smell the stale sweat on his collar.

"So you're the one," he said. "You don't look like much."

"Truth is, I don't feel like much right now."

"Well, we need you—I don't like it but we need you. So it's time to shave and shine your shoes and put on a big smile, Ransom. Or else."

"What is there to smile about? That's a question, Officer—what's going on out there?"

They had not been taking the trouble to keep me informed about politics, so I did not know.

"Fighting," he said. He began to pace. "It'll all be over soon. Only a matter of time. We'll take Jasper City—not that we want it, it's a f——ing cesspit, it's squalid beyond belief—but we'll take it back because that's what we do. The fighting won't matter. We have numbers, production, history on our side. Understand? We'll turn this place into a Station within the year, the Engines will come and go. Now listen."

"Where's Adela?"

"What I don't like about you, Mr. Ransom, could fill a whole file. Understand? But the one big thing is that we need you. Numbers, mass-production, organization, ideology—that's what wins. Or it should be. Understand? Ever since that Creedmoor business last year we've been concerned with *individuals.* Like Creedmoor, like the General, like you with your stupid smile, Ransom. It's the Folk, that's what I think—but it doesn't matter, understand? What matters is we need you. We can take the City but it'll fight back, it'll keep fighting us, and we can't afford that—not with what's going on in Juniper, down in the Deltas, out on the Rim—all the wheels coming off—we need continuity here. A human face. Greasing the wheels, understand?"

"I don't understand, Officer. I guess I don't understand you any more than you understand me."

"I mean, and this comes by order of the Engines themselves, who have taken an interest in you, you poor stupid bastard, that before Mr. Baxter died of his long unfortunate illness he was so impressed by your pluck and ambition and your devotion to Jasper City that he buried your dispute and the old man personally chose you as his successor."

I had nothing to say to that. In fact I was so surprised that I do not think I could have spoken at all without choking.

"Quite a promotion, understand? Heir to the whole enterprise. Order restored. Everyone gets in line. Everyone pulls together to get over this unpleasantness. Understand? We'll get you dressed up. You speak to the Senate in two hours. You do understand, right, Ransom? Damn it, he looks like he's choking."

I know that I have been accused of being a collaborator, a sell-out, and other such things. I do not intend to plead my case here because what I have learned over the years is that people believe what they want to believe, and that is what makes the world go. Never apologize—keep moving. But I will say that I did not say yes until Mr. Nolt had threatened Adela and my sister May, and even after that I did not say yes until he observed that if I did not say yes the odds of a peaceful transition of power in Jasper City would be lowered by a significant percentage, and the odds of atrocity correspondingly increased. You cannot argue with mathematics.

My clothes were chosen for me and my speech was written for me and I was driven to the Senate in the middle of a military procession of motor-cars. All I had to do, as Mr. Nolt kept telling me, was smile. I read from a sheet of typed paper and I spoke without listening to what was coming out of my mouth. I was too busy trying to think of ways I might turn this sudden elevation to my advantage and against the Line. I was sure I would think of something.

I recall that I stumbled over some of my lines—something about the long history of partnership between the Baxter Trust and Jasper City— and I looked up. The Senate chamber was half-full, and most of the assembled Senators had a look about them that suggested they were not entirely a willing audience. I wondered what might happen if I tore up my speech and told them a few of the things I could tell them about Mr. Baxter and about the Line. I doubted I would be telling the Senators anything they did not already know, but there were reporters in the balcony, taking notes. I wondered what would happen if I told them to fight. I was not greatly experienced in making speeches of a martial character but I reckoned I could learn quickly.

Behind me Mr. Nolt coughed quietly, and I thought about Adela, wherever she was. The Senators were staring at their feet or at the walls, anywhere but at me.

Maybe there is another world where I diverted from my prepared remarks, and said what it was in my mind to say. Who knows how things in that world would have gone. One day maybe I will know, because sometimes when the Ransom Process gets up a good head of steam it seems it might burn a hole right through the world so that you can see how things might have been instead of the way they are. But I do not know now.

The silence became so heavy I could not stand it anymore.

*Another time,* I told myself. There would be a better moment. If I bided my time there would be a better moment.

I wished that Mr. Carver was there to nod or shake his head or spit or curse and tell me what was right to do—or Liv—or anyone.

I coughed. Some of the Senators looked startled. I looked down and returned to my script.

After I had finished speaking, the Senators rose from their benches, slowly, as if prodded from behind, and gave me dutiful applause.

That evening my captors moved me from the basement cell and installed me in Mr. Baxter's penthouse.

※　※　※

The Amazing Amaryllis died in a mission hospital in Hoo Lai operated by the sisters of the Silver City. I regret to say that her passing did not make the newspapers—I know about it only because my friend the soap-inventor Mr. Lung was with her.

You may recall that Mr. Lung had helped her to the hospital in the first place, after the altercation at the foot of Baxter's Tower in which she got shot—in the leg as it happens—well anyhow he visited her a number of times after that. Love can blossom in the most unlikely circumstances. He sat by her bedside and they talked of his inventions and her growing fame and how they might leave Jasper and start over down south. When Jim Dark's mob took the hospital over as a headquarters and kicked out the Silver City sisters Amaryllis remained in her bed and Mr. Lung remained by her side. Dark's mob were the kind of men you would expect, recruited in haste from the city's worst sorts—it was because of laziness, not kind-heartedness, that Dark's mob did not evict the sick from their beds on the upstairs floors. They certainly did not bother to feed them. They occupied the lower floor and drank and schemed and boasted of how they'd win glory and take the city for themselves. They tormented the sick in their beds—thank fortune that Mr. Lung was there to protect Amaryllis. Food ran out, and medicine.

Mr. Lung did not sleep. His spectacles were broken in a scuffle. Then as the forces of the Line closed in block-by-block around them the men of Dark's mob started to shoot themselves. In the end Amaryllis died of infection. Mr. Lung assures me she passed in her sleep, and that he was there by her side—her last audience.

There is a story of heroism and suffering to be written about the mission hospital but that will have to be up to Mr. Lung. He is that story's hero, kind and patient and steadfast and strong and all that kind of thing. I was not there. I spent that week in the penthouse apartment of Baxter's Tower. I paced and talked to myself, still scheming of ways to turn my new position to advantage. It took me some time to admit that I could not think of anything.

I was imprisoned, but I was imprisoned in circumstances of such luxury I cannot begin to describe them any better than I could describe the town of the Folk I once visited. A poor boy from East Conlan does not have the words in his head. The bathroom alone—not to mention the four-poster bed and the Dhravian carpets and the discreet bell-ropes everywhere and the bookcases . . . The windows were not barred but you could not climb down from that sky-scraping penthouse, not even if you tied all the silk bedsheets together with all the bell-ropes and all the Dhravian carpets, and you may trust me when I say that I calculated and re-calculated that possibility to the last inch.

Mr. Lung escaped the city after Amaryllis died. Mr. Bekman, the inventor of financial instruments, perished in the fighting on the steps of the Bank; maybe he would have found that fitting. The rain-maker Mr. Angel Langhorne fled the city in advance of the Line's invasion. Later when I met him again I asked how he knew—he stuttered and looked at his feet and smiled and said that he had f-f-fine antennae for danger, it came from contemplating lightning and thunder-clouds all day.

Mr. Baxter's penthouse was electric-lit, of course. Lamps hung from the high ceiling and hissed and buzzed and whispered like they were laughing at me. Of course the lamps were the work of the Northern Lighting Corporation. I could tell by their design and if I stood on a chair I could make out the letters NLC etched on them. On my fifth day in the penthouse I decided that I could not tolerate them. I had to stand on a chair and stretch and swing at them with one of the old man's walking-sticks but in the end I got every last one of them. I could not escape and I could not rescue Adela and I could not do anything about what was happening outside in Jasper City but damn it I could show those lamps who was boss. Because of the demands of the fighting it was more than a week before they could be replaced.

✳  ✳  ✳

Mr. Nolt, who had replaced Mr. Watt, was replaced in his turn by Mr. Lime. In the time I spent as chief executive of the Baxter Trust—subsequently re-named the Baxter-Ransom Trust—I met a number of others like them. They came and went, they were promoted and removed, I stopped noticing their faces or remembering their names. Mr. Nolt was shot for incompetence after his men raided the Floating World.

I knew about the raid before it happened. Mr. Nolt came to me in the old man's penthouse that morning, while I sat at the old man's writing-desk reading his old correspondence. That was on the third day of my confinement in the penthouse, when I was thinking that maybe I might find something in the old man's secrets that could be turned to advantage. Mostly I was learning about old land deals that were of no use to anybody.

Mr. Nolt told me that his men were assaulting the Floating World that night.

"Informing you, sir, in your capacity as chief executive. You see some of the men to be used in the assault are detectives in the employ of the—in your employ, now."

"What do I care? But if you're—"

"You see, sir, the bitch has holed up there—who can be sure how many men she has with her. There are tunnels under that place or else we'd use rockets, you see. Who can be sure what kind of awful things go on down there. It'll be bloody, that's for sure."

I stood. I seem to recall I was wearing one of the old man's white nightshirts, finely made in the fashion of bygone decades, faintly malodorous.

"I don't care about your men, Mr. whatever your damn name is, but my sister Jess is up there. Down there. It's not her fault—"

"I know, Mr. Ransom, sir. We know very well where everyone is. Now I can't make any promises, this thing has to be done and it has to be done fast, but maybe we can make an effort to see she comes to no accidental harm—you see you can be sure we know what she looks like, you can be sure of that. But you see you'll have to be accommodating in return."

"I think I've been accommodating enough, Mr. Nolt."

"As you please, sir."

He turned to go. My nerve failed me.

"Wait—Nolt, wait."

He stopped in the doorway.

"Nolt—You'll see she comes to no harm?"

"Well," he said.

That is why I gave that speech at the premises of one of Mr. Baxter's munitions factories—now my factories. I dressed up in a fine black suit and I stood among the idle machinery and I spoke to the workers. Normal business would be resumed very soon, I promised them. The crisis would soon pass and order would be restored. Things would get better and better forever thereafter. Those who remained loyal and law-abiding would receive raises. As soon as the crisis was resolved there would be work for every able-bodied man in Jasper, mass-manufacturing the Bomb. Applause, cheering, stamping, caps thrown in the air. I am good at giving speeches.

The assault took place that night. A dozen of the Vessels converged from all four corners of the city—I watched from the window of the old man's Tower as smoke trails criss-crossed the night sky. The Vessels climbed the bluffs and circled around and around the grounds of the Floating World, shooting at windows and gunning down whoever they saw in the rose-gardens or canoodling on the benches among the ivy—it was Mr. Nolt's opinion, he told me, that nobody in such a filthy place could be innocent.

I did not see the fighting but I heard about it, because I was permitted to wait in the Big Office in Mr. Baxter's Tower while the assault took place, and the reports that came in on the telegraph machines were translated for me.

By the Big Office I mean the place where I first met Mr. Baxter. That was what we called it. It was full of telegraphs and Linesmen in uniform. I was still wearing the black suit but I had loosened my neck-tie.

Initial reports were promising. The Vessels encircled the grounds, preventing escape. A group of two dozen detectives approached the premises. They offered a warrant before smashing down the door. Girls screamed, Senators threw themselves on the floor and begged for mercy. The detectives took names and confiscated weapons.

"You see," Mr. Nolt said, nodding as he scanned the reports that came in on the telegraphs. "You see."

"What about my sister, Nolt? You promised she'd be safe."

"I promised we'd try, Mr. Ransom, sir. We'll see, won't we?"

The detectives broke into the cellars and hauled sobbing women out of their hiding-places. They wrestled hand-to-hand with Jen's men in the tunnels. They beat them with sticks to the floor. They strapped them to chairs and questioned them. Jen could not be found.

"Well," Mr. Nolt said. "She thinks she can hide? Run? We'll see about that. We'll see."

Not a single one of the detectives died for the first forty-five minutes. After that they started dropping dead like it was their job to do so, each one shot without warning in the back, with no sign of the shooter—which was blamed in the reports that came back to the Big Office on the fact that it was dark in the Floating World, and all the women were in red and looked alike, and the flames in the fireplaces everywhere flickered and made strange shadows, and kept rising and rising and could not by any natural means be extinguished, until the surviving detectives were forced to retreat into the gardens. Fire leapt from the windows. The grass withered and the roses turned black and the statues cracked with the heat. Girls fled, their hair on fire. Updrafts of hot air and smoke made the Vessels unsteady—the rotary-wing Vessels shook like boats in a storm and three of them crashed. Canvas wings caught fire. Nobody was exactly sure how Scarlet Jen escaped but one of the Vessels went missing. One of the detectives reported seeing her standing on the burning roof as the Vessels wobbled by—it's possible she stole it.

Mr. Nolt's face fell as he read the reports.

"I see," he said.

"What do you see? Look at me, Nolt. What about my sister? Nolt? What about my sister? You promised."

Mr. Nolt placed the reports in a neat pile and walked silently out of the Big Office.

❊　❊　❊

That was the first time I stood in the Big Office while the Linesmen worked—not the last. Standing in the Big Office I learned all about Gentleman Jim Dark's various skirmishes with the occupying forces. By the time the Floating World burned Dark had organized a mob of several hundred men and in the days after the burning they put on a pretty good show, if that's the sort of show you like. Mostly they burned and looted. Dark was everywhere in the city, rallying the mob, laughing and making speeches and handing out ill-gotten loot with aplomb. He invariably wore a top hat and a vest in the purple and gold of the Jasper City flag and in his speeches he compared his mustache to the horns of the Jasper City Bull. If there was any kind of strategic purpose to his activities I don't know what it was, and neither did the officers of the Line. Later he told the newspapers that it was all only sport and maybe that is all it was to him. He was never caught but soon enough his mob shrank to nothing, while the number of Linesmen in the city only kept growing and growing.

I never saw Nolt again. After the fiasco of the raid on the Floating World he was replaced by a Mr. Lime, like I think I said. I guess they shot Nolt, or he shot himself, or he was sent to the front somewhere. I do not know. After the Floating World burned I guess you could say my spirit was broken. I was dead certain Jess was dead and that it was my fault. I had bargained and sold everything I had, I had given the Line everything they wanted, and I had not been able to do any good with it at all. I could not save anyone. I could not eat or sleep. I stopped asking about my sister and I stopped asking what they had done with Adela. I was scared to hear the answer. I remember that Mr. Lime came to me in the penthouse and put papers in front of me to sign and I signed them just to make his face go away. Later they came to drive me somewhere to make a speech. I went with them without thinking twice. I did what I was told. It got easier every time. I stopped even day-dreaming of escape.

Two of the stagehands from the Ormolu died in the service of Jim Dark's merry band. I learned this later from reports filed.

Mr. Quantrill from the Ormolu died in a stampede of cattle on Swing Street.

I can tell you how a lot of what happened happened, but not everything. I don't know how come there was a stampede on Swing Street. All I know is that toward the end of the fighting somebody poisoned most of the cattle still penned in the Yards—I don't know who. I would say it was the work of Jim Dark's men but he always denied it. The

Linesmen were baffled too. Most of the animals died. Some escaped their pens, maddened and frothing, charging through the city, and a few of them made it all the way to Swing Street, where Mr. Quantrill according to eye-witnesses stood in the street with his cigarette hanging out of the corner of his mouth, frozen as the big beasts rounded the corner and came crashing down the street, like he was an actor playing at being a statue.

There were roughly one hundred Folk slaves in the Yards before the fighting started. Some time in the middle of things they escaped, leaving no tracks. I hope they made it out.

⁂

Mr. Elmer Merrial Carson remained in the city until the last possible minute, recording what he saw for posterity. At the time I wondered why he bothered but now I understand. After the *Evening Post*'s offices burned he moved into a house on the bluffs, from which he escaped by a back door when the detectives finally came for him. He fled the city by cover of night, taking only his typewriter in a suitcase. He has written about that better than I can.

⁂

I can tell you that it was the Agent Rattlesnake Renner who burned the Senate down. He was caught in the act and executed by hanging without delay. Of course his demon master could not be killed, the Linesmen not having either Liv's weapon or mine to hand—its vessel could be smashed, but the thing itself returned to the Lodge of the Guns, beneath the earth or up in the sky or out in the far unexplored West or wherever it is, if it is a place—returned to wait and brood until it was ready to take a new servant and return to the world.

"That's where you come in, Ransom," said Mr. Lime, who was as cheerful and friendly that day as any Officer of the Line has ever been.

"One day we'll burn down their Lodge itself, Ransom. One day. And that's where you and your Bomb come in."

He put a hand on my shoulder. That is the only time I have ever been touched in a friendly way by an Officer of the Line and I did not know how to respond.

"We'll settle business with the city soon enough," he said. "Then we'll get to work."

⁂

I've heard all the rumors about how in the last days of the fighting Liv and John Creedmoor showed up to join in the excitement. According to some accounts they had an army of Folk behind them, armed with sharp spears and strange magic, with storm and madness and evil eye, with dreadful old-world savagery, with a sound of terrible drumming. Some accounts say that it was their dreadful weapon that destroyed the Senate, or the Floating World. "Jasper will not fall to the Line," John Creedmoor said as he stood on the Senate's steps and wound the handle of his secret weapon, "it'll burn first," as the lightning struck on all sides of him and the Senate's roof cracked open like an egg. "This is the end of the world."

Well, none of that is true. I don't know where they were but they were not in Jasper City. There was enough destruction without them and nobody needed their help.

A troupe of Swing Street actors in Folk masks of white wood and horse-hair manes were mistaken for the real thing and that started a panic that ended in arrests and the closure of Swing Street by order of the Archway Engine itself—the Street was cordoned off at all entrances by barbed wire. By that time the Linesmen had taken just about the whole city and they were cordoning off streets as they pleased, and defoliating the parks.

The fighting did not last long. The whole Battle of Jasper lasted less than two weeks. That was thanks to the excellence of the Engines' planning, Mr. Lime assured me, but in a small way it was thanks to me. By stepping into Old Man Baxter's shoes and lending my name to the cause of order, he said, I had helped to smooth over what might have been a significantly more troublesome transition.

If I had done things differently then who knows, maybe Jasper would have fought back and won its freedom. Mr. Lime did not think so but maybe he was wrong. Maybe Jasper would have fallen anyhow, only more people would have died. I believe that I did what seemed best at the time, under difficult circumstances.

Gentleman Jim Dark fled the city like a rat from a burning building as soon as things went south for him. He rode out on the road west at evening, with a Vessel in pursuit and the last few gold bars from the sack of the Jasper City Bank in his saddlebags, and he spent the next six months drifting from town to town on the Rim, boasting of how he may not have won the Battle of Jasper City but damn it he'd let the bastards know they were in a fight.

Scarlet Jen was made of sterner stuff. I guess the way she saw things Jasper City was hers and had always been hers and she would not leave it, she would rather die when it did. I admire that.

In the Linesmen's files I read all about how she'd been in the Floating World for sixty years, seventy, or more, collecting secrets and scheming and blackmailing and whatever else Agents of the Gun do. The demon that rode her gave her long life and it made her beautiful. Don't think it didn't make her dangerous too. She cut her hair short and she wore trousers she'd taken from a dead employee of the Baxter Detective Agency and for ten days, even while the Linesmen's trucks roared into the city along every road carrying men and machines, she roamed free. Unlike Gentleman Jim Dark she had no mob and she didn't give speeches or pose for photographs or talk to the newspapers. Nor did she make demands or offer justifications or claim that right was on her side. She just killed.

Mr. Lime had a map made on the wall of the Big Office showing the place where she'd shot an officer from the rooftops, and another place where she'd murdered a whole checkpoint, and the place where she'd somehow cracked an Ironclad's shell and the place where a lucky Private Second Class had shot her in the leg and she'd limped away bleeding, cursing out loud for her demon to heal her. It didn't take a genius to see a kind of spiral drawn on that map, starting out across the river but coming in over the bridge to Fenimore, and around and around the outskirts of that occupied island, constantly probing and testing the defenses arrayed around the spiral's central point, which of course was Baxter's Tower.

Mr. Lime folded his arms behind his back, studied his map, nodded.

"She's coming for you, Mr. Ransom, sir."

"I guess she is, Mr. Lime. I'm flattered."

"Well, too late, isn't it? They've lost. You're with us now."

I waited in the Big Office for days and I watched them make marks on the map as incidents were reported in— always closer and closer—an inch here, an inch there. I'll confess that I was rooting for her to make it all the way.

She didn't.

"Good work, everyone," Mr. Lime said. With his thumb he pushed one last pin into the map, then stood back and examined it with satisfaction. "Good work."

My sister Jess survived the burning of the Floating World too, though I did not learn that for many months—not until long after Jasper City had fallen. The barricades had gone up and gone down again. The rest of the world called it the Battle of Jasper but in the language of the new administration it was the Recent Emergency, and whatever you called it it was over. I was so well settled into my new employment that I no longer started when an Officer of the Line called me *sir*, and whole days went by when I thought neither of escape nor suicide. Every morning I sat at the old man's desk—my desk—and I answered my correspondence— some days I no longer needed the Officers of the Line standing at my shoulder to tell me what to write.

I guess it must have been a mistake that the report regarding MISS JESSICA HITE, NEÉ RANSOM, was sent across my desk. The Line makes more mistakes than you'd think. Maybe it was a friendly power, still looking out for me in spite of everything. Anyhow the report said that Miss Hite had been seen down in a place in the Deltas that I won't name, under an alias that I won't write, and asked "whether action should be taken to retrieve her." I tore the damn thing up and ate it. That small act of rebellion gave me the strength to go on for another six months. I was still a prisoner but knowing that she was alive gave me the strength to start thinking again.

Neither the author of the report nor I had any notion how she'd escaped the burning of the Floating World, not to mention the military cordon around Jasper City. Maybe the world is not always as hard a place as it pretends. I never tried to track her down. That was the best thing I could do for her.

## THE FOURTH PART

# RANSOM CITY

## CHAPTER 28

# THE BEGINNING OF THE FOURTH PART

To my way of thinking the Battle of Jasper City ended on the day when Scarlet Jen died at a checkpoint on Zelda Street. As I write this that was four years ago almost to the day. It is not an occasion anybody ever celebrates or mourns, not even back in the Territory, maybe because since then so many places have fallen to one side or the other and then fallen back. Ever since we brought our secret weapons and our rumors of weapons and the Bomb into the world there has been a whole lot of History, more than anyone can remember. More than I could write down even if I had forever, and I do not.

Nobody in this country would remember the date anyhow—out here Jasper City is just a rumor of something ancient and magnificent back East, like how people in Jasper City thought about the old countries back over the mountains. They hardly even know who I am. I guess our visit to these parts must be the strangest thing they've ever seen.

We are far out on the Rim, not far from a little town I won't name and by the edge of a big west-flowing river I won't name either. It is not the same river I mentioned in Chapter Twelve. We are striking the boats.

The Beck brothers turned out to be first-rate boatsmen. They had told me they were boatsmen when they joined up but I had thought it was only bravado, because in addition to boat-handling they are fist-fighters and crack shots and they know what do with horses and sheep and rope and how to read direction from trees and stars and how to tell if there is gold in a river and Josh Beck even says with a wink that he knows a bit of Folk magic. Ransom City is lucky to have them.

By the by the boats were bought for us by Mr. Lung, who after Amaryllis died left the city and struck out north-west and to make a long story short he ended up making his fortune in Melville City, which has now put itself on the map as the Cleanest City on the Western Rim. He was in a coffeehouse in Melville City a couple of months back when one of his acquaintances among Melville's business elite handed him one of my letters. It was the letter that began:

TO WHOM IT MAY CONCERN
TO WHOEVER PICKS THIS UP
TO ALL FREE-THINKING MEN AND WOMEN OF
PEACE AND GOODWILL
I INVITE YOU TO JOIN ME IN THE CITY OF THE FUTURE

And et cetera.

He sold up fast and headed south—by motor-car at first—and he caught our trail near the county of Nabilac. His wife is a beautiful and spirited young woman from Melville City who was active in the Six Thousand Club there and who is eager to build our city too, though our goals will be more modest at first. Along the way they met up with Mr. Angel Langhorne, who had not prospered so well—as a matter of fact he spent most of the years since the Battle of Jasper in prison on the Rim for fraud, and some of them in an insane asylum, and when he met up with Mr. Lung he possessed only one shoe. He still shakes and stutters and cannot look you in the eye and smells of sweat and burned hair, but none of us are perfect. His rain-making device does not quite work yet but he assures me that it is showing promise as we get further out West, where the skies are bigger and the clouds are wilder and stronger kinds of animal. I believe him. We need not fear for lack of water in Ransom City!

For a while I hoped one of my sisters might see the letters and come find me, but they have not. I guess I don't blame them.

❊   ❊   ❊

We are camped out on the edge of the river, on the edge of the world. A little way past this point the river becomes un-navigable, even for the Beck brothers. There are a few more settlements alongside the river, with deep woods all around them—then nothing that has any name in our language. In the very far distance on a very clear morning you can see mountains. Ask the locals what they're called and they'll shrug. They reckon Folk live there, and they have all kinds of superstitions regarding them.

We got the Apparatus off the boat without incident except that Josh Beck slipped and soaked himself, and Mr. Langhorne laughed until he had one of his fits. The Apparatus hums constantly these days, like it is happy to be going home.

This is the last place from which we might send back mail, and even here for mail to get to any place that counts in the world it will have to pass through many hands—a ridiculous succession of improbabilities—like one of the complex contraptions Adela and I used to build back on Swing Street. I reckon the odds are better than even that this last part of the story will get lost, sunk in the river or eaten by wolves or stuck through with spears or tossed aside as worthless by bandits or left to bleach in the hot desert somewhere, going white like the unknown places on a map.

Miss Fleming caught sight of the smoke-trail of a scouting Vessel in the distance. I couldn't see it myself but others with sharper eyes and a more finely honed sense of danger saw it clear enough. It turned back east. They have spyglasses, so if we saw it it saw us.

We are far out beyond any lands controlled by the Line. But who knows these days. Everything is falling apart and it may be that some splinter of the Line's forces operates in this area, or they may be deserters or rebels. Who knows. They are not likely to be friendly. Whoever they are I guess I must get through my story pretty quick if I want to be sure of telling it all before they find us.

## CHAPTER 29

# MY TIME AT THE TOP

The Baxter Trust became the Baxter-Ransom Trust.

The transformation of the Baxter Trust into the Baxter-Ransom Trust was an operation on a military scale, surpassing even the invasion of Jasper for manpower and planning. It happened maybe three or four months after the fall of Jasper City to the Line. I had no say in the matter. I am told it was a policy decided at the highest levels, which is to say by the Engines themselves, who find it useful sometimes to operate through a human face.

The Trust's activities extended all over the western world, and it was essential that the transformation take place without disruption in the lines of power, and so an army of lawyers and accountants had to go out from Jasper City all across the Territory and out to the remotest mining towns on the Rim and the plantations of the Deltas and up into the cold north to handle paperwork. They even went into East Conlan. Soldiers of the Line went with them to suppress rebellious subsidiaries. I had no part in the planning of any of this except to sign my name to documents. Mostly what I remember of my first few months as President of the Baxter-Ransom Trust was signing documents. Once matters of money and power were taken care of I was presented for a public signing ceremony in Tanager Square. What was left of Jasper City's great men sat in chairs before me and the crowd gathered behind a chain fence and I spoke through electrical amplification, promising a new start under new management and a square deal for the hard-working man of Jasper, who had the good sense to knuckle under and do his job without complaint. Sometimes Mr. Lime sat behind me while I spoke but he did not often need to threaten me. Most days I was so settled into my routine that I could make those speeches and make them well without feeling a thing.

✳   ✳   ✳

The roads reopened. Jasper resumed trade, notably with Gibson City, which remained under control of the Line. There was a period of truce. Life in Jasper returned to something not so very different from what it had been before, except that production shifted to a war footing.

✳   ✳   ✳

When I was a boy I used to dream about being a rich man, a man of power and the freedom to do as he pleases—what boy doesn't? I tried to imagine what a man like Mr. Baxter did all day. I confess I sometimes got him mixed up with a king from a story-book about the old country, and imagined jousts and harems of a hundred beautiful women.

I slept in a four-poster bed that had previously belonged to Mr. Baxter, in the penthouse apartment that had previously been his. I was woken at six every morning, whether I liked it or not, by one of the succession of adjutants who served me or commanded me, however you chose to look at it. The adjutant's servant carried a silver tray which in turn carried coffee, a boiled egg, a heap of correspondence and legal documents, a copy of the *Jasper City Evening Post* from which most news about the War had been censored, and an arrangement of chemical tablets, the finest products of the Line's science, which I was assured would calm my moods and sharpen my thinking and regulate my bowels and prevent cancer. Anyhow I was not permitted not to take them. The newspaper was a courtesy and they did not care if I read it or not. There was little in it after the censoring except sport.

From six until six fifteen I was left alone in the bathroom, where I did my best to perform the Ransom System of Exercises. Mr. Baxter's bathroom was more spacious than most people's houses and so the Exercises suffered little compromise, I am happy to report. There were gold fittings and big-breasted women made of white marble and mirrors big enough for the vanity of a King. A row of ivory boxes and greasy-looking jars on a shelf along the back wall held relics of Old Man Baxter, such as his false teeth and his spectacles and his wigs and breathing-tubes

FELIX GILMAN

and syringes and his mechanical hearing-trumpet and his artificial foot. Sometimes I used to look at those and think of the failing sight in my bad eye and the various aches and pains I had accumulated out on the Rim and I contemplated the years ahead of me with dread.

At six fifteen if I had not emerged the adjutant opened the door regardless.

I signed legal documents for a period of time that varied from two minutes to half an hour, depending on whether I bothered to ask questions as to their meaning or raise any kind of futile protest against any injustice I saw in them. Sometimes I did—truth is, not often.

Then until half-past nine I sat at the old man's writing-desk and answered correspondence. The desk was heavy and made of a very fine wood that was so black it looked burned and in the middle of it sat the big triplicate typewriter, which so far as I know is the only one of its kind in the world. Most of the correspondence was about business, letters from Mayors or Senators or the executives of subsidiary operations of the Baxter-Ransom Trust, like the Northern Lighting Corporation or the Conlan Coal Company. If it was important the adjutants told me what to write.

In my first month at the top I got at least a hundred letters from creditors from back in East Conlan or all over the Western Rim who reckoned I owed them money, and I guess I most likely did. All plausible claims were paid promptly and with interest. A few ambitious fellows attempted to bring lawsuits against me personally or the Baxter-Ransom Trust but they got a quick visit from the detectives of the Baxter-Ransom Agency, who taught them a thing or two about how the world works. Soon enough all my debts were cleared. I had never been debt-free since I was a knee-high child and I cannot say I altogether enjoyed the sensation—I felt like my strings had been cut.

I got letters from small boys in far-flung towns all over the West who wanted to know how come I made it from a nobody like them to the top of the tallest tower in Jasper City and I told them anyone who worked hard and played the game by the rules could get ahead, just like it said in Mr. Baxter's *Autobiography*.

On days when my correspondence was done before nine thirty I was permitted to stand by the window and stare out over Jasper City. I watched the new towers go up to fill the holes the Battle had knocked in the skyline. The cranes were taller than redwoods, and they were constructed in the Station of Harrow Cross and brought south on the backs of trucks to Jasper City and assembled by workmen in my employ and leased to the city by the Baxter-Ransom Trust for a sum so staggering I shall not write it down or you will think I am telling tall tales.

At nine thirty I dressed in a black suit and was taken down in the private elevator to the room that contained the old man's fleet of black motor-cars. I shook the hand of whatever adjutant awaited me and said, "Well, Mr. whoever-you-are, where is it today?" Usually it was some factory somewhere, where I spoke to the workers, or a meeting with Senators to discuss the defense of the city, at which I sat quietly while the adjutant spoke.

Sometimes on these journeys my routine was enlivened by an attempt at assassination. The Agents Procopio "Dynamite" Morse, Black John Boles, Pearl Starr, and Red-Headed Dick all made attempts upon my life at one time or another. Gentleman Jim Dark returned to Jasper City six months after he first fled and boasted in taverns about what he would do when he got his hands on me, but I can tell you that he never did get up the grit to attack my car. Of all the Agents who tried it was Procopio Morse who got closest to success. With well-placed dynamite beneath a manhole on Seventh Street he managed to turn the car right over like a beetle on its back, and when he tore off the door I spilled out dazed and bleeding onto the street between his boots and I lay on my back looking up at him. He was a black fellow with a broad nose and a wild mop of reddish hair and a big black bow-tie and a brass-buttoned black coat and everything about him was handsome except for his hands, which were burned and club-like. Anyhow he stood over me and made a speech, which I guess was heart-felt and proud and impassioned from the look on his face but it was wasted on me because of the way my ears were still ringing, and it gave the Linesmen in the car behind a chance to shoot him. He fell on top of me. I recall saying "Thank you, well done, good work" to the officers who pulled him off me and helped me to stand.

At one I took lunch alone in the dining room of the old man's penthouse apartment. Paintings all around the room bore the likenesses of thirty-eight Engines, which all looked alike to me. I ate lightly. Mr. Baxter was an old man and had had little taste for rich food—the bill of fare was fixed and invariable. At least I did not ask them to vary it—who knows if they would have. Dinner was at seven under the same circumstances. Like me, Mr. Baxter was a Vegetarian. From two until seven I worked in a laboratory of the Northern Lighting Corporation, which had been given to me for the development and refinement of the Process. After dinner I continued my researches and correspondence at the old man's writing-desk, sitting beneath a circle of cold electric light, typing away on this very machine right here. The Line's finest chemical science ensured that I slept by midnight every night, and did not dream.

✳ ✳ ✳

The first time I refused to cooperate with Mr. Lime's instructions was, as I recall, when I was asked to sign a document authorizing the seizure and depopulation of certain territories on the South-Western Rim— well, I will say no more, for I have enough enemies. It was shortly after I had learned of my sister's survival, and I was starting to think for myself again.

"No," I said.

"No?"

"No, Lime. Take it away."

He waited very patiently for me to change my mind. You have never seen a more patient man in all your life. His face was as blank as a clock, ticking its way toward midnight. I flatter myself that my face was firm as well. When he saw that I would not easily relent he simply gathered up the papers and left me alone in the penthouse. He locked the door behind him and had the lights turned off. At first I thought I had won. It took me a while to realize that he had ordered no food or water to be brought to me until I changed my mind. I am telling the truth when I say that I held out for a long time before giving in—as a matter of fact I was so weak from hunger and thirst that I could hardly pull the bell-rope to summon him back. They did not come when I summoned, but waited until I was near-dead before opening the door, letting in a great blast of electric-light that at first I thought was the light of the next world, and they hoisted me on the shoulders of two heavyset officers and swept me down to the infirmary in the Tower's basement. While I lay on a bed down there I seemed to hear many voices talking to me, and I dare say all of them were really just nurses or doctors or Officers of the Line, but it seemed to me that I heard the voice of Liv Alverhuysen, counseling silence, cunning, and subterfuge, and I heard the voice of my old friend Mr. Carver counseling patience.

When Mr. Lime presented the document to me again, I signed it.

I do not mean to say that I rebelled that way often. I did not. Sometimes I pretended to be sick, retreating to my bed like a child—I am not very proud of that, but you play the hand you are dealt. When the discomfort of my situation became too great there were chemicals that the Line's doctors could provide, ones that would help to calm you or to take away anxiety or to narrow and sharpen your thinking. Sometimes I asked for them. For the most part I did not need them. The truth is that for the most part I cooperated, telling myself I was biding my time, waiting for my moment to escape or to turn the tables on the Line. I kept thinking that I could do some good with Baxter's money. I kept thinking that for longer than you might credit, but it is the truth. I used Mr. Baxter's money to establish the Baxter-Ransom Scholarship for Poor Boys and Girls, and although it only lasted for two years before everything fell apart it was not a bad thing to have done. I am not a fool and I do not imagine that it counts for much set against everything else.

Often, and more and more as the months went by, I forgot to resist, even in my own mind. I forgot that I was playing a part. I found myself taking pleasure in the triumphs of the Baxter-Ransom Trust, the way Mr. Baxter must have.

✳  ✳  ✳

My work in the laboratory kept me sane, or just about sane enough. I could forget about politics and I could forget about right and wrong. I could think about nothing except the work itself.

A whole basement floor beneath the Baxter-Ransom Tower was cleared out for the reconstruction of the Apparatus, and a couple dozen Line engineers were assigned to assist me. Some of them were from Harrow Cross, and others were formerly employed by the Northern Lighting Corporation. They could have given me a thousand Line engineers and they would not have been the equal of one half of Mr. Carver or Adela Kotan Iermo and I was not shy about telling them so. Nevertheless within a few weeks all the grimy and sinister stone corridors beneath the Baxter-Ransom Tower were lit by the lights of the Process, and the elevators were powered by it too—not that Mr. Lime was impressed.

"That's not what you're here for, Ransom."

"The Process is free-energy—it'll save the Baxter-Ransom Trust a substantial sum—I know, I've seen the books."

"You're here because of the Miracle at White Rock, Mr. Ransom. You're here because you promised Bomb-making."

"Never my words. And White Rock was an accident and not easy to replicate. These things take time."

"You're here because the other side has their secret weapon, and we must have ours. You're here because of what you found. You're here because of dumb luck. Never forget that you're replaceable, Mr. Ransom, that's my advice to you if you mean to survive in this life."

"Replace me then, Lime, and see how far you get."

Not long after that Mr. Lime himself was replaced. That was right about when I stopped remembering the names of the adjutants.

I guess that was about the time when the Concord of the Barons down in the Delta declared for the Republic, and so did the Territory of Thurlow. Dr. Lysvet Alverhuysen was appointed First Speaker of the Republic, second in rank only to the President himself. The Gloriana and Dryden Engines met their end. The Northwest Territory was swept by a wave of little rebellions. There was word that the abandoned town of White Rock had been taken over by a group of the Folk, who were not afraid of the transformations that had been worked on that place, and who were letting nobody across the pass. I guess they do not make the same mistake twice. The adjutants tried their best to keep news of the War from me but things slipped out. The rebellions in the Northwest Territory disrupted the Baxter-Ransom Trust's operations so badly that I was forced to spend hours signing documents. Anyhow by the time the historians sort out who did what when and how I will be long gone, one way or the other.

I guess should say a few words about Bombs.

The thing Liv and Creedmoor dug up from under the World's Wall Mountains was probably of the same kind as the thing I just plain stumbled upon in the woods outside of East Conlan. What I mean is that it was a word in the language of the world before people like me came over the mountains. I do not know how they learned how to use it. I guess the Folk must have showed them. I guess they made a deal of some kind. I wish they would have been so forthcoming with me, it would have saved a whole lot of hard work.

I never got the chance to see their weapon in operation with my own eyes and nobody knows better than me that the accounts you read in the newspapers are not always to be trusted, but I hear that it was more sound than light, like a great big drumming that makes everything in the world shake. I hear other accounts that say it was silent and still, that no warning sign of its operation could be detected except that suddenly Engines would fall still, Guns would fall silent. I heard other accounts that spoke of fire or a great dark cloud. Not all of those stories can be true at once and maybe none of them were.

At the Battle of Juniper it left the Gloriana and Dryden Engines as merely machines, tons of empty metal, so much junk.

There is a theory that a lot of people hold, myself included, but nobody much likes to write down, that the Gun and the Line are likewise powers of the world before. Some people will say that we drove them mad when we came here and put our names on them and gave them the shapes they wear now. There is a somewhat heretical sect of the Smiler Brotherhood who hold that Gun and Line are therefore a kind of self-punishment for our sins, and that all we need to do is forgive ourselves to be rid of them. I guess that hasn't worked so well so far but the Smilers are always hopeful, in fact that is their best quality.

What the Folk entrusted to Liv and Creedmoor must have been something like a cure, or a stick to tame wild beasts. I wondered why they had waited so long to share it and I guess they had no real reason to stir themselves quickly on our behalf. Or maybe they thought we might only make more trouble with it. If half of what you hear about the fighting that followed the Battle of Jasper is true then maybe they were right.

What I found was something a little different, and more. A more fundamental process—something that struck at the roots of the world. I had to learn how to make it work for myself, and what could be done with it.

By all accounts, the weapon Liv and Creedmoor found kills the demons of the Gun and the Engines of the Line, but leaves everything else as it is. That is not true of the Process. If you have ever read a newspaper in recent years you know what happens when the Process is fully let off its leash.

If I had to guess I would say that the Folk who permitted me to see it never thought I would make anything of it. They did not think I would understand. I would guess it was a kind of joke for them.

Another possibility is that they wanted to see this whole world we have carved out of what was here before blown away, and therefore entrusted this power to fall into the hands of an irresponsible boy. That they saw some madness in me, something unstable, that would take their old science and add something new to it and make something terrible. I guess they have their factions and their disagreements and their politics just like anyone else, and if the Folk I met outside Conlan all those years ago had a plan it is not necessarily the same as the plans of those Liv and Creedmoor met out West.

Or it was just an accident. Anyhow I played the hand that was dealt me as well as I could and I worked hard and I guess in a way I made something of myself, just like I always said I would.

I did my best. I had no choice but to work, but I gave the Linesmen as little as I could. I never wrote down enough of the Process for them to reconstruct it without me, and I introduced errors and impurities wherever I could. I spotted the sharpest minds among my engineers and filed complaints regarding their incompetence, causing seven of them to be relocated to the front before the adjutants got wise to what I was doing. They needed my mind intact or they would have drugged me or tortured me, I have no doubt.

Despite my best efforts we made progress.

An experiment with an early prototype of the Bomb cleared a whole city block of abandoned slums, but destroyed the Apparatus in doing so, and the effect could not be repeated. It was judged still too unpredictable for regular military application. I hear the Engines themselves gave the matter their attention.

I said before that the engineers that they gave me were no good. That was just bluster. The engineers of the Line were very good. All the resources of the Baxter-Ransom Trust and of the Line were behind my work. It was all I could do slow it down even a little. Often I forgot that I was trying to slow it down. The laboratory was a terrible temptation.

You may recall the ghost I called Jasper, who visited me in the basement of the Ormolu Theater as I worked on the Apparatus. A similar phenomenon repeated itself in the Baxter-Ransom Tower. This time it happened on a mass-production scale.

Like I said, I worked in the basement beneath the Tower. A whole floor of labyrinthine corridors and echoing windowless rooms had been given to me, and a couple dozen engineers in black coats. We filled the rooms with the wild rotating and humming machinery of the Apparatus.

There were, to be precise, twenty-three engineers working in those rooms at the time when the phenomenon began to repeat.

One of the foremen came to me and said, "Sir—I don't know how to say this, exactly—but there are too many engineers, sir."

"I've always said that myself."

"No, sir—Ransom—you should see this, sir. It's—peculiar, sir."

I followed him. There were, as he observed, twenty-six persons gathered in or at the door to Room Nine, not counting myself. Twenty-six engineers stood nervously by the door, while three supernumerary persons stood in Room Nine. They were dressed like engineers, but nobody recognized them and nobody knew by whose authority they had been admitted into the basement. So far as anyone knew, they had simply appeared, in a moment when nobody had been looking.

The three of them stood facing the Apparatus. Their backs were to us, and we could not see their faces clearly. All three of them had their hands up before them in various positions suggesting surprise or alarm. They said nothing and moved little and had a vague and indistinct appearance.

It does not do to look yellow in the presence of your men, so I entered Room Nine, and walked briskly toward the three and spoke to them in a no-nonsense manner.

"What are you doing here? Did Lime send you? I don't need any more of you people, I can hardly take a step here without tripping over some incompetent—are you listening to me? Do you know who I am? Answer when I speak to you. Listen—"

I put my hands on one fellow's shoulder and instantly all three of them retreated—or I should say they receded—their feet not moving nor their hands, their mouths still half-open as if about to say something, all three of them very rapidly leaving backward through the metal door to Room Nine and taking a sharp turn left to disappear down the corridor. I heard one of the real engineers curse. I cannot describe what it was like to touch that phantom.

There were more of them over the weeks that followed. By no means all of them looked like Line engineers. There were men, women, children. They appeared without warning, the same way Jasper used to, they said nothing, they disappeared. Some of them looked like soldiers of the Line and one or two looked like long-dead Agents I recognized from illustrations in the story-books. There were ladies in the fine gowns of the Delta baronies and there were hunched-over miners and there were red-faced ranch-hands from out on the Rim. There were Jasper City office boys with rolled-up sleeves and Keaton toughs and feather-bedecked Log-Town dancing girls and very old women in black who could have been from any place, any time. Not all of them had expressions of panic. Some of them stood all day in the same spot in a corridor, staring at a crack in the wall. The ones who didn't move were scarier than the ones who did, though you would think it would be the other way around. At first the phenomenon of the phantoms scared some of the engineers so bad that they could not work, and that pleased me a whole lot, but after a little while they got used to it. It is remarkable what you can get used to.

There were phantoms in fancy old-time wigs like Jasper used to wear. Some of them had an ever older look about them, with the tall hats and buttoned-up coats you see in history-books about the very first pioneers to cross the frozen mountains and settle the West—every one of them had the stern expression of a judge, passing sentence.

As time went by more and more of the phantoms were Folk, some of them in chains, most of them not—tall, finely painted, long-limbed, sometimes beautiful.

All the history of the West was there! We should have sold tickets.

Eventually the phenomenon spread beyond the basement and into the upper floors of the Tower, causing panic among the office clerks and secretaries. For a week a phantom man of the Folk stood in Elevator Six all day, splendidly painted, glaring in an accusatory way at anyone brave enough to get in with him, of whom there weren't many. He could not be moved.

One time I woke in the middle of the night in the old man's four-poster bed to see a figure staring at me from by the moonlit window—I would swear on what's left of my honor that it was Mr. Carver. As I ran to embrace him and apologize the window blew open and Mr. Carver vanished like he was swept away in the wind.

Until that moment I think I had imagined, without ever thinking about it, that the phantoms were men and women of bygone days. I had imagined that they were the long-dead, let back into the world by the holes the Process opened—or that the ghosts of the dead were always with us, and it was only by the light of the Process that they were visible. The strange thing was that though I knew for sure that Mr. Carver was dead, seeing him there made me sure he was no ghost, and therefore none of them were, but rather they were people who might have been, and might one day be, in a world that was made differently, and maybe better.

Well, who knows how strange things would've gotten or what other insights I might have had if we'd stayed much longer in that place.

❋   ❋   ❋

There was unrest throughout the Tri-City Territory, and everywhere else as well, and the Line's forces were overstretched and more paranoid even than usual, and so it took a full nine months for them to lay tracks between Harrow Cross and Jasper City, and to build a Station in Jasper fit to house an Engine.

They constructed it where the old Senate building had stood. They laid tracks right across the city, behind a barbed-wire fence, cutting streets and neighborhoods right down the middle. They built a new bridge. As for the Station itself they built it twice as tall as the Senate had been and three times as wide at the base. It was made all of polished stone and black metal and smoke and it was heavy-shouldered like a vulture. It made a hell of a noise at all times of the night and as it settled itself in it spread out, swallowing squares and parks. Inside there was a maze of corridors and a cavern they called the Concourse, that was big enough to hold an Engine and full of echoes and shadows and shafts of electric-light and foolhardy pigeons. The stone walls were thick as a mountain and built at the Baxter-Ransom Trust's great expense but they started to crack anyhow, the first time an Engine showed up in town.

It was the Kingstown Engine, the one that I'd seen back in the swamp all that time ago. Of course I was among the assembled Jasper City dignitaries there to greet it. I can't say I had any great enthusiasm for shaking hands and making conversation with an Engine of the Line but it beat another day with the phantoms.

I stood for three hours waiting behind a black railing, between a white-haired old Senator and the man who had been appointed to replace Mr. Carson at the *Jasper City Evening Post,* whose name I forget, and we all tried to keep our faces calm as the Engine approached— steam first, then noise, then shaking, then a wave of heat that made the skin of your face go tight, then finally the shape of the thing itself getting bigger and bigger, until it is so close and so big that you cannot believe it is real. The Senator's nerve broke and he turned his face away. I did not.

Behind me and the Senator and the newspaper man and the other assembled great and good of Jasper there was a huge mass of men press-ganged from all of Jasper's factory floors. They were all supposed to remove their hats in unison but I guess in the general panic some men jumped the gun and others froze, and there was whispering and shoving and then as the Engine loomed closer and closer there was a sound of panicked moaning—it reminded me of the Yards at slaughtering-time—but I still did not turn my face away from the Engine.

The Engine brought with it about seven hundred soldiers of the Line and more guns and wire and concrete than I can imagine anyone had any use for. If it still bore scars from whatever injury it had sustained that night in the swamp, I couldn't see them, but of course it was a mile long and kind of battered and dusty in places, and the far-off parts of the Concourse were in shadow. It sat and steamed while a ceaseless stream of soldiers silently de-boarded.

My adjutant gave me the signal that I should make my speech, so I stood up straight and approached the Engine, climbing the steps of a temporary scaffold so that I stood beside it, nearly as tall as it was.

It had no face, only a great black metal mask. I wonder if it knew who I was.

I cleared my throat, and forgot whatever I was meant to say.

The Engine was still as a mountain. Heat poured off it.

"Gentlemen of Jasper," I said.

Because I never got to say whatever I was going to say I could, if I liked, tell you that I intended to make a speech of heroic defiance—one that would make my adjutant's spectacles steam up—one that would tell the Engine exactly what it was, by which I mean that it was a monster, the nightmare of a bad few centuries, a thing that had no place in the new and rapidly-changing century to come—a speech that would give them no choice but to replace me.

Maybe I would have. Who knows?

I took a deep breath and I turned away from the crowd to face the Engine itself and I said, "Well—"

I was interrupted by the noise of a gunshot, and pain.

I guess it is because I turned when I turned that the gunman in the crowd only got me in the shoulder, not the heart. It hurt like a son of a bitch anyhow and I dropped like a stone to the floor of the scaffold and for a few moments I did not know what had happened.

I lay on my back. I rolled over to the edge of the scaffold and looked out over the crowd, in the middle of which a very large and very complicated kind of fight had broken out. Among the mass of men in gray and black waves and currents and whirlpools were forming. There was shouting and more shooting and men standing back-to-back and rallying others around them, though I could not tell who was who or what side they were on from where I lay. Sometimes a man in the crowd fell over and a space cleared around him and then was filled again. From my altitude and with my head throbbing as I bled on the scaffold it was hard to tell uniformed Linesmen from Jasper City factory workers.

After a minute or two of this the Engine quite suddenly lurched into motion, with no warning except a terrible screech, as jets of steam erupted all along its length. It was as if its mind had been elsewhere all that time but now it had fallen back with a thump into its body, like a man sitting down in a motor-car. It seemed to expand and then contract as it began to move backward out of the Concourse. Its sudden movement caused the scaffold to sway—the floor beneath me tilted—struts snapped and bolts shot loose—and I rolled back away from the crowd, bouncing on my wounded shoulder, and I rolled right off the scaffold, catching myself only at the last moment, hooking the elbow of the arm I hadn't been shot in around one of the teetering metal struts.

The arm I'd been shot in was no use and so I could neither pull myself up nor climb down. Instead I just dangled there over the hard & distant floor of the Concourse and watched the Engine slowly move.

I believe it was retreating. Retreat does not come naturally to its kind and you could tell that just by looking at it. Connecting and coupling rods like the arms of giants bent backward and strained to move wheels bigger than my father's house. It would have been faster maybe but for the fact that it was still loading and unloading all along its huge body and as it lurched back Linesmen fell from broken planks and rolled beneath its wheels—trolleys spilled cargo, and a lot of it was concrete or canned food or rifles but some of it was rockets, and some of those went off, at 60 yards down the length of the Engine, 160 yards, 300, one by one lighting up the shadows of the Concourse.

I swung my legs until I was able to catch my foot in a cleft between two struts, and then I tried to kick myself up onto the platform again. When I got my head up I saw that a man had broken from the crowd and was running up the steps of the scaffold—well he was not so much running as he was climbing and jumping. He wore a flat cap and a scruffy beard and a brown jacket and he carried a big red rock in his hand. As he passed me he kicked my arm, not quite hard enough to dislodge me—but then I guess he had bigger game in mind.

With a cry of, "The Red Valley Republic lives again!" he stood before the Kingstown Engine and he lifted the red rock over his head in both hands.

Nothing immediately occurred. In fact he had time to continue his speech, saying something about the rights of man and the future and freedom and peace and the little fellow.

Believe it or not I think I knew him—before the Battle of Jasper City he'd been employed by the *Jasper City Evening Post* as an editor of some kind, and I had met him in the company of Mr. Carson. But that's by the by.

Nothing continued to occur. He lowered the rock and held it in his hands and looked at it like it was very puzzling to him. Then he looked up and into the Engine's black mask, bigger than a barn, as big and round and blank as the face of the clock on the famous Territorial Tower that used to stand in Juniper City.

I guess I was born without much of a sense of danger but it is a muscle like any other and I had given it years of exercise. I did not know what was going to happen but it seemed to me better to take my chances with the drop than stay where I was.

I let go. As I fell backward through the air the Engine screamed and a big cloud of gray-white steam emerged from its vents and swallowed up the whole scaffold, stripping paint and warping wood and boiling that poor fellow right where he stood, rock in his hand.

I had the good fortune to land on an Officer of the Line. I broke my hip-bone but I was otherwise unharmed.

The Kingstown Engine withdrew from the Station, gaining speed as it went. In another few minutes it was gone entirely, leaving only smoke and heat behind. The fighting continued on the Concourse for a while but I was picked up by two Officers of the Line and taken to what they called safety, and I called captivity. With my hip-bone and shoulder broken there was little I could do except hang there with my arms around their shoulders and go where they steered me.

I said, "Who are they? Who are these people—what's going on— wait, hold on—"

I still do not know who they were. There were at least one hundred of them and my best guess is that most of them were working men from the factories and Yards of Jasper City, and that whatever connection they had to the Republic was only in their heads. That's all I can say.

Anyhow after that incident the authorities of the Line decided that Jasper City was too dangerous, and so they relocated me to Gibson City, and then six weeks later to Harrow Cross, along with Old Man Baxter's triplicate typewriter and my adjutants and all the engineers and the prototypes and in fact the entire Ransom Project, by which I mean the Bomb.

## CHAPTER 30

# INFORMATION

Too much has already been written about the sounds and the smells and the sights of Harrow Cross, oldest and biggest and foremost of the Stations of the Line—you could make a heap of words as tall as its tallest spike—I do not have the time or the inclination to add to that heap. The *Official Statistical Digest of the Surveyors of the Line* boasts of the Station's size and power—Harrow Cross is to Jasper City as Jasper City is to East Conlan. There is nothing bigger than it. It is as far as you can go in that particular direction. The mad poetess Miss Hermosa Goucher of Keaton City wrote a poem about the place called "The Scream" and though she never visited it but only saw it in a dream, I hear her poem is well-regarded, if you like that kind of thing—I must warn you though that it does not rhyme. Mr. Elmer Merrial Carson stayed for three months in 1874 in a hotel on one of the sky-scraping upper levels above the smog, and later he wrote a book about it called *On the Men Who Toil in Darkness,* that was banned in Line territories but I hear it sold pretty well elsewhere. I don't reckon much changed in Harrow Cross between 1874 and when I was there except that the smog level rose to engulf Mr. Carson's hotel and the thing was converted into tenements. I recommend it to you, the same way I recommend all the works of my friend Mr. Carson to you. May he write kindly of me when I am gone!

The Agent Jim Dark wrote an account of how one time he stole into the Station and fought through its labyrinth of lightless tunnels and wrestled with gas-powered pistons with his bare hands and outwitted an Engine in its lair and escaped in a stolen aircraft. It is called *How I*

*Fought in the Great War,* and officially it is banned in the remaining territories of the Line, but in reality it is freely available as an example of how everything the Line's enemies say is lies and bullshit and self-flattery.

Old Man Baxter himself or whoever wrote his *Autobiography* sang for many pages the praises of Harrow Cross's pistons and steam and smoke and industry and how every man there was sorted into his proper place, some at the top and some at the bottom, according to their nature. I am ashamed to say that when I read those pages as a boy I thought only about what it was like at the top.

This morning we saw the trail of Heavier-Than-Air Vessels overhead, criss-crossing, hunting. Miss Fleming was the first to notice the trails but I saw them clearly enough. They are fading now, which I guess means that the Vessels have moved on, or returned to their base to report. Back in Harrow Cross the sky was always dark with smoke but out here it is a very strange sight.

✳   ✳   ✳

They moved me from Jasper City to Harrow Cross by motor-car, under light guard, for reasons of secrecy. Ordinarily dignitaries such as myself would have been moved by Engine, but from the gossip of the officers who drove me and guarded me I learned that the Engines were no longer considered safe. The Engines themselves were targets now. This fact frightened the officers so much they could not stop themselves from talking about it, as if by repeating the absurdity of it they could prove to themselves that it was not true.

I did not want to go to Harrow Cross. I wanted to be free again. But though things were changing and the discipline of the Line was not what it once was, its officers could not be bribed to let me go. They just ignored all my offers.

They helped me out of the back of the motor-car and as they helped me to stand I opened my mouth to make one last attempt to bribe or cozen them but the noise and stench and hugeness of the Station took my words from me. They said, "This way sir," and they moved me from the motor-car bays of the Station's Arch Six up through a maze of corridors and elevators to a tower-top apartment, taller by far than Mr. Baxter's penthouse, from which I could look down from high windows into many-layered canyons of black metal, all the way down to the depths where I cannot think any daylight ever reached—the darkness crawled with what I think were men and women and machines.

✳ ✳ ✳

Officially the story was that I remained the head of the Baxter-Ransom Trust, and that I had been removed from Jasper City to Harrow Cross only so that I could be given the finest medical treatments available, after the injuries I sustained in the cowardly and underhanded and un-successful &c attack, in which I had bravely though unnecessarily stood between the assassin's bullet and the Kingstown Engine.

It was true that I had been injured. It was weeks before I regained the use of my right arm, and months before it was strong again, and I still have some pain in it. I had to learn to write my correspondence with my left hand.

My leg was not quick to heal either—I blame it on the bad air of Harrow Cross, and my conditions of confinement. For months I was stuck in a Wheelchair. This was a heavy contraption of metal and hard black rubber, a noisy rattling menace. It was never under any circum-stances comfortable, like a device constructed for the self-mortification of an old-country Saint. Its wheels constantly threatened to sever way-ward fingers, and once it started rolling sometimes the brakes could barely stop it and I was a danger to myself and anyone in my path. An adjutant was assigned to push me. This one was a woman, and she must have been stronger than she looked. I did not ask her name and she did not tell me. She addressed me as Sir, with contempt. Every day like clock-work she pushed me up and down the long electric-lit corridors and into elevators and across the expanse of concrete rooftop between my quar-ters and the laboratories where they were building the Bomb.

In Jasper City I had been a prisoner, but also a dignitary. I'd been the heir to the Baxter Trust, the man in the penthouse, a man of many phil-anthropic enterprises, the wealthiest and most successful fellow for miles around. It was all an illusion, but a powerful one, and often even I thought that it was real. In Harrow Cross they did not play the same game. I was not admired or adored or respected. I was not called on to give speeches to the masses. I was not quoted in the newspapers—there were no newspapers. In Harrow Cross there were no Great Men. They were beyond such notions. My job was to advise on the construction of the Bomb. That was all.

Truth is I had little to do with it. I had delayed and prevaricated and fed my captors false information for as long as I could, but bit by bit I had let slip too much of the truth, and now the engineers of the Line hardly needed me at all. The project was gathering its own momentum.

Tests took place and the results were reported to me in the form of a rapidly upward-rising line on a chart pinned to the wall of the laboratory.
The engineers were eager but silent young men who never questioned
what they were doing. They talked over my head. They looked forward
with quiet pride to the moment when they would win the approval of
the Engines, when the Bomb was ready to be used against their enemies.

When the phantoms started appearing again I was pleased to have
somebody to talk to, even if they never talked back, just stood there
looking stiff and wide-eyed and open-mouthed with alarm.

If you have never been in a Station of the Line you probably imagine
that every moment in a Station is spent in the presence of the Engines.
They are so immense—how could you not live in their shadow? Well,
they are immense but their Stations are bigger. Truth is I rarely set eyes
on one of the Engines while I was held in Harrow Cross. Sometimes I
saw their smoke as they approached or departed across the plains.
Sometimes I felt their vibrations through the floor or in my gut. Sometimes I got telegrams from the Engines themselves, full of bluster and
menace:

RANSOM. WE EXPECT PROGRESS.

RANSOM. DO NOT FAIL US.

RANSOM. WE ELEVATED YOU. IS THIS HOW YOU REPAY US?

EXPLAIN YOURSELF RANSOM.

Everyone told me this was a great honor but I did not enjoy it. Once
and only once I replied.

DEAR ENGINES. A PROPOSAL. PURPOSE OF BOMB IS TO
DESTROY THE DEMONS OF THE GUN. WE HAVE NO DEMONS TO
EXPERIMENT ON. NO COMPLAINT INTENDED BUT NONE HAVE
BEEN CAPTURED FOR US. GREAT OBSTACLE TO RESEARCH.
HOWEVER ANY SPIRIT WILL DO, & THERE ARE STILL A GREAT
MANY ENGINES IN THE WORLD. PERHAPS 1 OR 2 VOLUNTEERS
COULD BE SPARED AS EXPERIMENTAL SUBJECTS?

That resulted in a storm of telegrams condemning my blasphemy and making threats of terrible tortures and I would like to say that did not scare me but truth is it did.

I got telegrams from just about all of the Engines but most often from the Kingstown Engine, until I began to feel that we had a kind of connection, me and It, that we had been through difficult times together, back in the swamp and in Jasper City, and that a bond of adversity had been forged. There were times when I wanted to please it.

❋ ❋ ❋

I guess you would also imagine that in Harrow Cross every secret is TOP SECRET and nothing happens without the Engines knowing of it, not a word is whispered, not a sparrow flies without it being noted and logged somewhere in the cold recesses of the Engines' minds. Well it is true that no sparrow flies there, but that is on account of the smoke and the noise. It is not true that there are no secrets. In fact Harrow Cross contains so many files and spies and so much INFORMATION that it cannot be contained. It spills out. It falls through the cracks. The Engines banned loose talk—they required all mail to be censored—they forbade whispering and gossip and gatherings of more than four persons other than on official business—but when everything is forbidden nothing is forbidden. I am not the first to say that the Gun and the Line are more alike in some ways than they pretend.

I should have had access only to those files that I needed for my researches—that wasn't how it was. There were so many files! They had to go somewhere. An error of a single digit on a requisition form was the difference between EXPERIMENTAL OBSERVATIONS REGARDING THE AFTERMATH OF THE WHITE ROCK INCIDENT and REPORT ON THE COMMUNICATIONS CAPACITY OF THE RED REPUBLIC—an error of a single digit on a routing order was the difference between sending SOME PRELIMINARY PREDICTIONS ON THE EXPECTED GROWTH OF THE RIM ECONOMIES to me or to whoever's business it rightly was. The Ether was thick with telegraph-messages just like the air was thick with smoke, and no wonder that often they ran afoul of each other, so that the wrong man was sent to the front, or projects begun or ended for no obvious reason. Anyhow it is on account of this tendency toward error that I know so much about the population of Melville City and the history of Jasper City and about banned books and the exploits of Jim Dark and how motor-cars and Injunctions work and a hundred other things.

I guess if I had to describe Harrow Cross, that is how I would de-scribe it. I did not get out into the streets a whole lot and I never set foot in a factory. Harrow Cross was a deluge of numbers and orders and words and facts.

News of the War was forbidden in Harrow Cross, except for the maddening deafening moving-pictures stories of triumph that played in monumental black-and-white on the walls of the Station's towers and fortifications. The moving-pictures are sporting, I think—they tell you from the start that everything in them is a lie, because no ordinary sol-dier of the Line has ever been so tall or so square-jawed or handsome as those ten-foot-high faces on the walls. But I heard the truth anyhow, or fragments of it. The engineers whispered. I heard conversation in the halls. Even the adjutant could not keep her mouth shut. I heard about the siege of Juniper, and how the mercenaries of the Gun broke it. I heard the news about the Collier Hill and Arkeley Engines and how they were both removed from the world in the space of one day, when they confronted the forces of the Republic—the real thing that time. I heard about the defeat of the Line's armies at Chatillon no more than three or four weeks after everybody else in the world. I heard about how after the battle of Chatillon Dr. Lysvet Alverhuysen was no longer First Speaker of the Republic, though I heard a lot of different information as to whether she had stepped down, or been voted down, or shot, or got re-ligion and gone to work in a mission hospital out on the Rim.

❊  ❊  ❊

Anyhow I'd been in Harrow Cross for maybe a month when I got the first letter from Adela.

I was working in the laboratory. By that I mean that I was sitting in my chair in a shadowed corner watching engineers strut back and forth, shouting out numbers and waving their hands and bumping into phan-tom images of themselves, which were also waving their hands, though not shouting.

The laboratory was built in a hangar, constructed on one of the roof-tops high over the Station. It was windowless, and so huge that one of the prototypes could explode and it would not shake the walls or dislodge the electric-lights from the ceiling. It was bone-white and gunmetal-gray and the floor was tiled in the same kind of discomforting grid as the floor of the big office where I had first met Mr. Baxter.

The adjutant had left me alone. Two of the engineers came to me to ask me to resolve a dispute over the nature of the Process and I answered them without thinking or looking up at them. Another presented me with a series of notes and observations regarding a test that had been conducted at Black Lake—disappointing to them and delightful to me— the prototype had burned down a barn but done nothing else. A third engineer slipped a piece of paper into my hand and walked quickly away, and I could not turn the heavy chair fast enough to see his face.

> *Harry. I hope this note finds you. I am so sorry. If they tell me this gets to you I shall write again. If you do not want to read anything I write at all I will understand but I will write regardless. —A.*

But no more letters came from her for two weeks. I got angry with her and then hopeful and then sentimental and then angry again—last of all I got sad.

✳  ✳  ✳

It was the middle of the afternoon. Three of the engineers stood with their backs to me, a row of black coats and folded arms. One was a woman. I do not know her name. Their attention was fixed on a prototype of the Apparatus, the wheels of which were turning and turning and turning, its light casting shadows in which all kinds of phantoms big and small could be seen.

The engineers talked amongst themselves. They paid no attention to me, and I paid little enough attention to them. I sat in my chair thinking about Adela and getting sad. I was thinking about how I would surely never hear from her again, and I was thinking about how maybe she did what she did because of me—how if only I had saved the piano, she might not have been driven to that extremity that caused her to shoot Mr. Baxter. Maybe.

One of the engineers said, "Won't work."

"It was promising," said another.

"Dead end."

"Easy for you to say. Your team's working with the new data."

"They've got new data? What data?"

"Hush-hush. The latest raid. They brought back a half-ton of junk and the code-crackers have been at work on it—promising new leads."

"Huh. Not fair, if you ask me—why hasn't my team seen that data?"

"Strings. It's all about what strings get pulled."

"Favoritism, that's what it is—it's bad for efficiency and it's entirely improper. When did this happen? Why wasn't my team informed?"

"Last week. They say the Harrow Cross Engine itself carried the stuff in—a half ton of the usual junk and a dozen interviewees."

"Well, I'm going to complain. Why wasn't my team informed?"

I said, "What raid?"

They turned to look at me. Two of them blinked blankly and one removed his spectacles to polish them.

"What raid?"

"Hush-hush, Mr. Ransom. Sir."

"What damn raid? What do you mean? Don't look at me like that— you'll tell me, damn you—what raid?"

"There's no need for you to know, sir."

"You'll tell me or I'll never say another word to you. I won't be lied to. I'm in charge here. What raid?"

The one who had removed his spectacles put them back on.

"What did you think, Ransom? This thing you found—you found it in one of the hovels of the Folk. Everyone knows that. Creedmoor and the woman—whatever they found they found it in the same way you did. That's what everyone says. The Line's had men raiding every Folk cave and squat and forest within a thousand miles of East Conlan for the last six months. Seizing the carvings. Interviewing the inhabitants. Extracting the information. Good men have died. Now what are you looking so shocked for, Ransom? Did you think we wouldn't go digging too?"

I do not know what I said in response to this.

"We'll have what we need with or without you, sir. As a matter of fact I don't know why we keep you around."

The other two looked anxious about this speech. I guess I confused their sense of hierarchy. But they did not protest or apologize, and all three of them turned their backs on me again when the light of the prototype suddenly pulsed.

During this conversation the light of the prototype had steadily increased and at the same time the room's shadows had sharpened, and the number of phantoms had increased. Many but not all of them looked like Folk. I would swear that among them I saw Mr. Carver. The engineers and me were greatly outnumbered by those phantoms.

Later that day I attempted suicide. As it turns out the windows of the tall spikes over Harrow Cross Station are not made of glass, though they look like glass, and even in a heavy runaway wheelchair you cannot break them.

## CHAPTER 31

# ADELA

I was going to write a lot more about Harrow Cross and our experiments and how whatever people say about me I did not serve the Line willingly, and I did what I could to defy them. Well I guess you will have to believe me or not as you please. We have had more sightings of Line Vessels overhead. Deserters, perhaps, or scouts. Our camp has surely been discovered. I have no time to waste and I want to write about what happened to Adela.

I got the second letter from Adela about the same way I got the first. One of the engineers passed it to me. I did not see who. He moved quickly away and by the time I had turned my chair he was lost among a crowd of other engineers and secretaries and frozen phantoms in various modes and eras of dress.

A corner stuck out of the edge of a stack of reports and I saw her handwriting. I tucked the corner back into the reports and did not pull it out again until that evening, when the adjutant had returned me to my apartment and locked the door behind me.

*Harry—*

*I know by now that my first letter got to you and my messenger has kept his silence, at least so far. I will risk another letter. As a matter of fact I suppose there is nothing to risk.*

*Since we last spoke I have resided in Harrow Cross. From my window I can see the Spike where they tell me you are being held, at least on days when the smog clears.*

*They put me to work, just as they did with you. They do not think very well for themselves. It is not pianos or Orange Trees that they want me to make! But I have been here long enough that I know how things work and I believe this messenger can be trusted.*

*I was not honest with you from the start and so you must think I had no reason for what I did. I do not know if you are angry with me and I do not know if it will make any difference if I explain.*

*I do not want to know that you are angry, or how badly I have hurt you. I have told the messenger to take no messages back from you.*

*Much of what I told you about my childhood was a lie. Not all. It is true that my father was the Baron of Iermo. It is a beautiful country for all of its faults, and nothing like this place where we have found ourselves. I told you that I left because my father and my brothers would not tolerate my work; that I struck out for independence of my own accord. That was not true, though you are not the only one to whom I told that lie, and I suppose at times I believed it myself.*

*My father had debts. Every one of the Barons of the Deltas has debts; his were worse than most. He was ambitious and he wanted Iermo to grow. He loved his children very much. He became indebted to wicked men, and to free himself he called for help from wickeder men. He secured a loan for Iermo from the Baxter Trust. I imagine you know how the rest of the story goes. In the space of two years everything in Iermo belonged to the Line. Within three years Iermo was at war with its neighbors, and my father was a broken man. Most of my brothers were dead. I shall not say what became of the man I was to marry; it is too humiliating. I fled. All of this happened long before I met you.*

*I came north to become someone new. I had always been clever, and I had enjoyed building clever and beautiful things. My father used to say that I would make Iermo's fortune one day. I worked in Gibson City and I made the piano but then Gibson City fell to the Line too, and I lost the piano, and I was arrested. I understood that there was no escaping, nowhere in the world. When they let me go I came to Jasper City meaning to shoot Mr. Baxter for my family's honor and my own and so that nothing else would fall into his grasp.*

*I do not expect you to understand; we are not made the same way. But I could not go until I had explained.*

*Our time together on Swing Street was an accident—a distraction—a diversion—but you must believe me when I say that it was a very happy one. I am sorry; I always knew that it could not last. They would not let it. I lied to you, Harry—I lied for the sake of lying. I lied to be free of the truth. In the end I lied to you to get to Mr. Baxter, and I am sorry that I did any of that. It accomplished nothing. We should have run away together!*

*I remember how you babbled that morning about Ransom City. It was a good idea, though I would have made you change that name.*

Around that same time I got a letter from my sister May. That letter came through official channels, and May's outlook on life was such at that time that only a very few words had to be smothered by the censor's black ink. What I mean is that she wrote to tell me that she had abandoned the worship of the Silver City. She had seen that in these times of disruption and uncertainty the world had no use for airy promises of heaven, but needed instead the firm hand of Power and Authority, Here and Now. She had therefore petitioned to enter the service of the Engines at Archway. It was a hell of a long letter with a whole lot of words about the Power and Glory of the Engines and how they would prevail through these Difficult Times and how their enemies would learn a Hard Lesson, and none of it is worth recording for posterity. Sorry, May.

❋ ❋ ❋

*I could not go until I had explained,* indeed. I did not like Adela's implication. I had no intention of letting her go! I saw that I could do good for someone.

I summoned each of my engineers into my office one-by-one under the pretense that I wished to discuss the Process. Once I had the door closed behind them I said to each of them in turn, "I know it was you."

Well, there is hardly a man or woman in Harrow Cross who does not have a guilty conscience about some failure or infraction or sin. I heard a number of groveling confessions that would be of interest only to other men of the Line—half the time I could not even understand what rule or protocol they thought they had violated. I had to go through six such interviews before I identified the fellow who was Adela's messenger.

"The message?" he said. "Sir, I—"

"You," I said. "I knew it was you."

Truth is I could not tell him apart from any of his colleagues. He looked furtive, ambitious, scrawny.

"Don't tell anyone, sir. I'd get—"

"You take messages. You need the money or you're being black-mailed or who-knows-what—I don't care to know. You'll take a mes-sage for me."

"She told me—"

"I'm telling you. I'm your damn boss, whatever your name is. You'll take a message or I'll call down the Engines on you. Me and the Kings-town Engine are the best of friends. Now listen. Tell her—I don't know what to tell her—don't you try to get away damn you—tell her there is nothing to forgive. Tell her what's a few lies or a few hundred lies be-tween friends—I lied too. Tell her I was happy too. Tell her we will be happy again. Got all that?"

I was not born yesterday and it crossed my mind that any response I sent might be intercepted—what's more it was possible that the letter had been allowed to reach me precisely so that I might be encouraged to tell *my* story in return, and let slip secrets. It was even possible that the let-ter was not from Adela at all. I couldn't know. So when I collared the go-between the next day and made him take a letter, I said nothing in it except some harmless recollections of happy days on Swing Street.

One week later she responded in kind. There was no more talk of *going,* I was pleased to see.

I found that my hip was not hurt so bad as I'd thought. It was painful to stand but no more than I could bear. I demanded that the adjutant bring me a walking-stick. When she refused I made one myself out of a lever from an abandoned prototype. I sent the chair away.

I sent Adela another letter, written for secrecy's sake in the margins of an Encyclopedia. I got a letter from her written on the back of an invoice, in which she said that she was crying from happiness as she thought of my face. I wrote to her about East Conlan and about my father and she wrote to me about Iermo. She wrote to me about her work—she was working with a team of engineers on improvements to the design of the Heavier-Than-Air Vessel—and I wrote to her about mine. We wrote about the future.

Our go-between was called up to the front, on account of the fighting in the Northwest Territory was going badly, as the leaderless armies of the Stations that had lost their Engines were breaking every which way or striking out for independence. I found another go-between quick enough. Now that I was on my own two feet and limping around again I was a holy terror to the engineers of the Project, always threatening to have them sent away to the front if they displeased me, and they did not know if I could do that or if it was an empty threat. Neither did I. It is true that all three of the men who had spoken about the raids on the Folk in front of me had been called to the front, though who knows if that was because of my recommendation or not. Anyhow they all jumped when I told them to jump, and they took messages if that was what I demanded.

> A—It's me. Write back at once if this gets through. I have missed seeing your words. I have missed you. This has been one hell of a long week with no one for company except for the engineers and the phantoms and the threats of the Engines. What news? They tell me they tested the bomb at the front and it did not meet expectations. I do not think they will be satisfied until it is big enough to swallow the whole world. Maybe that's their plan. My leg is better. Last I wrote to you I said how when we are out of here and building the place you won't let me call Ransom City the avenues would be lined with Automated Orange Trees like we built back on Swing Street, only bigger. I am anxious to know if you consider this practical. Write back if you can.—H

> H—it got through. See? They cannot keep us apart. I wish I had told you when we were together that I loved you but I did not understand it then. I know better now. Write back a thousand times. I consider the Automated Orange Trees eminently practical. I shall draw up plans.—A

That was the first time either of us wrote the word *love* but not the last. Once you start it is hard to stop. We wrote *love love love* on diagrams of Heavier-Than-Air scopes and on the backs of requisition orders for top-range electromagnets and on cables from the front reporting experimental results. We made vague plans for escape. We promised that we would meet again and cover each other in kisses and walk hand in hand alone into the West. Once she confessed that she was no longer beautiful and I supposed she was talking about her wounds from Mr. Baxter's office and I said that whatever she meant I did not care. Truth is I could not imagine seeing her again. She was words now—she was the notion of love—I was intoxicated by those words. I was like a child again—I admit it. We spoke of marriage, children of our own. She disclosed her location to me—no more than half a mile from where I was kept but it might as well have been another world. Sometimes we were afraid to put our messages in writing—sometimes we were fearless and sometimes fear gripped us the same sudden way love had—and when that happened we would commit nothing to paper but have our go-betweens mouth words for us—I have seen a whole lot of strange things in my time but nothing stranger than a burly officer of the Line whispering to me, *"One day we will be married under the Western skies."*

I got letters about how the Baxter-Ransom Trust was falling apart everywhere, about how its properties had been seized in Thurlow and how its stock had collapsed in Gibson and how its operations out on the Rim were going rogue and all of that. I paid them no mind, and wrote love-letters on the back of them. We told each other that the free and perfect city of the future would be populated with boys and girls with her beauty, my way of talking, her courage, the combination of our mutual genius—yes, we flattered each other. Can you blame us? I guess this exchange of secret letters was the great romance of my life. I don't know. Now that I look back on it I cannot quite recover the intensity with which I felt for those words. It was everything to me at the time but it happened to a different man, somewhere in the margins of his existence. I think that I gave too much of my life to ambition and not enough to love. Maybe things will be different in the world to come. I am sorry, Adela.

❋　❋　❋

Adela wasn't the only person who got letters smuggled in to me. As the months went by I guess Harrow Cross's security got worse and worse. The War was—you could call things *uncertain,* I guess. Seven or eight or nine or none of the Engines had been destroyed, maybe forever, depending on which reports you trusted. Arsenal, Dryden, and Fountainhead Stations were in a state of open revolt—Gloriana Station's leaderless armies had declared for the Republic. I hear the original forces of the Republic were not always too sure of their new allies but they could not stop them. Anyhow it was open to debate who was the real Red Republic and who was not. Anyone could put on red and say they were fighting for the Republic and for what it stood for. Opinions differed on exactly what it stood for but it was generally agreed what it stood against, namely what was left of the Line. Strange times. Harrow Cross itself was in a state of uncertainty. For the first time in a long time there was crime in the streets of Harrow Cross. Painted slogans appeared on the walls. The frequency of moving-pictures was doubled, then for no reason that was ever made clear moving-pictures were abolished.

A letter from Dr. Lysvet Alverhuysen appeared one evening beneath my pillow:

> Harry. I was so happy for you when I heard you got rich like you always wanted, and so sad when I heard that you were working for the Line, like you always said you would never do. You picked the wrong side but I want you to know that it is not too late to make amends. The Red Valley Republic lives again but our struggle is dire. We need your Bomb, Harry. We need your plans. We have a contact and can smuggle them out if you . . .

I did not believe that was really from Liv. Maybe this letter was really from John Creedmoor:

> Ransom. This is from John Creedmoor. You damned son of a bitch, you traitor. I should have shot you when I had the chance. I saw them test your Bomb at Log-Town. Maybe one day I will shoot you.

And I do not doubt that this letter was from the Agent Gentleman Jim Dark:

> Professor Ransom. I have not forgotten our appointment. One day you and I will talk. Your friend, "Gentleman" Jim Dark.

And nor do I doubt that this letter was from Mr. Angel Langhorne, my friend the rain-maker:

> Mr. Ransom—I just want you to know that I know it's not true what they say about you. Our correspondence back in Jasper meant the world to me. One day I hope we'll meet.

I heard about the test at Log-Town, and how many men on both sides died. I was not there. I do not intend to write about it.

✳ ✳ ✳

Anyhow they moved Adela out of Harrow Cross and we lost contact. They moved her to Archway. While she was still en route the Archway Engine disappeared and that Station too fell into chaos and for a long time I could not discover where she had been diverted to. Before she departed she sent me a copy of her plans for the reconstruction of the self-playing piano. I still possess them.

✳ ✳ ✳

As it happens I was studying those plans at my desk in my apartment on the evening when the adjutant unlocked my door, and entered without a word of explanation or apology, with her pistol in her hand and an expression of bemusement on her face, and announced that there was a mob at the door to the laboratory.

"It's—sir, they're—"

"Well," I said, "whose side are they on? What do they want? We're under siege, is that it? Is it the Republic?"

She shut the door behind herself, and leant against it. She did not put her pistol away. I think I had sounded too hopeful and made her wary of me.

"No," she said. "It's—sir, they're nobody."

"They can't be nobody," I said. "If nobody were assaulting the laboratory it wouldn't be newsworthy. Do you mean you don't know?"

"They're just—people from Harrow Cross. Workers. Men and women of the Line. I've never—I've never seen anything like it. Not here."

I stood. I was still walking with the aid of my self-made walking-stick. I packed up the plans and some other papers in my briefcase, and I stood beside the adjutant at the door. The poor woman looked quite lost. I had never seen her that way before, and for the first time I felt a certain fellow-feeling for her, and I regretted that I did not know her name.

I put my ear against the door and imagined that somewhere over the constant din of Harrow Cross I could hear angry shouting.

"Numbers," I said.

"A hundred or more."

"Do they know where I am?"

My apartment was just a short walk from the laboratory.

"I don't know."

"Well," I said. "Well then. What do they want? To smash the Apparatus or steal it or—what?"

She thought for a moment. "Smash it, sir."

"They wouldn't be the first. What's their particular objection?"

"They say—sir, I shouldn't tell you this—shit, sir—the Harrow Cross Engine has not returned from the front. It's been a week. I don't know—its location is unknown, sir."

"Nobody told me."

"It's not publicized, sir. But it gets out regardless."

"I don't see how I'm to blame, or my Apparatus."

"They've heard things, sir—the Bomb to end the world, the Bomb that kills the Powers—they hear about the tests that go wrong—they hear about the—the things you call the phantoms—they're frightened, sir, and confused. Things are changing and they don't know what to do. I never thought I'd see it in Harrow Cross. I've lived here forty-five years, sir, and I've never seen anything like it."

"Well then. Well. I suggest we run."

"Run?"

"It offends your pride? Not mine. I don't have much pride left and I never did mind running."

I opened the door. She did not stop me.

The corridor outside was empty.

She followed me along two turns of the corridor to the elevator.

I said, "What *is* your name, anyhow?"

She didn't answer.

The elevator took us down to the rooftop. Its doors opened onto a broad expanse of concrete. In the red-gray perpetual half-light of Harrow Cross at night you could see the hangar that housed the laboratory, its tall locked gates. Outside the gates there was a crowd.

As a matter of fact I would say that there were at most a couple of dozen men and women. By the standards of Jasper City or the Western Rim it was not much of a mob. Many of them were in uniform. They were milling uncertainly—it was very strange to see people in Harrow Cross who did not know what they were supposed to do or where they were supposed to go.

Not much of a mob. But they had a good try at chasing us down anyhow, until the adjutant started shooting at them and then with a thunderous noise a half-dozen Vessels converged overhead. The wind of their blades whipped the cap off the adjutant's head and blew her gray hair wild. The wind knocked the mob off their feet. Their spotlights marked a clear white line across which the mob did not dare step.

Among the mob were a number of the silent phantoms conjured by the Process—fierce Folk with stone spears, soldiers of Jasper City with bayonets, women in pioneer bonnets and tear-streaked faces—the wind didn't touch them, the spotlights didn't scare them, and when the rest of the mob fell back they kept on running. The adjutant shot at them until her gun was empty and she fell to her knees on the concrete and they kept running. They ran right past us—when I turned to see where they'd gone it seemed they'd vanished.

The mob had their hands in the air. So did I. The adjutant was weeping. I lowered one hand very slowly to her shoulder to console her.

✳   ✳   ✳

It was true. The Harrow Cross Engine never did return from the front. After a few weeks the Kingstown Engine took its place. It moved out of Kingstown for reasons of safety and it traveled north to Metzinger. The tracks west out of Metzinger were broken and so was the route north. It moved itself into Dryden and then out of Dryden. All the Engines seemed to be moving themselves about like chess-pieces, each one in its own mind a king, as their enemies cut their lines and trapped them— well, somehow it was the Kingstown Engine that ended up in Harrow Cross. It inserted itself into the deepest darkest parts of the Station and it issued a torrent of orders and threats and it did not emerge into the light ever again.

There were rumors that the armies of the Republic, swelled by the men of the rebellious Stations of Archway and Gloriana, were approaching Harrow Cross itself.

The Ransom Project was moved, for safety, and under conditions of extreme secrecy, to a new location—another hangar, on a different rooftop.

We were located directly above the Kingstown Engine itself, and though there was a tall building between us and the depths the Engine hid in, sometimes you could feel the floor vibrate, as if the thing was shifting in uneasy dreams. I complained—it was bad for the Apparatus. I was ignored.

The adjutant was reassigned for the sake of her mental health and I never did learn her name. There were a whole lot of new guards outside the new hangar and my new quarters. They were grim and loyal-looking Linesmen, hand-picked. A new adjutant appeared. This one was also a woman, younger than the last one, red-haired and freckle-faced, pretty but stern and zealous. She informed me that she had personally requested to work with me, in light of the critical situation in the inner Territories and the need for urgent progress. A number of my engineers were transferred away and I was left only with the most loyal and the

most ambitious. And yet I had not been in my new quarters a week before somebody left a note for me, poking out beneath the edge of the
triplicate typewriter.

> H. It's me. They transferred me back to HC. But while I was out I
> made contact with the Republic. They can get us out. They can get
> us out together. They want you and your Process. It must be to-
> gether. This is our moment. Send back word.

## CHAPTER 32

# HOW I GOT OUT

*Is it you? Adela, is that you? I thought I'd never hear from you again. Where have you been? I heard you were lost en route to Archway. I feared you were dead. I hoped you'd escaped.*

*Will you come? There's little time. Are you with us?*

*I'm with you, Adela. I care nothing for the Republic or the Line or the Gun or anything else. How do I know you're really yourself?*

*Will you make me repeat all those words of love? I'll write them again. Will you make talk about music—that stupid piano you loved so much? The Republic's forces will be at the walls soon—we don't have time for games. Will you come?*

*Yes. Tell me what to do.*

That exchange lasted maybe two weeks. I have cut it short, because I am in a hurry now.

The young and freckle-faced new adjutant knocked on the door of my quarters. I let her in.

"I'm working," I said. "I'm always working."

She sat on the bed. She removed her cap and placed it in her lap.

"Sir," she said.

I stood by my writing-desk. By that time I no longer needed my stick to walk but I liked to lean on it anyhow. I felt it gave me a kind of authority. When I was a boy I had imagined the dignitaries of Jasper City, Mr. Baxter and the Senators and all those great men whose number I would one day join, all of them with sticks. I cannot say why.

"Another riot?" I said. "If you can't keep control of your people here in Harrow Cross then the War is over and our efforts here are futile."

"Sir," she repeated.

"Yes?"

"I pulled strings, sir, to work with you. I distinguished myself at Chatillon. I proved my loyalty."

"I don't doubt it."

"It's all falling apart, sir. I saw the test at Log-Town with my own eyes. I was in the Second Company of the Second Army of the Archway Engine. I saw the walls of Log-Town—I was a long-rifleman, sir. I was there when—that light, sir. Those shapes. What was left behind afterward. It spilled—not many from Second Company survived, sir."

"I'm sorry."

"Don't be, sir. It opened my eyes."

She leaned forward as she spoke, and her eyes were fixed on mine and full of a kind of frightening zeal.

"I heard all those stories about—and I heard about the Miracle at White Rock—and I didn't believe. The Engines said it was all lies. Nothing was new, nothing had changed. But it was true."

"Some of it was true."

"I believed in the Engines. I believed in them with all my heart, all my life, sir. I wanted nothing more than to serve them. But they're just—things, aren't they, sir? Just things after all. The Archway Engine's gone, sir. The Cross Engine's gone. How long before they all go? Just—history, sir. They lied to me."

I did not know who she meant by *They*. The Engines, I guess, or maybe everyone. I said nothing, just nodded.

"It's a new century," she said.

By the reckoning of most people we were still a few years off from the new century, but the Line has its own calendar. We count from a date of what I guess must be some kind of significance in the religions or history of one of the countries of the Old World but I cannot even tell you which country, and I do not believe I am alone in my ignorance. The men of the Line do not suffer from that kind of confusion. They count from the day the Engines spoke their first order. For them it was the Year 300, and it had been for quite a few months. There had been no celebrations.

"We can make a new world," she said.

"Yes," I said.

"There are people here in Harrow Cross who are working for the Republic, sir. Their armies will be here within the week. The Engines are too scared to fight back. They're *scared*. We'll get you out, sir, you and your Bomb—don't worry—but you must help us too."

"Adela," I said. "You've seen her? You've talked to her?"

She nodded, stood, and put her cap back on.

"We communicated through channels, sir. Sir—the Republic must have your B— your Apparatus."

"I see. That's their price?"

"Yes, sir. If you want to call it that."

"Then I guess I have work to do, don't I?"

✳  ✳  ✳

I do not have time to describe everything I did in the next week, and if I did have time you would not understand it, and if you did understand it you would be tempted to repeat it. All I'll say is that I worked in my laboratory without sleep for days on end.

I chased away the engineers—I was forced to strike one of them with my stick—I shall not deny that it gave me great satisfaction. He lodged a complaint. I did not give a damn.

"No wonder this thing hasn't worked," I said. "It's my damn fault it took me so long to understand it. It's you—it's your small minds, your lack of vision—It's a delicate process, the Process, it's as much magic as science—let us not delude ourselves, ladies and gentlemen—and your small-minded mean-spirited unbelieving presence is poison to it. Anathema. We are making new worlds and the end of old worlds. We don't need paper-pushers. We don't need anyone but me. Get out, the lot of you."

The adjutant enforced my orders. The engineers complained to higher authorities but the higher authorities had more immediate concerns, namely that the forces of the Republic, swelled by the vehicles and guns of Gloriana and Archway, had clashed with loyalist Line forces in the Stow marshlands not that many miles south of Harrow Cross itself, and the result was so far a stalemate. The Line was not accustomed to stalemate.

I worked day and night. I did not leave the laboratory. I slept hardly at all, ate next to nothing, drank less than I sweated. To make this possible I took one hell of a lot of those chemical tablets that the Linesmen love so much, the ones that can make you work for days without sleep but also make you grind your teeth and twitch your leg. They give you a wonderful cold sharp focus on your work but leave you numb and dazed so that you do not notice when someone is talking to you, and when you try to talk back your words are slow. Sometimes they fill you full of sudden rage or tears. After a long enough time they make you see and hear things that cannot be the case.

I had exiled the engineers from the laboratory, and I had told the adjutant not to bother me with anything but the most urgent news, but I could not banish the phantoms that the Process produces.

Back when I first met the phantom I called Jasper, down in the basement of the Ormolu Theater, I had thought of him as a real person—a man not unlike myself, conjured into being by the Process and silent and prone to vanishing but still a man. In later years I had seen the phenomenon repeated a thousand times over, and in all that time not a single one of them ever spoke, or communicated through sign, or even looked me in the eye. I had come to think of them as a kind of shadow, cast by the light of the Process. It operates by cycling power between one world and another—one time and another—one state of being and another—it drags some things with it. If they were people at all, they were people who had once existed in a very different time, or who might have existed in a different world, or who one day might exist—even if they could speak, I would not understand them. And they could not speak.

So perhaps it was the Line's drugs that caused me to believe that one night, while I was working on the Apparatus by the light of the Apparatus, I was visited by Mr. Carver, and he spoke to me.

He stood behind me. "Well," he said, in that familiar voice. I put down my wrench and turned to him, and at first he did not acknowledge me, just stood looking into the light of the Apparatus without speaking, and he was silent for so long that I began to doubt that I had heard him speak at all. Then he smiled and shook his head, and I knew that he had spoken to me. The light of the Apparatus shone on his face so that his skin was stark white and his beard and long hair gray and ghostly. Behind him towered his shadow and mine.

"Well, Mr. Carver," I said. "Well indeed."

"You've f——d things up pretty bad, Ransom."

"Indeed I have, Mr. Carver. Indeed I have."

❋  ❋  ❋

We talked for hours—maybe days. The laboratory was windowless and we were alone and I do not know how long we talked for. The clocks did not work—the Process is hell on clocks. The adjutant brought me food and water. There were rumblings from below at irregular intervals that suggested that the Engine was moving. If you do not know what it was like in the Stations of the Line I cannot describe to you how strange and unprecedented it was that anything at all should occur at intervals that were not perfectly regular.

I told Mr. Carver all about what had happened since we parted at White Rock, and how I hoped he was not disappointed in me, and did not feel that his sacrifice was in vain. I told him all about what I had learned about the Process, and about Adela, and I told him about my plans for our freedom, and about Ransom City.

He told me what it was like to be dead. Mr. Carver was never much of a talker and it took him a long time to explain. I asked him if he had met Mr. Baxter, now that he was dead and Mr. Baxter was dead. I asked if he had met the Harrow Cross Engine, if that entity was truly no more. He explained that the next world was not like that.

I asked him how he pulled off the trick of coming back from the dead.

"Practice," he said.

"I find that answer unsatisfactory, Mr. Carver. Not only as a scientist, but as a businessman. Coming back from the dead—there's money to be made in that, if you know how to do it."

"You're imagining me, Mr. Ransom."

I did not like to hear that, and I did not entirely believe it, but I did not want to argue with him and so I pretended I had not heard.

Throughout our conversation he was naked, and not ashamed of it. Neither of us remarked on that fact, as I recall. He looked thin.

"You knew," I said. "From the start—I mean that you knew what was in the heart of the Apparatus. Where it came from."

"Yes."

"Mr. Carver, there's been a lot I've wanted to ask you, ever since White Rock."

"Guess there must be."

"Well then?"

"Yeah?"

"Have I done right by this thing, Mr. Carver?"

He looked into the light of the Apparatus.

"Who the f— knows. Who knows, these days. This is something new."

There was a great pounding noise from the depths of the building below us. It made the dust jump. I remarked that noises of that kind were like weather in a Station of the Line, and Mr. Carver remarked that he missed weather, and we started talking about weather we had experienced in our travels, together or apart. It turned out that he had a lot to say about weather, because in life he traveled a lot, but also because now he was dead. He told me what a lightning-storm looks like to one perceiving it from the next world. I found that so interesting that I forgot to ask him anything further about his past or about his purpose in traveling with me. Instead we talked about lightning, and about electricity, and then about the Ransom Process, which I promised him I would rename the Ransom-Carver Process, and in fact for a while afterward I did try to call it the Ransom-Carver Process but by then it was too late: it was already too famous.

I wish that I had time to write down every word that he said, or that the drugs caused me to imagine that he said, because either way they were full of interesting and valuable information. But I do not.

We worked as we talked—Mr. Carver and I. Wherever I moved in the laboratory, he always stood behind me, which at the time I guess I put down to the natural modesty of the naked and of the recently dead—now it seems more characteristic of hallucination. Anyhow I did a lot of work in that week, with and without Mr. Carver's help. I made a number of quite radical adjustments to several of the numerous models of the Apparatus that stood in the laboratory. During the time when Mr. Carver was there—I cannot say how long that was—he made helpful suggestions, and encouraged me when my nerve was failing, and pointed out things I had missed, which once or twice prevented me from causing crisis sooner than I had intended.

Once I had finished those adjustments, I made a wholly new model of the Apparatus. The adjutant had told me that when we fled we would have to flee on foot. Therefore the Apparatus had to be shrunk down. Mr. Carver stood behind me as I worked. I took parts from wherever I could find them in the laboratory and I constructed a device that was hardly bigger than a suitcase—it was kind of reminiscent of an accordion.

"Back in the old days we could have gone door-to-door with this," I said to Mr. Carver, and he nodded. "We could have dispensed with the wagon. But I would have missed the horses."

He said nothing. He was a man who traveled a lot, and he was never sentimental about horses.

"I'm going back out there," I said. "Out and beyond. Into the unmade, out to the sunrise, out where it gets weird, and not before time. Me and her. And whoever else. Going to start over. Wish you could come with us."

"Maybe I will," he said, "Maybe I won't."

"It's your choice, of course."

He said nothing. I felt obscurely pleased, like he had given me his blessing. I felt that I would not be alone.

❋ ❋ ❋

"It's time," the adjutant said. "They're here."

I turned. I was crouching over my work and the adjutant stood behind and above me. She seemed for a moment inhumanly tall and the shadow she cast on the laboratory's gray and distant wall was larger even than Carver's had been.

Mr. Carver was gone.

I rubbed at my eyes, pretending to wipe sweat from them. Mr. Carver did not return. For a while I could not think of anything to say. I was aware of a foul taste in my mouth.

"I said they're here."

"Yes. You did."

I thought for a moment, and understood that she was talking about the forces of the Red Republic.

"Yes," I said. "All right. Where?"

"They massed across the river yesterday," she said. "Two days ago we destroyed the bridge—last night they bridged it again. They have the earthmovers and the engineers of Archway with them. The Heavier-Than-Airs on both sides engaged this morning. It was a stalemate."

Because of my exhaustion and because of the drugs, it took me a long time to understand what she had said. I tried to picture the events that she described. I could not. I was excited that I might soon be released. I was sorry that there would be more fighting. I felt one of those fits of drug-induced weeping approaching, and fought it off.

"Carver," I said. "Was here."

"Sir, are you—?"

"Yes. Quite all right, quite well, thank you. Reminiscing. Gets lonely in here, you know?"

"Sir."

"Well. The boys in red. Can they win?"

The adjutant shrugged. "Who knows? Not easily. In my opinion they're over-confident. They think the Engines are broken and maybe they are but they still have damage left to do."

"We are under siege, then."

"By order of the Kingstown Engine itself I'm here to escort you and the Apparatus to the front, where you are to begin the Process. Like the Log-Town test again, sir—they don't care who dies on either side. Not anymore—not if they ever did. They want you there personally."

She held out her hand to me and helped me to my feet. I was so tired after my work that I could hardly stand. I was locked in a crouch, like a rusted machine or a comic actor. My legs shook.

"I don't intend to do that, sir. The contact from the Republic got word to me this morning—we must meet them under Arch Six, by noon, no later."

"Will Adela be there?"

"Yes," she said. "So they say. She knows the contact—I don't."

"Then we should hurry," I said. "One thing before we go."

✳  ✳  ✳

Have I described the inside of the laboratory before? I think I have not—an oversight. I apologize. It was one very big room with walls made of gray metal and a flat gray roof from which hung lamps powered by the Process—sometimes trapped pigeons died on them like moths. From one end of the laboratory you could hardly see the other—it could be hot at one end and cold at the other. I would not have been altogether surprised if one day it started to storm overhead. I have been in towns that were smaller than the laboratory and considered themselves to be booming little towns on the go. A room like that was hell for echoes at the best of times and you can imagine that under the conditions of heavy experimentation with the Process, I mean the phantoms and the effects on gravity and time and distance, it was a strange and confusing place to work. Rows of desks and workbenches were laid out grid-fashion to the farthest wall. Between them was a chaos of machinery. The letters NLC were etched over and over into the metal whether I liked it or not. There were experimental forms of the Apparatus everywhere. Many of those departed wildly from my design—I did not understand some of them at all. Some of them were big as houses with magnetic cylinders like a miller's wheels and they disturbed the bowels of every person who

went near them. Sometimes a team of engineers would venture inside
and I cannot say for sure that they always emerged. Some were even
taller than that, and constructed like grandfather-clocks, with a great
iron weight that would drop with a terrible whooshing noise. There
were empty zones cleared by past frightening incidents where maybe
only an overturned bench or a single hammer lay on the floor. There
were half-constructed or half-dismantled designs lying on their sides
with their ribs sticking out. There were machines that were made to
monitor the efficiency of the other machines and I'll confess again—I did
not understand them. The enterprise had long since surpassed the understanding of any one person's mind. I do not think the Engines understood it either.

I guess I understood it well enough to break things.

For most of that last sleepless week I had been working on the various half-made Apparatuses that stood around the laboratory like crum-
bling ruins. I had rebuilt three of the largest models, readying them to
run wild. The Line wanted weapons. I had made weapons. They were
not weapons that could be controlled, but they did not need to be.

"Here we go," I told the adjutant.

I threw levers, turned wheels. There were signs on the three Apparatuses warning of DANGER if certain parameters were exceeded. I exceeded them.

"What will happen?" asked the adjutant.

"Nothing good," I said.

"Why?"

"I won't leave them behind for just anyone—besides this may give
the Republic's men a fighting chance. I believe in fair play."

"How long?"

"Half an hour? Maybe less. Maybe more. Sometimes it builds slowly
and sometimes it comes on at a rush. To be honest I thought it might
happen at once."

She was a good soldier, and said nothing, only stiffened slightly. I
respected her.

"Well," I said. "I guess we'll see."

There was a protocol in event of emergencies that called for the laboratory and all of the many-storied building beneath it to be evacuated.
It required both my key and the adjutant's. We activated it, causing
alarms to sound and telegrams to be rattled off from the machines of
offices everywhere—CLEAR THE BUILDING IN AN URGENT BUT ORDERLY
FASHION. . . .

The three Apparatuses were magnificent beasts, even if I did not fully understand them. I remarked to the adjutant that it felt like I was setting them free.

"Sir—we have to go."

✳  ✳  ✳

We left the laboratory and went down from the roof. Alarms blared. A panicked mob blocked the elevators, including my private elevator, which they would never be able to use. I confessed to the adjutant that I had not thought of that before starting the alarms—I blamed sleeplessness. We were forced to go down from the rooftop by one of the endlessly spiraling echoing staircases. We stumbled in the gloom. Crowds pushed past us. Already the Process as it built up in the laboratory was creating its phantoms—summoning them to it—and as we ran downstairs there were phantom people doggedly heads-down climbing the stairs as if the event upstairs was an appointment they had to keep, like it or not. There was that usual moment of electric uncertainty every time you bumped into one. Like always they were in a variety of styles of dress and like always they were silent. It was no use saying *excuse me* to them or *are you mad* because they were not really there.

We stumbled down the staircase. The adjutant and I carried the suitcase with the miniaturized Apparatus between us. The suitcase also contained a number of Adela's letters, and it contained a great deal of money and a fortune in letters of credit and stock in what was left of the Baxter-Ransom Trust. I had to leave Mr. Baxter's typewriter behind. I was somewhat sorry to leave the thing after all the time I had spent with it but when I suggested that together we might carry it out, the adjutant told me as respectfully as she could not to be a fool.

We quickly went further down than I had ever been—I had not touched ground level for months. There were noises and stinks of machinery. Below us somewhere in the subterranean levels the Kingstown Engine cowered in its lair. I wondered what it made of the alarms.

I followed the adjutant outside through a big open doorway through which hundreds of people were streaming—it led out onto a concrete plaza under a concrete sky. Everyone was running everywhere and shouting. By no means everyone running out there on that plaza was really a real person. There was a light up above on the roof of the building that was hard to look at but also hard to look away from.

It was just as we got outside and while I was still staring up at that light that a group of men in black coats stopped us. I only recognized

them as engineers from the Ransom Project after blinking and thinking
for a moment and after they called me *sir* in a menacing way.

"Evacuate," the adjutant told them.

"What's happening—where are you going?"

"I said, evacuate—didn't you hear the alarms?"

Well, they weren't fools and they quickly guessed that we were up to
no good. Two of them tried to seize the suitcase and the adjutant had to
shoot one of them in the leg. I wrestled the suitcase from the other and
swinging it I knocked him on the head. I do not know where I found the
strength to swing it like that.

The adjutant waved her gun and the other engineers scrambled
away. Addressing the crowd, she explained, "Traitors." Nobody seemed
to care—I am not sure who was on whose side anyhow. Harrow Cross
was in chaos. The streets were full of phantoms. Tall Folk in robes strode
brazenly down the Station's avenues. I saw the citizens of Harrow Cross
running, crouching in dark corners, screaming, laughing, looting, kissing each other right in the street—I saw people shooting the phantoms
conjured by the Process, to no avail—I saw people taking the phantoms in their arms and kissing them—I cannot tell you how strange
that was to see. The living and the dead, the real and the unreal, all running here and there in the maddened avenues—I remarked to the adjutant that maybe that was what the Process was for after all. All together
as one, I said.

The adjutant waved her gun. Above us, one by one, the windows began to break, all the way down the building. Below us there was a sound
like a great beast roaring, and the concrete shuddered beneath our feet.

❋   ❋   ❋

Light leapt from the earth to the sky and back again. A hole opened up in
the world. I do not mean that metaphorically. That is what the Process
did—what it does—I did not fully understand that until I saw it open in
the middle of Harrow Cross. It strips away the world and reveals the
energy that lies beneath. That is why it seems to make more energy than
you put in, and that is why it has strange effects on gravity and other
forces, and that is why its light casts ghostly shadows of men and women
from other worlds, and finally that is why it is so very dangerous.

An area about the size of White Rock right in the middle of Harrow
Cross vanished into bright light, like the world was a map and somebody was holding a candle behind it until the light burned through.

I do not know how many people died, and I do not care to offer an estimate. No more than would have died in the siege anyhow, I think, or I hope.

"Died" is not precisely the right word, but it is good enough. It would be more accurate to say that they ceased to exist. Small comfort to anyone, I know.

The Kingstown Engine was reported lost after the battle. Opinions differ on who can take credit for its destruction—I believe it was me. The radius of the devastation was so great that it could have reached even the subterranean levels where the Kingstown Engine hid. I believe that I thereby shortened the siege by days at least, probably weeks—and who knows, maybe without me the Station would not have fallen to the siege at all. Then who knows where we would be.

"When I was a boy," I said to the adjutant, as we turned our faces away from the light and crouched behind a motor-car, "I read the *Autobiography* of Mr. Baxter over and over. Do you know it?"

"No, sir."

"Well, he talked a lot about great men and how history was like a woman and seizing the reins of history. I guess he was thinking of horses not women but he was an old man and maybe confused. Anyhow when I was a boy, I was red-hot for being like him. I mean that I wanted to be a big man and I wanted to leave my mark on history."

"Sir," she said.

"I guess I've done it now. What do you think?"

"How long will it—it keeps growing, sir. Will it—?"

"Stop?"

It was hard to estimate the rate at which the light was expanding—it was hard to look at it. But it seemed to be expanding slowly but steadily, at perhaps the speed of a man walking, a tourist taking in the sights of the Station.

The truth is that I was not sure when the light would stop expanding. It had already exceeded my wildest predictions. I was not sure it would ever stop.

The car's windows burst, showering black glass on my shoulders.

"We'll be okay," I lied. "So long as we keep moving."

"Sir."

"What?"

"We should keep moving, sir. Now."

"Yes, yes, of course. Yes."

The adjutant and I ran through the avenues and corridors of the Station. She went first. We ran toward the appointed meeting-place. Arch Six, at noon.

✻   ✻   ✻

Arch Six was one of the Station's seven big entryways, big enough to encompass the biggest of the Engines. It was made of gray-black stone. It curved high up in the air over the tracks of the Line—tracks that ran east out of the city and once had run all the way out to Fountainhead and Gloriana and nearly all the way to the World's Walls. The forces of the Republic had cut that line. On the arch above there were fortifications and barracks—in the shadows beneath it there were warehouses and machines and people running to and fro. Along the tracks an army of phantoms came marching in old-time clothes from the first settlement of the West and sometimes in chains, their faces turned up toward the light in the middle of the Station.

The adjutant pushed through the crowds holding one end of the suitcase and I followed behind her holding the other.

Someone touched my arm. I turned to see a woman in a black coat. It was Adela. At first I didn't recognize her.

I didn't care about the scars—I had said that in my letters and it turned out to be true. I dropped my end of the suitcase and the adjutant cried out in surprise and aggravation.

Adela said my name—nothing else—we embraced for longer than the adjutant thought wise.

"You—," Adela said, and I said, "I—we—"

The adjutant interrupted us, demanding to know where the contact was, where we were going, what the plan was to get us out of the Station and into the safe and welcoming arms of the Republic's forces.

"This way," Adela said. "Hurry."

There was no time to say anything else.

I hefted my end of the suitcase. Adela led the way, the adjutant ran, I followed. We ran together down a narrow alley between two windowless buildings beneath Arch Six and into a small dark room where a man awaited us. He smiled to see us as we entered the room—he took off his hat and stretched out his arms in welcome.

"This man is working with the Republic," Adela said. "He—"

"No," I said. "I know this man. He once tried to shoot me. This is Gentleman Jim Dark, Agent of the Gun."

Mr. Dark had shaved his famous mustaches, perhaps by way of disguise, but I recognized his face anyhow. He did not deny my accusation, but smiled again, kind of like I had asked him for an autograph.

Adela made a noise of shock and outrage.

"Sorry, ladies," Mr. Dark said.

"The Republic," I said, "doesn't know we're here. Does it? It never did. I dare say it doesn't even want us."

Gentleman Jim Dark nodded, as if acknowledging that I'd made a fair point in debate.

"I told you one day we'd have a fair fight, Mr. Ransom. Well that day is here."

✳   ✳   ✳

The adjutant was well-disciplined. She did not waste her time crying out in shock or complaining about how she had been betrayed. She drew her gun and lifted it toward Mr. Dark without delay. She was not nearly fast enough—he shot her dead.

Then he smiled and shot Adela too.

I guess he shot her because now that he had me and the suitcase he no longer needed her. I did not ask him why he did it.

I shall not describe how it looked as she fell, or how she lay there afterward. I shall not say how I felt. I do not have the time or the words. It would cause me pain, and do you no good, and do her no honor.

Mr. Dark, having holstered his gun, was talking. I shall not record the whole long speech he gave me. Why should I? It was all gloating and posturing about his cleverness and how all the world might fall apart but the Gun would remain strong, or at least *he* would remain strong, to hell with the Gun, and how he was now the richest and most powerful man in the world so long as he held that suitcase in his hand.

"There are so few of us left, Professor—so few. These last few years have been bad. Soon there'll be none of us at all outside of story-books and history-books. Well, I won't have that—not me. I won't go gently. I don't know that I like this new century coming so much but I mean to have a place in it anyhow. Let's see. Let's have a look-see."

He kept his gun holstered and he turned his back to me while he examined the contents of the suitcase. Perhaps he was hoping I would attack him, so that he could have the satisfaction of shooting me as I fought back. More likely he simply did not care what I did.

I did not attack him. I stood where I was, and watched him roughly handle the Apparatus's delicate parts.

"Is that it?"

"Yes," I said. "It is."

"Doesn't look like much. What do you think?"

He did not appear to be talking to me, but to himself.

"It is terrible," I said.

He turned to me and raised an eyebrow.

"It is much more terrible than your bosses. Or the Line. Soon nobody will care about you at all. Then where will you be?"

He smiled at me. "Well now, Professor—I reckon we'll adapt. Resourceful, that's something I've often been called."

I did not want to argue with him. I had not meant to speak out loud at all.

When he saw I would give him no more entertainment, he turned back to the Apparatus. He touched a finger to one of the magnetic cylinders, and spun it.

"Is that it? Well, I guess I'm not the scientific type. Nor are the bosses. So long as it works."

He dug beneath the Apparatus, and pulled out the letters from Adela. "What are these?"

I told him. He did not trust me at first, but scanned a few and found them boring. He glanced over at the place beside me where Adela lay, and a theatrical expression of sorrow appeared on his face, making me wish I could somehow kill him.

He shook his head. "Too bad. Too bad. You know, Professor Ransom, I'm not a cruel man—whatever you may have read in the newspapers. I'm a sporting man—ask anyone. I know what love is. Here, take them."

I hesitated, and he shrugged and scattered the letters on the floor.

Beneath the letters, he found the money I had packed for my escape.

"Ah, now," he said. "That's something else. Professor, I'm no thief. Ask anyone—I'm a decent fellow. But I have a great many widows and orphans to support. I can't in good conscience let this go. But nor can I—well, now, here's a sporting notion—what say we share it? Partners?"

"Take it," I said. "Take it all! It has done me no damn good."

Jim Dark smirked and stroked his chin.

It seemed to me then that this ridiculous man was the agent of retribution for all the things I had done wrong in my life and all the good I had meant to do but I had not done.

From outside there was a thump and the light from the one high window shifted, illuminating a stack of rusty old tools. Now you know that I am not a religious man but I felt that that little shed was full of something bigger than both of us and that whatever it was it had worked out my fate. It was as if there was a plan to the world and it had nothing to do with my dreams and ambitions or the pride of men like Mr. Baxter or the machinations of Gun and Line or whatever the Folk might have in mind. Gentleman Jim Dark was a preposterous fraud and a bully and a crook and a small and mean man but perhaps he was what I deserved.

"Take it," I said. "Take it and be done with it."

He nodded, and stuffed it into his pockets. Then he stood.

"Now will you come with me quietly, Professor? Otherwise I'll have to shoot you too—I had a hell of a time getting in here and I'll have a hell of a time getting you out if you won't come quietly."

"No," I said.

"No, you will not come quietly?"

I nodded.

He shrugged, and drew. I closed my eyes.

The next I knew he pushed past me, laughing and slapping me on the back.

"You're a good sport, Ransom. It would be a waste to shoot you—I want to know what you'll do next. See you again, I'll bet."

He stepped lightly over the adjutant and Adela, and out through the door, leaving it swinging open behind him.

I had been mistaken. He was not the agent of my punishment. He was the agent of my deliverance. He had given me my freedom. I did not know what to do with it and I did not especially want it.

✳   ✳   ✳

I was wrong about the money too. I could have done a lot of good with it, certainly more than Gentleman Jim Dark would have done. I do not believe what he said about the widows and orphans for a moment. That is what comes of doing business when you are not thinking straight.

On the other hand the device he stole from me was just seventy-five pounds of junk. That is not because I had the foresight to expect that it would fall into the hands of the Gun—I won't lie to you. It was junk because I did not trust the Republic with the Apparatus either. I did not trust anyone with the Apparatus, and I still do not. Sometimes I am not sure I trust myself with it. Anyhow I had planned to trick the soldiers of the Republic with junk, then try to escape. What Mr. Dark walked away with whistling was just a suitcase full of junk, and though it looked clever it did nothing at all and there was nothing that anyone could learn from it except that you should not count your chickens before they hatch, and you should keep an eye out for pigs in pokes. Those are good rules in science, business, and life.

Since he has never come after me again I guess that some bad luck befell Mr. Dark in the fighting after Harrow Cross fell, and now he has passed into the history-books. Like he said, there are not a lot of his kind left anymore.

❋ ❋ ❋

I stayed with Adela and the poor adjutant for a while and I said my farewells until I could stand it no longer. Then I gathered up the letters and walked out into the streets of the Station. The light was gone. Some time during my conversation with Gentleman Jim Dark it had stopped growing, and fallen in on itself. I was not pleased. I had thought that I might sit on the sidewalk and wait for it to wash over me, or walk into it and be consumed. Its expansion had been unstable, and had collapsed. That seemed to me to be just one more of my many failures. Even my disasters were unstable.

In the darkening sky up above Arch Six Heavier-Than-Air Vessels circled each other and I guess they were fighting. I could not tell which belonged to which side.

There were no more phantoms. The door had closed. Now there were just people running in every direction.

I headed east, sticking with crowds. When all else fails you you can always follow a crowd and at least it will keep you moving. We were looking to get as far away from the fighting as possible. Eventually something exploded—masonry fell—I was not injured but someone behind me was and then people started running in a panic and I was knocked off my feet and hit my head on the concrete.

## CHAPTER 33

# LAST WORDS

I recall waking to bustle and screaming and stink and swaying lamps, then sleeping again. I recall that this happened a number of times—I cannot say how many—before I woke really and truly.

I lay on a hard camp-bed. I was in a tent.

I raised my hand to my head to feel my bruises and then I lay with my head in my hands for some time. I did not feel that I had escaped. I felt that I had lost everything.

After a while I stood. I saw that the tent was full of beds, and the beds were full of injured men and women and children, and many more of them lay on the floor. Some of them looked like citizens of Harrow Cross and some of them did not. It was hard to tell them apart. A woman screamed and a man shouted at her to be silent.

It did not seem that anyone was doing anything for any of us. My first instinct was to protest. I stood, unsteadily, and said, "I will—I'll see—don't worry." I took a few steps to the tent's door then fell.

When I woke again I was lying on the ground looking up at the stars. A woman stood over me. It was Dr. Lysvet Alverhuysen, or Miss Elizabeth Harper as I cannot help thinking of her, whatever the history-books may call her. She wore white and she carried a candle.

"Harry," she said, in a whisper.

"Miss Harper!"

"It is you, then." She did not look entirely pleased to see me. "I wasn't sure. You've changed."

"Well, it's been a long time since White Rock, and I haven't been out on the road in a while. I guess I may have put on weight. You've changed too."

She had. She was a little older. She was not so thin any more, in fact she was becoming somewhat comfortably heavy-set. She looked well, and she did not look so uncertain of herself or so driven and hunted as she had been out on the Rim.

"Last I heard you were First Speaker of the Republic," I said. "I was proud of you. A great role in history. I guess you're doctoring again now? Also a noble profession."

"It was ceremonial," she said. "I made speeches about the necessity for struggle until I could stand it no more."

She sat on the grass beside me.

"In the stories from back in—back in the old country—there was a spirit called the Mother of Battles. I began to feel—well, it hardly matters. Yes, I quit. Now I follow the army."

Later in our conversation she had some sharp-tongued things to say about the government of the reborn Red Republic, and about the administration of President Hobart IV. I guess she would prefer that I not repeat them.

"How is John Creedmoor?"

"I don't know what he's up to these days. We haven't spoken since Chatillon."

I guess she was talking about the fighting there. I never heard any stories about John Creedmoor at Chatillon, but that does not mean he did not do anything terrible there.

"Well," I said. "I'm happy you're happy."

"I know a thing or two about head injuries, Harry. You'll be all right."

"All right?" I touched my bruises again.

Something in my expression made her say, "You lost someone."

"Yes."

She did not look as sympathetic as I thought she might. In fact her face went hard.

She said, "Friends among the Linesmen?"

"I guess you could say that."

She sighed.

I sat up.

"Well now—what do you mean by that?"

She explained to me that right at that moment nobody but she recognized me, but as soon as the chaos in the aftermath of the fall of Harrow Cross subsided others would too. I was a very famous man indeed. Soon someone would see my face and jump up and shout, *It's him!*

She also explained to me that the way many people saw it, I was kind of a monster. A traitor. I was the man who by stepping into Mr. Baxter's shoes had brought about the surrender of Jasper City. I was the man who'd spent the last days of the war building terrible and blasphemous weapons for the Engines of the Line. The deaths at Log-Town were on my hands. I was known for my cruel and terrible experiments.

You will think me naïve and I guess I was, even after everything I guess I was, but I was stunned at the unfairness of this.

"Jasper was lost anyhow," I said, "and I had no choice—they held me by force. I did not work for them willingly. I fought to be free. Why, when I fell and hit my head as a matter of fact I was escaping from Harrow Cross to deliver the Apparatus into the hands of the Republic—I was coming to meet—well, an impostor as it turned out, but . . ."

She sat cross-legged beside me and she listened to me patiently, without judgment, and I do not know whether she believed me or not.

Soldiers went to and fro around us, some brisk-marching, some idling, some limping. I looked down at my feet so as to hide my face. Harrow Cross stood on the horizon in the dark and there was a whole lot of work going on. I think there was still fighting within the Station, die-hards holed up in the tunnels and so forth.

We were not far from the river. It seems I am rarely far from rivers. When I started this account back in the Territory I thought it was about Light but maybe it should have been about Rivers all along.

"I should report you," she said. "The officers of the Republic will want to question you."

"I have nothing to hide."

"There'll be a trial. It won't be fair. Passions are hot here. That light back at the Station—"

"My doing. I can explain. I brought down the Kingstown Engine with it. I won your damn battle!"

"Keep your voice down."

I sat in a sullen silence.

"I have work to do," she said. "You're far from the only injured man here. And very far from the worst. And we're moving on soon. It's a punishing pace."

"Where?"

"I don't know. I'm just a doctor now—I'm not privy to the plans."

"All be over soon, I guess."

"Maybe. In a few years, perhaps."

I asked her about what had happened to her and Creedmoor after White Rock and I asked her about the weapon they'd found and she said it was hard to describe. It was hard to describe the places they'd gone to find it. I acknowledged that the Process was hard to describe too. She gave me a small smile. I asked her if there ever was any weapon, or if it was all just a big hoax, if the Engines had just been scared to death by rumor and stagecraft. She did not answer, but told me that everyone has to decide for themselves what to believe.

"Easy to say," I said. "Not so easy to do."

She suggested that one day somebody should write a book.

"It won't be me," I said. "I don't know half of the truth of things. I think it would be for the best if the world heard nothing more from Harry Ransom for a while. It would be best if I'd died."

"Maybe it would have."

We talked a while longer. But soon enough she was distracted by the sound of screaming from the tent and someone calling "Doctor, Doctor," and she left me. I got up and walked away.

A little further down by the river there was a man who had a wagon and a heap of junk salvaged from the fall of Harrow Cross. He explained that much of it had floated down-river and he offered no guarantees as to its quality. He was wearing no uniform and I do not think he had any right to be selling anything. I was not interested in his rifles or flashlights or tin cans or automobile motors but I was interested to see the triplicate typewriter perched on top of the heap.

My great wealth was gone. I guess it had never really existed. I exchanged my watch for the typewriter. I regretted it later when I was hungry but I could not resist.

I introduced myself to the man as John—no last name.

I drifted south from Harrow Cross. I worked when I could. I made myself useful wherever I could. I attracted no attention. Word got around quickly that the terrible Professor Harry Ransom had perished in the taking of Harrow Cross. The story that the Republic told was that I had killed myself in the attempt to unleash my terrible weapon against the forces of the Republic—that I had blundered and blown up half of Harrow Cross's forces along with me. President Hobart IV himself celebrated my death in a speech on the floor of the Capitol in Morgan.

I do not much resemble the man in the stories. I am of no more than average height and I do not think my manner is cruel and I do not mean to be arrogant and I have never to my knowledge cackled or stroked my mustache in a sinister way.

✳ ✳ ✳

I went back to sign-painting after a while. A lot of people had moved to one place or another because of the fighting and so there was a demand for signs. I am good at it.

I joined up with a chapter of the Smilers who were doing good works near Gibson. I told them I wanted to make amends, and they asked what for, and I said that it did not matter, everyone had something to make amends for. It was hard work and accomplished nothing.

I made a little money in Keaton City teaching the Ransom System of Physical Exercises to rich young men. Of course I did not call it that and they did not know who I was. I told them I was teaching them the exercise secrets of long-dead Folk warriors, and mostly they liked that notion.

I had a lot of strange dreams for a very long time, which maybe is because I had stopped taking the sleeping-tablets too suddenly. Who knows. Anyhow I dreamed of the edge of the world, and of Mr. Carver, and of the Folk I had met back outside East Conlan when I was a boy.

I stopped hearing my name cursed as a villain. I started to hear my name made a joke. I do not quite know how it got around but soon it seemed there was a general view that there never had been any terrible weapon, that Professor Ransom was a fraud at best and maybe never existed. Some people said that the whole thing had been a decadent and deceitful and desperate ploy of the Engines in their last days. Others said that Professor Ransom was just a snake-oil salesman who had happened to cross paths with Dr. Alverhuysen and John Creedmoor, and who had subsequently taken credit for wonders they had performed. Still others denied the existence of Dr. Alverhuysen and John Creedmoor too. Soon enough there was a general view that the Republic had taken

Harrow Cross through good old-fashioned fighting spirit, without the aid of mysterious weapons or happy accidents or Professor Harry Ransom. I did not like that much. If nothing else I hope I have shown that it is not true.

I moved town a few times and after a while I stopped hearing my name at all. I did not like that either.

Miss Harper thought the war might be done in a matter of years, and the current fighting is like a fever before it breaks. I hope she is right but I do not know. I still do not understand politics. I do not think I like the Republic very much, and I do not think I like President Hobart IV, but I do not move in great circles anymore and I do not know him.

I think I said that in one of the letters Adela sent to me she described the operations of the self-playing piano. Well, I do not want to speak ill of the dead but her explanations were unclear, and it took me months of hard work to understand them, months more to make the thing that the Beck brothers have hauled out here. Even after all that work it is not half as wonderful as the original, in fact the music it makes is downright ugly. The Beck brothers compare it to cats and dogs and they are right. But I mean to keep trying. She had a lot of bad luck in this world and I hope things will be better in the next.

I built a new Light-Bringing Engine. It still does not work as well as I would like it to. Most of its weight is made of safeguards to stop it running wild, and safeguards to be sure the other safeguards are in order. I did not dare exhibit it, or patent it, or try to go into business. I did not trust anyone with it. I spent many long nights just staring at it, not daring even to make it run.

Eventually I was able to mend the typewriter too. Then I realized that I did not know exactly what to do with it. I did not have anyone to write to. But the white space calls to you. It demands to be filled. I wrote a very long letter regarding how rumors of my death had been much exaggerated and regarding how as I saw it I had been unfairly treated by History, and how I had won the Battle of Harrow Cross just about single-handed. I addressed it to Mr. Carson but I did not send it. I tore it up. It was no more than a half-truth, no better than what you might read in the newspapers.

Then one night I sat down and wrote

TO ALL MEN AND WOMEN OF GOODWILL
IT IS TIME TO BEGIN ANEW
I INVITE YOU TO JOIN ME IN THE CITY OF THE FUTURE

And *et cetera*. I signed my true name to it and sent it to the editor of the town's newspaper.

Not everyone who showed up at the meeting-place I had proposed was friendly to me at first. I guess most of them thought I was an impostor, and the rest were still mad at me for one reason or another. As a matter of fact one man threw a chair at me. But I always was a good talker. That man is still with me now and will be with us when Ransom City rises.

When Miss Harper and I talked, back at the camp outside Harrow Cross, I told her about Adela and about our letters and about how we had talked of building a new city, free of war and all the other problems of the world. She said that was a common enough notion in these times and I acknowledged that it would never happen, it was only words. I said that I did not trust anyone with the Process, and I did not trust myself, because sooner or later someone would find me and offer me money for it, or fame, and maybe they would promise me they would not misuse it, and maybe they would even believe they were telling the truth, and who knows what I would do then. I said that I had to go far, far away. She said that it would not be enough to go to the edge of the world, I would have to go as far as anyone has ever gone and keep going, and that that country had its own inhabitants who might not welcome me. I acknowledged that that was true too. She took pity on me then, I think, and she asked me if I remembered when we first met at Clementine, and I said of course I did, and she said that at that time she and John Creedmoor had recently completed their own long wandering in the wilderness, having got almost all the way out to the place where everything turns into Sea, and if I wanted she could tell me a few things about what was out there, almost like a kind of map, though I should not rely on it too much. I said that I was grateful to her, and I would take it all as it comes, and that I relied on nothing these days.

This is the END OF THE FOURTH PART. When I write again I will write from Ransom City.

# EDITOR'S AFTERWORD

## —EMC.

And there endeth, as they say, the sermon.

I assume that one of the copies of the Fourth Part of Mr. Ransom's letters was addressed to me, the same as all the others. It never came to me through the mails, and I have never found any trace of a copy addressed to me anywhere in the world. One of the copies was addressed to President Hobart IV. A few pages of that copy survive in the Public Library of New Morgan City. The rest of it is in private collections, or lost. In the years after the fall of Harrow Cross there was briefly hot competition for Mr. Ransom's letters, among those who had heard rumor of them, and who hoped that they might find clues as to how to reconstruct Mr. Ransom's weapon. That has gone out of fashion lately, and for the most part I have been able to indulge my hobby quite cheaply.

The third copy was addressed to the Baron Iermo, father of Adela. It reached him, and it remained in his possession through all the ups and downs that the Baronetcy of Iermo and the Deltas have suffered in the years since Ransom wrote; it was still in his possession last year, when I visited him in his rotting and vine-choked mansion. I had come all the way south to interview him on the subject of his daughter, but he was old, prodigiously so, older even than myself, and there was little that he could tell me, little that he remembered. There were no traces of her in the house. Some musical instruments; some rusting and overgrown machinery in the fields outside, the purpose of which was unclear to me. No marks of genius that I could see—but mine is an untutored eye. Yet it was not a fruitless expedition, because to my great surprise I discovered a complete copy of the Fourth Part of Mr. Ransom's writings rotting among the old Baron's papers. He was happy to give it to me, seeing no value in it.

I have never seen any Fifth Part of Mr. Ransom's writings, nor heard any rumor of any such thing. Moreover anyone can tell you that there is no Ransom City, and never was. You have only to look at a map.

✳  ✳  ✳

I had planned to return home to New Morgan once I had said my good-byes to the Baron, leaving before the rainy season came to the Deltas. It is not an easy matter to travel at my age, and I had business to take care of. But at the pier at the river my excitement at my discovery of the Fourth Part overtook me, or perhaps it was the spirit of young Mr. Ransom. I exchanged my ticket and I set out West. I visited a number of acquaintances I had never thought to visit with again in this life, and I saw a lot of sights between here and the edge of the world for what I suppose will be the last time.

I toured the sights of Mr. Ransom's autobiography. East Conlan and New Foley are part of one town now, by the name of Foley. The town of Kenauk is a busy little metropolis, and hardly anyone remembers the day Mr. Ransom came to town. White Rock is long gone; only the lake and the trees remain. The town of Mammoth still has its mammoth, and I have the post-cards to prove it. Melville City thrives, of course. Clementine is gone. The town of Domino, where Ransom boarded the ill-fated *Damaris*, was destroyed in the last days of the Great War, along with the nearby Line camp and the Fountainhead Engine; in its place there is a memorial.

The western edge of the world expands further and further and places that were wild in Ransom's day are respectable now. I wanted to set eyes one last time on the edge of things, and so I kept going, out past Melville and the crossroads where Clementine had grown and dried up and blown away, out past places that in Ransom's day had no names, but were now thriving little towns, well-marked farms, busy roads. I traveled all summer. Thank our lucky stars that the motor-car is no longer the exclusive property of the Line, or I would never have been capable of it.

Wherever I went I interviewed old-timers. Well, call it *interviewing*; perhaps it was just old men jawing about the old days. A few people remembered Ransom, and the day long ago in the time of the War when he and his band of deserters, misfits, and reprobates went by on their way out West. Nobody knew what had become of them. Most of them agreed that Ransom's band numbered twenty or thirty at most, not the hundred or more he claimed in his letters. Some of them still had copies of Ransom's letters and posters, his invitations to Ransom City, stiff and yellowed papers which they were happy to sell to me for pennies or tobacco.

I met a few old men who had come out looking for Ransom City, back in the days of their feckless youth, but never found it. The place was a joke, a drifter's dream; the paradise at the end of the road, always the next town over, where nobody works and everybody lives for free.

The people of New Jasper, which is a town of some five thousand souls and about as far from old Jasper as it is possible to get, will tell you a story, if you ask, about how their founder was a war hero, and a businessman, and an inventor, whose genius was the secret of their town's success. They cannot agree on the nature of his genius, though most of them will say *rain-making* if you ask them, and a few will say *electricity*. That gentleman, who went by the name of Rawlins, left town twenty-five years ago, headed west. There is no statue to him in New Jasper but by the accounts of the old-timers he looked a little like Mr. Ransom, though they remembered him as tall, which Mr. Ransom was not. New Jasper is a fine little town but its people work for a living like everyone else, and it gets dark at night.

From the town of Gourney there are no roads west, so I traveled by mule to the settlement of Sherlund's Water. It was one of the old men there who told me of a place nearby called Carver's Hill, where strange lights are sometimes seen at night, and where travelers in the woods sometimes meet ghosts, and where a madman lived on the hill. Apart from the small coincidence of the name, there was nothing to set those stories apart from those that you might hear anywhere on the Rim. Wherever you go there is always a haunted hill somewhere nearby, there is always a madman who lives in the woods. The coincidence of the name was enough to make me curious, and I attempted to hire a guide; but Carver's Hill is not just haunted, but also Folk territory, by the Treaty of 1911, and nobody would take my money. I set out a little way toward the hill myself but the going was too steep, and I was afraid— not because of ghosts, or lights, because I saw none, but for the most part because of the sheer remoteness of the place. My wristwatch stopped working as I approached the hill, and still does not work today.

After Carver's Hill I turned back East. For the most part I traveled by steamboat, and slept on deck in the sun. I returned to New Morgan, and to my house on Cuvier Street, which my housekeeper had kept for me in fine condition, and where, after I had bathed, and shaved, and dined, my secretary presented me with a heap of correspondence, near the top of which was a letter—no return address—hand-delivered— reading simply

*My Dear Mr. Carson,*
  *What are you waiting for?*

Yours, HR